Brothers Black

Ryan The Joker
Book 6

Blue Saffire

Perceptive Illusions Publishing, Inc.
Bay Shore, New York

Blue Saffire/Perceptive Illusions Publishing, Inc.
PO BOX 5253
Bay Shore, NY 11706
www.BlueSaffire.com

Publisher's Note: This is a work of fiction. Names, characters, places, and incidents are a product of the author's imagination. Locales and public names are sometimes used for atmospheric purposes. Any resemblance to actual people, living or dead, or to businesses, companies, events, institutions, or locales is completely coincidental.

Ordering Information:
Quantity sales. Special discounts are available on quantity purchases by corporations, associations, and others. For details, contact the "Special Sales Department" at the address above.

Brothers Black 6: Ryan The Joker/ Blue Saffire. -- 1st ed.
ISBN 978-1-941924-01-3

Laughter is medicine. If you can smile more than you stress you have mastered a great thing.

—Blue Saffire

Black & Nash

Ryan

A year ago ...

"Get out of here," Wyatt hisses at me as I play with his earlobe. He swats at me, causing me to huff and move away from him.

I'm bored. Toby and Dad are in that Alliance meeting with the other members. Since the meeting would be at my cousins' estate here in Ireland, I decided to come along.

Any chance to see the O'Briens is a chance to have some fun. However, this isn't as fun as I thought it would be. The air is somber knowing Logan isn't released yet.

I'll be glad when he's out. He doesn't deserve to be locked up in the first place. Well, not for some shit he didn't do.

"Ya want another plate?" my cousin, Connie offers.

"Nah, I'm good," I say. I grin as I find the opportunity for some fun. Teasing Connie is always rewarding. "So, you dating or did you eat another one of your boyfriends?"

"Shut yer gub, Ry before I cobbler ya," she hisses.

"I'm only asking so I can help. You're a pretty woman, but you've been a man eater for so long—"

"Ryan," Connie growls at me.

I jump up from my seat at the island and run out of the kitchen, laughing my ass off as she lunges at me. I've pissed her off and she'll make good on her threats to kick my ass. I don't put it past Con to try, and as Logan's little sister she might succeed if I let her.

The O'Brien family is full of scrappers. I burst into more laughter as a spoon hits me in the back of the head. I turn, rubbing the spot.

Connie's cheeks are red as she stands with her hands on her hips. I'm so busy laughing, I run into someone as I back away.

I turn and reach out for them as I steady myself as well. I grin when I see it's Kiyoshi Matsumara-Nash. This should be fun. I always get under this guy's skin.

"Matsumara," I croon and cup his face to kiss each cheek.

"Ryan," he mutters waving me off. "Why is it you have such little respect for me? Do you not understand who I am?"

I fold my arms across my chest and smile. "I know who you are. See, the problem is you're seeing my actions as a lack of respect. I see them as affection."

"I like you. I'm showing you how much."

"I will say this in a way I think you will understand. I have history with your family. Very old friends.

"It is the only reason I haven't taken your life. However, I'm going to thrash your smart ass soon, young Ryan. It's what you need," he says as he narrows his eyes at me.

I return the gesture. I step in closer to him to tower over him. He lifts a brow, opening his suit jacket and flipping it back.

"I like you, didn't say that couldn't change. Don't let the jokes confuse you, old friend. I'm not the one to threaten.

"When I take a threat seriously, I handle that shit. Don't fuck with our friendship, Nash."

His men step forward as if they're going to do something. I stand firm. Despite popular opinion, Braxton isn't the crazy brother.

I've already mapped out four ways to take all their last breath in under two seconds. Kiyoshi lifts his hand to ward off his men. He snorts and pats my cheek with the same hand.

"Yes, I like you too, Ryan Black. Only reason I don't kill you. Neruson, get your friend before I teach him a lesson," he calls to his son who hasn't moved an inch as his father and I have our little exchange.

Kiyoshi walks off, but not before popping me upside the back of my head. I turn and grin after him. I truly do like him.

He's a cool ass dude. He fixes his jacket as he walks off with a whole lot of swagger.

"You're going to push my father one step too far one of these days. He's plotting the day he gets your ass back for always getting on his nerves," Nelson says as he places a hand on my shoulder and gives a squeeze.

"He loves me." I shrug. "I bring color to his life."

Ne chuckles. "I will help you stitch up the wounds when he strikes."

"Whatever, Ne."

The female with their group catches my eye. She stands out among the men for a few reasons. I grin as I let my gaze roll over her, but Ne drops his hand from my shoulder and steps in my way.

"Don't even think about it," he says.

I look between the two of them. No, this isn't a family protectiveness. She's not family at all. However, this is a familiar relationship.

"Oh, didn't know you staked a claim, bro."

He frowns. "She is off limits to you."

"Gotcha." I smirk and tilt my head to the side. "By the way, don't you have a sister? Why haven't I ever met her? Old Kiyoshi scared I'll end up family?"

He glares at me. "You do know that I have a temper far greater than my father's. Are you sure you want to rib me?"

"Ry, my boy," Brooklyn croons and pulls me into a headlock. "Why'd they bring ya along? Ya know how to be a rash on everyone's ass, ya do."

"Tell me about it," my father says. "It's going to come back to bite you in the ass one of these days."

"Me, never. Everyone loves me."

"Anyone want my last born? I think I dropped him a few times too many?"

"I knew it," Toby calls out.

I flip him the bird and walk off mumbling as I glare at dad. He roars with laughter, grabbing my shoulder to pull me back into a hug. I resist for a few seconds before I wrap my arms around him like the spoiled brat I am.

"Yer mouth is going to get ye clobbered," he murmurs into my ear.

"Comes with the territory."

Dad laughs some more. Hey, you either love me or hate me. I don't care either way. As long as my family's good, I'm straight.

Carmen

"Mommy, why can't he understand that I'm not a child anymore?" I whine to my mother.

"Your father is well aware that you're not a child, Nene. However, you're eighteen. Our guidance is a blessing you're graced to have," she says with her slight island accent.

Both of my parents have been so Americanized, it's mostly in their anger that they have a slip of the tongue. It's when my grandparents come for visits that I get the biggest reminder that I come from such a rich heritage. Well, other than looking in the mirror and seeing the mix of my parents in my reflection.

I have a Japanese father and Bajan mother. I guess you can call my mother Bajan American. My grandfather is first generation to be born and raised in the States.

He met his wife, my grandmother, on a visit back home and they married a month later. They moved back to the States and my mother was born. When you look at me there's no denying that I have a mixed background.

It gets annoying to be asked what I am, but I've grown up hearing it. Most times I ignore it now. I pout and lean against the countertop.

"I'm going to be nineteen," I mutter.

"Yes, I give birth to you. I know this. That changes nothing that I've said."

"But I don't want to study journalism." I drop my head to the counter and bang my hand against it.

"Cheese on bread." She groans. "And this tantrum is going to get your father to change his mind?"

"No," I huff, and lift my head to place my fists against my cheeks.

"We will talk to your father again. I think he has a valid point. You would do well in journalism, and he has a job waiting for you when you're done."

"I'm not Ne. I want to do something else."

"Like what? You have told your father what you don't want to do, but you refuse to tell him what you want to do. That's why he runs you, you have to speak up for yourself.

"He's not as hard a man as you see him. He may surprise you."

"If I tell him, he'll shut it down."

"Listen, Carmen. You're about to wear my nerves thin, girl. When your father comes home, we'll talk to him. Now go on."

"Fine, no one listens to me except Auntie Mariah. Ugh," I storm out of the kitchen for my bedroom.

CHAPTER ONE

Carmen

Present …

"You're full of shit," Wyatt says to Johnathan and bursts into laughter.

We all start to laugh as John shrugs his shoulders. "Whatever you say," he replies with a sly grin.

"You know you can't believe a thing he says," Ryan says beside me. "John says all the right things to make whatever he needs work for him."

"Is that right?" the pretty girl sitting next to John says. I've had too much to drink to remember her name right now.

I lean into Ryan. "Is she John's girlfriend?"

Ryan gives a shrug before leaning into me. "Complicated. You're going to have to watch that one unfold like the rest of us. We're all still trying to understand them," he whispers into my ear.

I go to ask another question when my phone rings. I look at the screen and frown. I'm a little tipsy. However, I know if I don't answer my father will send out a search party.

I quickly slip out of the pub to answer the call before he hangs up. My head spins a little as I make my way out. Maybe I'm a little more than tipsy.

"Hey, Daddy," I answer the phone.

"*Kon'nichiwa*, Nene, how are you?"

"Hello, *Otōsan*. I'm fine."

He makes that humming sound he does. I bite my lip not wanting to talk too much. Aunt Mariah will kill me if I get us busted.

"What are you up to? Are you studying while on your trip?"

"I'm out with some friends at the moment. I will study a bit when I get back to the house," I say.

"Is your *oba* with you?"

"No. She and Kevin are out having dinner, I believe." I bite my lip.

That's a lie. Aunt Mariah and Uncle Kevin left to return to the States. She promised she would tell my father that she's still here with me.

"Hm, I will let you get back to your friends. We will spend time when you return. I'd like to hear all about your trip," he says.

I promise, I think I'm busted. His tone says that he thinks I'm BSing him. I rub at my forehead.

I hate keeping secrets from my dad, but they have become necessary if I'm going to follow through with film school. I guess wanting to have a little fun while I'm at it adds to the necessity. I inhale the night air and nod as if he can see me.

"I'd like that. I'll see you soon, *Otōsan*."

"Yes, you will."

I hang up and look down at my phone with my brows drawn. I'm too drunk to analyze that call. Maybe it's the alcohol making me paranoid.

"Hey."

I nearly jump out of my skin. I fumble with my phone as it almost falls to the ground. Clenching it to my chest, I sigh in relief to see its only Ryan.

However, my relief is short-lived as he closes the space between us. Those golden eyes pierce right through me. Holding up two beers, he tilts his head to the side.

"Come for a walk with me," he says.

I suck my lip into my mouth, drawing his gaze down to my lips. I should walk back into that pub and get back to the lively conservation I left. That would be the sane thing to do.

However, my head seems to be possessed as I begin to nod it. I'm only along for the ride as my body moves to his side. He laces our fingers together and begins to lead me away from the rest of our party.

"Your dad checking in?"

I roll my eyes and sigh. "Yeah. My father tends to treat me like a baby. Everything has to be his way.

"Sometimes, I feel like I'm in this glass bubble watching life. It drives me crazy. If I want to go left, he says it has to be right.

"And of course, because I'm a good little daughter, I'm expected to do what he says. Boy, if he knew the things I'm hiding. He'd lose his mind." I hiccup and clamp my mouth shut.

I didn't mean to say all of that. Yup, I'm way more than tipsy. I peek up at Ryan to find him smiling down at me.

He squeezes my fingers. "Finally, my girl is opening up to me. Don't stop, gorgeous. You're adorable. Tell me, what are you hiding from, Daddy?"

I chew on my lip. Again, I know the right thing to do here. However, what my mouth does is totally another story.

"I'm supposed to be here with my *oba*. That means aunt in Japanese."

"I know, I'm fluent," he says and winks at me.

"Oh." I let that sink in as I continue. "Aunt Mariah has gone home so I could live a little. Back home, I have to check in with my father every other day since moving into my own apartment.

"An apartment I had to fight tooth and nail to get. Ugh! If Aunt Mariah and her husband didn't own the building, I'd still live with my parents."

I pull a frown and turn to face him. I look up at him and those golden eyes. His expression is so open, I can't help but spill all my feelings. I continue as if he's pulling a chain to open the dam.

"I'm not like my brother. He's like Daddy's little soldier or something. He has done everything my father has asked.

"I don't want to work in print. Words are great, but there's no creativity in writing stiff articles like my father wants me to. Or, God forbid, falling into some rat race to get into the latest issue of some paper or magazine. I'd shrivel up and die."

I throw my arms in the air and spin. "I want to work in film. Yeah, I should be grateful for the opportunity to work for one of the largest international media companies, but my father isn't going to let me do what I want." I sigh and shake my fist as I continue.

"It's why I freelance for NY/LA Connections. They allow me to incorporate images and video in my stories. Their blog is progressive."

I drop down onto my butt in the grass. We've walked into a wooded area by a little pond. Ryan walks over to a tree that's facing me and leans his back against it.

He still has the beers in his hands as he crosses his arms over his chest. I look away from him before I get caught in his gaze and lose my thought. I need to get this off my chest. It's like I've had it bottled up for so long, it's bubbling over now.

"I don't think I could stand doing things my father's antiquated way. His Japanese background influences the business and how he runs it. He publishes magazines and newspapers, they have to start with audio-visual soon, right?

"Why is he so against live film and capturing the moment?" I shove my hand in my hair and tug. "I'm scared if I tell him I want to do film, he'll shut it down. It's not words, it's not scholarly.

"I have no choice but to hide it. Once I do something great though, he can't take it from me. He'll see that I'm doing something that's worth my time and he'll allow me to have this," I say with determination.

I collapse onto my back and look up at the stars. "It's my life. I'm going to do what I want eventually. One of these days I'll find the balls to stand up to my dad."

Ryan

She's so cute as she geeks out about film versus words. Same shit to me, but I can feel her passion on the subject. It's in her eyes and in the way she slurs her words for her love of film.

She spreads her arms and legs out across the grass, like a snow angel. The moonlight places a glow on her face as she starts to sing "Time After Time," bouncing her feet to keep rhythm. Maybe she doesn't need any more beer.

With a grin, I squat and place the two bottles on the ground. I keep my eyes on Carmen. I think I'm forgotten as she lifts her hands and frames them as if she's filming the stars above.

I take a seat on my butt and drape my arms over my knees. Carmen is smart, but she's also a little naïve. She has this innocence that slips out when she's trying to be all tough.

"What about you, Ryan Black? What are you hiding?" she sings happily.

I chuckle. "Nothing, babe. I have nothing to hide."

"I don't believe that. Everyone has something they're hiding. It's funny. You got your family to tell me all about them, but I know nothing about you."

"Which is why we're going to date when we get back home. You can learn all about me."

She sits up on her elbows. Our eyes lock. Her cheeks have a blush to them that accents the bronze tone of her skin.

"There's no time like the present. Tell me something about you."

"Like what?" I smile at her.

"What makes you tick? What's your passion?"

I go to give a slick answer, but I realize for once I don't want to hide behind jokes. I want Carmen to get to know me. It's an odd feeling, but I go with the flow as I have since I met her.

"I've never thought of it that much. I'm the youngest of seven. I think my interests got lost somewhere along the way. I go with whatever."

She tilts her head and bats those long lashes at me. When she sucks her lip into her mouth, I'm tempted to go pry it free and kiss her. Instead, I stay right where I am and watch her think.

"There has to be something you love. Something that makes you, you."

I shrug. "Not really. I go to car shows because that's Brax's thing. I like playing video games, but Felix is crazy about them and anything tech.

"Noah and Wyatt got me hooked on hardware and combat—"

"Hardware?" She wrinkles her brows.

"Guns."

"Oh, gotcha, duh," she says and hiccups. "What about John?"

I laugh to myself. "I'll show you what I picked up from John soon enough."

She eyes me cautiously. I wink at her, and she gives me a shy smile. I allow my gaze to roll over her.

"I think you have a passion for being a smart ass."

"Ha." I release a deep laugh. I speak through my laughter. "That's possible."

She tilts her head to the other side. "No, I think I've got that wrong."

"Oh yeah, how so?"

"I think the jokes are a cover. For what, I haven't figured out," she muses.

I nod. She may have a point. I think it over.

"Most people are too focused on what I say. They don't take time to notice what I see. I keep your attention on what I want while I observe."

"I can see that. Still doesn't tell me what your passion is."

"I guess you're going to have to stick around to figure that out," I say and start for her.

I crawl over her until she falls back and I'm hovering over her body. She looks into my eyes, surprise clear in hers. I brush my fingertips against her cheek.

"You're beautiful. Do you know that?" I breathe against her lips.

"No."

I shake my head at that. She has to be insane. I brush my thumb across her bottom lip. It's so full. I want to feel her sexy mouth against mine again.

"Carmen."

"Yes?" she says breathlessly.

"Give me one good reason we shouldn't be together. If you can give me one, I'll walk away. If you can't we start our forever here. So make it good, baby."

"You're going to ruin my life," she says without a thought.

I scoff and grin at her. Shaking my head, I wish I could say I feel sorry for her. I don't. That was the wrong answer.

"Ruin your life, nah. Not me. I'm going to enhance your life in ways women only dream of."

I nuzzle her neck before kissing it softly. I grin wider at the sharp intake of air that comes from her lips. "This dick though, yeah, this dick will ruin your life. That I can promise you."

This time I capture the gasp that comes from her lips. She moans into my mouth and locks her fingers in my hair. I take my time, gliding a hand down her side.

"Mmm," I groan as I deepen the kiss.

She tastes so damn good. I want this girl so fucking much. I begin to bunch her dress in my hand, lifting it up to her waist.

Breaking the kiss, I savor the flavor of her skin as I drag my lips from hers to her chin. Her thighs are so warm when I reach between her legs to caress them. Her skin is smooth and silky.

When I hook my fingers into her panties, I find her dripping wet. I growl and run my digits along her seam a few times before pushing into her. When she arches up into me, I nip at her chin and continue to play with her fat pussy.

Pressing my thumb to her clit, I watch as she writhes beneath me. She's perfection. The bewildered look in her eyes turns me on so much, I think I'm going to burst right out of my jeans.

"Can I have a taste, baby?"

She makes the cutest face as she whimpers and nods. Licking my lips, I move down her body. I spread her dress underneath her as a barrier between her and the grass. Swiftly, I pull her panties down her legs.

"Ryan," she whispers as I lower my head and take my first taste.

"Fuck," I groan into her folds. She tastes and smells like heaven.

Her thighs cradle my head as I feast on her. I hadn't planned this. I wanted to talk and get to know her more. There's just something about Carmen that makes me forget everything. I've wanted her for too long to deny myself now.

"Oh my God, yes," she cries out.

I chuckle, but I don't stop eating her out while I work her with my fingers. I'm tapping that spot. She's going to come soon.

I'm nothing if not proficient in the art of pussy. I'm good with my mouth, hands, and cock. Something Carmen learns fast.

She's tight and so wet. I can't wait to slide inside her warmth. Although, I'm determined not to take it that far out here. This sample will have to hold me over for now.

I lift her hips and push my face deeper into her core. Her cries mix with my slurping. When her legs start to tremble, I grin in satisfaction.

However, I'm taken by surprise when she squirts in my face. "Oh, shit," I exclaim as I back up and place her hips down.

I wipe at my face and look at my hand in awe. I look down and see that her dress is soaked beneath her. I've never had a chick squirt. I've seen it in a few films, but this is a first for me. I mean, chicks have come for me, they've been wet as fuck, but squirting.

She just gushed like a geyser. It's dripping down my face. I lift my gaze to hers. She bites her lip as she stares back at me.

"We're leaving. Now," I say tightly before fixing her clothes quickly and standing to pull her to her feet.

She looks at me with a confused and lost expression. I can't think to say what needs to be said. She'll understand soon enough.

CHAPTER TWO

Take Our Time

Carmen

I don't know what I did wrong. I'm too embarrassed to ask. My dress is soaked. It's sticking to my skin.

I was grateful when Ryan took his shirt off to wrap around my waist while he went into the pub in his T-shirt to grab my things. He then rushed us back to the house.

I've kept my head down the entire time. I just want to get to my room and hide. We walk into the house and voices can be heard coming from somewhere.

This place is so big, I'm not sure where they are, only that they're having a good time as laughter fills the air. I turn for my side of the house, but Ryan wraps an arm around my waist and tugs me in front of him. I look up at him finally and find lust in his eyes. He shakes his head at me.

"Too many people on that side of the house. Come to my room," he whispers.

I bite my lip as I stare into his eyes. His gaze drops to my lips. Before I can think about it, he plucks me off my feet and rushes to the stairs on the opposite side of the house.

I lock my arms around his neck, nervous and still confused. When we get to the top of the stairs, he pecks my lips and grazes his nose across my cheek. I close my eyes and take a deep breath.

"Ryan," I whisper. "What ... did ... um did I do something wrong?" I ask as he steps into his room and closes the door with his back.

He places me on my feet and pulls his shirt from around my waist. He looks into my eyes and tilts his head to the side. His gaze travels the length of my body.

"When?" he breathes as he moves closer, placing a hand on my waist and tugs me to him.

"You stopped. I ... I thought I did something wrong."

He cups my face with his free hand and leans in to kiss me. I drop my things to the floor and reach to lock my hands in his hair and allow him to devour me. Okay, so I've kissed guys before, but not like this.

Ryan kisses with everything he is. I feel his kisses in my toes. I've never had anyone go down on me like that.

Or at all, if truth be told. I don't know if what happened back there is normal or just a Ryan experience. I mean, I tried to get myself off once. It wasn't what I thought it would be, so I never tried again.

"Carmen?"

"Yes."

"Are you a virgin, baby?"

I twist my lips, bite the inside of my cheek and nod. His eyes soften as he brushes my cheek with a soft caress. He nods to himself.

"Twenty. Okay. We'll take this slow. I'll give you a pass. As much as I want you right now, you say the word and we'll do this another time."

My inner walls clench. There's no way I'm waiting. I want him to take care of this ache that's nagging at my body.

My nipples are rock hard as they press against my bra. I'm still wet and I have to clench my thighs together every time I think about him between my legs.

"No, I want this," I say in almost a whisper.

"That's my girl," he murmurs before taking my lips again.

Breaking the kiss, he slips the straps of my dress from my shoulders and slowly pushes the fabric to the floor. I heave out a nervous breath. Ryan reaches for my chin and lifts my head until I meet his gaze.

"Relax. You did nothing wrong. Your response to me was a turn-on. I want you. I want you bad." He licks his lips. Then he smiles that teasing smile. "I'm going to show you the world. You just hold on for the ride."

With that, he lifts me onto his waist and carries me over to the bed. Never once does he break our eye contact. A voice in the back of my mind tells me that I need to run out of this room and stop being a fool.

I'm not a virgin because I'm waiting until marriage or for the right one. It's more like I've never been turned on by a guy enough to go there. I have a habit of picking gorgeous jerks to date.

It's the reason I know this is bad for me. However, when Ryan touches me, it feels like my body is on fire. His intense gaze is only taking it over the edge.

"Open," he commands as he places his long fingers before my lips.

I open my mouth, and he sticks them inside. I suck on his digits until he pulls them free, dragging them down my chin, my throat, between my breasts, over my belly button, to the apex of my thighs. When he slips his hand between my legs, I start to pant.

I can't wait for him to give me another orgasm. That was so incredible. My pussy makes all kinds of wet noises as he pushes his fingers inside of me and starts to play with my body.

With his free hand, he pulls down the cup of my bra. My breast spills free and it's the first time he looks away from me. He dips his head and pulls my nipple into his mouth.

I cry out and lift my back off the mattress. I reach for his bicep, not sure if I want to pull him closer or if I want to stop him. It feels so good, but like too much all at once.

"Ryan," I gasp.

He moves to place his lips to my ear. "You like that?"

"Yes."

"Tell me what you want? I'm whatever you need. All you have to do is ask. Come on, baby, tell me exactly what I can do to make this pussy happy."

I moan. I don't know how to answer that. I like the way I feel, but I know I want more. I need more.

"You can tell me. Come on. Let me hear it."

"I need more," I whisper.

He licks beneath my chin. "That's a start."

I lock my eyes on the ceiling and grab for the sheets as he rubs my nub and works his fingers inside me at the same time. He plants a trail of kisses down the center of my breasts. His descent is painfully slow. I almost want to yell at him to hurry the heck up.

"I need you," I whimper the thought when he still doesn't reach where I need him most.

"I'm going to give you everything you need. Hold tight."

I moan and try to call on my patience. He moves to kiss my hip and licks at the skin there. He's killing me.

The slow licking and sucking he does to my hip and thigh is maddening. He works his way to my inner thigh. Just when I think he's going to get to my core, he shifts to the other leg and starts to kiss and work his way around the other thigh.

"Please."

He chuckles and makes his way back to my center. His fingers are still doing all kinds of delicious things to me. I want something I don't know how to ask for and I'm desperate to figure it out.

When his lashes lift, revealing those golden eyes that look straight through me, I bite my lip and hiccup. His lips spread into a wider smile. I should've known he was going to strike.

I cry out and suck in a deep breath as I lift and grab the top of his hair. He attacks my center mercilessly. I try to scoot away, and he locks his hands around my thighs tight.

My stomach caves as I wiggle and try to hold myself together. He only dives deeper. My eyes roll in my head.

I plant my feet and try to buck him off. It's no use. I gasp for air and try to take it.

When he flattens his tongue to my clit and then flicks quickly across it, I'm so not able to hold it all together. I flip over onto my stomach, trying not to kick him in his head. However, it's no reprieve.

Ryan attacks my pussy from behind. He lifts my hips until I move to my knees and he buries his face in deep. I don't think I helped myself out at all.

I need to grab the sheets again to help me stay in my body. I'm right there. I'm going to come.

"Oh my God," I scream out.

"Fuck yeah," he growls as I start to come and spray him like out in the meadow. He nips my butt cheek. "You're so sexy, baby."

I'm left panting and sagging into the sheets as he shifts around doing something. I don't have the strength to open my eyes and see what. That is until I hear him curse.

The bed dips under his weight. I push my hair out of my face and turn to look at him. His cheeks are red, and he looks frustrated.

"What's wrong?"

He locks eyes with me. "I don't have condoms. I had a box to put in my bag, but just remembered I left them on the damn dresser. I totally forgot. Fuck."

"Can you ask someone else for one?" I ask hopefully.

He looks at me with a pointed glare. Yeah, almost everyone here is married and I'm not sure I want anyone to know about this if they weren't. This could be a problem.

I bite my lip and bury my face in the mattress. I want this so bad. I'll never have this chance again once we're back home.

My dad is always in everything. He's another reason I don't date or have sex. I growl into the mattress.

Decision made, I look back at Ryan. He has one hand shoved into his hair with the other palming his erection. My eyes widen. I almost change my mind.

"Have you been tested?"

He turns his head to me slowly. His eyes are narrowed. He looks me over, still on my knees with my ass in the air.

"Yeah," he says. "Last results came back clean."

"Have you been with anyone since?" I suck my lip deeply into my mouth.

He shakes his head. "I see where you're going. You've been drinking. I think we should wait."

I wiggle my butt at him and smile. "Are you sure? I know what I want. I thought you wanted the same thing. Maybe I'm wrong."

"Oh, don't play with me, Carmen. I'm holding on by a thread as it is."

"What happened to all your jokes?"

He moves lightning fast, capturing my face and taking my lips. I can taste my essence on his lips. I smile and suck on his bottom lip. He groans.

"You're mine," he moves to my ear to say. His lips brush the shell as he grins. "Let's see if I can perfect my pull-out game."

He places a hand on my back and glides it up to release my bra. Flattening his heated palm between my shoulder blades, he turns me over so I'm on my back once again. I cover my breasts as I look up at him.

He shakes his head. "Don't hide from me. I want to see you. All of you."

He brushes my hair out of my face and lowers to kiss me again. I'm lost in his kisses as he lines up with my entrance. He's in no rush. He makes his way to my neck and starts to suck and kiss there.

Right when I think he's going to set another slow torture in progress, he starts to slip inside me. It's slow, but he's big and my body isn't having it at first. He licks my neck and backs out to push in again.

This time I take a little more of him. He groans and grabs hold of my hair. The action both surprises and turns me on.

He locks those eyes on me, and I know it's coming. He thrusts forward. I claw at his back. Ryan stills and pecks my lips.

"So sorry, baby. I promise it'll be nothing but pleasure from here."

I nod and tug him into me to bury my face in his neck. He's pulsing inside me. It's a weird feeling but it feels good too. A few beats go by, and he starts to move. I gasp and groan.

Ryan places a hand behind my thigh, pushing my leg back into me. I open to him fully and as he promised, my body comes to life and the feel of him stretching and filling me is like nothing I've ever felt before. He's all I can focus on.

"Ryan," I breathe his name like a prayer.

"Damn, your pussy is insane. You feel so ... oh, shit. Don't do that," he pants and places his forehead to my cheek.

I freeze. I hadn't meant to clench my walls, it just felt right. I rub a hand down his sweaty back. He keeps moving into me, but I can feel him trembling.

I don't know how, but he's swelling inside me.

I moan and tighten around him again. I giggle when he looks at me with wild eyes. I can't help myself. I squeeze him again.

"Really?" he pants and lifts a brow.

He pulls out and flips me onto my stomach. He palms my hips and tugs me back. I look over my shoulder and our eyes connect. He guides himself back into me.

"Ah," I cry out.

He leans over me. "Let's see if you can handle me now."

He covers my mouth with his hand right as he starts to plow into me, hard. I widen my eyes at him as he grins down at me. His smile is straight savage.

He knows what he's doing to me is brutal seduction. I curl my toes and reach for his thigh behind me. I scream into his palm as my pleasure goes through the roof.

When he reaches between my legs, my brows shoot into my hair. I fly right into the sun. It's bright and blinding and all-consuming.

Damn, I should've kept running.

Ryan

I've never had someone respond to me like she does. This warm, wet pussy is so damn good. I can see the surprise in her eyes as I get ready to take her over.

I'm close, but I fight my release back. This is for her. I bite my lip and grunt when I feel her about to come. One more flick of her clit and she's done for.

She passes out in my hold. I'm stunned at first. Then a grin comes to my lips. I peck her forehead and release her mouth.

"You should've kept running," I murmur. "Now, I'm never letting you go."

Carmen Black.

Damn. I'm not supposed to fall in love.

CHAPTER THREE

Abandoned

Ryan

I'm knocked out with a hand hanging over the side of the bed when my phone starts to vibrate. It takes a minute for the sound to break through to my brain. This is the best-sated sleep I've ever had.

I swear, for once in my life I want to ignore the damn thing. I'm exhausted. I spent the night devouring Carmen.

Hell, her thick warm body is snuggled into my side with my other arm around her. I'm actually napping before I take her again. Yeah, I've been greedy.

Something I shouldn't be since we haven't used a single condom. I sigh and lift my hand to grab my phone. I turn my head to open my eyes.

The text is from Felix. I sit up quickly. I read the text over at least three times.

I swear shit like this has the worst timing. Then again, this would happen when everyone thinks our attention is somewhere else.

Half the Alliance was present for Noah's wedding. I had my money on someone making a move during the ceremony. It's what I would have done.

"Fuck," I mutter.

I turn to look at a passed-out Carmen. I smirk. Her snores are cute.

I wore that ass out. I don't want to wake her. I get up quietly and go take a quick shower.

When I return to the room, she's still fast asleep. I chew on my lip for a second before I go to find her things she dropped on the floor last night. I can leave her a message on her phone. If it's not locked, I can get her number and text her.

I don't have much time. I need to be on the move. Her phone is in her purse. When I find it, it's dead.

I curse and toss it back into her bag. I should've gotten her number last night. I look around and move over to the desk in the corner.

I open the desk drawer and look over my shoulder. She's still asleep. I turn back and find a Post-it cube and a pen. I jot down a note and get frustrated with each word I write.

I don't want to leave like this, but hopefully, I'll be back as soon as we handle this shit. I don't have the logistics yet. All I know is our target and that we're about to be on the move.

Carmen should be fine with the girls. Noah will probably be staying behind. It's his honeymoon after all.

I turn and move to the bed. I think about waking her anyway, but my phone buzzes again. I'm out of time.

I place the note on the pillow I slept on and lean to kiss her forehead. I take one last glance at her sexy body resting beneath the sheet. I start to get hard and know I need to go now before my father and brothers kill me.

"See you soon, baby," I whisper.

Carmen

I wake to the sound of little voices. I turn my head slowly and find Lulu and TJ sitting on the bed on their knees watching me. I yelp and turn to sit up and tug the sheet around me.

"This is Uncle Ryan's room. He's not here."

"Um, maybe he went to the kitchen for breakfast?"

Lulu shakes her head and giggles. "No, silly. He's not here, here. He went bye-bye with daddy. We'll see them when they come home. Mommy's packing so we can go home," she says as if I'm the child.

"You were sleeping loud," TJ says, tilting his head as he peers at me.

"Oh, sorry," I say and try running a hand through my hair.

My head is throbbing. Actually, everything is throbbing. Last night starts to come back to me. I had sex with Ryan.

Suddenly, everything starts to snap into focus. We had sex and now he's gone. I can't believe he just left.

Wow.

I'm such a fool. I can't believe I fell into the trap. I knew I never should've slept with him.

He didn't even have the courtesy to say thanks or whatever. I'm left here feeling like a fool and embarrassed. His niece and nephew are sitting here wondering what I'm doing in his bed.

I groan and mentally slap myself. Yeah, it's time to cut this trip short. I'm such a goofball.

I would get myself into the walk of shame to end all walks of shame. I can't blame anyone but myself. I knew Ryan's type before I made the decision to sleep with him last night.

I'm not even going to try to blame the alcohol. TJ cups my cheek.

"Hey, why you crying? My mommy has band-aides she'll kiss your boo boo."

"I don't think she has a boo boo," Lulu says. "She has the sads."

Lulu stands up on the bed and puts her hands on her hips. "Where'd they go? TJ and I will kick their butts like Uncle Noah taught us. Show us."

A laugh slips out even as the tears fall down my cheeks. I wonder if they'd still be willing to fight if they knew it's their uncle who caused my sads. They're both adorable.

TJ wraps his arms around my neck and Lulu follows. "It's going to be okay. You have friends. Grandma baked cookies too."

"Lu ... TJ," Kamara calls out. "Where are you guys? I'm getting tired of chasing you two around this place. Come out now."

"Ut-oh. We're in trouble. We'll see you later," Lulu whispers and tugs on her brother's shoulder to get him to follow her. They both jump off the bed and run from the room. I palm my face and have a full-out cry.

I'm so humiliated. I have to face a house full of people after last night. It's not like they all know what happened, but I can't help feeling like someone will know.

I sniffle and blow out a breath. I have to get myself together and get back to my room. If I can do that without being seen, then I'll deal with the rest of my feelings later.

"It's time to call Aunt Mariah."

***

An hour later and I've returned to my own room, showered, dressed, and called my aunt to ask her to get me home as soon as possible. I've been hiding in my room, waiting for my ride to arrive. Courtney is at my side, holding me in her arms as I ball my eyes out.

"It's going to be all right. It's his loss."

I wipe under my nose. "I feel so stupid."

"Maybe there's more to it. I could go down and see if I can find out more," she offers.

"No. I want to be done. I don't want anyone to ask for me. I'm so embarrassed as it is. We can leave when our ride gets here."

"Are you sure?"

"Yeah," I say as my phone rings. I pull it out to see that our ride is out front. "Come on. Let's move fast."

We collect our things and move for the front door as fast as we can. I don't look back once our things are in the trunk and we're settled into the back of the car. I swipe at my tears and sink down into the seat.

"It's going to be okay."

"Yeah, I just need to get home."

He abandoned me. I thought for a moment that I was special. I allowed myself the fantasy.

Never again.

Cassy

"Lulu, what's that stuck to your butt?" Nellie asks as Lulu and TJ get up to run out of the kitchen after breakfast.

Lu stops in her tracks to look over her shoulder. She takes what looks to be a note from the back of her skirt. A guilty look comes over her face and she quickly clenches the note to her chest.

"Nothing," she says innocently.

Before I can get after her and find out what she's hiding, she takes off. These little ones are beginning to become little terrors. They're going to give their parents a run for their money. Nora is a little stinker too.

She sits in Nellie's lap looking all innocent with her face covered in syrup, but she'll be making trouble of her own in a few.

"I'll be packed faster if you can watch Nora for me," Nellie says to a pouting Bean.

"No problem," she grumbles.

"Please, who are ye fooling. Yer in a pissy mood because yer husband took off and ye look a little green this morning. Morning sickness started?"

Bean gives a little smile and nods.

"You're pregnant?" All the girls say at once.

Bean looks around at the other nine women in the room with us. Her cheeks take on color. I've known for a bit now. She glows with my next grand. She bites her lip and nods.

The girls and my sister-in-law break out into congratulations. Heather catches my eye as she looks down at the table. I smile. I don't blow her up. I wait patiently.

"So, I guess that means we're due around the same time then," Heather says.

A collective gasp fills the room. "I was waiting for ye to speak up," I say. "We have tons of new life coming into the family. I see a few more weddings coming too."

All heads turn in the same direction. Although, I don't doubt they're right with that one. That's not who I'm talking about.

It's the lass missing from the room that's going to make the next man out of my boys. The one boy who swore he'd never fall. My baby.

Speaking of which. "Has anyone seen Carmen or her little friend?"

"They left. I thought you knew that," my special little bird says.

This one is an unusual lass, but she'll survive this family. I furrow my brows at her words. Ryan said that Carmen was sleeping and asked me to make sure she ate and relaxed today.

I popped him upside his head when he made the request. I know that boy tainted the wee thing with his filthy hands and dirty cock. She's sweet, but I've noticed that she's a bit young.

Ryan is a whole handful. I worry for the poor thing. Ye never know what ye'll get messing around with one of my brats. That last one is a special one.

"What do you mean, she left?"

"They had their bags. A car was outside. They're gone."

I purse my lips. I may have to kill Ryan. He's going to have a full out breakdown when he finds out she left.

He may not know it yet, but he's gone for the lass. She's a pretty one. I can't blame him. All my daughters-in-law are gorgeous women. My boys did well.

I'll wait until I hear from Joe to send Ryan a message that she left on her own. Pity, I had looked forward to picking her brain on the ride home.

I'm well aware of who her father is. If Ryan plans to pursue her, I want to make sure the lass is worth the trouble.

"All right then. Let's get our things together. I'll get ye all home and we can wait for the word from there," I order and turn back to the kitchen.

I have cookies baking for the wee ones for the trip. I smile as I think of all the babes that will fill my home for the holidays. I raised good boys, I did.

I can't say I'd trade a single one of them.

CHAPTER FOUR

Mission

Ryan

"Fuck you," the dirtbag snarls.

"No, fuck ya." Logan puts a boot in the asshole's chest as he swings from the ropes, hanging upside down.

It's hot as fuck in here, but the one who's feeling the heat is the one about to meet his maker. This trip had a purpose. A purpose that has become personal to the men standing around me.

We've all been waiting for this motherfucker to come back up on the radar. He finally got ballsy, and the reaper was ready to greet him. Austin Mc Wien is a scumbag.

He deserves what's coming for him. The way he treated his own daughter, Camille, and the shit he did to Logan. Yeah, he's had this visit coming to him. It was only a matter of time.

Logan has a sinister grin on his face as he stands before Mc Wien. He has him tied upside down by his feet in the old bungalow a few friends of ours offered. I think I'm getting used to this Alliance idea. Costa Rica welcomed us with open arms.

We walked right in and handled business. Cleaners are already working on the bodies we left behind at Mc Wien's place. He was guarded like Fort Knox, but his men never saw us coming.

I look around the room. LaSalle, my dad, cousins, and brothers all wear the same expression. I get pissed every time I think of all the things Logan has lost because of this piece of shit.

Three years of his life, gone. He'll never get that back. The woman he loved.

I can't even imagine what that must feel like. I think of the woman I left behind in my bed. My anger rises.

I'd destroy a motherfucker for her. Logan squats before Mc Wien and grabs him by his graying hair, tugging him forward. The look in Logan's eyes goes from sinister to crazed. His rage bounces around the room.

"So ya thought ya could keep me behind bars? Ya helped my grandfather take pieces of me away. Do ya see how none of that worked?" Logan snarls.

"Your Alliance will never work. Bloodshed will fill the streets. You're not built for what you're asking for," Mc Wien says through swollen lips.

"He still talks shit, he does?" Brooklyn scoffs.

"Aye, that he does," Logan says.

LaSalle pushes off the wall and steps forward. "If I were him, I'd say something worth speaking with my last breath."

"You will fail. That's worth its weight in gold. You think you're the only ones who has been planning for this?" Mc Wien retorts.

"But here's the thing. It's already working. Ya all will meet the same fate.

"Every last one of ya that are tone-deaf and don't hear the signs of the times. I'm not fucking playing. Yer going to serve as my first example. The first head on a stake."

"You can't do this. If I die, you open the floodgates. You have no idea what I've been keeping from your doorstep."

"I'll take my chance," Logan says right before pulling a machete across his throat.

Welp, that's the end of that. Although, a feeling in my stomach tells me it's not. No, this is only the beginning.

There's no turning back now. The Alliance has been born, and we all have blood on our hands for the cause.

"Have everyone on alert," LaSalle says.

"Aye, I'm no one's fool. His words weren't rubbish to toss aside."

"I heard them loud and clear," LaSalle says. "I will make sure everyone at the table keeps their head up. If this is going to turn ugly, it's coming soon."

"We'll handle it. We've been getting ready for this," Logan says. "Uncle Joe, thanks for stepping in. We appreciate ya."

"Aye, not a problem. Do ye mind if I talk to Kiyoshi?"

"Suit yerself."

"Thanks. I'll handle getting him the information."

"Grand. Let's go."

Dad nods. He turns to me. "You're with me."

Great. I won't be getting back to Carmen anytime soon. Fan-fucking-tastic.

CHAPTER FIVE
Old Friends

Joe

I rub my tired eyes. This has been a trying week. No, make that month.

I would have loved nothing more than to see my son get married and enjoy my family and time with my wife. I knew the moment Toby requested a seat with the Alliance the lines would blur for good. We were always heading for this.

My nephews are nothing if not ambitious. I don't doubt them. Hell, they have the power behind them in bloodline alone to make this happen.

I sit back in my seat in this dimly lit bar as this tiny lass wiggles her ass around on the shiny black table before me. I have no interest in her. Cass would cut my balls off if I even thought about it.

Not that I would. I found the woman that gets my blood going years ago. That red hair drew me to her like a flame.

I grin as I think of my Cass. I can't wait to get home to my wife. I plan to remind her how we made seven boys. The woman still has that fire in her.

"I see you are having a good time." I look up from the whiskey in my hand. Kiyoshi stands before me.

I put my drink down and stand. I wanted to make this visit personally. Kiyoshi is a friend. I want to address him as such.

"I was musing on our youth," I say to him as I stand and bow.

He waves a hand at me and tugs me into a hug. I smile. Yes, a very old friend. He releases me and we take our seats.

"Sorry about the choice of location. I thought this would be the safest place."

I nod. What others don't know about this place is that any one of these girls will pull a sword or gun from thin air and clear this place out. This is a safe place for allies of Kiyoshi, until it's not.

"It's fine. We can talk freely here."

"Speaking of talking freely. I ran into Ryan at the bar." He tilts his head to the side. "Why does your son have a death wish?"

I chuckle. I wonder if he means the fact that my son is after his daughter or if Ry has been getting on his nerves again with his smart-ass mouth. I give a hearty laugh as both thoughts cross my mind.

"You entertain him. As long as he can get a rise from you, he's going to try you."

"Yes, this much I know," he says with a small grin. I think he enjoys Ryan's teasing. "One of these days I will have the last laugh. Anyway, down to business. You are here in person. This must be serious."

"Mc Wien has been removed from the equation. The Alliance has played its hand. They're coming."

"Ah, yes, I've heard the rumors." He leans back in his seat.

"This will get ugly before the balance is met. Our families, those close to us, they all will be targets."

"Ha. My wife is a dangerous woman. I wish them luck," he says with a smile.

I look my friend in the eyes. Kiyoshi has a tendency to live within the bubble of his creation. Untouchable. This is why I'm here. I believe he has something of value to my boy.

"Aye, I know she is." I lean forward and level him with my gaze. "However, she's not my concern."

"Ah, you're speaking of my daughter that thinks I don't know what she's up to," he says.

"Yes, as you know she was at another wedding and this time she spent some time with my lot."

"I'm very aware. What aren't you telling me, my old friend?"

I sigh. "You do know that this has the potential to reveal you to her?"

He narrows his eyes slightly. All humor leaves. He leans forward in his seat.

"She is protected."

I shake my head. "I want you to think about the threat that's coming. She knows nothing of who you are. You have babied the lass."

I lift my hand when his nostrils flare. "I mean this with all respect. I understand. You wanted her to live a life outside of all of this. However, we've all changed the course of our lives the moment we aligned ourselves with the Alliance. I've said nothing, ol' lad, but this is going to come back to bite you."

"My daughter is not as weak as it may seem. I've always prepared her for anything, even if she doesn't know it. What is the point you are making?" he asks with a calm that I know is false.

I chuckle. "She's a bright, lass. She's also inquisitive."

"What are you saying?"

"Ryan is keen on your daughter. *Kare wa kanojo ni taishite, kare ga mada shitte iru yori mo fukai kanjō o motte imasu.*"

It's the truth. Ryan has feelings for Carmen. Feelings I don't think the lad has realized are rooted deeply.

Kiyoshi's brows shoot into his hairline. I watch and wait as he processes this. I'm not expecting the slow smile that comes to his face. This time I sit back in my seat and observe.

"Is that right? And you feel that my daughter returns this affection?"

"I do."

His smile widens. "Yes, I see opportunity here." I side-glance him. I'm not sure I follow. "I have been wondering how far my daughter will go with these lies.

"I'm a fair father. I would have given her a chance to express her wants. No. She goes behind my back with my sister repeatedly. I believe I've raised a spoiled child."

"And what does this have to do with Ryan?"

"I now have something that your son wants. Ryan taunts those around him because he has no reasonability. My friend, I'm not the only one with a coddled child. As the youngest, Ryan has gotten away with quite a bit."

I nod. "Yes, Ry is a brat. Cass and I know this. The whole lot of them are."

"Yes, but they have all grown to be men you and Cass can be proud of."

He frowns and sits in thought for a moment before he continues. "I still don't believe this world is her place. Carmen is destined for a world of her own making, but I do see your point. I think your son and my daughter will learn a lesson as I show them both a master trickster."

I laugh. My friend is about to find out that my son will have the last laugh once again. I don't tell him this. I think I'll sit back and enjoy this one. It shall be entertaining.

"Are you sure about this?"

"Yes, they both need to learn this lesson. Nene lies to me and believes I'm a blind man. This will teach them both."

"This may blow up in your face."

He shrugs. "Worst that could happen, you and I will become family in a deeper sense. Ryan is a smart young man.

"He sees things others don't. His humor can make you want to throttle him, but it's a cover for his wisdom. I like your son very much. However, he and Nene don't need to know."

I sigh. "As you wish." I should have gone into the security business. It seems like we do more and more of it these days. I shake my head. "What's your plan?"

CHAPTER SIX

Knock-Knock

Carmen

"Yes, Daddy. I'm going to stay in for the night." I sigh into the phone.

I swear my father is onto me. He's called me two times a day since I've been back, even with my visits to the house. I can't even lick my wounds in peace.

"I hope you are looking after your studies."

"Yes, I've been studying. Everything is as it should be."

I could run through my classes without opening a single book, but I won't tell him that. I study anyway because if I ever fail, he would give me the lecture of my life.

"As a Nash, you never fail."

I roll my eyes and pick at invisible lint on my T-shirt. "Very good. I have a business trip, but I'll be back soon. I will see you when I return. We will celebrate your birthday then, I promise."

"It's fine, Dad. I get it. You're a busy man. I'll survive."

He sighs. "I want you to continue your visits with your mother." I slump down on the bed and kick my feet like a toddler.

Not that I don't plan to go see my mother while he's gone. It's the fact that he feels he has to tell me to like a child. Or maybe, it's really the fact that he expects me to check in at all.

"Okay," I say into the phone, hiding my frustration.

"Love you, Nene."

"Love you, *Otōsan*."

"*Oyasuminasai*."

"Goodnight. Have a safe trip."

We end the call, and I stare up at the ceiling. My life is so lame. My birthday is tomorrow and I'm here in my apartment alone, instead of out somewhere partying.

I look over to the stack of books on my desk. I have five exams to study for. Two for film school and three for my journalism degree.

Thank God, finals are coming up soon enough and I'll be able to take a breather. No more double life for the summer at least. However, I'm not even remotely in the mode to move.

I frown as the front door opens, signaling my roommate's return. She has a date with her from the sounds of it. I roll my eyes.

It's about to get loud in here. It's the main reason I purchased noise-canceling headphones.

Grr.

Too bad I left those out in the living room. I huff and punch the bed. I don't feel like getting up.

I wiggle around until I'm under the covers and pull them up over my head. Soon moans float from the bedroom next to mine. I wish this place were designed differently.

Our beds are pushed to the same wall so I can hear everything that goes on next door. I start to think about my one night with Ryan. I grin when Gigi's moans don't sound half as enthralling as mine had.

She might even be faking again. My nipples tighten as I think of the way Ryan devoured my body and made me scream for him. I've tried not to think about that night, but it's been so hard.

I can't forget his strong body over mine or the way his forearms caged me in while I stared at the Brothers Black tats on them. I wanted to lick the ink and savor all things Ryan. A moan comes from my roommate's date, and I laugh to myself.

Ryan's groans and growls were deeper and sexier. This guy sounds like bad porn or something. I laugh at the thoughts.

I've never seen porn in my life. I don't know what a bad one would sound like, but this guy has it down.

"Oh, boy," I huff.

It doesn't sound like they're going to call it quits anytime soon. I chew on my lip. Maybe I should go get my headphones and check out some porn. It's the closest I'm going to get to any action.

Nah.

That's not going to help me to stop thinking of Ryan. I can almost feel his weight over me as I try to imagine that night all over again. Watching videos on my phone will only be torture.

I flip over on my stomach and groan, squeezing my thighs together. My body needs to get on the same page as my heart. We don't need to think about Ryan. He abandoned me and made me feel like a complete idiot.

I don't ever want to see him again. Another ten minutes go by and Gigi starts to cry out. Yeah, I can't take any more of this.

I force my body out of the bed, shoving my glasses on to stumble out into the living room. I snitch my headphones up and turn back for my room.

The doorbell rings and I lift a brow. My brother had said he was going to stop by this week, but he would have called first. If Gigi forgot about another date and I have to cover for her again, I'm going to be pissed.

Gigi and her date choose this very moment to go silent. Shaking my head, I toss the headphones back down and go over to the door to peek out and see who it is. My mouth drops open as I see the tall figure outside my apartment.

I step back like the door is hot. Wringing my hands before me, I try to figure out what to do. I can always go back to my room and blast my music in my ears and pretend I never heard the door.

The bell rings again and I jump. I palm my forehead and look behind me. I don't know who I think is watching me.

I turn back to the door and shake my hands out. Okay, I don't want Gigi to know about my shame so I should answer before she does. I step forward, unlock the door and snatch it open.

My intention is to glare at him and serve up attitude. That doesn't happen. When I open the door, he stands with his arms braced above his head on the doorframe and those golden eyes fix on mine right away.

He gives me one of those sexy, heated smiles and I nearly melt right at his feet. However, the pain of waking alone brings me back to earth.

"What do you want?" I hiss.

Ryan

I'm a little thrown by her reaction. Mom told me Carmen disappeared without a word. I was pissed and frustrated.

I didn't have her number, and we never got to talk. Lucky for me, her father was more than willing to give me all her information, address included.

As her new bodyguard, until this Alliance shit calms down, he was willing to tell me everything about her. Sure, Nash has plenty of men of his own, but if Carmen sees one of them following her around, she'll have questions. I can slide in, and Carmen won't think anything of it.

At least, that's how Dad and Kiyoshi put it. I don't give a fuck either way. Time with my girl is all I care about.

Sure, I was told to keep my hands off her, but when the hell have I ever listened to what I'm told. Besides, that sexy body has been mine since Ireland.

"I was expecting a much warmer greeting than that, baby," I say as I watch her closely.

"Get away from my door, Ryan."

I frown and take a step closer. I cup her face. "What's wrong?"

"Are you kidding me?" she replies. "You screwed me, then took off without saying a word. Like, wow, Ryan. Seriously?"

I work my jaw in frustration. "Babe, I left you a note. Your phone was dead, I couldn't call myself to get your number to text you or call."

"I didn't get any note."

I knit my brows. "I left it on the pillow—"

I cut off when a guy appears behind her in his boxers, scratching his head. I see nothing but red. I look down at Carmen in her panties and T-shirt then back at this guy.

"Hey, which way is the bathroom?" he asks.

I black the fuck out. "I'll kill you," I roar as I push my way into the apartment.

"Oh my God, Ryan, no," Carmen cries as she wraps her arms around my waist.

The dude starts to back away as his eyes bulge out of his head. I keep moving as Carmen calls my name and tugs at me. Some chick runs out with a sheet wrapped around her. She places herself between me and the guy in his boxers.

"Really, Ry?" Carmen says shoving me toward the room next to the one the girl in the sheet ran from.

I move in the direction of the room she pushes me to, but not without tugging her in front of me and covering her with my body. I turn to look back at the pussy in his boxers. He's not worth the ass whipping. He looks like he's about to piss himself.

"What's wrong with you?"

I look around the bedroom and shrug. "I thought he touched what's mine."

She looks up at me incredulously. She's so cute. Finally, I get to see her in those glasses.

I can't wait any longer. I need to kiss her. Smoothly, I close the distance and cup her face in my hand. Then I dip my head and take her full lips.

I groan as soon as I taste her. I wrap an arm around her and pull her into my body. Damn, it's only been a few days, but I missed her. I deepen the kiss as she stops pushing at me and tugs me closer instead.

"Did you miss me?" I say against her lips.

"No."

I nip her lip and chuckle. "You're still mad at me? I swear, I left a note. I told my mother to look after you for me. If you didn't run off, you would've known that."

"What did the note say?"

I can see the caution in her eyes even as I sway her body in my arms. She feels so good in my embrace. Better than I dreamed up while away from her.

"It said that work called me away. I would be back as soon as I could."

I take her lips again before she can reply. This time she melts into me immediately. I slide my hands down to her ass.

I need to be inside her before I go crazy. With that thought, I slip my palms into her panties and squeeze her cheeks.

She moans and lifts onto her toes. Kissing my way to her neck, I savor the feel of her body next to mine. I lift her onto my waist and climb onto the small bed. Small to me at six seven.

"Ryan, wait," she pants.

"Huh," I reply as I bury my face between her breasts.

"Do … do you have condoms this time?"

I look up at her and grin. "Damn right. I came prepared. It's going to be a long night, baby. I missed you. Happy birthday."

Carmen

"You're so silly." I giggle as Ryan swirls whip cream around my breast and tops it with a cherry.

"I almost missed your birthday. I didn't have time to get you anything. I have to make up for that," he says, tossing the can aside.

He cups my waist with one hand as he lies on his side beside me. He pecks my lips before he moves to my breasts. I bite my lip as I lift my head to watch him.

"Make a wish," he says as he hovers over one of the cherries he placed on each mound.

I twist my lips and feign pondering the question. I tap my lip. He flexes his fingers on my side. I laugh and grin at him.

"Okay. I made my wish."

He looks at me through his lashes. My lips part as I watch him lick from beneath my boob, up through the whipped cream then take the cherry and my nipple into his mouth at once. I reach to run my hand through his hair.

Ryan catches my hand and brings my fingers to his lips. I watch the heat in his eyes as he sucks them into his mouth. I smile back at him shyly.

We had sex twice already and I still want more of him. I don't know how we haven't broken this bed. Ryan gets into the task every time.

I follow his movement with my head as he moves to hover over me. Dropping my gaze down to his chest, I marvel at his chiseled body. I reach to trace the tat on his right arm.

Meanwhile, he starts to nuzzle my temple. I close my eyes and relish the feeling. He places a kiss to my eyelid, causing me to open my eyes and look at him.

"What did you wish for?" he murmurs.

"Not telling you. It's my wish," I say.

He chuckles. "Then tell me what you want for your birthday."

I smile at him and reach down for his length. He laughs loudly, reaching to remove my hand. He brings my fingertips to his lips.

"You can have that anytime. Tell me something that will put a smile on that pretty face."

I pout and puff my lips out. He pecks my mouth and turns onto his side again. This time he traces my skin with his fingertips.

He leans over to clean the rest of the whipped cream up before it drips off. I'm distracted as I watch him use his tongue to raise goosebumps across my skin. When he's done, he nips my chin and looks down at me expectantly.

I find my thoughts. *My birthday. What do I want for my birthday?*

"I don't know," I say and laugh.

"Yeah, you do. I see it in your eyes. It's something expensive. That's why you don't want to say. What is it?"

I look at him. I don't know how he could know that, but he's right. I do have something that I want.

"It's a camera."

He turns for his phone and swipes at the screen to unlock it. He then hands it to me. "Find it."

I look at him for a moment but take the phone eventually and search for the camera. I find it and hand the phone back. I observe him closely as he swipes and taps around on his phone.

He reaches over the side of the bed and retrieves his wallet. I watch in awe as he puts his card information into the phone. When he's finished, he tosses his wallet and phone on the nightstand by the unused condoms.

Turning to me, he pecks my lips once again and cups my face. "It'll be here day after tomorrow."

"Thank you," I say breathlessly.

"Anything for you," he says as he searches my face. "When do you have class?"

I groan. "You had to ruin everything."

He chuckles. "I want to go out to dinner with you. I'm only trying to figure out your schedule so I can make reservations. Twenty is a big deal. I want to celebrate with my girl."

I look at him and smile. I reach to adjust my glasses on my face. He has called me his girl a few times. I'm not sure how to feel about that. It makes my heart flutter every time he does.

"I have class tomorrow night."

"Okay, so I'll cook for you tomorrow. What about the day after?"

"I have morning classes."

"Perfect. We'll go out then."

He tugs me into the crook of his arm. Suddenly, my lids are super heavy. I yawn.

He kisses the top of my head. "Go to sleep. I'll clean you up."

CHAPTER SEVEN

Dinner

Carmen

I walk into my apartment to find Gigi sitting on the couch drooling all over herself as Ryan moves around my kitchen shirtless. I stop in my tracks and have to wipe up my own drool. Thank God my brother got a call and had to leave me downstairs to take care of some business.

If he'd come up with me to find this, I would've had a lot of questions to answer. Heck, I have my own questions. Ryan dropped me at my school's library this afternoon in his Mustang and said he'd see me later.

I know he said he would cook for me, but I expected to get home and have time to freshen up and clean the place a little. Gigi can be a bit messy. Although from the looks of it she straightened up some for our guest.

Especially her own appearance. It's seven in the evening and her face is beat to perfection. Jealousy and anger burn inside me.

She has enough boyfriends of her own. She doesn't need to sit here ogling mine.

Boyfriend.

I'm still getting used to saying that's what he is. At least that's what I think he is. I bite my lip and start to fidget with the flap on my bag.

Ryan looks up right at that moment. I smile a little when I see he has on my headphones. He takes them off and saunters his tall sexy self over to me.

He looks so good with his jeans riding low on his hips, showing off his V. Man, it's like his muscles have muscles. They're so defined and sculpted. Ryan's not bulky, but he's lean and toned to perfection. Not too skinny, not to thick. He's just right.

"Hey, baby," he croons in that sexy voice of his.

I don't get to answer. He palms the back of my neck and plants a searing kiss on my lips. I lift on my toes to meet him halfway. He tastes like tomato sauce and something sweet ... honey.

I moan into his mouth, and he wraps his other arm around me. I melt right into him. When he pulls back, I look up at him all dreamy-eyed.

Gigi clears her throat, causing Ryan and I to turn in her direction. She gives me a pointed look, her eyes bouncing back to Ryan. Ryan turns back to me and takes my bag from my shoulder. He kisses my forehead before he walks off into my bedroom with my things.

"Oh my God," Gigi whisper-squeals. The walls in this place are paper-thin and sound bounces off them. "You didn't tell me you were seeing someone."

"He was here last night." I shrug.

She palms her face. "I was totally wasted. Like, I heard you two going at it, but I thought it was my imagination or something. Shit, I kicked Frank ... Derrick ... Evan.

"Oh hell, I can't remember his name." She waves a hand in the air. "I kicked him out because I was faking it and you, honey, didn't sound like you were pretending one bit. And I can see why not. He's hot as fuck."

I blush and turn to look toward the bedroom. He hasn't come back out yet. I turn back to Gigi and inhale. The place smells wonderful.

"Has he been cooking long?"

"Not really, he rang the bell like an hour ago. Said he was your boyfriend and walked into the place like he owned it. Once he walked right to your bedroom, I figured he must have been here before."

I palm my face and laugh. That sounds like Ryan. He has a way of making himself at home even if not invited.

Since Ireland, I feel like he's doing that with my heart. I blink as that thought crosses my mind.

"Carmen," Ryan calls.

I turn to face him. He has a big box in his hands. I wrinkle my brows and stare at the box. My camera isn't supposed to arrive until tomorrow.

"What's that?"

He hands me the gift and plucks me from my seat to take mine and pulls me into his lap. I turn to look at him. He sits expectantly, waiting for me to open the box.

Since he doesn't look like he's going to tell me what's in it, I turn back to the box and start to pull the bow and lid off. My mouth falls open when a camera bag comes into view. It's personalized with my Japanese name on it. Most people think Nene is a nickname, which it's not.

It means many things according to which Kanji characters are used. My father chose superiority and heart. Ryan could never know what the use of that name means to me.

The bag is even in my favorite colors, yellow and teal. He must have noticed all the yellow and teal stuff in my bedroom. He's definitely observant.

I clench the bag to my chest and turn back to face him. Ryan searches my face as I look into his eyes. A slow grin turns up his lips as he takes in the smile on my face.

"Thank you," I say softly.

"You're welcome. How was class?"

I shrug. "Class. Boring and uneventful."

He laughs. "Wish I could say that about my day, but your friend with the puddle of drool at her feet has made my time here interesting. I swear, she's like two seconds off trying to feel on me," he says.

My lips twitch as I try not to burst into laughter. "Well, you are shirtless in our apartment. Can you blame her?"

He tilts his head to the side as if thinking. He then turns to look at Gigi, who's sitting with her mouth hanging open. I lift the bag over my lips as I let my laugh spill free.

"I guess you have a point," Ryan says. "I didn't want to get sauce all over my shirt." He winks at Gigi. "I'm taken, sweetheart. It's kind of rude to stare like that."

I can't. I cannot hold it in any longer. I burst out laughing. Gigi's cheeks glow and she pouts, causing me to laugh more.

"I wasn't trying to stare."

"Yeah, you meant to stare. It's okay. Get it out of your system."

I slap his shoulder. "Stop it."

He chuckles. "Okay, I'm sorry, not sorry. Would you like to have dinner with us?"

"It smells good." Gigi looks at me with longing in her eyes. She can't cook to save her life. I'm sure she had plans to order something in tonight.

"I don't know. You were checking out my man," I tease.

"Babe, be nice. She's your roommate. Not everyone can be as lucky as you. You saw what she had to deal with last night," Ry says.

Gigi palms her face. "Ugh, don't remind me."

I laugh and shake my head. I haven't been in this light a mood in so long. I hug my camera bag and sigh.

"I guess you can eat with us. As long as you keep your drool to yourself."

Ryan snorts. "That's going to be hard to do."

"Oh, shut up." I giggle.

"Nene has never had a boyfriend as far as I've known. Shit, she's never had a hook up for as long as we've been roommates. I think I was in shock."

Ryan stands and places me back in my seat. He rushes into the kitchen and starts to cut off the burners and stir whatever's in the pots. Gigi scoots closer.

"Where'd you guys meet? Does he have a brother?"

"Six," I reply. "And they're all taken as far as I know. Well, there's one I'm not sure about, but I think he is. We met at the wedding of one of his brother's."

She groans and falls over into me. "I'm hanging with all the wrong people."

"I thought you and that Jack guy were getting along."

"Pfft." She lifts her head and places her hands on her hip. "Found out he's been sleeping with my lab partner. The George she thought he was always going to see was actually me. Prick."

"Sorry," I say and frown.

She waves me off. "It's not your fault the guys I date are assholes."

She runs a hand through her jet-black hair. Gigi is Korean. When we first met, I thought that she was everything I wanted to be.

Carefree and full of life. She does everything her parents tell her not to do. My father would hang me from the roots of my hair if I were anything like Gigi.

"I like this guy. His blunt humor is attractive."

I feel that jealousy creeping up again. Gigi is a gorgeous girl and way more experienced. I don't know if I like having Ryan around her.

"Come here, baby," Ryan calls from the kitchen, breaking into my thoughts.

I turn to find him holding up a spoon. My heart lightens and I smile. It's my birthday and Ryan Black is in my kitchen cooking for me.

I guess I don't have much to worry about. I tuck my bag back in its box and head into the kitchen. With confidence I didn't know I had, I walk up to Ryan, wrap my arms around his waist and kiss his chest. The look he gives me in return makes my heart swell. It's a huge boost to my ego as well.

Ryan

When Carmen walks over and kisses my chest, something about it causes a shift within me. I look into her eyes and get lost for a second. I haven't done the relationship thing much, but with Carmen it's something I want to more than explore.

I meant it when I said I wasn't letting her go. Little things like the kiss on my chest and holding onto me tightly make me long for something I never knew I wanted.

Fuck. They were right.

I will be the brother to fall the hardest. But look at her. She has on those cute glasses again and she looks so happy.

I feel like an asshole for having to lie to her. Yeah, I'm here because she's my girl, but this is also a job for me. I spent all morning with her and watched over her before and during her classes.

Ne was to pick her up from class and get her back here to me. We're trying to make this as natural as possible.

"What's wrong?" Carmen says and her smile starts to fall.

I place an arm around her and dip my head to kiss her lips. If her roommate weren't here, I'd say fuck this food and eat her. My cock grows in my pants, swelling against her belly.

"Nothing. Just thought of something I need to take care of."

"Oh, was work busy today? You guys are bounty hunters, right? That can be dangerous."

"We do bounties and private investigations. No more dangerous than walking outside."

She gives me a side look. "Somehow, I doubt that," she says. "I've heard stories, remember?"

"Here, taste this."

Yup, I change the subject. I don't want to talk about work when she's my assignment. I've learned a lot more about Carmen after sitting with her father.

All the pieces have fallen into place. I wondered why I never met her before. Then there were things I learned about her, when I looked her up after we first met that didn't make sense to me at the time.

Like the fact that her family makes trips to Japan that she rarely if ever accompanies them on. Carmen is usually sent on trips or to spend time with her aunt Mariah.

Kiyoshi has kept a tight seal on the world that Carmen is exposed to and what the world exposes to her. Now it's my job to protect the bubble she's been placed in, which includes keeping her from what I do for a living.

"Mmm," she moans around the spoon as her eyes light up.

She licks her lips, and I follow the movement with my gaze. Man, I should have gotten rid of the roommate. Damn.

I shake my head and turn to place the food on plates. I get everyone a helping of pasta as well as the bread I talked Mom into baking and get the plates to the table. Once I have them set up, I go back into the bedroom for my shirt.

When I return, both Carmen and her roommate are moaning and devouring the plates in front of them. Carmen looks up and reaches to adjust her glasses. I bite my lip and grin.

I have no idea why that shit turns me on so much, but I'm a straight sucker for a girl in glasses. With a girl as gorgeous as Carmen, it's icing on the cake. Everything about her is perfection.

Her little nose, her slanted eyes, her full lips, her bronzed brown skin—it's all a perfect complement to her curvy body. Carmen is the type of stunning that makes you stop in your tracks to stare and possibly even follow after her.

I'm drawn to her as I move to the table and peck her lips. Again, Kiyoshi's voice plays in the back of my head. *'Do this for me, Ryan, but don't touch my daughter.'*

I never made that promise. I agreed to watch over her. I never said anything about not touching her.

CHAPTER EIGHT

Gaming & Calls

Carmen

"Yes," I cheer and pump my arm in the air.

I turn to find Ryan staring at me with a sour look on his face. I've kicked his butt at *Call of Duty* three times in a row. I sit on the couch and do a happy dance.

"I don't know what I was thinking," he says. "I opened that cabinet and found a gamer's wet dream. Why didn't I think you'd kick my ass?"

I shrug my shoulders. "Because I have a vagina. Most guys don't think I can play. It's one of my favorite things to do when I'm not filming or studying."

"Obviously," he mumbles.

I laugh and put the headset and controller down on the coffee table. I crawl across the couch and straddle his lap. Ryan grins up at me and places his hands on my waist.

Gigi went out after dinner, but Ryan has been too busy trying to beat me at the game to focus on anything else. While playing is fine, I have something else in mind.

"You're a sore loser," I say as I look down at him.

"I never lose."

"You did tonight."

He smiles. "Not from where I'm sitting."

I cup his face and kiss him. Ryan takes over the kiss and holds me to him. Things are starting to heat up when my phone rings.

I groan and fall over onto my side. I know it's my dad. It's his time to call. I reach over the edge of the couch and grab the phone from the end table.

"Hey, Daddy," I say.

"*Kon'nichiwa*, Nene. Happy birthday."

"Thanks."

I have a genuine smile on my face. I almost forgot it's my birthday. Ryan has made this feel like a regular 'hang out and chill' night.

Not that he hasn't made a fuss with dinner and a cupcake, including a candle. Ryan is just so laid back. It's been fun with no pressure at all.

"What are you up to this evening?"

"Some gaming before I study."

Turning onto my back, my legs are on Ryan's lap. He leans over me to push my T-shirt up and kisses my stomach. I wiggle beneath him and mouth for him to stop distracting me.

He ignores me as his eyes dance with mirth. Fixing his gaze on me, he licks from my belly button up to my breasts. I close my eyes, trying to block him out.

"How was school today?"

"It was good. Nothing new."

I totally have to commend myself for my voice coming out so smoothly. I bite my lip and open my eyes to see the intense look in Ry's eyes. I shake my head at him and smile. He's trouble.

Stop it, I mouth again.

"Hm-mm. I have a nice boy I want you to meet when I return."

I sit up and toss my legs over the edge of the couch. I must be hearing things. I pull the phone from my ear to look down at it.

"What?"

"Nice boy. He comes from a nice family. You'll like him. He's going to be a surgeon."

"Daddy, um… I don't think I need help finding a date."

Ryan stiffens next to me, and I peek at him to see the murderous look in his eyes. It's like last night all over again. I think I even see smoke coming out of his ears.

"You are twenty. It's time we find you a nice match. A nice boy to marry and start a family with."

"Um, I think I can handle finding my own dates, Dad. Thanks though."

He makes a sound on the other end of the phone. "You will meet him."

My mouth drops open. This is how it always is. My father tells me what he wants. It never has anything to do with what I want.

I'm so frustrated, I almost toss my phone across the room. I want to FaceTime him and let him see my boyfriend sitting right next to me, but I know I'll do none of that. I rub my temple instead.

"Can we talk about this when you get back first?"

"Yes, you come to the house, and we will talk before he arrives for you to meet him," he says.

Ugh, why do I bother? My mother's words ring in my ear. I'm going to have to stand up for myself.

This is one step too far. I've done everything my father asked me to. This isn't fair. My love life should belong to me. It's not a degree or a major that I can have on the side. I want to pick someone I want to be with and fall for.

That golden gaze stares back at me. I sigh into the phone. I'm going to have a problem when I hang up. I can already see it.

"I'll talk to you later, Daddy. I want to get some studying done."

"*Watashi wa, anata o aishiteimasu.*"

I sag my shoulders. Now I feel like a jerk. My father does these things out of love. Ne tries to tell me that all the time.

"I love you too."

We end the call, and I keep my focus on my lap. I can feel the anger rolling off Ryan. I wait for him to say something, but it never comes.

When I chance a look at him, he's not looking at me. He's staring at his phone clenched in his hand. I watch him closely as he responds to a text then puts his phone away.

"Everything okay?"

"You should tell your father you're seeing someone. It's the safest thing for everyone."

I'm a little taken aback by his words. Is he threatening my father? Me?

I'm not too sure I like this side of him. I go to scoot away from him, but he reaches for me and places me onto his lap. He strokes my cheek and leans in to peck my lips.

I can see the war happening within his eyes, but I'm not understanding it. Whatever it is he's battling with, he lets it go and buries his face into my neck. I relax as I feel the tension leave his body.

"Are we good?"

"Yeah," he breathes against my neck. "I've never shared well. It's what got my ass tore up all the time. I'd push Toby and Braxton around for touching my toys."

I snort. "I'm not a toy."

"No, you're something way more precious than that."

"My father means well. I'll talk to my mother. She's the best at reasoning with him. If I can get her on my side, this meeting will never happen."

Ryan scoffs and kisses my neck. "It's never happening regardless. Don't sweat it."

I go to ask him what he means, but he silences the question with a kiss. Soon my father and his nice boy are forgotten. I have a hot man right here in my arms.

Ryan

I look at the text on my phone. Kiyoshi thinks he's a funny motherfucker. I was straight with him when he asked me if I was interested in his daughter.

"Yes, very," I replied.

"I see. You do know that she's younger than you?"

"Yes, I'm aware. She's only four years younger than me."

He nodded as he held my gaze. "I need a favor from you. I need you to watch over Nene while we address the coming issues. You can insert yourself into her life as a friend."

I smiled at him. "I have no problem with that."

"When I say a friend, I mean a platonic friend."

I frowned and my brain shut down from there. Yes, I had every intention of inserting myself into Carmen's life, but not as a damn friend. I can't believe he's trying to set her up with someone.

I wanted to lose it while she was on the phone with her dad, but I held it together. Carmen has no idea that I know her father. If I'd said the wrong thing, I would've blown it all.

Instead, I texted Ne and asked him what the fuck his father is up to. He responded with a shrug emoji. That's not good enough.

If I have to get Felix involved to find out who this guy is so I can pay him a visit, I will. Whatever happens, one thing's for sure Carmen isn't meeting anyone. The text from my brother is the confirmation I need to calm the fuck down.

Felix: Find out what you can. I'll handle the rest.

"Is my bed too small?"

I look down at Carmen as she lies on my chest. I rub a hand down her smooth sexy back. She smiles and snuggles closer to my chest.

"It's the tiniest bed I've ever been in, but I'm fine. It means you have to stay close," I reply.

"It is not the tiniest bed you've been in." She giggles. "Although, seriously. What are you, six seven? This has to be uncomfortable for you."

I lift a brow. "Are you saying you want to go to my place?"

Her cheeks start to glow. "No. I just want you to be comfortable. You haven't fallen asleep."

I lift my shoulders. "I don't sleep much as it is. I'm not complaining." I brush a lock of hair out of her eyes. "You were knocked out. You want some help going back to sleep?"

She places a kiss on my chest and that feeling from earlier returns. I search her face as she looks down at the spot shyly. Reaching to pinch her chin, I lift her head.

"I woke to go to the bathroom."

"But you're still in bed with me," I tease.

"You're warm. I don't want to move."

I chuckle. "I'm into a lot of kinky shit, but golden showers isn't one of them. You better get up."

She laughs and slaps my chest. I peck her lips before I let her get up and go to the bathroom. I watch her ass sway as she goes to grab my T-shirt to slip over her head.

Damn, I'm a lucky bastard.

I prop my head up on my hands as I stare at the ceiling. This bed is small. I'm tempted to talk her into going back to my place, but I know that's out of the question. Kiyoshi's men are surrounding the neighborhood keeping watch.

I grin. He's probably steaming from reports of me staying overnight. I'm only doing my job. It's better if I protect Carmen up close and personal.

My phone rings, grabbing my attention. I turn for the bedside table and pick it up. My lips turn up higher when I see who it is.

"Hello, Matsumara."

"Why are you still there?"

"We're celebrating her birthday. You do know that friends do that?"

He makes a sound in the back if his throat. "At two in the morning? Go home."

"Dad, I'm not feeling the love. You asked me to do a job. I'm doing it."

"You are testing me. If I were your father, you would know better."

"Ah, but you're going to make such a good father-in-law."

He scoffs. "My daughter has better taste. Go home."

"Yeah, she does taste good."

"Don't make me kill you. If you're not gone in five minutes, I will send my men in."

"To get killed? Nah, you don't want that. I'll leave, but Matsumara?"

"What?"

"Stop trying to set her up. I told you I'm interested. I'm not playing. I'll take his head off. She's mine."

He laughs at me, causing me to get pissed. I'm not joking. Carmen is off-limits.

"You make bold claims, Ryan. Respect would have you come to me and ask to date my daughter, not demand it."

"I'm dating your daughter."

He laughs again. "See. No respect. You still approach me as a friend and not the father of the girl you wish to pursue. She will meet who I choose."

With that, he hangs up the phone. I grind my teeth and sit up. I will leave, but only because I want to make rounds through her neighborhood to familiarize myself.

"Were you talking to someone?" Carmen asks as she enters the room with a frown.

"Yeah, it was work. I have to go."

The disappointment on her face makes me reconsider staying the night. I'm surprised I didn't get a call last night. Yeah, I'll be making rounds and checking to see how alert Kiyoshi's men are.

I stand and pull her into my arms. I take her lips in a deep kiss and hold her close. I love that she melts into me. The fact that I tower over her is a turn on too.

"I'll call you in the morning. We still have plans tomorrow. Make sure you have plenty of nasty, dirty dreams about me."

She releases that sweet laugh. "Will do."

"That's my girl."

CHAPTER NINE

First Date

Carmen

I run my sweaty palms over my dress and look in the mirror. I couldn't focus in class today. All I could think about was Ryan.

I'm nervous about our official first date. I don't know what to expect and I had no idea what to wear. I turn to face Gigi, and she has a big goofy grin on her face.

"You look awesome. That dress fits you perfectly," she says.

Thanks to her I have something to wear. She had this dress in her closet with the tag still on it. It's not something I'd normally buy, but I do like it.

It's a black bodycon dress that stops mid-calf and hugs all my curves but also flatters what I feel are my imperfections. No matter how much I work out at the gym, my tummy rebels and stays pudgy.

I've tried all the clean eating advice. None of that works for me. It's been this way all my life. I accept the skin I'm in. I know for a fact Ryan does.

I bite my lip. I wonder if he'll like this dress. "Maybe I should change."

"*Nooo*," Gigi drags out and falls back onto my bed. She starts to kick her feet like she's having a tantrum. "You look great. Don't do this. It's perfect."

I sigh and turn back for the mirror. She's right. It's a perfect balance of dressy and casual. I'm ready for whatever Ryan has planned.

"Okay, you're right," I say right before the doorbell rings.

"I'll get it," Gigi sings and shoots off my bed for the front door.

My heart is pounding. I shouldn't be this nervous. We've already had sex more than once. That's the hard part out of the way, right?

My phone buzzes with a text. I pick the phone up to see it's my mom. I groan and read the message.

My nerves are already shot. I don't need one of my parents to make me a freaking mess for the rest of the night.

Mom: *New Tachis came in. See you in the morning.*

So like mommy. I can almost feel her excitement through the phone. I smile.

Okay, I'll be honest. My mother and I have a weird way of bonding. The woman has gained some interesting hobbies from marrying my dad.

Hobbies that she's shared with me since I was a little girl. My mom is totally badass. I shoot her back a text as I get a little excited for tomorrow's visit.

I'm sure she's going to make it a long one. It's in the middle of that text that I hear a groan that pulls my attention. His heat hits my back before I can turn.

Ryan places a hand on my waist and turns me to face him. With his other hand, he grasps my chin between his fingertips and lifts my face. My lips are crushed by his almost instantly.

Ryan aims to devour as he consumes my mouth. I wrap my arms around his waist and give in to the kiss. His mouth is warm and welcoming. The taste of something citrusy flavors his tongue.

"Hey," he says against my mouth when he breaks the kiss. "You look amazing."

I give a shy smile. "Thank you. You do too."

He does. He has on a suit and tie. I wasn't expecting that. It brings a huge smile to my face. I'm more confident in my choice of dress.

He groans again. "Let's get out of here before I hem you to the bed and forget about going out."

He takes my hand and entwines our fingers and leads me out of the room. My belly warms and dips a little before the butterflies take flight. Gigi has a big smile on her face as we pass her in the living room.

She waves and I give a wave back as Ryan opens the door for me. We make it to his Mustang in silence. It's not until he's behind the wheel that he turns to me and looks my face over. He leans in and pecks my lips.

"I'm going to have to kick someone's ass tonight if they stare too long. Brax always has my bail money," he says and winks.

"You're kidding, right?"

"Nope," he says and starts the car.

Ryan

I don't know what I did to deserve this, but Carmen is perfect. She's funny, gorgeous, and smart. I've never had so much fun on a date.

Dinner was enlightening. Not only is Carmen shy, but she's also fascinating to watch. It's like she's always looking for the camera angle into the lives of the people around her.

Even as she blew out the candle on the slice of birthday cake I ordered for her, she watched the waitress with curiosity. Granted, our waitress was distracted. Carmen and I both figured out why as we observed her.

"She has a crush on that waiter," Carmen whispered across the table once the waitress stumbled over her own feet and blushed to her roots.

"Yeah, I picked that up too."

We looked at each other and laughed. It was then that I realized how at ease I feel with this girl. She's not like girls I've dated in the past.

For example, now she's in a batting cage in three-inch heel, and that fucking dress that's an added turn-on. The craziest part is that the dress covers most of her body. I've never seen someone show so little skin and still pull off looking so sexy they've kept me semi-hard all night.

I bite my lip as I watch her swing the bat. The blue lighting casts a glow against her face and it's hot as fuck. I'm going to kiss John for suggesting we all chip in for this place.

It's our personal playground. When we want to blow off steam outside of the range or the ring, we now have this place. A batting cage, golf range, arcade, paintball—we're not finished, but the place is shaping up to be exactly what we all wanted.

Most of all, it's private. There's no one else here as Carmen and I have a great time.

Dinner was great, but this part—getting to see her smile and relax—has been the best part of the date. Her laugh rings out as the bat connects with two balls in a row. She's not bad at all. I think my girl has a competitive streak in her.

I like it.

"Did you see that?" she sings as I pause the machine.

She turns to me with a bright smile on her face. The helmet on her head not taking a thing away from her beauty. I step inside the cage and saunter over to her.

She tilts her head back to look up at me as I tower over her. Palming her face, I look into her eyes. I can't help running my finger across her full lips.

"I saw it," I breathe. "You're gorgeous no matter what you're doing."

She lowers her lashes in that shy way I love. I take the helmet from her head and the bat from her hand and drop them to the floor. The music muffling the loud clattering sound they make just a bit.

Carmen lifts her hands to my chest as I wrap my arms around her and start to sway her to the music. It's an old song, but sexy as fuck in this moment. "Knockin' da Boots" by H-Town fills the air around us, I bunch her dress up until I can bend my knees and wedge a leg between her thighs.

Our slow sway turns into a slow rock and grind. Our gazes are locked together and her lips are parted. The look of awe on her face is priceless.

Yeah, we had a simple slow dance at the wedding, but it wasn't enough for her to know how serious my moves can get on the dance floor. As I keep her hips swaying and dance her around the batting cage, her face lights up.

"You're a really good dancer," she says.

"I haven't shown you my best moves yet."

She gives me a side-glance. "Why do I get the feeling you're talking about more than dancing?"

I lick my lips. "Take it how you want to take it." I wink at her and watch as her cheeks glow and her pupils dilate.

She shakes her head. "You're nothing like I thought you would be."

I lift a brow. "How so?"

"Yes, you're arrogant when you want to be, but you're also sweet, funny, and …" She shakes her head again. "I don't know. I expected you to be a dick, honestly. You know, the guys who get what they want and they ghost you. Guys like you never stick around with girls like me."

I dance her over to the cage until her back is pinned to it. Dipping my head until we are nose to nose, I look her in her eyes. I don't know where she gets this idea from that she's such a forgettable being.

All I think about when she's not around is her. How could I walk away from her?

"To most people, I probably am a dick," I say against her lips. "But that's something you never have to think about. When it comes to you, I'll be everything you want me to be, everything you need me to be. I told you, baby, this is for keeps."

With that, I take her lips and lift her hands to pin them over her head. I don't think I can keep my hands off her any longer. I wanted to hold out and make this date about having fun, but having her in this cage, I have some other fun in mind.

She whimpers into my mouth, and I take the kiss deeper. I can never get enough of her sweet mouth. Her full lips drive me crazy. I want to nip, lick, and suck at them all night.

I lose focus and my restraint slips. I wrap my hand around her throat and squeeze. It's a move I shouldn't use with her yet. Or so I thought.

"Fuck me," I growl.

She convulses and releases a long moan. I look down at her with wide eyes. Her response to me keeps surprising the hell out of me. I remove my leg from between her legs and find my slacks soaked.

"You've got to be kidding me," I whisper to myself. I lift my gaze to hers. "You liked that, baby?"

She looks back at me with those big bright eyes and nods. Oh, hell yeah. All bets are off. I've been keeping my freak wrapped up. Not anymore.

I back up and widen my stance. I let my gaze roll over her body. Slowly, I lick my lips in anticipation of what I plan to do to her.

"Take the dress off," I command.

She looks at me shyly at first but nods and begins to peel her way out of the dress. I grunt as her black bra and panties come into view. I'm not sure what I want more. To be between her thick thighs or to bury my face in between her breasts.

I loosen my tie and pull it from my neck. The buttons of my shirt are the next thing I work. Shrugging out of the fabric, I grin at her and drop the shirt to the floor.

Closing the distance, I keep my eyes on hers. She lifts her chin and pulls her shoulders back. I give a full-on smile.

With the tie still between my fingers, I run the back of my hand between her mounds. Her skin is so soft. The way her lips part and she looks up at me with a plea in her eyes turns me on so much, I'm ready to burst through my pants.

Carmen places her hand on my chest and pushes me back. I lift a brow but move to see what she's up to. Before I can say a word, she drops to her knees before me.

I shake my head. "Oh, baby, you sure you're ready for that?"

She wordlessly releases my belt and unzips my pants. I bite back a smile as she reaches into my slacks and pulls me free. I've been wanting to see those lips wrapped around me for the longest.

She takes me in tentatively. I can tell she's not sure of herself. I remain still, allowing her to find her comfort.

When Carmen looks up at me for confirmation, I nearly come in her mouth right then and there. It's the trusting look in her eyes.

"Damn, baby. That's good. Just do me a favor. Use your tongue more for me." She nods and starts to swirl it around my crown. "Fuck yeah, just like that."

She smiles around me as I put my hand in her hair and start to guide her. My brows shoot up when she starts to bob more confidently. Confidence starts to ooze through as she rolls her neck and wraps her palms around the part of my shaft her mouth can't reach.

I groan and let my head fall back. Oh my God, she's killing me. When she slurps and takes me to the back of her throat, I drop my head back down to stare at her through hooded lids.

This is going to get messy if I don't stop her. Palming her chin, I pull from her mouth. She pouts up at me and I swear I'm tempted to let her finish.

Instead, I bring her to her feet and back her into the cage once again. I lift her hands above her head and secure them to the fencing with my tie. My blood is pumping pure fire through my veins as I look at her.

I lower to my knees and tease her thighs with my fingertips. She widens her legs as if begging for me to touch her fat pussy. I don't take the bait.

Instead, I reach for her panties and peel them down slowly. I mean, real slow. Carmen looks down her body at me and it's so sexy.

I lean in to kiss her tummy and my chest swells when she doesn't get that insecure look in her eyes. I love her body just the way it is. All this shit is mine.

Every curve, every fleshy inch of perfection belongs to me. I wouldn't change a thing about her. I grasp her thighs and run my thumbs along the sides of her inner thighs.

Her pussy drips for me, calling for my attention. With my eyes on her, I lean in and take my first lick. I moan and it mixes with her cry.

Bringing her leg over my shoulder, I support her weight as I really start to feast on her. And feast I do. I grin when my girl starts to ride my face, and she creates a song of her own.

"Ryan, oh my God. I'm going to come," she pants.

I know she's about to come. I can feel it. However, I have no intentions of allowing it.

I back off and push away from her, sitting on my behind. Gripping my shaft, I look up at her. She stares back at me as if I've lost my mind. I stroke myself and smile at her.

"Dance for me, baby."

"What?" she breathes out.

"Close your legs and grind for me. I promise it's going to feel good. Rock those sexy hips for me."

I've left her sensitive as fuck. I know she's going to spark off this. Reluctantly, she slides her legs together. At first, she rocks her hips tentatively.

I see the moment she gets what I want for her. Her mouth opens and she moans. The rhythm of her hips changes as she begins to clench her thighs and roll her hips more vigorously.

"Yeah, you feel that shit," I say as I stroke myself. "Come for me."

Her eyes grow wide as her peak comes for her. She looks like a goddess, tied up to the cage, dancing her way to bliss. The blue light highlighting her skin and creating the perfect glow.

I move swiftly, standing to go to her to tug her bra cup down. I tug her nipple into my mouth, and she screams as her orgasm swallows her.

She's convulsing again. All while I continue to jerk off. I feel my release coming. I back off just a little and aim at her hairless mound.

Locking eyes with her, I bust my load all over her. I start to grow hard within seconds as I look down at her stomach and pussy covered in my nut. I want to roar at the top of my lungs.

It's like I've staked my claim. I'm two seconds off pounding my chest. However, my baby girl is out to take my knees from under me with her sexy request.

"Can I taste it?"

My gaze shoots up to hers and I narrow my eyes. Oh, yeah, my girl is perfect for me. All that's missing from this moment are those sexy glasses.

I think she would have had me on my knees crying real tears if she had those on tonight. I draw a finger through my cum covering her pussy and lift it to her lips. She sticks her tongue out and pulls my finger into her mouth.

She cleans every last drop as she moans. I reach into my back pocket with my free hand. I need a condom, *now.*

Pulling my finger from her mouth, I get the rubber on as fast as my shaking hands will allow. Yes, she has my ass shaking.

What the fuck?

Suited up, I shove my pants farther down my hips and grab her thighs to lift her onto my waist. Angling her body, I slide inside of her, and she detonates on my cock as soon as I push in to the hilt. I pause and throb inside her while I wait for her pussy to calm.

Taking her mouth, I kiss her hard. I groan and start to move inside her. The intensity between us has grown. This feels so much different.

Fuck. I'm falling for her hard. No. I'm in love with her. That's the only thing that can explain this.

I break the kiss and look into her eyes. Damn, yeah, I love her. And to prove it, I make love to her against the cage wall pressed to her back.

"You're mine, Carmen," I breathe in her ear thirty minutes later as we come together one last time.

CHAPTER TEN

Dad Interruptions

Carmen

"This has been so much fun," I say in between bites of my hotdog as we sit watching the go-karts race around the track.

We've already been around it at least five times. I've laughed so much my ribs hurt. That is when I wasn't concerned Ryan would lose his temper.

He actually told one guy that if he cut me off one more time, he was going to throat punch him in front of his girl. The guy was an asshole. I wasn't the only one he cut off.

A few people were getting pissed because he wasn't getting flagged and he seemed to only target the women and teenagers. Apparently, the workers are friends of his and weren't doing their jobs.

Ry put a stop to that when he went over and whispered something in one of the guy's ear. The jerk got flagged and parked the next time he did something stupid on the track. Despite that, it's been great.

"Yeah, it has," Ryan says around the bite in his mouth.

He swallows and his golden gaze locks on something behind me. I turn to see what has his attention. It's the girlfriend of the guy that Ryan threatened. She's storming out of the door.

"Finally," Ryan says. I turn back to him with furrowed brows.

"That guy is an asshole. I told her about an hour ago she should leave his ass. He talked to her like shit. I hate guys like that. His ass isn't worth the sperm his father wasted."

I nearly choke on the piece of hotdog I just bit. I shake my head at Ry as I chew. My heart warms as I see he's truly concerned for the girl.

"That was nice of you to say something to her. I had wondered what you were saying."

He makes a sour face. "I hate that shit. If I have daughters, they're going to know to date guys who give a shit about them and respect them."

Oh my God, I think I just fell in love. He said that without thinking about it. It was a genuine from the heart statement and all his heart was in it.

He turns back to the track and continues to eat his hotdogs. Seriously, Ryan can eat. I guess as big and tall as he is, he needs the fuel.

I smile and reach to wipe mustard from the corner of his mouth with my napkin. He turns and locks eyes with me. It's like we're lost in time for a moment.

It's not the first time he's looked at me this way after I perform a simple gesture, like a kiss on his chest or touching his arm. Almost as if he's surprised by the actions or something. I go to retract my hand, but he catches it and brings my fingers to his lips to kiss them.

I smile and lower my head. We sit silently for a bit as we finish our food and drinks. I'm lost in thought, trying to figure out how I got here.

A few weeks ago, I was boyfriendless and spent most of my time with a book in my face or in an editing room. If not, I'd hang with Courtney and her friends. Not always my cup of tea.

Courtney is my best friend, but I don't like her other friends much, so I stay to myself. These last few weeks with Ryan have shown me so much about myself. I've been questioning a lot.

School, my future, what I plan to do once I tell my father about film school. Heck, I've been questioning everything.

"What are you thinking about?"

He brushes a lock of hair behind my ear. I lift my gaze to his and stare for a moment. He gives me a coaxing smile.

I bite my lip and figure what the heck. It's not the first time I've spilled my guts to him. I blow out a breath and go for it.

"Have you ever wondered what your purpose in life is? Like, sometimes I feel so out of place. I haven't found where I fit in."

He looks at me pensively for a moment. "Yeah, I've been there before."

"I don't think I noticed how long I've been here until recently. You remember I said I was going to hang with Courtney yesterday?"

"Yeah." He nods and takes a sip from his straw.

"It was weird. Like having an out of body experience. I love that girl, but I didn't feel like I belonged.

"Her friends were making mean girl comments about people, and I was grossed out. I wanted to leave. At one point, I was sure if I wasn't with them, they'd talk about me."

"Fuck them," he says and shrugs.

I nudge him with my shoulder. "You're missing the point."

"No, I'm not. I get how you feel. My point is.

"You're not hanging with the right people. If they make you feel uncomfortable, only hang with Courtney when it's you guys. Her toxic people don't have to be your toxic people.

"You find people who keep a smile on your face. Fuck the rest of them."

I look at Ryan and once again I see something in him I wasn't expecting. He's right. It's the toxic people who make me question my friendship with Courtney, not Courtney.

He adds. "It's okay to outgrow people. It happens all the time. You're moving forward with your life. Goals change; friends change. It's all a part of the process."

Wow. If he didn't just reach into my brain and pull out all my thoughts. I lean in and kiss his cheek. He gives me that bright, sexy smile of his.

I look him over. I love the way his brown hair is neatly blown out on top and parted on the side. It gives him a polished feel to the mysterious and rough side of his appearance. Sort of like, I'm supermodel gorgeous, but I'll still kick your ass.

I smile. "Thanks for the advice."

"No problem. You can pay me in sex later," he teases, giving me a heated stare as he licks his lips.

"Perv."

He leans to nuzzle my neck. "Only for you," he whispers.

He tugs me into his side and places his chin on top of my head. There's that feeling again. The feeling of being cherished, cared for, protected.

I absorb it and ignore the little voice in the back of my head that whispers it's too good to be true. After a few minutes, he presses his lips to my temple before he stands. He stretches and his T-shirt rides up to reveal his tanned skin.

"Ready to go at it again or do you want to head out?"

I've been nervous about this date all day. I've been nervous about the others, but this one is different. He's taking me to his place after.

I won't be spending the night, but still, I'm going to get to see his space. I have so many ideas of what his place must look like. However, my nerves have been all over the place as I think of actually stepping foot on his territory.

Although, after this date. I'm ready. I've gotten to know Ryan a little more and I want to see what's next.

With my eyes still locked on his bare flesh, I give my answer. "I'm ready to head out."

Ryan

"Why do you look so shocked? What am I, an animal? I'm feeling some type of way here," I say as I watch the look of awe on Carmen's face as she looks around my place.

I'll admit, I wasn't sure about buying this house after Brax moved out of our condo, but I was the only one without a house. A place that one day could house a family. It felt like the thing to do. Even John has a house of his own.

Carmen laughs and reaches for my arm, pulling me to sit with her on the couch. "It's a really nice house. I don't know what I expected. This is ... it's grown up."

I narrow my eyes at her. "When did I leave you to think anything about me isn't grown up?"

She rolls her eyes at me. "You know what I mean. This is a family home. It's decorated like a forever home. It's so warm and inviting."

I pull her into my arms and smile at her. "So you approve of our home?"

She turns away shyly. "Hey, my contacts are drying. You mind if I take them out?"

"If that means you're putting your glasses on, be my guest. The powder room is at the front of the hall. It's a good idea to learn your way around our home. You'll be chasing our babies around here."

"Whatever, Ry." She shakes her head.

She gets up and grabs her bag to go to the bathroom. I watch her go, loving having her in my home. She thinks I'm joking.

I'm not. This will be our home together. I get up to go in the kitchen to heat up the food I prepared for us yesterday while her brother took over looking after her.

I'm starving. We made a stop at the mall before coming to my place. Those hotdogs have already burned off.

I'm probably the best cook out of all my brothers. I like cooking for Carmen. She seemed to enjoy the birthday dinner I made for her.

"It smells so good in here," Carmen sings as she reenters the living room.

I look up from the shrimp I'm searing. It's the only thing I didn't cook last night. I only did the prep work for those.

The shrimp are forgotten as I take in Carmen in her glasses with a curly ponytail piled on top her head. A yellow tank and distressed jeans complete the sexy look. She looks like a dream.

"Come here."

She smiles as she moves into the kitchen. I wait until she stops in front of me before I take my eyes off her. I only look away long enough to cut off the fire before I burn our dinner.

When I turn back to her, I grasp her hips and bring her into me. Slipping my arms around her waist, I hold her close. She reaches up to fix her glasses.

"What did you cook?" she asks, peeking over into the pots.

"Shrimp, red beans and rice." She turns back to me and lifts a brow. "What?"

"You're telling me you're about to feed me red beans and rice? Ryan ... are you sure you want to take this risk?"

"Oh, so we have jokes?" I say, sliding my hands down to palm her ass.

"Your pasta was good. I'll give you that, but red beans and rice? Come on."

"Okay, let's make a bet. If it sucks, I'll sit through that whack ass movie you wanted to watch. If dinner knocks your socks off, you'll let me teach you something new in my favorite room in the house."

Her eyes sparkle as she looks up at me. She's seriously doubting my skills. I see the moment she confidently takes the bet.

"Okay, you're on."

"You really think I'm Karen in the kitchen. I'm wounded."

She laughs, reaching up on her toes to wrap her arms around my neck. She kisses my lips. When she pulls away, I place my forehead to hers.

"No, I think you're capable of anything you put your mind to. However, I'm looking forward to filling my belly and losing this bet."

"Oh, I plan to fill your belly all right."

I take her lips, and we get lost in a passionate kiss for longer than I intend. When I finally let her up for air, I get us two bowls of food and lead her to the stools on the other side of the island. I watch her as she takes her first spoonful.

"Oh, you have to be freaking kidding me," she moans. She looks at me with wide eyes. "Who are you, Bobby Flay's nephew?"

I burst into laughter as she digs in for more. She continues to moan and eat at the same time. I sit back and fold my arms over my chest, my own hunger forgotten as I become hungry for something else.

"I'm going to gain so much weight dating you."

A smile curls my lips. I lean over into her ear, allowing my breath to fan her skin. "I can't wait. More flesh for me to pound," I say. "Now hurry up. I have nipple and clit clamps waiting for you."

She freezes with the spoon halfway to her mouth. She turns her head slowly to look at me. There's lust in her eyes.

Oh, yeah. I love that my girl is game for whatever. I'm going to enjoy tonight.

I go to say something else dirty when my phone rings. I frown and pull my phone from my pocket. It's Kiyoshi. My frown deepens.

"Everything all right?"

I kiss her forehead. "Yeah, baby. Let me go take this call. Eat up. You'll need your energy."

I answer the call on my way out of the room. "Ryan."

"You have my daughter with you." It's a statement, not a question.

I roll my eyes. I noticed his men when we left the go-kart track. They weren't that close, but close enough that I was able to make them out.

"You know my father lets me do my job. He never bothers me like this."

"I'm not your father. We had a deal. You wouldn't interfere with my daughter's studies."

I give a cocky grin that he can't see. "I'm not interfering. I'm very much a part of her education."

"End the evening, Ryan. She has finals coming."

I frown. I already know this. It's why I had her bring her books along.

I sigh. He's right. I'll only be a distraction to her.

I've been thinking about all the ways I want her in my bed since I picked her up for our date. I've had her out all day as it is.

"Fine," I mumble. "But let's be clear. I'm doing this because she needs to study. Not because you're a pain in my ass."

"You will learn to respect me," Kiyoshi says tightly.

"I talk to you which means I already do. It's when I go silent that you'll know I have no respect for you."

This time, I end the call before he can hang up on me. I'm horny and pissed. I know if I take Carmen even once, it will be hours before I want to let her out of my bed.

"Shit."

CHAPTER ELEVEN

Sunday Morning

Ryan

"Stop looking so nervous," I say and squeeze her hand. "You've been around my family before."

"Yeah, but I wasn't your girlfriend before and I hadn't run off after having sex with you," she murmurs.

I stop in front of my parents' front door and turn her to face me. I cup her face and kiss her lips. I'm tempted to get lost in the kiss, but I stop myself.

Placing my forehead to hers, I hold her tight. "I promise they won't bite. You mean a lot to me. They won't give you any reason to try to run from me," I tease. "Maybe."

Her eyes sparkle as my words sink in. I haven't told her that I love her yet, but it's coming. For now, I don't want to scare her off.

However, it almost slipped a few times when we've been hanging around her place or on the few occasions, she has come to my place. Oh, how I love when Kiyoshi sends me pissed off texts about his daughter hanging at my house.

"Are you sure it's okay for me to be here? You said this is a family thing," she says.

I growl at her, and she starts to laugh. The front door opens before I get to say another word. Mom stands in the doorway with a smile on her face.

"Ye thinking about running again?" she says.

Carmen blushes and her mouth falls open. I groan and tuck her under my arm before she does take flight. I start into the house as mom backs up.

"I'm so sorry I didn't tell you I was leaving," Carmen says.

"I'm pulling yer leg, lass. It's good to see ye again," Mom says and pulls Carmen into a hug.

Carmen visibly relaxes. I smile and reach for her hand. She looks up at me with that shy smile on her lips.

"Come on. The lot of them are vultures. If ye don't get a seat at the table and some food on ye plate, ye may not get to eat."

"This is a beautiful home," Carmen says.

"Thank ye. Now that I don't have seven little fuckers tearing it up, I can keep it looking respectable."

I snort and shake my head. We never tore up Cassy Black's house. That's some straight bullshit if I've ever heard it. She'd have us in headlocks while whipping our little asses.

"Don't believe a word she says," I whisper to Carmen.

We follow mom into the dining room. All my brothers and their women are surrounding the new table Mom bought. We've grown as a family and need more seats these days.

"Hey," my brothers cheer as we walk into the dining room.

Carmen gives a little shy wave. My chest swells to finally have my girl at the table. I pull her chair before taking the one beside her.

All the women welcome Carmen right in. My brothers are their usual selves, joking amongst each other. I notice Brax piling food on a plate for Heather and smile.

I'm going to be an uncle again. There are three pregnant women at this table. Nellie looks like she's ready to pop even though she has a little longer to go.

I look to Bean and find Noah leaning in her ear as his hand rests on her tiny bump. Damn, I didn't know I wanted to be a father until now. It hits me hard that I want to watch Carmen swell with my seed inside her.

"What?" she asks as she looks up at me.

"Nothing." I dip my head to peck her lips, then kiss her temple.

"Congratulations, Carmen," mom says into the chatter. "Ye got an A for the video from the wedding I hear."

"Yes, ma'am. Thank you."

"Two degrees from two different schools. Ryan brags about ye. I'm proud of ye."

"Thank you," Carmen says. "I'm not done yet. I still have a year to go in both programs. It's not that big of a deal."

I reach under the table and squeeze her thigh. "You have to be kidding me, right? Neither of those programs are easy. You go to two of the best schools and remain an honors student at both."

She shrugs her shoulders and her cheeks glow. I'm so proud of her. I know she hasn't told her father about film school, and last time I asked she told me she wasn't sure when she would.

I have her back whenever she's ready to. I think she's amazing and should follow her dreams. It's her life and she should be happy in whatever she wants to do with it.

"Ry, I think you're embarrassing her," Dad says.

I reach for her chin and turn her face toward me. Looking into her eyes, I wait for her to focus on mine. When she does, I make something very clear.

"You're amazing. There's nothing to be embarrassed about. I'm proud of you. You should be proud of yourself."

I then kiss her soft lips quickly. She stares at me when I back away. I turn back to the food and dive in.

The chatter starts again and soon the girls have invited Carmen to hang out. I love the way her face lights up as they bring her into the fold. She looks like she belongs.

Carmen

I look up at the sky as we sit in the backyard of the Black family home. What was breakfast turned into a daylong affair. I have Nora in my arms as I sit around the fire pit with the ladies.

"I'm so sleepy," Nellie groans. I look to her and she's widening her eyes as if she's trying to keep them open. "Someone tell my husband he has to stop playtime to take me home."

We laugh at her. Wyatt has gotten lost with his brothers. I love the closeness of this family.

I thought maybe they were close in Ireland because it was a vacation or something, but they're really tight knit. I look down at Nora in my arms and smile. She's gorgeous. I can't help wondering what a daughter with Ryan would look like.

"They're always cute while they're sleeping. Don't do it to yourself," Nellie teases.

"I can't wait to see what our baby looks like," Bean says with a bright smile as she holds a hand over her little bump.

She must have been pregnant at the wedding. It's only been a few weeks and she's showing. Not a lot, but enough for me to notice.

Time is flying. Next week will make a month since I've been dating Ryan. An entire month, but honestly it feels like so much longer. It's so surreal. We've fallen into a relationship so easily.

"Do you want children?" Heather aims at me, pulling me from my thoughts.

I think about it for a second. "I never thought much about it before. I guess someday."

"Have you not seen the way he looks at her. She'll be knocked up as soon as she lets him hit it raw," Roni says.

She's always so quiet. It surprises me when she speaks up. I look at the pretty woman. She's both mysterious and alluring.

"You're so right." Nellie giggles.

My cheeks heat. I've already let him have sex with me without a condom, but I don't make that announcement. Instead, I give a shrug.

"I think we have a ways to go before we get to that point."

They all make a humming sound and burst into laughter as they realize they've done it at the same time. Nora stirs in my arms and nestles closer. I can't help but smile.

No, I wouldn't mind having a baby. When the time is right, that is. Especially one as cute as the twins or Nora.

Nellie yawns. "That's it." She pushes out of her seat with her big belly. "That man is taking me home. *Wyatt.*"

She wobbles off, calling after her husband. I get up to follow her, so they don't have to come back for their baby. When I get inside Ryan is in the kitchen with a smile on his face.

He and his mom look like they were having an interesting conversation. He stands and walks over to me to kiss my forehead. I crane my neck to look up at him as he moves behind me to wrap his arms around me and Nora. He starts to sway us, pecking my lips before he looks to his mother.

"Look at this, Ma. Tell me we wouldn't make a beautiful family," he croons.

"Run, love. Don't let him get anywhere near ye with his filthy pecker," Cassy says with a smile.

I know I blush instantly. I've let her son put his pecker all over me. And I mean all over. There isn't a part of my body Ryan's penis doesn't know.

Cassy throws her head back and laughs. Ry kisses the top of my head and Nora wakes, looking around the room. Cassy covers her mouth as her eyes sparkle with mirth.

"Hey you," Ry croons and reaches to take Nora out of my arms.

She goes right to him. I turn to look at him holding his niece in his big strong arms. It's a hot look on him. I can totally see Ryan being a sexy daddy.

Nora cups his cheek as they start a little conversation. When Ry makes a goofy face and Nora starts to squeal with laughter, I think I lose my heart. His eyes twinkle as he makes her laugh.

"Bro, you woke her?" Wyatt groans as he walks into the kitchen with a sleepy Nellie at his side.

The protective hold Wyatt has on Nellie's belly reminds me of their story. They have so much love for each other. It makes me all warm and fuzzy to see them together.

"I didn't wake her. Mom did," Ry replies.

"Sure she did."

"This time I did," Cassy says. "I'll make it up to ye. Take yer wife home. I'll keep the wee one for the night."

Nellie perks up. "Bless you. Bless you and all you love." Cassy laughs and shakes her head. "Let's go, Wy, before she changes her mind."

"You don't have to tell me twice," Wyatt says and kisses the top of his daughter's head. "See you in the morning, munchkin."

"I'll distract her," Ry says when Nora's little face crumples and she reaches out as her father backs away.

"Hey, sweetpea," Ryan croons and nuzzles her neck before he blows a raspberry against it.

Nora bursts into giggles. Soon she's focused on her uncle and her parents rush out before she can turn back for them. Ryan keeps her busy for the next ten minutes and it's amazing.

I take a seat and watch him with her the entire time. Cassy brings me a cup of hot chocolate and some cookies. After a while, it feels like she's watching me and not the two of them. I turn to face her.

"Yer falling," she says.

"Huh?"

She smiles at me. "Yer falling for my baby. It's never easy to watch them grow up and not need ye anymore. However, there's something about watching them fall in love. He be me baby. The last one to need me."

I smile at her. "I don't think you have anything to worry about. Ryan and I are just dating. It's still really new."

She gives a short laugh. "Ye sell yerself an apple in a butcher shop. My babe has fallen for ye and I'm pretty sure ye have fallen for him. But that's none of my business."

She gets up with a smile on her face and goes to take Nora from Ryan. Ryan kisses his niece's cheek before handing her over. He bends to kiss his mother's cheek as well.

"See you later, Mom."

"See ye later, love."

When Ryan turns to me, he has a heated look in his eyes. I squirm in my seat as I get caught in his gaze. He holds out his hand in a silent command and I find myself on my feet, moving to him.

He cups my throat and runs his thumb across my lips. Leaning in, he places his lips near my ear. "You would look so good with me growing inside you."

When he backs away and looks into my eyes, I stand there stunned, turned on, and pretty sure I'd have his baby if he asked me to.

CHAPTER TWELVE

Changing Tides

Nellie

I nearly stumble into the house as Wyatt unlocks the door. I could kiss Cass for taking Nora for the night. I don't remember being this exhausted with my last pregnancy.

This time around I nod off wherever I am. Sitting, standing, it doesn't matter. If I'm still too long, I pass out.

"Wyatt," I yelp as he lifts me into his arms and carries me to our bedroom.

"You're tired. Let me pamper you for a bit," he murmurs against my forehead.

I smile and bury my face in his neck. He carries me right to the bed and places me at the foot. I sigh deeply when he takes my shoes from my feet. I can't even see them anymore these days.

He sits on his butt on the floor and starts to massage one of my feet. I look into his eyes, and it dawns on me that he's been rather quiet since we left his parents' house. At first, I thought he was giving me time to nap, but something in his eyes tells me it's more.

I go to pry, but he shuts his face down. It's his way when he's not ready to talk about something. I chew on my lip, debating on whether or not I should push anyway.

I get totally distracted when he takes the massage to the next level. He's hitting the spot. He's not playing fair.

I'm too sleepy to fight the relaxation he's sending my body into. With no bath time for Nora and no bedtime story, I can drift off and sleep without worrying about waking early to take care of my toddler. I let everything melt away and take advantage of this gift.

I may miss her already, but I'm grateful for the rest I'll get. I'll take all I can get before this new little one gets here. Yup, I sure will.

I lean back on my palms and throw my head back. Allowing my eyes to close, I relish in the feel of his strong hands as he rubs my foot. I live for moments like these.

The sound of his movements fills the room as he uses one hand on my foot and the other disappears. I don't even bother to look to see what he's up to. I sink back onto the mattress to lie flat.

When soft music fills the room, I smile. That's what he was up to. "Why I Love You" by MAJOR plays.

Of course, I start to cry as my hormones make a mess of me. My husband does everything intentionally. I know he picked this song with purpose.

Wyatt kisses my foot before switching to the other one. I can't stop crying as the song plays and he massages my other swollen foot. Tears roll back into my ears as I keep my eyes closed.

I'm carrying his child, and my body feels like it hates me, but I wouldn't want this with anyone else. He kisses his way up from my ankle, calf, thigh, over my belly and hovers above me. I look into his golden eyes and get lost.

"I love you," he says softly.

However, there's so much intensity in the words and his gaze. Again, I get the feeling that something is weighing on him. I search his face as I reply.

"I love you too."

He brushes my cheek with his fingertips. Dipping his head, he nips my lip and tugs at it. Then he kisses me softly, the total opposite of the nipping he initiated.

I lock my fingers into his hair and keep him close. He's careful not to place his weight on me as he deepens the kiss.

"Are you too tired?" He flicks his tongue against my bottom lip.

I shake my head. "Never," I whisper.

He gives me a sexy grin and reaches for the straps of my sundress. He moves to kiss my shoulder as he slides the fabric down. I lift up to help him peel the dress from my body.

He gets it over my belly and down my legs, then tosses it aside. He removes my panties and bra next, taking his time to kiss my belly with each removal. I'm bare to him and his appraising gaze.

I watch as he backs away to stand from the bed and starts to strip from his clothes. My lips turn up as his newest tat comes into view. He has Nora's baby picture on his right shoulder.

He's an amazing canvas. His muscles move so fluidly beneath his skin. However, none of that is what gets my heart racing.

It's the look in his eyes. I see his love for me. I move back on the bed, and he climbs back on.

With his strong hands, he turns me onto my side. Brushing my hair from my neck, he starts to place open-mouthed kisses there. I smile when his tongue ring brushes against my skin.

As tired as I am, my body awakens to his touch. I tilt my head to the side, giving him more access to my neck. A moan slips from my lips as he palms my breast in one of his hands.

"Ah." I release a breath.

His touch is like having life breathed into me all over again. I don't know what I did before Wyatt. It seems like life started the day I stopped before him in that airport and looked up into his golden eyes.

If you'd have told me then that I would marry Wyatt Black and have two children with him, I would have laughed to the point of tears. Now my tears are because I'm so loved I can feel it in every cell in my body. As he slides his hand over my belly, down to the apex of my thighs, I can't help but feel his love for me.

I lift my leg to give him access to my center. "Nellie," he whispers my name in my ear as he finds me wet and ready for him. I wiggle my butt against his growing erection.

"Wyatt, please."

He kisses my shoulder. I go to plead with him again, but he slides into my heat, cutting off my words. Instead, a moan fills the room.

I bite my lip and reach for his hand still between my legs as he rocks into me. We lace our fingers together and place them over my bump. He grunts but keeps the slow and steady pace.

He makes love to me to the song he left on repeat as if he plans to drill these lyrics into my head. He loves me. This is his way to show me that love.

We build together slow and steady. Our hands locked tightly together over my belly. Our baby starts to move, and I burst into more tears.

We made this life together. With all I've lost and all we've been through, my husband continues to show me that our love can make anything better. Every pain, every concern, every challenge, Wyatt is always there to make sure I come out on the other side.

"You're everything to me, Nellie. I love you," he says as he lifts our joined hands to thumb away my tears. "Don't cry, baby. Come with me."

"I love you, Wy," I say breathlessly.

If I could describe this very moment, it would be like the culmination of a long journey. A road that ends with all our heart's desires. My heart blooms as if it has grown wings.

They spread and soar. Every nerve in my body answers to my heart. They stand at attention and salute the love that's surrounding us in this room.

When I reach my peak and feel the warmth of Wyatt's release, it's as if we've awakened a spiritual connection that can't be touched and will never be broken. He cradles me in his arms as I come down. My eyes close on the final note of the song and I fall into a blissful sleep.

Wyatt

I hold my wife as she snores. I haven't said this out loud to anyone else, but I don't like this Alliance shit. It puts my entire family in danger.

Not only those at the head of it but everyone. It's unpredictable. I have this gut feeling that it's going to test all of us.

I have too much at stake to allow it to get out of hand. Toby's seat at the table may not belong to me, but the responsibility to protect my brothers and our families does. It would be my life before any of theirs and because I love this woman in my arms too much to leave her and my children without me, I'm on top of this shit.

My phone buzzes, pulling me from my thoughts. I look at the time. It's a little past midnight.

When I see the name of the caller, I know it's even later for them. It's after 3:00 a.m. in New York. I'm instantly alert as I answer the phone and slip out of bed.

Nellie mumbles my name in her sleep and reaches out for me. I lean to kiss her forehead before leaving the room.

"What's up, Nate?"

"You told me you wanted to know if anything moved wrong. We can now officially count the Sato family as an enemy."

"Yakuza, fuck. Give me the details."

I close my eyes and run a hand through my hair as he runs down what's going on. Japanese mob. Great, this shit is coming for our door.

Carmen is a priority for me and my brothers. We all agreed on that when we saw the way Ryan looked at her at Mom and Dad's. My little brother is in love.

Anyone who touches Carmen or her family has a big fucking problem now. Kiyoshi isn't a man to be played with, but he's just gotten a hell of a lot more dangerous now that my brother is in love with his daughter.

More dangerous than the Alliance will ever be because we're built on love and blood. I can say for a fact that every single one of my brothers will bleed every last drop for our family. I'm more determined than ever as I step out into my backyard and look up at the sky.

"If this is our destiny let's play," I say into the phone once he's done.

"Figured you'd say that. Keep your eyes open and heads up. This is only the first test."

"Yeah, don't I know it."

I hang up and send a text to my brothers. I'm not surprised when my phone rings. I blow out a breath and answer.

"What the fuck?" Ryan barks before I can speak a greeting.

"You knew this was a possibility. Kiyoshi is in Japan on Alliance business. This is the first wave. They're going to test this shit," I say.

"So you're telling me they're on their way here?"

I shake my head. "I'm telling you that they are the first to rebel against this. It's time to look alive because someone's going to try us all. Carmen's father is a seat holding member of the Alliance. You went big, bro. You couldn't have picked a girl with more shit in her backyard—"

"Wyatt," he says on warning.

I heave a heavy breath. "Relax, I'm not saying that's a bad thing. I'm saying that this is going to put some hair on that chest.

"It's time to man up. We protect what's ours. You know Noah, John, and I will never let shit happen to you.

"She's now a part of you. We saw the way you looked at her. We get it. We're here."

There's silence on the line for a beat. I know my little brother. He's working out his feelings and his plan.

"Thanks. I'll be on the lookout."

"We all will. Love you, Ry. We have your back."

"Yeah, I know. I love you too, Bro."

"Later."

CHAPTER THIRTEEN

Not Sure

Carmen

I sit in the sand with my new camera, recording Ryan as he surfs with his older brother, John. I thought I'd feel out of place. I'm the youngest out of everyone.

However, no one ever makes me feel like a baby or like I'm not on their level. Actually, I think I fit in with Ryan and his crowd better than my own friends.

I was surprised to get the call from Roni asking if I wanted to hang. I like her. She can be detached at times, but then there are moments that her true personality seems to shine through.

At least, I think it's her true self. She's quiet, down to earth and funny. Although, I'm still trying to figure her and John out.

"That's awesome," she says beside me as she peeks at my camera screen.

"Yeah, it is. The lighting is everything. I wish I could get closer."

"There's an extra board. The camera is waterproof, right?"

I shake my head before she can get the words out. "I'm not going out there. I have a fear of oceans. Like, I can totally swim, but I won't step foot in that water," I reply.

"Seriously?"

"Yup. It's crazy because my mom and dad could swim out to the buoys and back. I swear I'm adopted."

Roni laughs. "Hey, we all have our thing."

I stop recording and put the camera away. The sun has finally set. I have a ton of great footage.

Roni digs into the cooler and pulls out a beer. She holds it out to me. I bite my lip and wince.

"I'm not twenty-one yet," I murmur.

She makes a show of looking around us before she turns back to me. "Okay, and who's going to tell? The police aren't coming for you for a beer."

I laugh and reach to take it. I go to open it, but it's plucked from my hand before I can get the top off. Ryan looks down at me with a frown. I didn't even notice that he and John were heading our way.

I look to John and Roni and John's scowling at Roni too. I turn my gaze back to Ryan. He hands the beer to John who puts it back into the cooler.

"What?" Roni says.

John leans down to murmur something in her ear. I don't know what he says, but whatever it is has her squirming on her beach towel. When he lifts back to his full height, he has a knowing smile on his face.

"Fine," she says breathlessly.

"Those were for Felix and Toby before they bailed," Ryan says. "We have plans tonight. You'll want to be sober."

The anger that was about to build fizzes away. Ryan plans the best dates. We've gone on a ton of them, that is when I'm not studying.

I can't get pissed if that's his reason for taking the beer from me. I actually get excited to see what he has in store. Sure, I should be studying.

My father has been sending email reminders about my finals. I'm so ready for the semester to end so I can breathe.

I push all thoughts of school out of my head. "What are we doing?"

He gives me a playful smile and winks. "Wouldn't you like to know?"

I fall back on my towel. "The torture," I say dramatically.

He chuckles and takes a seat beside me. When I sit back up, he shifts my body to sit in between his legs. Roni and John take off down the beach. It's so interesting that they don't hold hands like a couple, but they ooze sexual tension.

"I'm still trying to figure those two out," I say.

"You and everyone else. Save yourself the brain cells," Ry says into my hair.

"We should get out of here after you finish your finals."

"Huh?" I say and crane my neck to look up at him.

He fixes those eyes on me, and I get lost for a second. I shake my head clear and wrinkle my brows. He pecks my lips and smiles.

"I want to take you away. A vacation somewhere," he says the words like he's thinking out loud.

I scoff and shake my head again. This time it's because I know that's not going to happen. My father still doesn't even know I have a boyfriend.

Besides, I haven't told my father I'm taking the summer off. I need a break. I want to take a moment to breathe before the fall semester starts.

"I don't know about that."

"Why not?"

I go to answer, but my phone rings. I move to take it from my camera bag. Seeing the bag Ry bought me for my birthday brings a smile to my lips. A girl could get spoiled.

I nearly groan when I see it's my dad. However, I don't dare ignore his call. I pick up and put the phone to my ear. I think about talking in Japanese, but my father will become suspicious. Then, I remember Ryan speaks about seven languages fluently.

"Hi, Daddy."

"*Kon'nichiwa*, Nene. How are your studies coming along?"

"They're going great. Exams start this week. I'll be ready," I say.

It's not a lie. I'll be ready. I just haven't been studying much.

One more week and I'll be finished with all my exams. I'm more than ready. I'm tired of the lies and the crazy workload. Not that it's hard, it's tiring mostly. I want time to do twenty-year old stuff.

"Very well," he says with a hint of something I can't place. "I look forward to the transcripts. I'm very proud of you."

I can't help but smile. It's not often that my father says he's proud of me. However, I do feel the sting of my lies more deeply as his words sink in. I wrinkle my brows at the use of transcripts, but I brush it off. My dad is Japanese. It wouldn't be the first time he misused or said a wrong word or tense.

I'm paranoid. All of this is starting to weigh on me. I've been so worried I'll get caught and now I'm dating Ryan and I've yet to tell my father about him either.

I swallow my crazy thoughts. "Thanks, Daddy."

"I'll be home soon. It's time you begin to think of marriage, your career."

"Dad. I have time for all of that. I'm twenty." I pause as the wheels turn.

Ryan tightens his arms around me, and I gain a little courage. I've been thinking about my options after I finish film school. I don't know if I truly want to finish my other degree.

I'm on track to graduate at the top of my class, that's an advantage, right? Now would be the time to show my father the value of what I've been doing.

If only I knew what I want my next step to be. I don't think I'll ever get him to change how he runs Nash Media. However, maybe, just maybe he'll hear me out. My heart starts to pound as I approach this cliff I plan to jump off.

"Hey, Daddy. Could we talk about an idea I have when you get back?"

He's silent for a moment. I sag my shoulders, immediately thinking he's going to shut me down. When he does speak again, his voice is warm.

"You are welcome to talk to me about anything your heart desires, my Nene."

Tears well. Perhaps my mother was right. I should've fought harder and told my dad what I wanted last year before I went behind his back.

"Okay, great. I will see you when you return."

"Yes, you shall. I will talk to you later. Make sure to study, Nene."

Again, I get the feeling he knows everything. The fact that I've been spending all my time with Ryan. That I've been living a double life.

I sigh. "Yes, Daddy. I will."

We end the call, and I sit staring off at nothing. I almost forget that I'm in Ryan's arms. He remains quiet as I think to myself. I'm the first one to break the silence.

"Ever since I was a little girl, I've wanted to please my father. He's not like your mom and dad. He's not open with his emotions or affection. We've always gotten that from our mom.

"But I've seen him so affectionate with my mother, and he's always kept my brother close. So, I used to think it was me. The only way I could make him happy was with my studies."

"You're doing great in school," Ryan murmurs.

I give a little smile. "Yeah, but I have no passion for it, not for Journalism anyway. Can I tell you something?"

He tightens his arms around me. "Anything."

"If it were up to me, I would drop out of both programs. I'm starting to wonder if film is a hobby." I shrug my shoulders. "Honestly, I think this has been my way to rebel.

"I've done everything he's asked and still, I feel like an outsider in my family. Like everyone's in on a secret that I'm not. Film school was *my* secret. My way to say I don't need to be in on theirs."

Ryan stiffens behind me and I'm a little confused by the action at first. I think over what I've said and still can't place his reaction. I frown and wonder if I sound like a spoiled brat.

"What makes you think they have a secret you don't know about?"

I blow out a breath. I think over my life. I never get to go on the trips to Japan my father takes with Ne. Sometimes my mother goes, but I've never been.

Sure, I've gotten to go to some really cool places during those times. Mostly with Aunt Mariah, she's always been like a big sister to me. However, I've always felt left behind or something. Like, they didn't want me with them.

"I don't know. It's a feeling I have."

"What made you start a program at a different school? I checked, you could have minored in film where you already were," he says.

I turn to look at him. "You checked? Really?"

"I was curious."

I laugh. "I'm going to give that a pass." I shake my head. Dating a PI has been interesting, to say the least. "I didn't think I would be able to pull it off, to tell the truth.

"If it weren't for my aunt, I wouldn't have. If I would have taken it on as a minor my father would have known. He's invested in my education. He gets a copy of my schedule every semester. Enrolling in a different school helped me hide it."

"That makes sense." He nods. "So, when do you plan to tell your father?"

I turn my body until I'm sitting between his legs but facing him completely. I look at Ryan. Really look at him. He never named his passion, yet he's content with his life.

"I want to be more like you. I want to be happy with whatever I do with my life. I used to think I was on that path, but now I see most of what I've been doing has either been to please my father or rebel against him.

"Until now, I've never had the courage to speak up. I don't know, being around you and your family has changed that for me. I want to be honest with my dad. I want to tell him that I need to find my own way. I think I'm going to tell him when he gets back from his business trip."

"I'm here if you need me. If you want me there when you tell him, I'll stand by you."

My heart fills with hope from his offer alone. It means so much to me. Not that I'm ready to tell my dad about him, but the offer still means a lot.

I tilt my head to the side and study Ryan. He's nothing like I imagined and I'm falling in love with who he is with each day. I know it's fast, but it's happening whether I want it to or not.

I go to tell him just that, but Roni's laughter rings through the air. I turn and find her standing over John as he lies flat on his back in the sand. I smile. I hope I get their story one day.

"I think you found your passion. You just don't see it." I turn to come nose to nose with Ryan. He's closer than I thought.

"What?"

"People open up to you. They give you their raw emotions and they're willing to do it on your camera. You have something. You only need to step out of pocket to look at it."

His words hit their mark. I turn to look at John and Roni as I ponder Ryan's words. Maybe he has a point.

CHAPTER FOURTEEN

Sharks

Ryan

I'd like to think that I would plan all these dates for Carmen even if she weren't my assignment. The fact of the matter is, these dates, hanging with my family, it's all a part of us working to keep her safe.

I want my sisters-in-law to like my girl and bring her into the fold, so I asked the guys not to tell them. I want their interaction with Carmen to be real. Well, with the exception of Roni.

She knows, which is why I was a little annoyed when she offered Carmen that beer. Carmen isn't like the others. She can't hold her liquor for shit.

Not like Bean and Heather can. Roni seems to be able to hold her own around those two, but I don't think that will ever be Carmen.

With Roni, she's always alert and ready. We don't have to tell her to be. The beers were left over from my brothers.

It's their weekend off and a few beers wouldn't have kept them from springing into action if need be. My girl did not need that beer. It would have ruined the night and my plans.

Tonight feels different for me. I think this will be something special between us.

"Hey, where are you?" Carmen says, bringing my attention to her as she places her hand on my thigh.

I glance over to her before training my eyes back on the road. "Thinking."

"Penny for your thoughts."

"Nah, you don't want those. We're almost there."

"Where is there?" she says excitedly.

I grin and turn to her once more. She has that gorgeous smile on her face again. I wish I could lean to kiss her. Instead, I focus on the road and feed off her excitement as it fills the car.

"You'll see."

She huffs. Out of the corner of my eye, I can see she's pouting with her arms crossed over her chest. I chuckle and hit the signal to turn into our destination.

"You have your camera, right?"

"Yeah," she says.

The car falls silent until I turn into our destination. Carmen gasps, I turn to glance at her. Her eyes are lit up.

"The aquarium," she says softly.

"Yeah."

"But it's closed. What are we doing here in the middle of the night?"

I place a hand to my chest to feign shock as I use the other hand to turn into the parking spot. "Babe, do you not know what my last name is? I got connections. There's no such thing as closed to a Black."

She laughs and shakes her head at me. I wink at her before I hop out of the car and head to open her door. I hold out my hand and she places her soft palm in mine. Once she's out of the car, I tug her in for a quick kiss.

I release her to grab her camera bag from the back seat. When I close the car door, I take a look around. To anyone else, nothing would seem out of place, other than us going into the aquarium after hours.

I, on the other hand, see Noah's truck tucked away, out of plain sight. Brax is walking the grounds in a baseball cap and uniform as if he works at the place. I nod to myself. My girl will be safe here.

"We're really going inside?" she asks.

"Yeah, why not?"

I tap on the side entrance door. Cornell, an old buddy of mine opens up. He pulls me into a one-armed hug before he turns to give Carmen an appreciative look. I wrap an arm around her waist and tug her into my side possessively.

Cornell gets the point. Before I break his jaw and black one of his eyes, he turns to lead the way to the setup I have waiting for us. The lights are low, the light from the fish tanks illuminating the way, and causing a romantic ambiance, or at least I hope it is.

When we reach the table set for two, Carmen stops and looks up at me. The dreamy-eyed look she gives is better than I'd hoped for. She places a hand on my chest and reaches up on her toes to kiss my lips.

"Thank you, Ryan. Your dates are always perfect."

Guilt consumes me. I hate lying to her and the more time that goes by the more I feel like I'm lying. I'm getting sick of this shit. Her father needs to come clean as much as she does.

I force a smile and kiss her forehead. "Come sit with me."

I walk her to the table and pull her chair. She sits and I place her camera bag beside her. I take the seat across from her and watch as she looks around, taking in the Aquarian life that floats all around us.

We already had dinner. The setup before us is simple. More of a late dessert. Sparkling cider and chocolate covered strawberries.

Carmen lifts her glass to her lips but frowns after taking a sip. I laugh and she glares at me. I shrug and sit back in my seat.

"I will not be serving your underaged ass any alcohol," I tease.

"Screw you, Ryan." She pouts.

"Oh, baby. I plan for you to."

She rolls her eyes at me and finishes off the glass of cider. I pick up a strawberry and lift it to her lips. She takes a bite as I keep my eyes fixed on that sensual, sexy mouth of hers.

"Why here?" she asks after she's finished chewing.

I look around and smile. "You asked me for my passion." I shrug.

She tilts her head to the side and her brows knit. She's trying to make the connection. I point to her bag and wave her to follow me as I stand.

I lace my fingers through hers and lead her to the shark tanks. I guide her to sit and move to lean against the rail.

"Take out your camera."

She nods and gets the camera out. I wait and watch the excitement that oozes from her. Carmen may think she doesn't know what she wants to do, but I've seen her passion in her eyes for learning about people and figuring out their secrets.

The camera is her vehicle for that. She made my siblings amazing wedding videos. They tell a story, not just stolen moments of a day.

"Ready," she says.

"You wanted to know what my passion is. I've been thinking about it since you asked."

"You love sea life?"

I shake my head. "No."

Her face crumples. She looks at me in confusion. I'm going to be honest with my girl. I'm going to tell her my truth.

"I have a passion for the hunt," I say. "I'm a hunter and protector."

Her eyes light up. "Like a shark," she says, looking down at her camera screen.

"Exactly. I protect what's mine and if I need to hunt or protect, I do my job. I've never thought twice about working for my dad because it's in me to do what we do. I thrive off seeing what no one else sees.

"None of my brothers have been able to hide their secrets from me. I see it all. It's a part of the protector in me.

"I have a passion to take care of and look after those I care about, those in need. I wouldn't change what I do, because it's a part of who I am."

"I think I get it," she breathes. "Like that girl and her boyfriend. You didn't know her, but you wanted to protect her."

She lifts her gaze to look at the tank behind me. Her thoughts play across her face. I observe her, everything from the slow blink of her eyes and the slow slide of her tongue across her lips. She knits her brows and seconds later they shoot up as if she's had an epiphany.

"You have been a protector since the first time I ran into you," she says, turning her gaze back to me. "I remember you being concerned about my safety and you didn't even know me."

I shrug. "I wouldn't have wanted to see you lost out there even if I wasn't instantly attracted to you." She blushes, making me smile. "I love that shy shit."

She laughs and puts her camera aside. Patting the empty space beside her, she nods to it. "Come sit with me."

I saunter over and sit next to her. She snuggles into my side. I wrap my arm around her and kiss the top of her head.

She giggles after a while, and I look down at her. She gives me that smile, her eyes twinkling. I lift a brow in question.

"Between your brothers and your cousins, I can totally see you all as sharks." She laughs loudly this time, and I laugh with her.

"Whatever."

"You're a protector because you're a family man," she says as if musing.

She's right. I am. I'm all about my family. I allow that to sink in and think about it for a bit.

She turns her face up to look into my eyes. I'll never get tired of looking into those eyes. I peck her lips.

"Do you still think we have nothing in common?"

She searches my face for a moment. "I don't know. I think I'm still learning about you, Ryan Black. You surprise me every day."

Carmen

That was by far my favorite date so far. Getting to know a part of Ryan I know he hasn't shared with others made the night incredible. The aquarium, strawberries and the walkthrough we took before calling it a night were just icing on the cake.

I sigh and lift my hands over my head to stretch as I lie in my bed. I wish Ry were here with me, but a call came in and he had to go. I miss him already.

A smile comes to my lips as I think of the last month. I want to pinch myself. I'm falling more and more, but I'm too afraid to say the words out loud.

I turn onto my side and get ready to force myself to sleep. I have finals the day after tomorrow. I actually plan to study all day tomorrow.

My phone rings and I laugh. It's Ryan. I know because he programed "Drop It Off" by Little Duval as his ringtone. I totally can't deal with him.

"Yes," I say as I answer the call.

"Is that any way to answer your future husband?"

I pause and suck my lip into my mouth. When he used to say things like that, I ignored him. Now when he says stuff like that, I start to imagine what it would be like to actually be married to Ryan.

I shake it off. I know he's only joking. I release a sigh.

"Hello, handsome. How can I help you?"

"Ah, getting there, but I think you can do better."

I laugh. "What's up, Ryan? Did you forget something?"

"I can't miss my baby? I wanted to hear your voice. The night came to an end faster than I wanted."

My heart stutters as he says he misses me. I turn onto my back and look up at the ceiling. I inhale and smile as his scent fills my nostrils. Most of my things smell like him these days.

"You do know I'm not a baby?" I say.

He snorts. "Did you hear the way I had you cooing for me last night? You're my baby all right."

I laugh. "I remember no such thing."

"So, you don't remember when I had your legs pinned back with my face buried in your pussy for like an hour." I cover my face with one of my hands. "I can still taste you. How many times did you come for me? I think I lost count."

"Ry," I whine and squirm in my bed.

He chuckles. "Don't worry. I'll let you sit on this face tomorrow."

Oh God, can tomorrow hurry up? My nipples tighten beneath my T-shirt. A day of studying doesn't sound like such a good idea anymore.

"Hey, I have to study for my finals," I groan.

"That's fine. I'll spend the day cooking for you. Fuel for the brain. I'll make sure my baby is fed and focused. I've got you."

I bite my lip. I know I should tell him that I'll see him in a few days once my finals are over, but I can't fix my lips to tell him any of that. If I were bolder, I'd pack an overnight bag and head to his place.

"Are you home?"

He pauses for a second. "No, on the job."

"Oh." I pout.

I seriously was going to try to get up the nerve to go to his place. I'm super disappointed. I'm also curious. It's late. I wonder what kind of case he's working on.

"I need to go, baby. Sleep tight. I'll see you in the morning."

"Goodnight."

"Night, gorgeous."

CHAPTER FIFTEEN

Knowing Mommy

Carmen

I bend over and pant as sweat drips down my face. Looking up through my lashes, I see my mother is totally unfazed. I can't believe I'm so winded.

"What's going on with you?" she says as she wipes sweat from her face. "You're tired already? Come on."

"Are you serious?" I reply and frown.

My lungs are burning, and I feel like I've been jumped. This woman is out to kill me. I know she hasn't changed a thing about our routine, but for some reason today it feels like she has turned it up a thousand notches.

"Come on, Nene. You're so dramatic."

I make a sound in the back of my throat and drag my body over to my water bottle and phone. This gym isn't big enough for the attitude I have right now. I wasn't looking forward to this visit to begin with.

Ryan and I had a late date last night since I had a final yesterday morning. He took me to the movies and dinner. According to him, we were celebrating me crushing my finals despite the fact that I'm not done yet.

He's so sweet when it comes to things like that. I mean, I'm not nervous about my exams, but he insists on pumping me up and telling me how great I am. It's an extra boost of confidence that does bring a smile to my face in the middle of exams.

Ryan has made me feel super special since we've been together. I would've never thought that he could be so sweet and sensitive. I think my favorite moment was the day he showed up at my class with a dozen roses. I was embarrassed and happily surprised at the same time.

"What's that smile about?" my mother asks as I look down at my phone in my hand.

Ryan has been texting me while I've been spending time with her. He is a whole fool and nasty to boot. I tuck the phone behind my back before my mother can see the dirty things my boyfriend sends me.

"Nothing."

"When have I been a fool, eh? I know you and that's not a nothing smile."

I shrug my shoulders. "I've been in a happy place lately. School is almost over for the semester. I'll be done for good next year, and I have my life to plan before me."

"Hm," she hums, sounding just like my father and sucks her teeth. "You know your father wants you to meet someone. How is that going to go over with your boyfriend?"

"Oh my God. He's going to flip out if …" I trail off feeling like a butthead. She got me.

"That's what I thought."

"Mommy, I really like him. I think I know how to pick my own boyfriends. You have to tell Daddy that this is something he needs to back down on."

She gives me a pointed look. "How many times do I have to tell you to talk to your father yourself? He'll listen."

"No, he won't," I huff.

"Then you don't want to date this boy you're with."

I roll my eyes and frown. "But you could make this so much easier. He listens to you."

My mother is the only person my father listens too. She has this way with him that I've never seen anyone else duplicate. My father will walk into a room with a scowl on his face, but as soon as his eyes land on my mother, his entire being lights up.

She pinches my chin between her fingertips. Her gaze bounces across my face. I don't know what she's looking for, but she narrows her eyes as she finds it.

"Nene. Child, you found your way into something you're going to have to be an adult about. My words aren't going to help you." She clicks her tongue. "You don't even know, do you?"

"Huh?"

She shakes her head. "Come, let me feed you."

Suddenly, food sounds like a great idea. My stomach growls and my mouth waters. I had breakfast. I don't know why I'm suddenly so hungry.

We put our things away and head to the kitchen. I sit at the kitchen nook as my mother starts to make us lunch. I nearly leap from my seat when she pulls out roti skins and a stew pot.

My mother makes the best curry goat and her curry chicken is even better. I don't know which is in the pot, but I'll be happy either way. I'm near drooling as the aromas fill the kitchen while she heats it all up.

When she brings two piping hot dishes over and places them down, I grin like a little kid on Christmas. Mommy gives me a smile as she watches me dig in. Yes, curry chicken, beans and rice, and steamed vegetables.

"Ry would love this," I croon as I chew happily.

"Ry?" she says and lifts a brow. "Is that the young man's name."

I blush and nod. "Yes, Ryan Black."

I swear, a look crosses her features so fast, I have to wonder if I saw it. I'm sure I did though. I place my fork down and stare at my mother.

"What?"

"I said nothing."

"You didn't have to. It's in your face. Just say it, Mommy."

She places her elbow on the table and looks at me with a grin. "I remember when I first met your father. He was a fine man even then. I was waiting in a restaurant to meet a friend for lunch.

"Your father walked in, and he had this authority and power about him. I watched as he started for the other side of the restaurant. I could tell he wasn't as tall as me, but he walked like he was seven feet tall."

I giggle. My father isn't taller than my mother. He is about an inch or two shorter than her six-foot height. She's right though.

To this day, when they stand next to each other, my father holds this presence that would make you think he were the taller one. She continues as she smiles at my laughter.

"As if he felt my eyes on him, he looked my way. He stopped in his tracks and took me in with those dark assessing eyes."

She laughs and sits back in her seat. Her eyes are distant as if she's there at that table, watching my dad all over again. She tosses her hair over her shoulder and cups the back of her neck before she continues.

"That look." She narrows her eyes. "It was so intense. He changed course and headed straight for my table, pulled the chair across from me, opened his suit jacket, flipped it behind him and took a seat before me. I lifted a brow as I took him in. He was so smooth."

She laughs again. "He leaned into the table and said. *I hope you don't mind if I am so bold. You are stunning. One look at you and I know I have found my wife. Tell me what I shall call you?*"

"Seriously?" I say with my mouth hanging open. I didn't know my father had game.

"Yes. He had me right there. I knew he was my husband in that exact moment. Now, my question to you. Do you know who this Ryan is to you?"

I don't have to think about her question. However, I won't admit it to her or Ryan. I've fallen in love with him.

I know it's been super-fast and that scares me a bit, but I feel like I've known him for so much longer. We've found this easiness about our relationship. His humor and teasing have grown on me.

"You don't have to answer me. As long as you know, that's what matters. That's where the courage to tell your father what you want will come from."

"I think you will like him. Ryan is smart and caring. He listens to everything I say. It's one of the things that I love most. I know he's listening."

"I can't wait to meet him," she says with a secret little smile.

I can't help the feeling that she's not saying something. I let it go as my stomach starts to complain and demand I finish the food in front of me. My mother makes sure I'm nice and full before I leave.

Okay, I may be a little spoiled.

Ryan

I start my car when Carmen steps out of the house to get into hers. Before getting into the driver's seat, she hauls a black bag into the trunk, tugging at my curiosity. She's been with her mother from this morning, well into the afternoon. I've gotten used to her routine, which includes visits to her mother at least three times a week.

"Did you hear what I said?" Felix asks from the Bluetooth connection.

"Yeah, I've got you. I'll be there for the fitting tomorrow. Ne already agreed to cover for me and spend time with his sister."

"How is that working out?"

"It's fine."

Felix goes silent. I groan. I don't need him in my business. I'm doing my job. That's all that counts.

"What aren't you saying?"

"Now I get why you guys think I'm annoying."

He chuckles. "You're not the only observant one. You're my little brother. I know when something's bothering you. What's up?"

I blow out a breath and turn on my signal to turn at the next light along with Carmen's car. I've had a lot on my mind in the last few weeks. Things that have started to eat at me.

"I'm lying to her. This shit is going to blow up in my face. She means too much to me for me not to protect her, but I'm digging a deeper hole with the lies with each day that passes."

Felix releases a long whistle. "Yeah, that can be a big problem. For now, though, her safety is the biggest concern. If she cares about you as much as it sounds like you care about her, then it will work out."

I snort to myself. Care about her. I'm in love with her.

It's like that shit came out of nowhere and hit me with a bat. It's only been a few weeks, but she's all I think about, and I can't wait for the moments I get to spend at her side.

"I hope you're right."

"Yeah, it sucks to be in love with someone and know you have shit between you that can threaten it all."

"Yeah."

Felix falls silent again. I frown as I ride a few cars behind Carmen's car. I glance to make sure the call is still connected.

"You do realize you just admitted to loving her?" he finally says.

I shrug as if he can see me. "And? You know I don't play that shit.

"She's mine. I made my peace with my feelings. She's what I want. Why fight it?"

"Excuse me." Felix chuckles. "You'll figure this out. Keep her safe."

"That's what I'm doing, genius. I don't need you to tell me that."

"Bro, that pissy attitude isn't going to change the situation. It's only going to get your ass kicked."

"Who's going to kick it?"

"Me."

"Yeah, you can sniff the crack of my ass. If you don't need anything else I'm out."

He laughs and hangs up on me. I don't much care. We've arrived at Carmen's apartment building.

She parks and gets out. I park and get out of my car causally as if I'm arriving at the same time by coincidence. Carmen looks tired as she steps from the driver's seat.

I walk right up to her and tug her into my arms. She looks up from her phone surprised. I kiss her parted lips and she smiles that sweet smile.

I could stand here staring at her all day. Instead, I tuck her under my arm after she gathers her things and lead her to her apartment.

"You finished work early again?"

"Yeah, got most of it done this morning."

She tips her head back. "Hm. I'm going to have to ask your brothers about this. I think you're the slacker in the family."

I chuckle. "Whatever, baby. How was your time with your mom?"

She groans. "I think she was trying to kill me today."

I knit my brows as I look down at her while she unlocks the door. She pushes the door open, and we both walk inside. Carmen drops her bag and heads to the kitchen.

"She tried to kill you?"

She waves me off and gets a glass of water. I wait for her to give me a real answer. Placing the glass down, she chews her lip as if she's thinking over whether she'll explain.

"We work out together when I go over," she says but I know there's more to it than that from the way her eyes won't settle on me.

I decide to let it go for now. She truly looks exhausted. I round the counter and lift her into my arms.

She wraps her arms around my neck and places her forehead to mine. I've waited all day to have her in my embrace like this. I take her lips as we enter her room.

It's a slow kiss. I'm not looking to deepen it too much. My plan is to get her into the bed so she can take a nap.

"You're the best." She sighs as I put her on the bed and remove her shoes from her feet. "Ugh, I need a shower."

"Nap first. We can shower after."

Her lids are too heavy for her to protest my words. Her shoes barely hit the floor before she's snoring. I laugh and kiss her forehead. She'll probably be hungry when she wakes.

I head to the kitchen to find something to cook for my girl. While I'm searching, I think back to her hesitance to reveal what she and her mother do on their visits. Secrets. I hate them, yet we seem to have a few between us.

CHAPTER SIXTEEN

Carmen

I wake to the smell of something delicious in my apartment. I look at the clock on my desk and groan. I can't believe I've been asleep for so long. I don't remember passing out.

I slip off the bed and start to strip from my clothes. As good as that food smells, I need a shower. I put on a robe and start to collect my things to head to the bathroom.

"Hey, sleepyhead." Ryan appears leaning in the doorway.

I smile. "Hey. I'm going to shower and change. I'll be right out."

He pulls his shirt over his head. "I thought we agreed we'd take that shower together."

I bite my lip as I stare at his chest. Yeah, a shower with him does sound better than one by myself. I move closer to him and place my hand over his heart.

When I look into his eyes, I can't help but wonder if he knows I'm falling in love with him. He has to know. This connection between us has been steadily growing.

He brushes his fingertips across my cheek. Those gorgeous eyes seem to look through me as he searches my face. He tilts his head toward the bathroom.

"Come on."

I nod and follow him as he takes my free hand in his and leads me to the bathroom. Once we're behind the closed door, he takes my things from my hand and places them on the countertop. I move to the sink and brush my teeth.

Ryan moves behind me and removes my robe from my shoulders. While I brush and rinse my mouth out, he hangs the robe on the back of the door. I turn and lean against the sink as I watch him.

A part of me can't believe that I'm standing here naked before him as he loosens his belt and unfastens his pants. I bite my lip as he steps out of his jeans and tosses them aside. I move closer to him as if my feet have a mind of their own.

Placing my hands on his stomach, I make eye contact with him. Slowly, I glide my hands up his warm smooth skin. He dips to kiss me and palms my backside.

It doesn't take long before he lifts me onto his waist and starts for the shower. I almost forgot why we were in here in the first place. I slide down his body and reach for my shower cap.

One side of his mouth turns up. He shakes his head. I lift my shoulders. We've been together long enough. He knows better.

"You already know the deal," I say.

"You look like Marvin the Martian," he says.

My mouth falls open. I swat at his chest as he laughs. Turning my back, I tuck my hair into my cap. I turn on the water and ignore him standing behind me.

The water feels like heaven as it starts to cascade down over me. Ryan wraps me in his embrace and buries his face against my neck. I still don't respond to him.

"You're mad at me?" he says into my ear. "You're a cute Martian. Come on, baby. Don't be mad at me."

He sucks the skin on my neck into his mouth. I have to press my hands to the shower wall to hold myself upright. He groans as he continues to suck on my flesh. His length presses into my cheeks as he grows harder by the second.

"Ry," I whisper.

"You forgive me?" he says then licks my neck.

I don't even remember what I was mad about. I turn to him and grab his face. I kiss him hard. He returns it, taking over to deepen the kiss and devour me.

My back hits the shower wall as he grabs my breasts. He pinches my nipples and rolls them with his long fingers. I gasp and whimper as he breaks the kiss and dips his head to capture one of my hardened peaks.

"Tell me what you want, baby," he says against my breast.

I go to reply, but I suddenly feel dizzy. I put a hand out to steady the spinning room. Ryan looks up at me with concern. He straightens and looks down at me. Cupping my face, he observes me closely.

"Are you all right? What's wrong?"

"I don't know. I feel a little dizzy."

Without another word, he cuts off the shower and lifts me into his arms. He puts me down long enough to wrap a towel around his waist and to place my robe back on my body. After, I'm back in his arms he takes me back into my bedroom.

He sits, bringing me into his lap. Pinching my chin between his fingers he lifts my head, his gaze bounces across my face.

"Did you eat lunch?"

"Oh *no*. I left my leftovers on the counter. Mommy packed some for you too. I wanted you to taste her roti."

I left the bag she made for me right on the kitchen counter. I don't know how I forgot it. I had it in my hand at one point. Darn it.

"Focus, baby. So you did eat."

"Yes." I nod and pout as I think of the food I left behind.

A little smile comes to his lips. He sucks the bottom one into his teeth. It's so sexy to watch, I lose my breath and my lips part as I stare.

"I'm going to ask you some questions. Don't freak out when I do," he says, bringing my attention back to our conversation.

"Okay."

"Are you on birth control?"

I laugh. "Yeah right. Between classes and studying, I've never had time to date. Not seriously. Besides, my father doesn't make it any easier. I'm like a princess in a bubble—" I stop talking when I realize I'm rambling.

"Sorry. No, I'm not on birth control," I say.

He nods. "Carmen," he says slowly. "Baby, when was the last time you had a period? I've been inside you almost every day since I showed up on your doorstep that first night. It's been over a month ..." He lets his words trail off.

"Oh my god." I jump up and tug my shower cap off. I stare at my feet as my mind races. "No, no, no. Ryan no."

I turn and race to my drawer and pull-out panties and a bra. I throw them on quickly. I find a pair of leggings and tug them on too.

"Where are you going?"

"I need to get a pregnancy test. I can't be pregnant. My father is going to lose it."

"Baby, you need to calm down. If you're pregnant, the last thing you need to do is stress out and run off."

The gentle tone of his voice causes me to stop and turn to face him. He's looking at me with a twinkle in his eyes. I cover my belly and stare up at him.

"I could be pregnant, Ry," I say the words in almost a whisper.

"Yeah, babe. Which means, my pull-out game is trash."

I twist my lips and roll my eyes at him. "Really?"

He shrugs. "Facts. Your pussy was so good that first night. I'm not surprised I fucked up."

He moves over to me and wraps me in his arms. I can't help shaking my head at him. He kisses the top of my head and gives me a little squeeze.

I sigh. "So this is a fuck up to you?"

He pulls back enough to look down at me. His face is the most serious I've ever seen. There's something there that I can't put my finger on.

"That's not what I meant. I meant that I was supposed to pull out, not get you pregnant. Now that you are, I'm happy as fuck.

"My baby is having our baby. Told you our story would be the best yet." With that, he captures my lips in a searing kiss.

I moan and cling to his damp hair. He slides his hand into my bra and starts to knead my breast. I whimper and he turns us for the bed.

He lowers me to the bed and climbs on over me. I pant and squirm beneath him as he kisses his way down from my collarbone to between my breasts. I go to help him with my leggings when the doorbell rings.

I growl and punch the bed. I'll kill Gigi if she lost her key again. Ryan mutters under his breath as he allows me room to get up.

I quickly find a shirt and make my way to the front door. When I pull it open, all the blood drains from my face. Ne and his assistant, Yui, are standing before me.

My heart starts to pound as Ryan's naked body in my bedroom pops into my head. His jeans are still in the bathroom.

"What are you doing here?" I breathe as I find my voice.

Ne looks at me like I'm crazy. "What kind of greeting is that?"

"I'm sorry. I … um. I wasn't expecting you."

"Well, mom wanted me to drop off the food you forgot." He moves into the apartment before I can stop him. I groan under my breath and close the door as he and Yui move into the living room. "I remember when my little sister was always happy to see me."

"I'm happy to see you," I say. "Um, give me a second."

I rush to the bathroom for Ryan's pants. I need him to get dressed before my brother sees him. Ne may be on my side most of the time, but I don't think my naked boyfriend will go over so well as an introduction.

I grab the pants and rush to my bedroom. Ryan is lying on the bed with his arms behind his head as he looks up at the ceiling. He looks so sexy, I can't help taking a moment to take him in.

He turns to look at me and gives me a smile as he holds a hand out to me. I shake my head quickly, clearing it of my lust and toss him his pants and underwear.

"My brother is here with his assistant. You have to get dressed," I say quickly.

Humor lights his eyes. "Babe, why do I get the feeling you're ashamed of me? Are you going to introduce me to your brother?"

"Ryan," I warn.

"Okay, okay." He sits up and starts to tug on his clothes.

I push a hand into my hair. This day is turning out to be crazy. I'm still processing the fact that I could be pregnant.

This is so bad. Hiding film school was one thing. Hiding a baby isn't going to work out.

Not even Aunt Mariah can save me from this one. Or maybe she can send me somewhere to hide me. First, I need to get through my brother meeting my boyfriend.

One thing at a time. I wipe my sweaty palms against my leggings.

"You look like you've seen a ghost. Relax, your brother will love me."

"Ry, I swear. I'll kill you if you start with that smart mouth. Let him get to know you first."

"Handling my mouth is part of getting to know me. I'd never ask you to be anyone but you around my family."

I palm my forehead. This is going to be a disaster. Ne has always been laid back, but he has a temper. Ryan can try the patience of a saint.

"Relax," he repeats.

I blow out a breath as he kisses the top of my head. I nod and turn for us to go out and face the music. I'm shaking as we walk out into the living room.

"Ne," I say as we stand before my brother sitting on the couch. "I want you to meet my boyfriend, Ryan."

Ne narrows his eyes at Ryan. His gaze drops to our entwined hands. To my surprise, he stands and crosses his arms over his chest. He keeps his glare on Ryan.

"Why is your hair wet as if you've come out of the shower?" Ne says to Ryan.

"Your sister only has one of those shower caps and she was already using it."

I squeeze the hell out of Ryan's hand and dig my nails into his skin. I go to talk my way out of this mess. The last thing I need is for my brother to run to my father to tell him that I have a boyfriend I'm sleeping with. Not that that's not going to come out soon enough.

However, Ne's phone rings and I'm saved. With a frown, my brother excuses himself to take the call. I chew on my lip while I watch him go.

When I turn back to the couch, Yui sits looking between the two of us with a secret smile on her face. Like Ne and I, you can see her Japanese heritage, but her African American roots show through as well. Her pretty dark skin has always been something I envy. Yui brings to mind Taral Hicks and that movie *Belly*.

"We will talk soon," Ne says as he returns and nods for Yui to follow him.

"I look forward to it," Ryan replies as if my brother is talking to him.

I elbow his side and glare up at him. I swear, I'm going to choke him. I wait until my brother is out of the door before I spin on Ryan.

"What was that?"

"I think we're going to make one big happy family," he croons and places a hand on my belly.

Why me?

"Ryan?"

He narrows his eyes. "What?"

"We can't tell anyone. If I'm pregnant, we have to keep it between us until I can talk to my father."

"If you are pregnant, we need to talk to your father."

I palm my forehead. "Please, Ry," I plead.

He's silent for a moment. When he embraces me, I look up at him. His jaw is tight, but he concedes.

"All right. We won't say anything until you talk to your father, but Carmen."

"Yes."

"We're not lying to my family. You already know how that shit hurt them with Toby. I'm not doing that shit. You figure out your dad, but we're telling my family."

"Okay," I whisper. "Okay."

CHAPTER SEVENTEEN

Followed

Carmen

Maybe it's the stress of my little secret or having back-to-back finals today and reaching the end of one of my goals, but I swear it feels like someone's watching me. It's a feeling I've had since walking out of my class. I try to shake it off for the millionth time as I walk to the garage to get to my car and head to my first doctor's appointment.

Ryan comes to mind. He's going to meet me there. He's so sure that I'm pregnant. I get ready to text him, but my phone rings.

I smile when I see it's Aunt Mariah. I've been thinking about telling her about everything, but I'm still waiting to find out for sure.

"Hey auntie," I chirp into the phone.

"Hey, Nene. What's up?"

I shrug as if she can see me. "Nothing much. About to head home from my last final."

She squeals on the other end of the phone. "I'm so proud of you. You did it. Your father will be proud when he finds out how well you've been doing with two programs."

"First, I have to prove that it was worth it."

She sighs. "I don't know why you're so afraid of Kiyoshi. He's a big softy when it comes to you. He will be proud, no matter what."

"We'll see."

My little cousin squeals in the background and my heart swells. He's so adorable. Uncle Kevin and Aunt Mariah made one handsome little guy.

"Aww, give my little chunk a kiss for me," I coo.

Aunt Mariah laughs. The sound of her shifting around on the other end comes through the line. At first, I'm greeted by breathing.

"Say hi to Nene," Aunt Mariah coaxes.

"Hi," Kevin Jr. says.

"*Hi*," I sing, causing him to laugh. I can just imagine those hazel-green eyes lighting up as he does.

"Phew, this little boy is a handful. So, have you thought about what you want for your birthday gift? I'm still waiting. Anything you want, sweetie, you ask."

I smile from ear to ear. My aunt truly does spoil me. I'm still not sure what I want.

Ryan already bought the camera I was going to tell her about. I hadn't told her about it even though she's asked me a number of times to pick something. Maybe she can get me out of the country, so my father doesn't kill me if I'm pregnant.

"I'm still thinking."

"Okay, you know how to find me when you decide. This little guy is getting fussy. Give me a call later. Love you."

"Love you too."

I hang up and turn to look over my shoulder right before walking into the parking structure. Even during the call that feeling didn't go away. There's a guy walking a few yards behind me.

I swear I noticed him before. My hackles are up. I turn back around and pick up my pace. I'm not that far from my car. I parked up one level.

I pull up my brother's number and get ready to call him. However, when I look back again, the guy I thought was following me is gone. I shake my head at myself.

I blame Ryan. He made me watch that horror movie last night. I'm going to kill him.

I brush off the crazy feeling and walk up the stairs instead of taking the elevator. However, I don't slow. Something still feels off.

I don't want to annoy my brother, so I put my phone away and pull out the key fob for my car. I catch movement out of the corner of my eye when I'm a few steps from my car.

Okay, I'm not crazy. My instincts kick in. My mother's voice rings in my ear.

Always trust your instincts, Nene.

I pop the trunk and toss my bag in. Faster than I can think I unzip my gym bag I take for my workouts with Mommy. If someone plans to attack me, they're in for a rude awakening.

Ryan wanted to know what my mother and I do for workouts. We sword fight in the traditional styles of the samurai. My father has trained my mother to be lethal, and she's been teaching me since I could hold two of my own swords in my hands.

My double scabbard is on my back in one fluid motion. I slam the trunk closed and spin into a stance. Lightning fast, I pull both swords from my back.

"What do you want?" I hiss at the two men in front of me.

Ryan

My blood boils as I watch this motherfucker follow after my girl. He's closing in on her and doesn't know I'm closing in on him. I signal for Roni to move into the garage after Carmen.

I've already sent Ne a text to get his ass here ASAP. I knew something was wrong when this asshole first showed up on campus. He's been keeping his distance watching.

Once Carmen emerged from her class he started to follow her. I wanted to rush in and stomp his ass into the ground, but he was too close to Carmen. I warred with blowing my cover but decided against it.

"I don't like this, Ry," Felix says in my ear. "Put him down."

Carmen has entered the parking garage, and this guy is heading straight for her. I close the distance between us and wrap my arms around his neck now that we're in the shadows of the garage. He's a big guy and he tries to struggle, but I put his ass to sleep.

I contemplate putting his lights out permanently, but Kiyoshi gave orders that I bring him in. We need to know where this guy came from. There are a number of enemies on the watch list. I drop him to the ground once he's out like a light.

"Ryan, get your ass up here," Roni says through the earpiece.

I don't stop to think. I step over the body I just dropped and head for the stairs. I race to the next level where I watched Carmen park before class.

When I get up there and through the exit, Roni puts a hand to my chest to stop me. I go to shove her hand away, confused as to why she's hiding behind an SUV and not keeping my girl safe.

"Don't blow your cover. Look," she says low.

My jaw ticks as I look around the truck. My eyes go wide. Carmen has two badass swords in her hands, moving like a character out of a Bleach episode or something.

She slashes her sword through the air, cutting one of the guys before her, then spins bringing the other sword through the air slicing off the hand of the guy aiming a gun at her. Just as quickly as she slices their asses up, she sheaths both swords on her back. Her chest heaving.

Carmen looks around wildly before rushing to her driver's side door, slipping the swords off her back and tossing them into the car. She jumps in and peels off before I can rush to her. I shake the shock off and rush to the handless guy rolling on the ground.

Stepping on his handless arm, I lean in with all my weight. He howls in pain. I look to Roni.

"Follow her," I bark.

Roni nods and takes off. Pulling my phone, I shoot off a quick text. I grind my teeth as I realize Carmen has gotten a good head start.

"I have eyes on her, bro," Felix says as if reading my mind. "Nelson is heading in now."

Tires squeal right as he gets the words out. Ne and a few other men jump out of a black van. The men collect the guys at my feet while Ne scowls and stops at my side.

"There's another one downstairs. You should be able to get something from one of them," I say, working my jaw in anger.

"I will take care of them."

I get in his face, toe to toe. "What the fuck? Your sister just disarmed two men with fucking samurai swords on her back. When did you guys plan to tell me about that?"

He shrugs. "When do you plan to tell my father, you're sleeping with my little sister?"

"Come on. Two totally different things."

"It looks like she saved herself, which means you weren't there. I'd be happy if I were you. My father has not hidden that Nene is able to protect herself. He tried to warn you and your father of this."

I tighten my fists at my sides. I know Roni kept her hands off to watch Carmen in action. She was ready to take the kill shots if she had to. Roni was also right. I would have blown my cover if I'd stepped in.

"We were on it. She didn't *need* to protect herself."

"Hmm, yet that guy's hand was severed by one of her blades."

"Are you saying I'm not doing my job?"

He narrows his eyes at me. There's a brief moment of silence as he regards me. I wait him out as I seethe.

"This is more than a job to you," he says. "It's personal."

I get the feeling he wants to say more, but he doesn't. I'm not going to get into how personal this is for me. I roll my shoulders back.

Both Kiyoshi and Ne already know what Carmen means to me. I'm not a fool. I've already caught on to Kiyoshi.

It's why I taunt him with my long nights at Carmen's and taking her to my place. He's called me to tell me to take my ass home almost every night I've been at her place.

Ne nods and pats me on the shoulder. "I am not your enemy."

He's right. He's not. In all honesty, I'm more pissed with all the secrets around here than my girl being able to slice a motherfucker up.

I return the nod. "Where's your dad? Did he land?"

"Yeah, he's back for a few days. Arrived this morning. He should be in his office," he replies.

I turn and head for my car to put an end to the lies. Things have just changed for me. This threat is real and there's a real chance that the woman I just watched become a little warrior is pregnant with my baby.

There's no way I'm playing these games with Kiyoshi a second more. "Let me know what you find out," I call over my shoulder.

"Without question."

This fucking Alliance is going to cause us all to have a head full of gray hair. If it were up to me, we'd bring this shit to their doorstep first. However, I get why we're not.

Too many smiling faces with knives behind their backs. We don't know who to trust or who plans to challenge this new alliance. Until we figure that out, we're all walking targets.

Too bad I've never been one to lie down and take an ass whipping. Won't be starting that shit now. Damn, my girl is a fucking ninja.

What the fuck?

CHAPTER EIGHTEEN

Take Her Away

Ryan

"I think we're beyond this game you wanted to play. She's in real danger," I snarl.

Kiyoshi glares at me. He then turns to my father. "I have sent visitors to those who sent those pieces of trash after my daughter. I'm sure my message will be heard loud and clear by all."

"That doesn't mean they're going to stop coming," I growl in frustration.

"No, it doesn't," my father says.

Kiyoshi sits back in his seat and steeples his fingers together. He finally turns his attention back on me. "What is it you suggest?"

"She's finished her classes. We'll go away for a bit and lay low. You're an Alliance member.

"They want to hurt you the most. Carmen is a way to do that. If they can break you guys up before you fully rise to power it will serve them best."

"Dad, he's right. You were saying the same thing already. Carmen would be better off somewhere else for now," Ne says.

I clench my jaw. Carmen is at my house waiting for me. It's where she ran to after the attack at the garage. Roni has had eyes on her since Carmen got there. I'm trying to make this quick so I can get to her.

Thank God I thought to tell her how to get in if she ever needed. I can't say how good it felt to have her go to my home for safety. However, I've been worried because she's yet to reach out to me.

Kiyoshi purses his lips. "The point of the Alliance was not for us to begin to live like cowards. I don't like this."

"No one's living like a coward. You're living safe. You don't want Carmen to know about any of this, you better do something about it. Which means she needs to disappear away from all of it."

Kiyoshi bangs his hands on the desk and stands. "Ryan, you take my calm for kindness. There are times when you take things too far. Now is one of them."

I stand. "Your daughter and her safety are important to me. If I ruffle your delicate feathers, oh fucking well," I bark back.

Dad stands and places a hand on my shoulder. He gives a warning squeeze. I shrug him off and turn to leave the room. Before I'm out of the door, I call over my shoulder.

"She's my responsibility whether you like it or not. I'm not going away, and neither are the feelings we have for each other. Allow me to protect her. This isn't a game to me."

"Nor is it a game to me," Kiyoshi seethes. Silence fills the room for a beat. "I will allow you to take her on a trip for the summer break. It will give me enough time to establish my hand with the Sato family and any others who plan to become foolish.

"I will talk to her aunt and have her offer Nene a trip for herself and a friend. I have a place—"

I spin to face him. "No, it has to be somewhere I know. Someplace I can control."

Kiyoshi glares at me for a moment before giving me a nod. "Under no circumstance are you to reveal who you are or what's going on. You protect her like a precious treasure."

I nearly break my teeth from the tight grip I have on my jaw. More lies. I thought we would be done with this shit after what happened today.

For now, I'll take my victory. I'm getting to take Carmen away from this shit for a while. I'll keep her safe away from here.

"I don't think you've been listening to me. She's the most precious thing in my life. I don't just care for your daughter, I love her."

With that, I leave out of his office and head for my car. I need to get to my girl. Then, I'll get us out of here, but first, I have one stop. There's something she and I need to clear up.

Carmen

I sit on Ry's couch with my swords on my back and my knees pulled into my chest as the tears roll down my cheeks. I think I'm in shock. I haven't moved from this spot since I arrived.

I didn't know where else to go. I cut a man's hand off and I'm pretty sure I wounded the other guy fatally. I reacted to save my life. It was the only thought I had once they drew guns on me.

Oh my God. The cops are going to come for me. I'm going to go to jail. If I'm pregnant my baby will be born in jail.

I sob harder and curl more tightly into a ball. My entire body is trembling. I'm so deep in my panic, I don't hear when Ryan enters the house, causing me to jump when he appears before me.

"Oh my God," I yelp and leap from the couch into his arms.

"I'm going to take the scabbards off your back," he says softly.

I nod and turn so he can slide the straps that are holding my swords on my back off my shoulders. He tosses them on the floor, and I turn back into his arms. He tugs me into his embrace and kisses the top of my head.

"I did something bad. I'm going to be in so much trouble, Ryan. They're probably looking for me. I don't know why I ran. I panicked. I should've waited for the cops to come."

"Shh, baby. I'll take care of it. My family will make it go away. Calm down for me."

I take a deep breath. I'm still trembling, but I feel safe in his arms. He tightens his hold and leads me out of the living room to go upstairs.

I follow as my mind races over all the ways this can blow up in my face. My father is going to lose it. I've never used my swords on an actual person, not in real combat.

"I never thought I'd have to use my swords. I reacted," I say absently to Ryan. "What if he bled out? What if both the men are dead? Oh my God, Ry. We have to go back and check."

"Carmen," Ryan says firmly.

I look up at him as we stand in his bedroom. His face is tight with emotions, anger being one of them. Oh no, he's mad at me. Coming here was a mistake.

"I'm sorry. I shouldn't have come here," I whisper.

He pinches my chin between his fingers. "You are right where you're supposed to be. I need you to calm down for me. You never go back to the scene of a crime.

"I need you to strip from your clothes. Give me everything. Once you're undressed, you're going to get into the shower and we're going to scrub you.

"While it's still fresh, I want you to retrace all your steps after the incident for me. Then I want you to tell my everything that happened before the incident."

I lick my lips and nod my head. When I look down at my clothes I see I have blood all over me. I hadn't noticed it before.

"Oh, no, did I get blood on the couch."

"Focus, baby. I'll take care of all of that."

I nod again and start to peel out of my clothes. I hand them over piece by piece. When I'm completely naked, Ryan takes my hand and leads me into the bathroom to turn on the shower.

I step inside and the water runs over me, bringing a soothing calm with it. Ryan strips from his things and steps in behind me. He takes my hair from its ponytail and kisses my forehead.

I look up into his eyes. I still see anger, but this time I don't think it's aimed at me.

"I'll be right back," he says gently.

"Okay."

It only takes him a minute or two to return. My clothes are no longer in his hands. Ryan sits on the bench seat in the shower and pulls me onto his lap.

Once I'm settled, he starts with washing my face. His touch is gentle but firm. When I see the rag come away with blood I gasp.

"It's going to be fine. Did you come straight here without stopping?"

"Yes, I remembered where you told me the key was. I came in through the back. I was too scared to stop.

"I felt like someone was following me after class. When I got to my car, I saw a guy moving out the corner of my eye.

"I don't know what made me do it. My mother's voice was playing in my head. I just strapped on the blades and turned to protect myself.

"When they drew their guns, I freaked. I did everything my mother always taught me to." I stop talking as I see that man's hand fall to the ground all over again. My lips tremble.

Ryan tilts my head back. He kisses me softly. "You did the right thing. You're here and you're safe."

He pecks me gently again. This time his lips linger on mine a little longer. When he pulls back, he looks in my eyes and reaches for my hands.

I don't realize how much they're shaking until he cups them in his and covers them with the rag. He scrubs at my hands as he holds my gaze.

"It's going to be fine. I'm here. I'll take care of everything. Relax, baby. Can you do that for me?"

"Yes."

"Good."

He continues to care for me. The more he does, the safer I feel. I've never been robbed before. Nothing like this has ever happened to me.

I'm sure I could've handled it better. However, knowing that Ryan says he'll make this all better speaks to something deep within. I believe him.

I know he'll make this right. Once he starts to wash my hair, I relax even more. His long fingers soothe me. I don't even know when I drift off against his chest.

CHAPTER NINETEEN

Come Away

Ryan

After carrying Carmen's naked body into the bedroom, I dried her off, placed her in one of my T-shirts and tucked her into the sheets. She fell asleep while I washed her hair. I could tell when she started to come out of shock.

The anger that ran through me threatened to explode from within. She was shaking so hard when I got here. I never want to see her like that ever again.

I felt so helpless and pissed. I barely hid my anger from her. It's been about an hour since I kicked off my shoes and climbed in bed with her.

I'm still coiled tightly with anger. My thoughts have been racing as I plan our trip. Placing a hand on her belly, I think about the pregnancy test I stopped to pick up.

I think I probably would've tossed all caution to the wind had I known for a fact she's pregnant. I swear, I still almost shot that fucker in the head even after she chopped his hand off. I probably would have if I weren't in complete awe.

"I'm hungry," she mumbles sleepily right before her stomach grumbles.

I kiss the back of her head. "I'll order something. You want pizza or Chinese?"

"Pizza sounds good. Oh, wait. You want to do one of those other delivery thingies and get Greek or something?"

I snort. "Fuck out of here. So the driver can take a shit with our food or eat half our shit?

"Have you seen some of those guys? I swear they deliver food to case your place and come back to rob you later. Nah, I'll pass."

She giggles and it's the sweetest sound in the world. It loosens some of the tightness in my chest. It's welcome after the way I found her.

"Seriously, Ry?"

"What? Man, babe, you're already taking a chance with your life with the kitchen staff at the restaurant. No telling when the cook wants to spit in your food.

"Now you want me to add another person to the process who's even in the food industry and has no regulations. Nope."

She laughs louder. "You know you just ruined all delivery services for me?"

"Good. I can't have you taking chances with our baby." I pull out my phone and order a couple of pies from my usual place.

Carmen turns to face me. "My appointment," she gasps.

I peck her lips. "Don't worry about it. I called and canceled. When you're ready, I left something in the bathroom for you."

She wrinkles her brows. She was so out of it earlier. I don't think she saw when I put the two test boxes on the counter. I nod my head toward the bedside table.

"There's some water."

She turns to look at the bottled water. Reaching for it, she chugs half the bottle. She falls silent, snuggling into me.

It doesn't escape me that she doesn't head into the bathroom. I think she's in denial about the reason she's been dizzy a few times and has yet to have a period since we've been dating. Honestly, a small part of me has too, so I don't push.

About thirty minutes pass as we wait for our food. We lie there as I hold her until the doorbell rings. I kiss her head and climb out of bed to answer the door.

Not wanting her to have to get out of bed, I head into the kitchen for plates to take up to the room with the pizza. When I get back to the room, Carmen is no longer lying where I left her. I put the pizza and plates down on the dresser and turn the TV on. I get ready to find something on Netflix when a pale-faced Carmen stumbles out of the bathroom.

"What's wrong?" I rush to wrap my arms around her.

She looks up at me. Her lips parted, but no words coming out. I brush her damp hair back off her face and search her eyes.

"We're having a baby," she says just above a whisper.

I don't react for a few moments. I heard her. Deep down I already knew, but it still doesn't keep the shock from registering for a beat.

"Damn, my pull-out game really is trash."

"Ryan," she groans.

I kiss her lips. "I'm sorry, baby. Wow, I'm going to be a father," I croon as it begins to set in.

"Ry ... I ... this is not going to go over well with my father. I haven't even told him about you."

"Well, baby, you're going to have to tell him sooner or later. Listen, I still want to take you away. How about we spend the summer someplace where we can really get to know each other? We figure us out and when we get back, we can worry about everyone else."

She's shaking her head before I can get the words out fully. I already knew this was going to be a challenge. I can't tell her what's going on and she's afraid of her father.

"I can't, Ry."

"Yes, you can. You're an adult. Heck, baby, we're about to start a family.

"You and I need this. Your father is going to have to get over it if he has a problem with us. I'm not going anywhere."

"You don't understand. My father is strict—"

"You're twenty, Carmen."

She stops and bites her lip. I get it. Different cultures, different upbringings. I know her brother well enough to know that her father and mother raised them a lot different from how I grew up.

"I don't know."

"Hey, did you know that Wyatt's really good friends with Nicholas Lincoln and his wife is a friend of mine. Six degrees of separation. It was meant to be," I say. She looks at me curiously. "Your aunt works for Nick, right?"

"Yeah," she says cautiously.

"Good, Nick will vouch for me. If you think your father is going to have a problem with you coming away with me for the summer, we'll get your aunt to cover for us," I say.

I know I don't need any of this, but she doesn't know that. After all, her father doesn't want her to know, so I go with it. It's what I've been planning in my head since I left her father's office.

The wheels turn as she thinks my words over. I grin when she slightly nods her head. Her eyes light up as something crosses her face. I've got her.

Carmen

I nod my head. "Okay."

After what I did today, it might not be a bad idea to disappear for a while. Ryan is right. If I talk to Aunt Mariah, she'll cover for me.

Question is, do I want to tell her about the baby? Should I tell her she's covering for me to spend time with my boyfriend? Should I get Uncle Kevin and Nick involved?

"I'll give Nick a call," Ryan offers.

"No." I lick my lips and cover my stomach protectively. "I'll call my aunt.

"I'll handle it. She's the best with my dad after my mom. She'll know what to do. I don't want to get you into this."

He searches my face for a moment. Next thing I know, he's consuming my mouth. I lock my fingers in his hair.

When it dawns on me that I'm pregnant with his baby and I'm pretty sure I'm in love with him, I give back as good as I'm getting. Ryan grabs my backside and pulls me into his erection.

I moan and suck his tongue into my mouth. He makes a rumbling sound in the back of his throat, but my stomach growls back at him. Ryan breaks the kiss and places his forehead to mine.

"You need to eat," he breathes. "Then, I'm tearing that pussy up and putting you to sleep."

My mouth pops open. I still don't think I'm used to him saying things like that, but he wouldn't be Ryan if he didn't. I shake my head. I noticed my phone on the nightstand earlier.

While Ry gets us pizza, I move to grab the phone. I call my aunt to set things in motion. I chew my lip as the line rings. It takes a few rings before she answers.

"Hey, you," she sings into the phone. "What's up?"

"Hey, auntie."

She laughs. "What can I do for you, Nene?"

Yup, I'm a spoiled brat. I pull the auntie card whenever I need something. I'll admit it.

"You asked what I wanted for my birthday," I reply and pause to bite my lip. "I have something I want. It's not something you have to buy. It's more like something you can do for me."

"Okay, I'm listening," she says.

"I want to go away for the summer. I don't plan to tell my father where or with who and I plan to take the summer off from school. Do you think you can cover for me?"

There's a pause on her end. I hold my breath. If she says no, I'm going to have to face my father much sooner than I would like. I'd rather run from all of this. I'm scared as shit.

"This is the last time, Nene," she says my name with the Japanese intended pronunciation. "You're getting too old for this. I will not place a wedge between myself and my brother because you don't want to speak up to him. You will have to face him from here."

My heart sinks. She's bailing on me when I need her most. However, a small voice in the back of my head tells me she's right. I'm going to have to grow up. I have a baby of my own to think about.

"Thanks, Auntie."

"Hm," she says sounding so much like my dad it sends a chill through me.

I'm going to have to face the music once I return. By then, I probably won't be able to hide the pregnancy for long. If I'm right, I'm around six weeks pregnant as it is.

This would only happen to me. One night, one night I decide to be reckless and this is the result. I wish ... no, I don't think I would change that night.

As Ryan comes over and places a plate with pizza in my lap, I know I wouldn't. I watch him as he turns and plucks up a slice as he texts with one hand.

"I'll call you with more details soon."

"Okay, I'll figure out what to tell your father when I know where you're going and with who," she says.

I palm my forehead. I should've known that was coming. I nod as if she can see me.

"All right. Call you later."

We hang up and Ryan comes over to sit on the bed already on his third slice. I pick up my pizza as my mouth waters. I'm starving.

"Don't worry about packing. I'll run by your place to get you a few things. John is coming over to pick something up for work.

"He'll sit with you while I'm gone. We fly out first thing in the morning."

"Will I need my passport or anything?"

"Yeah, you're going to need it."

I smile. I should be freaking out. I may have killed two men and I'm pregnant, but honestly, I'm excited about spending an entire summer getting to know Ryan better.

As he looks at me with a hungry gaze, I can't help getting excited about all the sex we'll get to have. Ryan makes sex something I want to put on my daily planner. He's just that good at it.

As if reading my mind, he reaches between my legs and starts to massage my already wet lips. I moan around the pizza I'm chewing. He leans to whisper in my ear.

"You have no idea all the ways we're going to get to know each other. I can't wait." He circles my clit with his thumb. "My baby is inside you. I'll never let anything happen to you."

And I believe that. With everything I am, I believe him.

CHAPTER TWENTY

Heading for Love

Carmen

I sit on the beach with a virgin pina colada in my hand and the sun beaming down on my face. I've been having way too much fun on this island. I wish this was my life twenty-four seven.

I've felt like a princess since we arrived two weeks ago. Ryan has waited on me hand and foot. A small staff has been in and out to clean and stock up the place, but they don't say much or bother us.

We've been here relatively by ourselves. We spend mornings and afternoons on the beach. We make love throughout the day whenever Ryan sees fit to peel me out of my clothes and make me cry for him.

Good tears. Tears of pleasure and oh so much joy. I think my orgasms are getting better the farther along I get in the pregnancy.

I should be about two months pregnant now. That's still so insane to me. When I return home to California, I'm going to have a lot of explaining to do. I close my eyes and sip my drink while I place my hand over my stomach.

"You look so fucking sexy."

I open my eyes to find Ryan standing over me in soaked board shorts. He's been swimming all morning. I think of the shark tank and smile. He's a shark all right.

"Are you ready to go eat?" He bends to peck my lips then my forehead. "Are my babies hungry?"

"Yes," I groan.

"Let's go. We'll get dressed and head into town."

I put my drink down, throw my hands up and do a little dance. I've been wanting to go for some Caribbean food. I miss my mom.

We text, but there's nothing like spending time with her and eating her cooking. I go to stand and Ryan lifts me into his arms. I wrap my legs around his waist and he starts for the house. My face hurts from smiling.

When we reach our bedroom, he takes us straight into the bathroom. Soon he has us both naked as he backs me into the shower. From the smile on his face, I know it'll be another hour before we leave.

I don't mind.

Ryan

I love the smile on her face. This trip has been great for our relationship. Carmen has been carefree.

Back home her father was always a part of her decisions and hesitation. Since we've been here, she's been living life for the moment and not what she thinks her father would want. I haven't pointed that out, but I've noticed.

"Full?" I murmur against her temple as we ride back to the house. I place my hand on her belly and kiss her soft skin.

"Yes," she groans covering my hand. "I totally overdid it."

I chuckle. "My little guy needs his strength," I tease.

"Little guy? You think it's a boy?"

I grin. "Yup."

She turns her face up to me and smiles. "Want to bet? I think it's going to be a girl."

I shrug. "You're on. What do I get when my boy arrives?"

She taps her chin and her eyes sparkle. "I don't know. It has to be something good. I think I want another vacation or something when I win."

I peck her lips. "You're on."

"What do you want to do when we get back? It's still pretty early. Are you going back into the water?"

"No. I want to lie back and chill. I never noticed how much I'm always moving. This is the first time I've been still."

I think about that for a moment. While it's a half-truth, it's true. I'm always alert for danger, but it's still not half as busy here as it is back home in the office.

I've been able to think more here. Don't get me wrong. I miss the office and work, but the quiet time has made me take the time to think about what's next.

We have a baby coming. I want a future with this girl. The more time I spend with her the more I know I've fallen in love and I'm ready to take that next step.

However, there are huge lies dangling over our heads. I can't help feeling like with one string pulled, it will all fall apart. I frown at the thought.

"Hey, where'd you go?" her soft voice brings me back to the present.

"Nowhere."

She searches my eyes. I smile at her and tug her closer to my side. She snuggles in, placing her hand on my thigh.

"You promised me a game of scrabble. You ready to lose?"

I laugh. "If you promise not to cry when I whip your ass, sure, we can play."

She scoffs. "You are so on."

Simple. That's the word for how easy our relationship has become. I didn't know how much I needed Carmen until I found her. Slowing down, smelling the flowers, that's what's been missing from my life.

We climb from the car and head into the house. I look around and nothing seems out of place. I chose to come here because we've used this place a time or two for training.

My dad has gotten creative with practice missions since we were old enough to start training. I also chose it because it reminded me of Carmen. Her Barbados roots stand out as much as her Japanese ones. I thought she'd like coming here. The privacy was also a huge factor.

"I'm going to drop a deuce. Get the game set up," I say as I head for the bedroom.

"TMI. Thank you."

I shrug. "It's human nature. You'll be wiping my son's ass soon enough. We're all family."

"Crazy." Her laughter follows me as I keep walking.

Twenty minutes later, I rejoin her in the living room. I chuckle when I find her passed out on the couch. She's been napping a lot in the last week.

I leave her to rest and head to the back study to make a call. I need to check in. It's hard to do when we're always together.

"Hello, son," my father answers the phone.

"Hey, Dad. Anything new?"

"It's been pretty quiet. Wyatt hasn't gotten any updates from Nate so far. How is the lass?"

I sigh. "She's good."

"Good. Your mother is driving me crazy. She wants to come stay with you and help."

"It's still early. She hasn't had any morning sickness or anything. I don't think we need any help." I chuckle. "Tell mom thanks, but we're okay."

"I'll let her know. You may want to give her a call when you have time." He pauses for a moment. "How are you holding up?"

"I'm not complaining. I want this to be over so I can move forward with my life. I hate having secrets. I know our relationship is happening super-fast, but it feels right. It feels like we've been together for forever," I reply.

Dad gives a small chuckle. "*Lorg a h-uile duine leatha agus cùm i leat leat fhèin.*"

"Yeah. She's worthy. I've found the one I plan to keep for my own. I just need all this other shit to go away."

"In time. It will all work itself out in time."

I sigh. "He's going to want to kick my ass, isn't he?"

Dad gives a hearty laugh. "Aye, ye have gotten yerself into one there."

I cringe as dad's accent comes out. That means I've done it. I may give Kiyoshi shit, but I like him. I want to go to him as a man about the baby.

"It is what it is, Dad. I love her and that's our baby. I'm going to ask her to marry me as soon as I can."

"Aye. You do what you need to do. Kiyoshi will surprise you both."

"Ryan?"

Hearing Carmen call after me, I turn to look at the door. "Hey, Dad. I have to go. Call you soon. Let me know if anything changes."

"Will do. Keep your eyes open and be careful, son."

"Always."

I hang up and head to the front of the house. I furrow my brows when I don't find Carmen on the couch. The back door is open. My heart races as I rush to it.

I sigh in relief when I find her by the pool. She has her dress tucked between her legs and her feet in the water. I smile as I think of the fact that she refuses to go next to the ocean water, but here she is with her feet in the pool.

I go over and sit beside her. Bumping her shoulder with mine, I kiss her cheek and place a hand on her thigh. She covers my hand with hers and links our fingers together.

"Have you been thinking about what we're going to do?" she says after a few moments pass.

I turn to look at the side of her face. She keeps her gaze straight ahead at the beach. I study her face contemplatively.

"I meant it when I said my home is yours. When we get back, we'll move your things in. We'll start visits to the doctor for the baby. You need to have a conversation with your dad. Then we start to plan what kind of wedding we want to have," I say.

She snaps her head in my direction at the mention of a wedding. Her gaze bounces over my face. I wait for her response.

"Wedding," she whispers. "Ry, I know we weren't planning to have a baby. I'm not going to force you to marry me because I'm pregnant."

"First, who said you're forcing me to do anything? Second, I'm not marrying you because of the baby. I—"

I'm cut off by her phone. I was about to tell her I love her. That's why I want to marry her, but the words are stuck in my throat as she takes a call from her father.

I know it's him because of the tense, scared look she gets whenever he calls. She truly fears him. I'm reminded again that we're four years apart.

I stop to wonder if I could be pushing her too fast. When she places her hand on her belly, I shake that thought away. Yeah, we're moving fast, but it's us. We have a family to think of. We'll figure the rest out. We have to.

Carmen

I stare in the mirror and try to figure out the woman looking back at me. Ryan wants to get married. I've been thinking about it since he said it by the pool.

Having a baby is one thing, getting married is another. What if I'm not ready for that? I haven't even found the nerve to tell my father about my boyfriend let alone the baby I'm carrying.

I feel like a fraud. I'm living the life of someone I would love to be, but I don't feel like I belong here.

"Baby," Ryan calls.

"Yeah?"

"You okay in there?"

I smile. "Yes, I'm fine. I'll be out in a second."

"Did that spicy ass food get to your stomach too?"

I laugh. "No."

Humph sounds from the other room. "That shit fucked my stomach up. We're not going back to that place. I can handle spicy food, but that stuff. I don't know what they put in it."

I shake my head and continue to giggle at him as I finish putting on lotion. I can't help but think that we sound like an old married couple. Maybe that's what's so odd to me.

We fit together effortlessly. I keep waiting for there to be something out of place or wrong with Ryan or our relationship. When I walk into the bedroom, he's lying on his back with his hands behind his head. He devours me with his eyes.

"You're glowing," he says, holding a hand out toward me.

I move to the bed and take his hand. He pulls me to straddle his waist. Sitting up, he captures my lips.

When he breaks the kiss, he silently looks into my eyes. My breath catches. I must be tired.

There's no way … that look. The one I've seen his brothers give the women in their lives, it's in Ryan's. At least, I think I see it for a moment before I chide myself and shake that thought away.

I cup his face as a distraction from my wandering brain. Placing my forehead to his, I kiss his lips softly.

"Do you think you can make me glow some more?"

CHAPTER TWENTY-ONE

You Don't Know

Ryan

I roll over and groan. Reaching out I find the bed empty where Carmen should be. I open my eyes and look around the room.

She's normally snuggled under my heat until I get too hot for her, then she rolls to the other side of the bed. The light in the bathroom is on. I reach for my phone to check the time.

I frown. It's still the middle of the night. I go to sit upright as the sound of retching comes from the next room.

I'm on my feet before I can think about it. I push into the bathroom and find Carmen hugging the bowl. She looks up as I enter and her face is covered in tears.

A mix of exhaustion, embarrassment, and agony crosses her features. I grab a towel and wet it under the sink. Once the towel is damp, I move toward her and sit with her between my legs.

"I'm okay," she tries to sob and wave me away.

I could give two fucks that she's blowing chunks again once I wrap around her. I rub her back and move her hair from out of the way. As she heaves, I press the damp towel across the back of her neck like mom used to do us when we were little.

"Damn, baby. I'm so sorry. I thought you were going to make it without morning sickness," I murmur once she has a reprieve.

"I don't know where this came from. One minute I was sleeping. Then I woke up hungry, so I went to get a snack. Now my stomach feels like it's trying to turn itself inside out," she groans. "Ry, this is so gross and embarrassing."

"Baby, I've eaten your pussy and your ass. You've been butt ass naked bent like a pretzel while I've pounded you out and I know for a fact I've heard that pussy farting on a number of occasions.

"Not only am I unbothered by this, I need to be here to support you because you didn't get pregnant alone. While you were giving up all that good pussy, I was taking and this is the result," I reply.

She turns her head to look at me and stares. I shrug my shoulders. No lie was told.

Hell, I think I remember exactly when I slipped up. I was hitting it from the back, staring at her thick ass, she started to throw it back and grind her hips. Yup, I know exactly how my son got in her belly.

"You know. I don't think you shock me as much as you used to. I think now I expect it. I know you'll always tell me the truth," she says.

I school the frown that automatically tries to come to my face. Instead of responding, I return to wiping her face with the towel. She closes her eyes and groans.

I take the time to look away and react. I hate lying to her. I hate this situation I'm in.

Fuck it. I'm going to tell her. I can't have this between us. It's not how I'm built.

"You know, I think I'm probably having the morning sickness as a result of stress," she whispers right as I get ready to spill it all. "My dad called again while you were cooking in the afternoon. We've been here for a month, you would think I'd relax by now, but every time he calls, I get nervous all over again."

I blow out a breath. She has been relaxed and having a good time, but I did notice something was up after lunch. Kiyoshi is still pissed at her for not telling him about me and for having her aunt make up a story so she could come away with me.

"Say nothing, Ryan. I want to see how long my daughter will keep this up," he hissed over the phone the day we left.

And now, because she thinks she's sick because of the stress, of course, I'm not going to say shit. Damn. The last thing I want is to put stress on her or the baby.

"Babe, at some point you have to decide whose life this is. I get that you love your dad, and you were raised to respect his opinions on your life. I'm not mad at that.

"I think it's cool that your father is so involved, but Carmen. You need to realize you're not a little girl. You need to go to your father as an adult and talk to him."

"Easier said than done," she mumbles.

"Personally, I think that's all in your head. I think that if you talk to him, you'll find that he's a father who wants the best for his daughter, no matter what that is."

"You don't know my father," she snaps in frustration.

I bite my tongue. I don't want to fight and she's wrong. I do know her father, but I can't tell her that.

I climb to my feet and start out of the bathroom. It's best if I walk away. I can't say what I want, and things are only going to escalate if I continue to bump my head against this wall.

For now, I'm done talking. One thing I know from growing up with six brothers and becoming a PI. You can't change someone's beliefs or perception.

We see what we want to see, we believe what we want to believe until we decide otherwise. Carmen's not ready to see herself as a grown woman that's in charge of her own life. I'm her man, but it's not my job to force her to see anything she's not ready for.

My job is to love her. I don't know what else to do beyond that for now. I can only hope that she sees the truth before it chips at what we're building.

I climb back into bed and lie on my back, looking up at the ceiling. It's cooled off for the night and a breeze is coming into the room. I need the cool sheets beneath me and the airy breeze to keep my temper at bay.

When Carmen enters the room and climbs into the bed, I remain quiet. I can feel her eyes on me, but I don't turn to give her my attention. Not until she speaks.

Carmen

I think we're having our first real fight, and I hate it. I didn't mean to yell at him. I was frustrated.

He keeps telling me to talk to my father, but he doesn't know him. He doesn't know what it's like.

"My father is ten years older than my mother. He grew up in Japan and only moved to live in the States permanently after meeting my mother. He was in his late thirties and set in his ways by then.

"My mother tells stories all the time about my father being the most stubborn man she's ever met, but she fell in love with him just the same.

"In his culture, he was raised strictly. My aunt Mariah, she's closer to my age and her father was more lenient with her than dad's father was with him, I guess. My grandmother remarried in America after my father's dad died.

"Different eras different cultures. Talk about apples and oranges. My mother and my aunt have always been in my corner.

"Because I can be timid and shy, they have stood up for me when my father tends to be more heavy handed." I pause and blow out a breath.

Ry places a warm hand on my thigh as my legs are crossed in front of me. "Babe, all I want for you is the best. I'm not trying to tell you to go against your father, I'm telling you to talk to him.

"How we see things when we're younger is not how they totally are from the outside looking in. This is something I'm telling you I know. It's like a gift, I see shit other people don't."

"I'll think about it," I say not wanting to fight about this anymore.

Ryan didn't grow up in my house. I don't expect him to understand. Having a Caribbean mother and Japanese father was no picnic in the park.

Two very strict cultures but in two very different ways. Somehow, my mother and father balance each other. I've admired that.

As I look at Ryan's hand against my thigh, I want that with him. I want to be the *In* to his *yō*. I smile.

That's the way Yin and Yang were adopted in Japanese. Same concept, different words. I never thought to think of my parents that way, but it applies.

Ryan and I can be that. It's what I want. To be the translation of him.

To be our own language, the way my parents are. I lift my eyes to Ryan's.

"Our baby will be special. It will have so much culture and so much of the world inside of it. Whatever happens, I look forward to that. I don't want to fight with you, Ry. I don't like it."

He sits up and kisses my forehead. "I'm not here to fight with you either." He places his hand on my belly. "You and this baby are all I care about. Whatever else comes our way, we'll deal with it. I need you to remember something for me."

"What?"

"Everything, and I mean, everything I do, I do for you and this kid. You got that?"

I smile up at him. "Yeah, I got that."

"Good, now, shut up. That toothpaste isn't masking much," he teases with a smile on his lips.

I swat at his shoulder, but he catches my hand and kisses my fingertips. Tugging at my hand, he brings me to his chest. When I fall into him, I wrap my hands around his neck.

"You're an ass." I chuckle.

"Heard it all before. How are you feeling?"

"I don't know if I can go back to sleep now," I murmur.

He rubs circle across my back, and I second-guess those words. The motion has my lids growing heavy. He kisses the top of my head.

"We could always make good of this time in bed," he croons.

"My breath stinks, remember?" I say dryly.

"Who said that?" he mock gasps. "Besides, I could always gag you. You seemed to like that last time. I had the staff stock some honey. Oh, babe. The shit I can do with warm honey."

My nipples tighten even as I get sleepy. The idea of Ryan, gags, and honey triggers a flood between my legs. You wouldn't think I was hugging the toilet moments ago. I smile sleepily into his neck.

"I think I'm going to fall asleep before you can get everything and come back. Tomorrow? Promise?"

He kisses my head again. "Promise."

"Ry?"

"Yeah."

"Tell me more about what it was like growing up with six brothers. Do you think we should have more than one?"

His lips turn up against my temple. He tightens his arms around me slightly.

"I sure hope we have more than one. First, we need to get some things straight and get this one out of the way. Then, we'll talk about the team I want to build with you."

"Team?" I chuckle, forcing my lids open. "I never said anything about a team."

"Ah, babe. Something you have to learn about those with multiple siblings. We're competitive. Wyatt's already on his second. The rest of us are going to catch up. This means we have to have at least two more."

I burst into laughter. Even my sleepy brain knows that's insane. However, it totally makes sense when I think of Ryan and his brothers.

"I want pancakes in the morning, with honey and butter," I mutter.

"I've got you. I'll even make you honey butter. How does that sound?"

"You can make me honey butter?" I ask excitedly.

"Is my mother Cassy Black? Go to sleep. You'll have your pancakes and honey butter in the morning."

I smile and snuggle into his warmth. *I love you.* I think the words I'm too tired to say. I've fallen so deep in love with Ryan I know I'll figure the rest out.

CHAPTER TWENTY-TWO

Moment to Shine

Carmen

I giggle as Ryan spreads my cheeks and dips his tongue between them before sucking a piece of fruit into his mouth. I've been his personal fruit platter for the last ten minutes. We're on our private beach as the sun beams down to kiss our skin.

I'm lying on a beach blanket on the sand. Ryan has covered my back and butt in pineapples, grapes, and strawberries. I've become his human fruit salad. Fruit juices have dripped into the crack of my butt and Ryan has taken his time, lazily eating half the fruit and feeding me the rest.

"Mmm, I think I've eaten too fast. All my fruit is gone, all I have is juice and a very wet pussy. What should I do now, baby?"

I keep my eyes closed as my head rests on my folded arms. This bubble we're in is going to burst soon. The real world is waiting, and this is coming to an end in a week. For almost two months, I've been getting to know Ryan and falling in love with him.

"You should clean your plate, babe. Never waste a single drop," I tease.

I've been feeling bold these last few weeks. After that night Ry found me in the bathroom something changed. We've become closer.

I haven't allowed my father's calls to get to me. I've found a new confidence that I like. I've also had time to explore my sexuality.

I mean, really explore it. There's so much more I want to try after the baby is born. Ryan nips my butt cheek.

"Oh, I plan to clean my plate, baby. Are you ready?"

"I'm always ready," I say, knowing I'm never ready for the way he puts it down.

This man never disappoints. He gives me something to gasp for every time I give myself to him. It's never just sex.

It's like Ryan is determined to show me what pleasure is meant to be. Not his pleasure, although I can always see the ecstasy he gains from our intimacy. No, Ryan educates me on my own pleasure.

He's a master at showing me the ultimate experience of my own body and all the ways it can serve me. It's not about him pounding his way to his release. Ryan will drag our lovemaking out for hours so he can take me from level to level of joy and bliss.

"We'll see about that," he says with a hint of darkness to his words.

His breath fans my skin as he speaks. I don't open my eyes as my smile widens. He kneads my cheeks before spreading them.

I wait with bated breath for him to flick his tongue out for a taste. When his warm mouth connects with my core, I moan and suck my lip into my mouth. It's as if I heat up from within.

He's slow and deliberate about sucking on my folds one by one, working his way back and forth. He knows I'm going to run so he palms my cheeks and holds me still before I can start to wiggle away. Then he goes in, and I mean in.

I moan and grab at the blanket beneath me. Trying to scoot away, I lift my hips and wiggle. Ryan only takes that as an offering.

He scoops his arms under my legs from in between my thighs and lifts me in the air. I'm in the position to start a crab walk, which I try, but Ry pulls me back and holds me to his face.

"Ry," I cry out.

He laps at me until my arms and legs start to shake. However, he's not rushing me to a finish. No, he takes his time, but it doesn't matter.

My body rushes toward my first orgasm spiraling to bliss so fast my head is spinning. Ryan goes in for another, but my annoying phone rings. The roaming charges on this bill are going to be crazy.

I'm here and my father says he is still in Japan. Thank goodness I don't pay the bill.

"Ignore it," Ryan groans.

"You know I can't." I sigh and answer the call.

"Hello, Daddy."

"*Kon'nichiwa*, Nene. Your aunt says you've been enjoying your vacation. Have you two been having a good time?"

"It's been fun."

It's not a lie. I am having fun with Ryan. The fact that Aunt Mariah isn't here isn't something my father needs to know.

She had an actual trip to make with Uncle Kevin, Nick, and the baby. Things have worked out perfectly.

"I'm glad you are enjoying yourself. Kiss the baby for me."

I frown. I don't want to add to the lies, so I try to change the subject.

"Will you be returning home soon?"

"Yes, I believe I will. I'll be there when you return."

Ryan starts slow, licking kisses from the back of my knee up my thigh. He's totally distracting me, but then something happens. Ryan brings me so much confidence when it comes to sex.

I can't help but wonder what would happen if I borrowed some of that confidence for something I've been thinking about. I take a deep breath and go for the leap.

"Daddy, I was thinking." I have been thinking a lot. I'll be four months pregnant when school starts. I don't know if I'll even finish the semester with the baby on the way. "I've been wanting to take a break from school. Maybe a semester or two."

"You already skipped the summer semester. You're almost finished early. Why the change?"

"I'm not sure I'm doing what I truly want."

He makes a sound on the other end. I hold my breath because this is usually the point when he shuts me down. However, his next words blow me away and place me on edge all at once.

"You have a plan, I will listen. But you better be ready to tell me the whole truth with all the details, Nene. I will not have you wasting all your hard work."

I turn over on my side and look at Ryan with wide eyes. I chew on my lip. For a moment, I wonder if he knows I'm not with my aunt and that I've been lying about school all this time.

I shake that thought off. We've been so careful, and I've passed all my classes with A's. He can't be upset with me for something I've done well.

Can he?

"Yes, I have a plan. I'll tell you everything when I get home."

There is a pause for a moment. I look at Ryan and he smiles proudly back at me. It's slowly setting in that I've spoken up for myself.

"Nene, you are one of my greatest treasures. I've shown you love the way my parents showed me. Sometimes, there are times I believe I should have followed your mother's lead.

"However, I want you to know that I love you and want only the best for you. I will see you when you return," he says.

"I love you too, Daddy. I'll see you when I get home."

I hang up with a mix of emotions. I feel guilty, but at the same time, I'm elated that my father listened to my wants and will continue to listen when I get home. I lock eyes with Ryan and launch into his arms.

"Thank you, thank you, thank you," I squeal.

"For what?" He chuckles as he gives me a little squeeze.

"He's listening to me. I had the courage to say something. You helped me with that.

"You listen to me and make me want to speak up for myself," I say. It sinks in that my father's going to hear me out and I squeeze Ryan tighter. "I love you."

The words are out before I can stop them. Ryan pulls away and those golden eyes connect with mine. This time when I see it, I know it for what it is.

That look. The one I've seen his brothers give to the women they love. Joe even gives Cassy that same look.

It's the look I never thought I'd see from anyone, but especially not Ryan. It's so intense and all-consuming. It's not lust or desire.

It's something way deeper than that. It's a look that says love isn't a strong enough word to place the feelings within. As if to prove that point he blows my mind with his words.

"*Anata o hontōni aishiteimasu,*" he says in Japanese. Then he says something in a language I believe to be Gaelic. "*Fad mo bheatha bidh gaol agam ort, agus an uairsin a h-uile latha a chaitheas mi san uaigh.*"

I smile. "You said you love me so much in Japanese, but what did that last part mean?"

"All my life I will love you, and then every day that I spend in my grave."

"Wow," I say and start to tear up. I'm not sure if it's my hormones or his words but I start balling like a baby.

Ryan laughs. "Baby, I'm not sure this is the right reaction. At least it's not the one I expected."

"I'm sorry." I wipe at my nose. "This is all happening so fast. The baby, falling in love with you. Now my dad is willing to hear me out. I'm a mess."

He cups my chin and pulls me closer to him. "You're adorable and having my baby. I'm so proud of you, Carmen. I know how hard that was for you. Come here and let me give you a reward."

Ryan

She says that she can't see the pregnancy when she looks in the mirror, but I can. It's in her face and in the feel of her tight walls. Even her pussy tastes of my child growing inside her.

Now, as I devour her lips, I can't stop thinking of the fact that she's pregnant and I'm in love with her. I love this woman more than I ever thought I could. Watching her finally speak up for herself has been such a turn-on, I have to finish what I started.

"Love you, baby," I say against her lips. "Now turn around for me."

With a smile, she turns back into her stomach. I groan as her ass jiggles with the movement. Damn, I'm about to tear that shit up.

I want to hear her say she loves me again while I'm inside of her. I pull the strings to the top of her bikini, allowing it to fall to the blanket. I discarded the bottom a long time ago when I first wanted to devour her ass and the fruit I placed on her. I lick my lips and taste the pineapples and strawberries on them.

"Are you just going to look at me?"

I slap her ass and watch it wiggle. "Watch that mouth. I'm taking my time. No more interruptions and I'm not going to be rushed."

"So bossy. You're lucky I love you."

I can't help the smile that comes to my face. I feel like a little boy with a crush, and this is her first time telling me she likes me too. Damn, Carmen has me so fucked up. I'd make the world spin in reverse for her.

"I love you more," I say as I straddle her thick thighs.

I grab my hard cock and stroke it. My shorts have been lying with her bikini bottom. I had plans to slip inside of her right before her phone rang.

With my other hand, I test her folds to find her still wet for me. Slipping two fingers inside, I torture us both a little. Carmen lifts her ass up in offering. I bite my lip and remove my hand to grasp her ass cheek as I guide my way in.

"Baby," I breathe as I slide in to the hilt.

She's tight and this position has my balls tingling already. I still and grind my teeth. She whimpers beneath me, wiggling. I release a short laugh. "So impatient."

Reaching beneath her, I find her clit and start to move in and out as I stroke it. I know this body like the back of my hand.

I'm going to build her slow and take her to new heights. I kiss my way across her shoulders. She smells like a mixture of her sweet scent and my cologne.

I can't help sticking my tongue out for a taste. I lick from one shoulder blade to the other. Her moans increase as I stroke my cock deeper and then let up a bit.

Placing a palm on her hip, I dig my fingers in. I love the way she fit my palms, no matter where I touch her. I lift her up until we're both on our knees.

I shift my body until my legs are on the inside of hers and I'm sitting on my heels.

"You like that?" I say huskily as she starts to cry out and shiver.

"Yes. More please."

I place my palm on her ass and guide her up and down on my shaft as I squeeze it. I nearly lose it when she starts to scream more than cry out, but I reel it in and continue to guide her slowly. I only lift slightly to get the right angle as I continue to drop her back down on my waiting cock.

I slap the cheek I was palming with the other hand. The way her ass jiggles around me as her pussy takes me in is a sight that I'll never get tired of. I slap her ass again just for a repeat.

"Yes, Ry. Yes. I love you so much," she cries out and my heart nearly explodes.

I reach for her hair and tug her head back. When I connect with her brown eyes, I tell her all the things I feel inside without using a single word. Tears spill down her cheeks, revealing she understands.

I cover her lips with mine and show her the same thing my eyes have told her. This is like a first kiss. It packs that power and smack that makes your heart stop. Her salty tears are only a reminder that she's emotional because of our baby.

I wrap my arms around her and place my hands on her belly as I thrust up into her from beneath. I latch onto her neck and slide one hand back down to her clit. I close my eyes as I feel her clench around me. I come at the same time, releasing her neck to bare my teeth and growl.

"I was made to love you," I whisper against her skin.

"I don't want this to end."

"Oh, trust me, I'm not done."

CHAPTER TWENTY-THREE

Unexpected Guests

Ryan

My legs are burning from the last two hours I spent inside Carmen, but I can't stop smiling. I have an arm around her waist and the blanket we used tossed over my arm as I carry the little cooler that held the fruit and a little something I couldn't leave behind. Carmen leans into me with her head resting against me.

"I'm hungry now," she says and gives a little yawn.

I lean down to kiss the top of her head. "How does steak and potatoes sound? I've had the steaks marinating since this morning."

She moans. "That sounds so good. Oh, do we have any more of those green beans? They were so good."

"Yeah," I say to her absently as we get nearer to the house. Something's off. "Why don't you dip your feet in the pool while I get dinner started?"

"Ugh, I was more thinking of taking a nap." She yawns again.

I bite back a curse and go to reach for the gun hidden underneath the bottom of the cooler. I place my body in front of hers as I scan the house through the glass panels. That's when Roni pops up and pulls the door open.

I purse my lips and stop reaching for my gun. Instead, my brows wrinkle in confusion. I wasn't told that anyone would be dropping in.

"Eww, you two are nasty," Roni says with teasing in her voice.

Carmen peeks around me and gasps. "Please tell me you didn't see us out on the beach."

Roni snorts. "I saw enough. John wouldn't let me watch though," she says with a smile. "Two hours and twenty minutes. I timed it. You two are little freaks."

"I know you and my brother have something going on. So there's no way I'm going to be embarrassed because either one of you saw me in action. I'm sure we were PG compared to you."

"Are you kidding?" Roni tosses back. "That one move with her legs in the air before you ate her out for the tenth time—"

"Wait, I thought you weren't watching," Carmen says incredulously.

"I said he wouldn't let me watch. Doesn't mean I didn't peek a few times." Roni lets her gaze roll over me. "I see that shit runs in the family."

"What?" I lift a brow.

"Nothing." She bites her lip and laughs as she walks away.

Carmen and I step into the house. I look around for John. He's sitting on the couch with his head thrown back.

"Thank God, you two finally gave it a rest," he grumbles.

"What crawled up your butt?"

"You try having her in a room while your little brother is on the beach putting on a show. I swear. She defies me to get punished."

"Whoa, whoa. My girl's not on that level. Keep that kinky shit in check," I taunt. "Wait, hold on. I knew it. What's up with you two?"

"None of your business," they say in unison.

"Fine. What are you doing here?"

Carmen kisses my arm before she takes off into the kitchen. I watch her walk off in her bikini and frown. I'm not that comfortable with her walking around like that with my brother here. As if sensing that, she heads to the bedroom.

"Okay, spill," I whisper-yell once she's gone. "What the hell are you two doing here? Is something going on?"

"Well, yes and no. Nothing is coming your way, but a ton of shit is going on back home with some of the other families. They've tried some of the lower seats," John replies.

I scoff. "That's not smart either way you look at it. There are no *lower* families," I say using air quotes.

"You know what I mean, but I'm not here for that. Mom wanted someone to check-in in person, and she sent something for Carmen. I think we're all missing your goofy ass."

"Speak for yourself," Roni says as she plops down on the couch with a jar of peanut butter in her hand. "Dude, what's up with those steaks. I'm starving."

"You guys plan to stay here?"

"Don't worry. We won't get in the way of all that nasty shit you've been up to." Roni snickers.

"Are you guys staying with us?" Carmen returns in shorts and a tank top.

"Yeah, Roni needed a break. I thought hanging with you guys would be cool."

I look at Roni, really look at her this time. "Everything all right? Are you okay?"

"I'm fine." She waves me off. "What's up with those steaks though?"

I grin and look back at my brother. "Oh shit! Really, John."

He shrugs. I get ready to light into him, but the atmosphere shifts and I lift my head just in time to see Carmen grab a knife. That's when I see the full picture.

"No," I call out, but it's too late. My eyes grow wide as Carmen grabs two more knives and takes a stance as she glares at Torque who's collar is nailed to the wall by the first knife she threw. I cover my face and laugh into my palm while I shake my head. "This guy."

"I thought I told you to stay in the car," John grumbles.

"I needed to go to the bathroom."

"You guys know him?" Carmen asks as she straightens and starts to chew on her lip. "I'm so sorry."

"Shit like this always happens to him." Roni shrugs as she licks peanut butter from her finger.

I walk over to Carmen and take the knives from her hands, placing them on the counter. I kiss her forehead and pull her into my arms. I don't miss that she's trembling a little.

When I think about it, we never dealt with the trauma she went through in that parking garage. We took off right after and she never had to talk about it or think about it. I totally get her reaction to Torque. She's never seen him before.

"This is Torque," I say. "He belongs to John."

"Why do you always say it like that?" Torque mutters. "I don't belong to anyone."

I snicker. I say it like that because it pisses both Roni and Torque off. I'm still trying to figure out how John ended up with two charges. I get the Roni thing a little more than Torque, but I'm minding my own business. The extra hands have been coming in handy back home.

"Sorry about that," John says. "Forgive, Torque. I'll keep these two out of your hair."

Roni lifts a brow at John, and they do that silent thing they do. I knew he was tapping that. Wait until I call Brax. I wonder if he knows about this.

"What did I do?" Torque says breaking into their moment.

Roni glares at Torque the way a big sister does. "You get yourself pinned to a wall with a knife and you ask what you've done? By the way, how exactly didn't you see that coming?"

"I saw it," he says, pulling the knife from the wall. "That's how I dodged it."

Roni shakes her head and rolls her eyes. "Let me get something to eat and we'll train. You're slacking."

"Yeah, that's not happening. Or have you forgotten?" John says as his glare homes in on Roni.

She looks down into the peanut butter jar in her hands and pouts. She sighs. "Fine."

"Is it okay if I use the bathroom now?"

"Yeah, go on and then we'll get our things out of the car," John says with a nod. "We'll head out to get food of our own too."

"You don't have to do that there's plenty of food here. I have extra steaks I was going to save some for tomorrow, but there's more than enough to share," I say.

"You sure? I know we're dropping in on you."

"Bro, honestly, it's good to see you. Give me a minute with my girl and I'll help you guys get settled," I offer. "Oh yeah, you two are going on the farthest side of the house. Won't be corrupting my girl with your shenanigans."

"Again, two hours and twenty minutes. Poor Torque almost pissed his pants waiting for you guys to be done. Not the best way to look alive by the way—"

"All right, let's go pick bedrooms," John says, cutting Roni off before she can say another word.

As they head for the other side of the house, I take Carmen to our bedroom. I sit on the bed and pull her into my lap. She has a distant look in her eyes.

"Talk to me. Are you okay?"

"I could have hurt him. I just reacted. I don't even know why.

"You guys were talking and he walked in looking lost and I saw the gun holster. I freaked. It was like I was in that garage again. They're all going to think I'm crazy."

"I doubt that. Like I said, they work for John. Torque is young.

"Roni can be protective of him. Long story. She was more annoyed with Torque for getting pinned, not that you were protecting yourself from what was a threat to you.

"You didn't know him. Your attack first, ask questions later is something my mother would do." I chuckle. It was kind of hot too.

She runs a hand through her hair. "I think I'm going to take a nap," she says without looking me in the eyes.

I place my fingers under her chin and bring her face to meet mine. "Hey, you did nothing wrong. Not out there and not back home when you were attacked." I kiss the tip of her nose. "Get some sleep. I'll be in to check on you after I get the food going."

"Okay."

I peck her lips and watch as she climbs into the bed. I have an ache in my chest as I watch her become detached. The happy woman I made love to for hours has retreated into herself.

I wish I could tell her that she's not wrong in her instincts to protect herself. We are in hiding for her safety. Nothing is wrong with her protecting herself.

However, I have to bite my tongue because of her father. I don't like it, but I suck it up, not wanting to put any more stress on her. Once she's under the covers, I move to kiss her forehead. She looks up at me with those big pretty eyes.

"I love you."

She gives me a genuine smile this time. "I love you too," she says softly.

Carmen

I'm full and I feel a lot better. I've apologized to Torque a number of times. He only smiles and tells me it's okay.

Now that I look into his face, he looks to be about my age. I don't know what made me think he was a threat. He has the most innocent face.

"Mom sent you a gift," John says, bringing me from my thoughts as I sit on the couch in Ryan's arms.

Torque moves behind the couch and lifts a large gift bag, bringing it over to place it in front of me. I crane my neck to look at Ry. He gives me a smile and winks at me.

"Open it," he says, placing a hand on my belly.

I haven't started to show much. However, Ryan always has his hands on my tummy. I suck my lower lip into my mouth and turn back for the teal and yellow gift bag.

I pull out the matching tissue paper and place it on the table. Peeking inside, a huge smile comes to my face. I reach in and pull out the big teddy bear. It's so adorable. He has a T-shirt on that says, *Baby Black.*

I get choked up. This baby is already so loved. I take the card from the side of the bag and open it. Tears do spill when I read the text.

"Welcome to the family, love," I read aloud.

Ryan kisses my cheek. "Everyone's excited about our little guy. Mom knows I'm going to give her the cutest grandkids of them all."

I start to laugh. When I look at John he's scowling at Ry, causing me to laugh harder. Ryan wraps his arm around me and the bear and starts to rock back and forth.

"It's going to be a girl." I giggle.

"Whatever."

"I just want to know how you're not showing," Roni says with a pout. She stands and I can see her tiny bump.

I missed it earlier because she had a hoodie on. Now, it's hard not to see it. It's so cute on her.

John looks at her stomach and smiles. The smug grin makes me look at him more closely. There's something about John, I haven't put my finger on it yet.

"I think it's time for bed," John says, standing up to follow Roni.

"I was only going to the bathroom," she protests.

"Goodnight everyone," John calls over his shoulder.

Torque shakes his head. "I'm going to take a walk on the beach. You guys need me to clean up or something before I go?"

"Nah, we're good," Ryan says.

"Cool," he replies and slips out the back door.

I look after him. "He's a sweetheart. Why do I get the feeling there's another story there?"

"There is, but again. That's John's world. One thing to know about my brother.

"He fixes shit. Our kid will always be able to run to John if they need protecting or something made right.

"It's like his specialty to make things whole again. Roni and Torque needed fixing, and John has been their person," Ryan says, he pauses thoughtfully then continues.

"However, when I think about it. I think Roni is Torque's person and John is by proxy. Like, my brother was there for Roni and when Roni was there for Torque, John was there for him too. At least that's what I get from them."

"Yeah, I can see he's like a little brother to them. He looks up to John."

"We all look up to John." Ryan chuckles.

"What's that supposed to mean?"

"Nothing," he says. "Are you feeling better?"

I hug the bear in my arms tighter. It brings me comfort I didn't know I needed. I think over his question, searching for the truth within.

"A little."

He kisses the top of my head. "Never feel ashamed for protecting yourself."

"It's not that. At first, I thought running away would make it better. It did for a while.

"I pushed it to the back of my mind. Now, I can't help wondering what happened to those men. Did I kill them? Were they able to reattach his hand?"

"This is one of the reasons that I love you. Those men were out to attack you, and you're concerned about them," he murmurs into my hair. "I wouldn't worry about them if I were you. Justice has been served. Let your conscience be free of all of that."

I bite my lip and let his words sink in. I guess he's right. I release a sigh.

"I think I'm tired. Let's go to bed." I stand with the bear in my arms.

"Are we going to name the bear?" he asks as he stands up behind me.

I chuckle and turn to look up at him. "No, but we can go talk about baby names."

His eyes light up. I love when he gets excited about baby stuff. It makes me fall for him even more.

CHAPTER TWENTY-FOUR

Wrong Move

Paloma

My daughter must think I'm a fool, eh. I know all about the baby. I saw it in her face.

At first, she didn't have a clue, but I've been waiting for her to tell me the truth since. The girl is not that slow. Humph, my child isn't slow at all.

She's too smart for her own good. She's just like her father in so many ways. I'm sure if she were a boy, Kiyoshi would have trained her to take over for him alongside Ne.

He is so proud of her and all she's doing behind his back. I think my husband is more hurt that he's not celebrating with her, instead of waiting for the lies to stop.

"Carmen why must I drag things from you?" I huff into the phone as I sit in the back of my car.

I've been out shopping and when I absentmindedly walked into the baby store I got ticked. It's been two months since she's been gone. She's at least three to four months pregnant. The child is trying to make me bop her upside her head.

"Wh-what do you mean?"

I suck my teeth at her. She's testing me I tell you. She wants to push this too far.

I step out of the car in front of the house and roll my eyes. My husband has been waiting as long as I have for her to come clean about this boyfriend of hers. Maybe longer.

I think he likes the boy. However, I get the feeling he's angry as hell with the two of them. Carmen will be adding fuel to the fire when Kiyoshi finds out about the baby. I haven't told him because he's going to hit the roof.

"You keep playing with fire, girl." I'm so annoyed, my accent starts to ring in my own ears. "You're going to see me in a whole new light. You think I don't know you let some boy carry you to my home? He giving you doggie and you think you should lie to me about it?"

"What? Mom did you just say Ryan's giving me peni—"

"Wait, child. I have to handle something. I'll call you back."

I cut the call and nod to my companions. Bekia and Calu give me slight nods as they reach for their weapons. They have seen the same movement I have.

We form a circle in the driveway, back-to-back. I toss off my lightweight gray duster and it sails through the air before hitting the ground, revealing the two Katana swords on my back.

With all that's going on with my husband, I've been wearing knives like accessories. The twenty-three-inch blades will do nicely for this. I grin as the thrill of combat rolls through me.

The blades sing a sweet song as I reach at my lower back to pull them from their scabbards. Being a tall woman has its advantages. Calu is the first to shoot at the intruders, taking one down. Bekia and I jump into action with our swords.

Swiftly, I run at the tall one who reveals himself. I spin away from his first shot and use my blade to redirect the second toward one of the others. I know the bullet pierces his neck, but I have no time to relish in that.

I keep heading toward my original target before he can manage another shot. With the momentum of my charge, I run up his torso and backflip, bringing my sword up through his middle.

I land on my feet in a crouch. Sensing more than seeing the one who runs up behind me, I cross my blades in front of me and thrust them straight up. My attacker cries out as the blades pierce their body.

I spin out, pulling my swords free as I turn and lift. With a hard kick to the gut, I send the man flying. A woman with blonde hair jumps in front of me.

Her Japanese heritage is clear despite the dye job. She has a cocky grin on her face as if she believes my Bajan ass isn't about to serve her up.

"You sure you want to do this?" I taunt her. "I haven't broken a sweat you know. You can't want to be in a body bag this badly."

My girls are still battling to protect me. Kiyoshi has surrounded me with trained companions since we married. The innocent looking young women who travel with me are lethal.

These people have made a grave mistake today. The tiny blonde begins to toss kunai blades at me. I block the first few small blades and dodge two others.

She's fast, I'll give her that. But don't let this age fool you. My husband has taught me everything I know, and he was a master in many forms of combat way before I met him.

Kiyoshi makes sword-fighting look like child's play and I'm an excellent student. He would even say I've surpassed him. No, that would be our shy daughter.

However, she sees this as sport and exercise. She doesn't know that we've been training her for times like this. Blonde girl rushes me, pulling me from my thoughts.

She gets a kick into my ribs. I take it in stride. I've been kicked harder while sparring.

I go on attack. I twirl my swords at my sides before spinning to return the kick, then I slash her with one of my blades.

Grabbing her arm, I lock it under mine and tug her into my chest.

She goes to pull another kunai, but I'm faster. I use my other sword to knock it from her hand, then point the tip of my blade beneath her chin.

"Who sent you?" I snarl. She narrows her glare but doesn't say a word. I push the point into her flesh, drawing blood. "Answer me."

She says nothing. Bekia walks up right before I push the blade in farther. I don't take my eyes off the woman in front of me. Although, I do note the silence that now surrounds my home.

"Their tats suggest they are from the Sato family. I will call Matsumara-sama. He will want to know."

I shove the woman in my hold toward Bekia. "I will call myself. Take care of this."

Kiyoshi

I am a man of many talents, but I've yet to master the art of leniency. This attack on my wife, it will not go unanswered. I will show them why I've been asked to join this Alliance and why I felt I have enough power to do so.

This could have been a peaceful transition. We had no intentions of removing anyone's power as long as they work within the sanctions we've presented. There is still enough opportunity for everyone to remain wealthy and in power with their families.

However, you always have those who don't want to follow rules or feel as if they have been dishonored. It is a dishonor to me that Hayate Sato sent assassins to my home after my wife. He knows I'm here in Japan.

I sat with him to see if I could smooth this over before this war. His father was a friend of mine and I wanted to honor that. Now, Hayate will learn a valuable lesson.

"Ready," Ne whispers to me.

I nod. "Cut the lights."

Screams and cries fill the house as my men and I descend upon the darkness. This message will be clear. These cries will be heard around the world.

My position is not to be tested. I am not the weakest link in this Alliance and I will not fold. Yes, I'm probably the oldest member with a seat, but my bones have not withered and neither has my ruthlessness.

I grab Hayate by his hair and lift his head close to the blade in my hand. This one is new. It was to be a gift to my wife for her sword collection. Now, Hayate's head will accompany it.

"There is no honor in what you have done. I can assure you. Your father has watched you fall with sadness."

With that, I pull the blade across his neck. Silence falls and the room fills with my warriors. It is done. I have made myself clear.

CHAPTER TWENTY-FIVE
Change in Plans

Ryan

My phone vibrates, pulling me from my sleep. I frown and reach for it as Carmen stirs beside me. My frown deepens as I have to get out of bed to avoid waking her. I look at the time.

I would have woken soon anyway. However, when I see the name of the caller, my hackles go up. I answer as I pad to the bathroom to brush my teeth.

"Hello."

"Ryan, I don't believe it's time for Carmen to return. You will keep her there a little longer."

"What's happened?"

The line is silent at first. I grind my teeth as I wait for him to answer. My grip on my phone is so tight my fingers start to hurt.

"There was an attack on my wife."

"Fuck, is she okay? Can my family help?"

He gives a short chuckle. "You will learn that my wife is the one to fear. She is fine. The problem has been dealt with. However, I want the smoke to settle."

I twist my lips thinking about this. I have no problem with keeping Carmen all to myself a little longer. However, it's time she starts her doctor's visits soon.

I want to make sure she and the baby are healthy. We were expecting to be back home for that.

"How much longer are you thinking?"

"A month or two," he grumbles.

"Kiyoshi," I bite out low, looking toward the bedroom. "You want me to lie to her for two more months? You have to be kidding me."

"She has lied to me for much longer. At least I do it for her safety."

I bite my tongue instead of telling him that we should return home because she needs to take care of herself and the baby. My family will guard her with their lives if we return. My mother alone would empty a clip for her.

However, I know Kiyoshi can indeed be stubborn and this isn't an argument I want to have over the phone. I have to think rationally and not with my emotions. I have Carmen and the baby to think about.

"She's not stupid. What am I supposed to tell her? She'll have questions. My job, her school, what's the plan for all of that?"

"She wants to take a break from school. I will grant her request this afternoon. You are the wise Ryan Black. Come up with the rest."

If I weren't so pissed off, I'd probably laugh at his sarcasm. I'm not finding any humor at the moment. I hate this shit with a passion.

"Yeah, I've got it." I snort.

He sighs. "Ryan."

"Yeah?"

"Thank you."

I nod as if he can see me. "I'm doing it for her, but you're welcome."

"Goodnight."

"*Oyasumi*," I reply.

He chuckles. "*Oyasumi*, Ryan-san."

I hang up and look in the mirror. Everything is changing but it's not. Not within this bubble we're in.

If we stay here, we're staying in a lie. A lie that's going to burn from every end. The Nash family is out to turn all of my hair gray.

Carmen needs to come clean with her father and her father needs to tell her the truth. As long as they continue with this I'm caught in the middle, and I don't like it.

I brush my teeth and relieve myself. I might as well go start breakfast. Everyone else will be up soon.

I can clear my head while I cook. I need to come up with something. I don't know what, but I'll figure it out.

"If this isn't some bullshit," I mutter to myself and I pad into the kitchen.

When I get there, John is already at the island scrolling through his tablet. Standing across from him, I flatten my palms on the counter and release a deep breath. My mind is racing with all the things I need to sort out before Carmen wakes.

John lifts his head from the tablet and narrows his eyes at me. "What's up with you?"

Yeah, worst thing about having older brothers, they can see right through you. Not that I'm hiding my frustration well to begin with. Locking my hands behind my head, I look up at the ceiling and ask myself how I got into this mess.

"There was an attack on Paloma Matsumara-Nash. Kiyoshi wants me to postpone our return," I murmur low enough for only my brother to hear.

John releases a low whistle. "And she's still to remain in the dark?"

"Yup."

He heaves a heavy sigh. "I feel for you, kid. I know how much lying is eating at you, but the job comes first. Trust, we'll handle anything that comes once this blows over."

Lowering my head, I level my eyes on him. "Yeah, but how do I convince her we're staying here for another two months?"

"You don't," he says and shrugs his shoulder smoothly, like this all is so much simpler than I'm making it. "We change locations. Use what you know to your advantage."

I knit my brows and start to think. Pushing aside all the lies that have been told, I search for the truths. It's like a lightbulb goes off. I know instantly how to handle this.

"Her dad's going to handle the school thing, but I have to fit together the rest. She's been questioning her career, but I know she's made for finding a story and making it something special."

"Didn't Nick get her that job with NY/LA Connections?"

"Yeah, from what I know he pulled the strings for her aunt."

John nods and he starts to tap away at his tablet. A smile comes to his face, and he lifts his eyes back to me. I know that look. He has an idea.

"We don't want to go near any of the Alliance, which will be difficult since they're everywhere, but I have an idea. Remi and Ramses have been running a Con. It's not connected to Club Desire and not many know that they're behind it.

"It's been moving from continent to continent. They'll be in Cali at the end of the year. NY/LA Connections would love a piece on something like this.

"Carmen does good work. She gives the story without giving too much away. We can call in some favors, get her the assignment and head to Sydney."

"Let me get this straight. You want me to take my girl, my pregnant girl to a BDSM convention in Australia. Get the fuck out of here," I say and frown.

He rolls his eyes at me. "This will be the last place anyone will look for any of us. She'll get a story out of it, and you won't have to sell it because it will be work. It will buy us time to secure another location or return here for a few weeks if you can pull off a reason."

"I thought the point was to stay away from the Alliance. You know this is right at the triplet's back door, right? Aren't they out there right now?" I lift a brow.

John nods. "Yes, and I'm well aware of that. It's the other reason I think it will work. We don't want to be connected to the Alliance and the trouble surrounding it, but we don't want to disconnect either.

"If something comes up, we want the manpower to back us up. You know them. They're going to look out as soon as they hear we're on their soil."

Dragging a hand down my face, I try not to admit that this isn't a bad idea. It's a good one, but I'm still not sure I want my girl at a BDSM Con. Leave it to John to know some crazy shit like this and to actually make it work in his favor.

I point a finger at him. "You know this is work. Your kinky ass better not get caught up in any shit."

He sits back with a grin, folding his arms over his chest. "It's work for you. I'm on a vacation."

"Bite me."

"I'll make it all happen. It's 3:00 a.m. in Cali. I'll give Nick a few more hours before I call. He'll be the one to get us invites to the Con and he'll plant the seed for the blog to assign her. I'll take care of everything else," my brother says.

"I didn't say I agreed to this," I mutter.

"You're welcome," he replies. I don't get to retort because I feel the moment Carmen enters the room. I flip John off as she steps behind me and wraps her arms around my waist.

Carmen

"I'm so hungry," I breathe against his bare back.

When I woke and he was already out of bed I brushed my teeth in hopes that he'd have breakfast waiting. I'm starving this morning. It's like I can't stop eating in the last few days and my belly has seemed to pop overnight.

"You want anything special?" Ryan asks.

Kissing his smooth skin, I think on his question. "Oh, yes, sugar cookies and caramel sauce and bacon."

He turns in my arms as he laughs. "Babe, you had that yesterday. I think you need to chill with all the sweets. How about I make some of Mom's fresh homemade biscuits and bacon?"

I pout, but then my stomach grumbles and his offer starts to sound really good. "Can I have cheese on my biscuits?"

He gives me that sexy smile and kisses my nose. "Of course, you can. Anything else?"

"Nope. Oh, wait. Hot chocolate."

He chuckles and squeezes my butt. With a wink, he releases me to start on my breakfast. I round the counter to take a seat next to John.

"Good morning," he says and with a broad smile.

I like when John smiles. It brightens his face. I've noticed that of all the brothers John is the prettiest. Not that they aren't all handsome. However, Johnathan has a softer face. Handsome in a pretty-boy way. Not as rugged as his brothers.

"Good morning," I chirp back. "I bet you guys are bummed to be going back so soon."

He shrugs. "We might stick around here for a bit more. Haven't decided yet."

"Oh, that's awesome. I wish I had more time." Placing my chin on my palm as I rest my elbow on the countertop, I pout.

I have to admit. I'm nervous about returning home tomorrow. It's like the last few days rushed by.

While I'm excited to talk to my father about my plans and taking a break from school, I'm going stir crazy wondering if he'll notice my belly or the changes in my face.

"Ry will have to bring you back sometime."

I grin widely. "I'd totally be up for that. I had such a good time the last two months."

"Duh, you were with me," Ry says. I roll my eyes. "Nothing but good times when I'm around."

"It has been fun. Not what I expected." I tilt my head at him. "Do you think it's because we were in our own shell? Like, seriously. We haven't had many other people around until last week. Do you think we'll click as well once we're back home?"

Ryan stops in the middle of making the dough for the biscuits, which by the way were amazing last time he made them. His gaze locks on mine. The weight of his stare almost leaves me breathless.

"We work anywhere, anytime, around anyone."

My cheeks heat. I cannot help wondering what my parents will think of Ryan. His humor can be cutting at times.

My father rarely shows he has a sense of humor at all. I think my mother will like him. Although, I can see her trying to fatten him up with her cooking.

Not that she will succeed at that one. I've watched Ryan eat plenty and he still doesn't gain an ounce.

"I hope— Hold on." I frown and lift a finger as my phone pings.

I pull it from my shorts and see it's my dad. I mentally do the math. It's late night for him, unless he has returned home a day early.

"Hello."

"*Kon'nichiwa*, Nene. How are you doing?"

"Hey Daddy, you sound so tired. What's up?"

"I want to have a talk with you."

My heart starts to race. Has he found out my secrets? I plan to tell him, but I wanted to wait until we were face-to-face.

I slip from my stool on shaky legs and walk into the living room area. Sitting on the couch, I cross my legs and take a deep breath. Nodding my head as if he can see me, I bite my lip.

"Okay, what's up?"

"I've been thinking about what you said. I think this break from school may be good for you. I spoke to your mother.

"She traveled the world between her Sophomore and Junior year in college and again between her undergrad and Masters."

"Really?" I say breathlessly. This is not what I thought he was going to say.

"Hm, yes. We have talked. She believes you should do some travel.

"You are ahead of your classes. I believe this will be good for you. Think about it. I will call again after I have some sleep, and we can discuss your plan."

"Okay, sure. Rest well, *Otōsan*."

"I love you, Nene. *Atode mata hanashimashou*."

"Talk to you later. Love you too."

I hang up the phone and stare at it. This is so unreal. Pushing a hand in my hair, I tug at it, trying to comprehend the last few minutes.

"What just happened?"

"Babe, you okay?" Ryan calls out to me.

I turn toward the kitchen. "Yeah, I think I am," I say with a smile.

Yup, I sure do think I'm going to be great. Maybe my father is turning soft in his old age. Hope blossoms. He might not totally disown me after all.

CHAPTER TWENTY-SIX

Best Day Ever

Carmen

I've been so happy all day. Even as I pack to leave in the morning, I can't stop smiling. I don't know how this happened, but I've been working my plan over in my head to make sure it's airtight and my father can't change his mind.

Looking out of the window at the beach, I sigh. I wish we could stay here for a little longer. I almost asked Ryan if that would be okay since John mentioned he, Roni and Torque would be sticking around.

"We need to get home to get a peek at you, don't we?" I say as I place a hand on my belly.

My phone rings startling me. I laugh at myself for jumping. Ryan would've totally made fun of me if he were in the room.

He and John have been working on something together all day. I guess it's time for him to go back to work. I groan when I see the name on my phone.

Looks like I need to get back to work too. I may be a freelance reporter, but I've taken a long enough break from accepting assignments.

"Hello," I answer the call with a smile as I laugh at myself.

"Hey, Carmen," my editor Karl replies. His voice holds a ton of excitement that's so unlike him. "I have a great opportunity for you, kid. This one is perfect for you."

"Oh, okay. I'm returning home in the morning."

"No, no, no. I need you on a plane to Australia in the morning."

I cover my belly with my hand. With the baby and Ryan—not to mention, school, my father still wants to know my plans—I don't know if this is the time that I can take an assignment like this. I was able to cover the weddings because I had breaks in school.

I don't normally cover events outside of the country. I furrow my brows.

"Karl, I don't know if that's possible. I have so much going on."

"Listen to me. You can't even get into this event without an invite. It's exclusive and private.

"I know you'll handle this with care. I need you to do this for me. Two weeks, that's all I'm asking. I'm sure you won't miss much with school."

I purse my lips, not telling him that I may not be returning to school. Australia. My interest is piqued. I can't help myself. I need to know more.

"What's the event?"

"Are you sitting down?" he says with a smile in his voice.

I sit on the edge of the bed. "I am now."

"It's a BDSM Con in Sydney. With an elite guest list. I need you to get this story for me.

"They'll be here in California at the end of the year. This will be great exposure for the blog. First the Black weddings, now this. Come on, kid. You have to do this for me."

I blow out a breath. "Can I talk to my boyfriend and dad about this first?"

"The invite is open to you and your team. Take the boyfriend with you."

Ryan enters the room as if he's been summoned. I chew on my lip as we lock eyes. He lifts a brow at me.

"I'll email you once I decide. Give me an hour or two. Okay?"

"All expenses are covered. This is the chance of a lifetime. Don't pass this one up, kid. You never know what you'll learn."

I roll my eyes. "I'll email you as soon as I decide. Thanks, Karl."

I end the call as Ryan pulls me into his arms. I don't even know where to begin with this. I'm sort of excited by the possibility and the event itself has me more than curious.

"What's up?" Ryan says as he searches my face.

"*So* ... NY/LA Connections has offered me a trip to Australia. I'll be covering a story for a conference there," I say.

"That's great, right? It'll look good on your resume. Why do you look so reluctant?"

"Well, there's us and the baby."

"Me and the baby can come with you. When is it?"

My heart skips a beat at the thought of him coming with me. "I would have to go straight from here. I won't be returning home. Don't you have to get back to work?"

"I can work remotely if I put in the request. Felix will set me up and Heather will assign me non-field work." He gives a shrug as if it's that simple. "I'll change the flight plans tonight. Perks of flying private."

"What about my dad?" I wince. "I don't know if he'll go for this."

"Baby, you're making excuses. Call your dad and tell him this is a part of your plan. You can tell him that your boyfriend will be with you to look out for you."

I snort. "I'll call about the job, but the boyfriend bomb will have to wait." Ryan's expression hardens.

"I'm going to tell him. I just think it will be better to do so when I get back home. Especially with the baby and everything."

He frowns but nods. I call up the courage to tell him what the Con is for. He may change his mind after I tell him.

"What?" He narrows his golden gaze.

"The conference is a BDSM Con," I whisper and bite my lip.

Something mischievous crosses his face. He places his forehead to mine. I hold my breath as I wait for his response.

"I like the sound of this trip. I love a little rope play." He groans and bites his own lip. "What I'd give to see you trussed up."

"Seriously?"

He gives me a heated stare. "When do I ever play about pussy?"

I bury my face in his chest. "I'll call my dad. If he agrees to this ... I don't want to jinx it. This will be so freaking amazing."

Ryan kisses the top of my head. "Call him. I'll take care of the travel arrangements. Where in Australia did you say it will be?"

"Sydney," I breathe into his chest.

"Cool. We can shop when we get there."

Oh my god. It starts to sink in that I'm going to Australia. I smile when I think of my camera that Ry bought me.

I wonder how much they'll let me get footage of. The story will be one thing, but if I can get real live footage.

I squeal before I look up at Ry. He smiles back down at me. It's like my life is changing right before my eyes and I don't know what to do with myself.

Ryan

I've never seen Carmen this happy before. It makes me hate that I'm lying to her even more. Of course, I knew her father would agree to her going to Australia.

However, her infectious joy over having this opportunity has caused me to have conflicting feelings. I want to see her happy, but the lies that are behind it chafe my nerves to no end. After dinner, I needed to take a walk.

I have to get my head cleared before we leave here. I've controlled this trip and our environment for two months. Things will change once we're in Sydney. I'll have to keep my eyes open.

"You took off in a hurry," John says from behind me. I don't bother to turn or reply. "You're doing what needs to be done."

"If this were Roni, would you be okay with this?"

I keep my eyes on the waves as my arms dangle over my knees pulled up in front of me. He's silent. At first, I don't think he's going to answer me.

He takes a seat beside me in the sand. "No, can't say I would be, but I'd also do whatever it took to keep her safe."

"Keeping Carmen safe and these lies aren't one and the same. One is necessary the other isn't."

"I know this goes against everything in you, but if you want to earn her father's respect, you're going to have to bite this bullet."

"What about her lies to him?" I work my jaw to dial down my temper. John only wants to help. "I've seen what lies do to people.

"Not just with our clients. Look at what Toby's lies have done. Heather and Brax were hiding some heavy shit from everyone for years. I watched it eat at Brax.

"I never knew everything, but I knew enough to know it was big enough to weigh on him. Now here I am in the middle of a bunch of damn secrets. She's so happy and she's finding her way into her own, you know? What's going to happen when she finds out the truth?"

John grunts before he speaks. "There's nothing like watching a woman you care about come into her own. It's like watching a flower bloom.

"But here's something I've learned. You can't hover because you become a shadow and kill the light that's feeding that growth. Allow her to have this time.

"How it's coming about isn't important. Her happiness is. Focus on that. Watch her shine in the light. It's all you can do for now."

I hear his words, but I don't want to accept them. There has to be another way. How can I build a life with the woman I love when I'm lying to her?

As if reading my mind, John answers my thoughts. "You're doing this out of love. Besides, she can't hide my niece or nephew for too long. She'll have to tell her father soon enough."

I smile as I think about our baby growing inside her. "Dude, I'm trying not to be a total ass, so I haven't mentioned it to her, but do you see her baby bump. I swear it's like it came out of nowhere. I love that shit."

"Best feeling in the world, isn't it?"

"Fuck yeah." I grin and turn to look at my big brother. "Wow, we're all going to be fathers. Three years ago, I would have called bullshit. Now, I'm so ready for this."

John frowns and this time he turns to the ocean to stare. My wheels start to turn, and I look at my brother more closely. Suddenly, the pieces start to click.

"She wasn't just threatening you with suicide. There was a baby involved," I say aloud.

He nods. "At least that's what she told me. I trusted her at first. I took her word for truth.

"However, I'm a PI. At some point, the pieces didn't fit and I started to dig. She was never pregnant like she said.

"Her roommate was. She used her pregnancy test to fool me. When we had that fight ...." He pauses and swallows. "We had an argument.

"She started it, I don't even remember what it was over. One minute we were arguing and I left. The next morning, she claimed to have lost the baby.

"I felt so guilty and she used that against me. It was like her own personal weapon for years."

I release a long low whistle. "Bro, I knew you hated her for some reason, but I could never figure out what the heck was going on between you two."

"I didn't want you to. I know you all too well. I kept it to myself.

"The guilt turned from me wanting to help her through her grief to loathing her for using it against me. The relationship had been over a long time ago.

"And when Roni came into the picture you admitted the truth to yourself?"

He shrugs and turns to look me in the eyes. "I think I was ready to walk away and deal with the consequence before Roni. Meeting her sped things up. Everything about my relationship with Missy was toxic."

He stops to frown. I grin as I read his thoughts. "See, lies. I hate them."

He gives a dry chuckle. "Damn, you have a point." He runs a hand through his hair. "If you decide to tell her, I'll back you up."

"Thanks. That means a lot. I'm going to do as Nash asks for the time being.

"Carmen's not ready to face him. I don't want to lie, but I don't want to be the catalysis that throws the ball in motion on this either." I pause for a beat to ponder on that. "I don't think."

"I understand that. Come on, she looked upset when you left out. You don't want her to think you're upset about the trip. Everything fell right into place. Don't mess it up now."

"Don't worry, I'm not going to blow your chance at kinky heaven."

"Fuck you." He chuckles.

"Nah, I'll leave that for Roni and the freaks in Sydney."

I stand quickly and dart out of the way before he can hit me. John hits too damn hard for me to let him catch me slipping. I laugh all the way back to the house as he chases after me.

When we step inside, he tosses an arm around my shoulders and leans to whisper in my ear.

"You're going to make a great husband and father. She knows that. It's in the way she looks at you. Stop worrying so much."

With that, he squeezes my shoulder and heads to break up the squabble Roni and Torque are in the middle of. I swallow past the lump in my throat. I look up to all my brothers, no matter what I might say. Hearing one of them put so much faith in me means a whole lot.

"You got this, Ry," I mutter to myself.

CHAPTER TWENTY-SEVEN

Power in Mastery

Carmen

I sit in the private box wide-eyed, staring at the scene before me play out. I don't have my camera. Over the course of the conference, I haven't been able to record any scenes where the participants didn't want to be recorded or if their faces are bare. The couple in front of us not only refused to be on camera, but their gorgeous faces are bare as well.

"Makes you want milk and cookies, doesn't it?" Ryan chuckles in my ear.

I palm my cheeks. "Oh God, Oreo cookies have popped in my head a few times," I groan. "Is that terrible?"

"No. Not the way he's feasting on her cookies. Shit."

I shake my head at Ryan, but I can't tear my eyes away from the couple before us. So many thoughts are running through my head. I've never thought about what Ryan and I look like to the outside world.

His skin is much paler than mine, but I can't say that I've given that much notice during sex. However, this couple ... they're breathtaking. Their contrast reminds me of Toby and Kamara.

The guy below on the stage is white, white. Like, I'm sure he hasn't sunbathed in a while, not that that wouldn't help, and the woman, she's the color of onyx with a glow to her dark skin that's amazing. Total opposites.

Running my hands across piano keys comes to mind. After all, these two move in perfect harmony as he seeks to give her pleasure and she gives herself over to it. I've been riveted to this beauty for the last thirty minutes.

I watched with awe when her master poured oil on her skin. Her body became a picture of liquid glass. I've never seen a more beautiful sight.

As his pale hands danced across her flesh, I felt like I was watching something too intimate for the rest of us to see. Now, as his head is buried between her thighs and the silver nipple clamps are fastened to her hardened, dark chocolate peaks with the beaded chain he keeps tugging, my breath is caught in my throat. It's a sight that's awe-inspiring, to say the least.

"He's showing so much restraint," I whisper.

Ryan places a hand on the back of my neck and starts to massage. My already aroused body tightens with need and anticipation as if I'm the one below ready to come. I ball my fists and try to concentrate.

"Restraint becomes simple when all you want is your partner's pleasure." My pulse quickens as his breath fans my skin. I hadn't realized he moved so near.

The little viewing sofa is spacious enough that Ryan hadn't been so close. He had been sprawled out, his arms across the back of the sofa and his long legs spread comfortably. Now he's so close I can feel his body heat against my side.

I've been avoiding glances at him. The leather pants he's wearing are sexy on him. They're tight enough for the imprint of his dick to show through.

It's not helping that he's shirtless. It's the suggested attire for tonight. Every event has had one.

As I register his words and his nearness, I start to breathe harder. A shiver rolls through me. Sucking my lip into my mouth, I look down into my lap.

"You speak as if you know more from experience. It's been that way for the entire Con. None of this is new to you, is it?"

I've been wanting to ask for days now. I brushed off his rope play comment before we come here as Ryan being Ryan. However, once we arrived and started to go to the workshops, I began to see my boyfriend in a new light.

He knows a lot about this life. John and Roni seem to too. Torque has been like a kid in a candy shop.

I've seen him get involved in workshops and the after parties as well. The sparkle in his eyes has been quite telling.

Ryan shrugs. "I've had an experience or two. Let's just say someone thought it was a good idea to allow John to be in charge of my eighteenth birthday." He chuckles.

"I don't think I want to know the story behind that one."

He kisses my temple. "No, you don't. Carmen?"

I force my eyes away from the couple below. Turning my head slowly, my gaze is met with golden eyes that are blazing with lust. He places his fingers beneath my chin and lifts my head.

His lips are only a breath away from mine as he speaks. "We can continue to watch this, or we can take advantage of this viewing suite. I know you're wet. I can tell by the way you're squeezing your thighs.

"It's nothing at all for me to fulfill your fantasies. Ask and I'm yours. I promise what he's doing down there has nothing on me."

My pussy gushes in my panties. The deep rumble of his voice and the way his breath tickles my lips combined are enough to have me panting with want and need. I reach up to push his overgrown hair from his face.

He hasn't had a cut since we arrived here in Australia. Sometimes, I feel like he's afraid to let me out of his sight or something. Back in Barbados, a guy would come once a week to cut it for him.

I secretly like seeing his hair untamed. It speaks to the real Ryan. Yes, he's smooth and put together when he wants to be, but there's something unhinged about Ry that you can't deny.

A *rough around the edges, do as I please, handle my business and dare others to get in the way* vibe. All things I promised myself I didn't want in a boyfriend. Now, I wouldn't want him any other way and I love him just the way he is.

I lick my lips. "Talk is cheap, Black. If you can do better than that, show me," I say boldly.

"That's my girl. Talk shit and see what happens. I love a challenge." He retorts with a wicked grin on his lips.

Yes, I know I just signed a check my butt can't cash. Oh well. That's what soaker tubs are for.

Ryan

That defiant spark in her eyes is something new that I like. It matches the Carmen I know. The one who's been defying her father and secretly defining who she wants to be.

Before the actions were there, but not the confidence to own them. However, in this moment, as I look deep into her eyes it's all there. The defiance and the confidence that she didn't have two weeks ago.

That's what I love about the BDSM life. There's something empowering about it. Not only for the Dom but for the Sub as well.

I always tell people not to knock it before they try it. There's so much more to it than the books and movies. That shit isn't the life.

Knowledge is key and the life gives you knowledge. Knowledge of self, knowledge of pleasure, knowledge of give and surrender. Not my Sub's surrender to me, but our surrender to each other and the release of the chaos that can consume our minds.

I stand and move before her view of the stage below. "Come here," I command as I lock eyes with my woman.

She stands with that adorable look of awe on her face. She looks sexy as fuck in the pink satin robe and red heels they gifted all the women tonight. However, it's the little outfit beneath that I want to get a look at.

She takes the few steps to close the distance between us. I don't move an inch. I watch as her chest begins to heave with anticipation.

"Release the ties. Take the robe off, slowly."

She nods and reaches for the ties. I like that she keeps eye contact. She had gotten into the habit of not looking me in the eyes after the first few nights here.

That doesn't feel right for us. I read her through her soft orbs. I'm not on that kind of power play.

It's fine when we're out in the parties and general events, but when we're alone I won't accept it. She peels the ties apart and slowly pulls the fabric from her shoulders. The pink satin floats to the floor and her beautiful body comes into view.

Her swollen belly is on display, causing me to smile inside. My baby has been making itself known in the last few weeks. There's no way she's hiding that bump from her father. She's lucky I'm not taking her back to Cali yet.

"So beautiful," I murmur and palm her stomach. "It's important we communicate. It's always important during play, but we have our little one to think about.

"If anything is too much or uncomfortable, we stop. You have to let me know. I won't put you or the baby at risk."

"Should we be doing this?" she asks, concern crossing her face.

"It's fine, as long as we communicate and take our time, it will be fine. It's no more risky than all the shit we already do."

That brings a smile to her lips. I tap my lips. Following the silent command, she lifts on her toes to kiss them.

I look over toward the display in the room. These suites are set up for this. You can view the action below through the two-way mirror or create your own.

Some do both. For us, the scene below shall be forgotten. I'm not going to lie.

I started to get a little jealous. Carmen has been intrigued by a lot of the scenes and workshops, but those two down there know how to command a room. Hell, even I was captivated until my woman grabbed my attention.

Watching her has been the biggest turn-on of the night. The way her full lips parted in awe. David and Christena are a gorgeous couple, but they have nothing on me and my girl.

Lifting my other hand, I finger the strap of her lacey bra. I ordered this set special for her. The corsets they gifted everyone else weren't safe for her and Roni so John and I took care of it.

Goosebumps rise across her breasts. Licking my lips, I can't wait to taste her skin. One of the gifts in the basket for tonight was flavored lotion. On the first day, we filled out packets with our preferences for each night. I remember the choices for tonight because of the caramel flavored lotion.

I dip my head and lick her neck for a taste. A groan leaves my lips. The flavor is more intense than I expected. She really tastes like caramel.

"Ry," she whispers.

"Sh. No talking. I want you to listen and feel."

She pouts a little, but she doesn't protest. I have a reason for this. I want her to understand the sacrifice a man in love is willing to make.

"Restraint is your power, not mine but yours. Watch and learn." I take a small step back. I lift my chin and give the command. "Turnaround."

She does as I say. Damn, I'm a lucky man. The black lace thong she has on is swallowed by her ass. Those round globes alone could end this night. I want nothing more than to bury my face between them.

"Take the bra off."

Again, she obeys without question. I'm so hard, I have to unfasten my pants. No matter how much pain I'm in, I'm not rushing this.

There's a change in Carmen and I want her to see what I see.

Carmen

I can see him behind me in the reflection of the mirrors that surround the room. I want to cover my belly and shy away, but the look of lust on his face makes me feel sexy. I went from not having a baby bump to not fitting any of the jeans I purchased the first day we arrived.

It's the look that he's giving me now that has kept me from freaking out. Every night we fall asleep with him palming my belly no matter how I lay. I'm honestly in awe of my body and the fact that there's a little person growing inside of me. I think it's finally starting to hit that I'm going to be someone's mommy.

The more I think about it, the more I want to stake my claim on the life I want to live. Sure, I still fear what my father will do and say, but I'm ready to face it. *I think*. Okay, maybe not completely, but I'm getting there.

"Where have you gone?"

I yelp and jump as Ryan's voice rumbles in my ear. He places his hands on my hips to steady me. I wobble on my heels.

"Kick the shoes off. I want you and the baby comfortable."

I nod and will my heart to stop racing. Stepping out of my heels, I lock my eyes back on him in the mirror. He looks down at me with a smile in the corners of his lips. It's sexy and dangerous at the same time.

I bite my lip nervously. I'm never sure what to expect, but this feels so different. The atmosphere is charged and change lingers in the air.

I can't explain it. I know he's about to change me. I'm just not sure if that's a good or a bad thing.

"Stop thinking," he says as he palms my breasts.

His touch fires off straight to my core. My thighs are so slick with my arousal, I can hear the moisture when I shift my legs. Clearing my mind of anything but his touch, I anchor myself to the moment.

In one of the classes I sat in on this week, the Mistress did an entire presentation on remaining in the moment with your partner. I start the breathing exercise she shared with us and immediately Ryan's touch becomes so much more potent.

"That's my girl," he says in my ear as he rolls my nipples between his fingertips. "Don't make a sound, baby. Your only job is to feel. Only time you speak is if you need me to stop or if you're uncomfortable."

I want to fuss at him and ask how the heck am I supposed to remain quiet. My panting already sounds so darn loud in my ears. I clench my fists as he releases my breasts and glides his hands down my body.

He fingers the garter around my waist. I had reservations about the lacey piece, but Ry helped me into it to show me that I still looked sexy.

"This looks so good on you," he says, bringing a smile to my lips.

I love it when he does that. In the time that we've been together, he has shown me time and again that he's in tune with me. I never knew how much I wanted someone that gets me, like really gets me.

He kneels behind me and unfastens the thigh highs from the garter. I almost moan when he chases the fabric down my leg with his tongue. He sucks a patch of skin into his mouth, causing me to bite down on my tongue. I don't know about this not making a sound business.

"Lift," he says, wrapping my other leg with his arm for support.

I lift my foot so he can get the stocking off. Ryan repeats the same action with the other leg. Only this time when I lift my leg, he steadies me as he licks my inner thigh where my juices have dripped.

"You taste so fucking good. I'm buying you a case of that lotion."

I try not to giggle. I think that's their point. There has been a price list and order form in the bottom of every basket.

Whoever throws these events really knows what they're doing. I've enjoyed everything. Every detail on every day.

Ryan slowly peels my soaked panties down my thighs. It's tortuous how he drags the fabric and his fingers across my skin. Yet, I take it in silence as I watch him.

I nearly whimper when Ryan stands and his body heat leaves my back. He leaves me standing in the middle of the room as he crosses to a basket that was left here for us. He filled out all the questionnaires the first day. I've been surprised by all his choices.

So imagine the look on my face when he removes the ribbon from the basket and plucks out ropes and oil. He reaches for a blindfold but shakes his head and leaves it. Sifting through the rest, he purses his lips in thought.

I nearly burst into laughter when he places the items back into the basket and lifts the entire thing up to carry over to the table in the center of the room.

I noticed the large round table when we first entered earlier. It drew my attention because nothing was on it and no chairs surrounded it. I found that odd in the bedroom-like suite.

He looks at me and shrugs his shoulder. "What? We're going to need a lot of this stuff. Some I'm undecided about." I shrug my shoulders back and smile at him. "Come here."

I move toward him, but he meets me halfway as if too eager to wait. He pinches my chin and devours my lips. I almost moan into his mouth, trapping it in right before it slips free.

He breaks the kiss with a smile on his lips. Pecking my forehead, he runs a finger across my lips. Those golden eyes search my face.

"*Kinbaku* is my favorite practice. The art is breathtaking in itself. On you, I know it will be so sexy and irresistible. It just so happens to be a Japanese art. Here it's called *shibari.*"

He palms my butt and draws me into his erection. "I won't get too intricate with the ropes." He drags a finger from my throat down the center of my breasts. "You're going to look so beautiful."

Releasing me, he leaves me standing breathless as he walks over to the panel that controls the lighting and sound system. After pressing a few buttons, the sensual sound of music flows through the air. I don't know the song, but it's raw and sexy. And this is why I love Ryan.

He starts to sway his hips and dance his way to me. God, he's gorgeous. Most men his size don't own his confidence and smoothness.

Ryan moves toward me like he owns his body and everything about it. When he reaches me, he dances around me in a circle. This time a little giggle does slip free.

When he stands in front of me again, he grasps the back of my neck and crushes my lips with his. As he devours me, he backs me up as he deepens the kiss. I cling to his neck and follow his lead until my butt bumps into the table he placed the basket on.

Ryan breaks the kiss and plucks me from my feet to place me on top of the table as if I'm no more than a toy. I sit on my knees before him. Even on the table, I have to tilt my head back to look up at Ryan at his six seven height.

He drops a kiss on my lips before reaching for the basket. Grabbing one of the ropes, he shows it to me. I nod my head and lick my dry lips. He pecks them again.

"Relax. You're going to love this."

I give another nod and take a deep breath. He holds my gaze until he sees I've fully relaxed. With a smile, he starts to caress my skin with the ropes.

They're softer than I thought they would be. I think that knowledge allows me to relax a bit more. He reaches for one of my wrists and starts to wind the rope around it.

"These were treated for comfort. It was another of the new products in the basket. I think you can write your article on all the toys and new products they have alone.

"We're packing all this shit to take home and I'm placing an order for a ton of stuff," he says with a teasing smile.

I roll my eyes at him, but the smile remains on my lips. It's once he has my wrists linked behind my back somehow connected to ropes that are crisscrossed above my belly, right under my breasts, and down the center of my back that I realize his mundane chats have been a distraction. While he talked of placing orders and what he plans to do with all the new toys, he trussed me up to his liking.

I glance in the mirror and I'm surprised by one, how turned on I am, and two, how beautiful this is. It's intricate yet simple. The knots and crossing of the ropes show Ryan's attention to detail. I want to tell him how beautiful it is, but I remind myself to watch and listen.

He takes a step back. "Stunning. Damn, baby. Look at you," he says the words as if he's in awe.

I sit as straight as I can. There's something about having him look at me like this. I feel … empowered.

It's clear that even though he released the fastening of his pants, he's still straining against them. The outline of his hard length is on full display. The leather pants are open revealing the hairs surround that delicious dick of his.

Just when I think he's going to put us both out of our misery he walks off and grabs a chair to drag back across the room to sit before me. Ry takes a seat and slouches down in the chair. A grin takes over his face as my chest starts to heave in earnest. The anticipation is stifling.

"I just want to look at you. Have I told you how adorable you look with your little bump? Don't speak, use your head."

I shake my head, causing him to frown. "I'm sorry, baby. I should have told you by now. I love watching you swell with my life in you. You were gorgeous before, now, you're simply exquisite."

I smile at him as it's all I can do. The lust and desire in his eyes as they roll over me solidify his words. He leans forward in his seat, placing his arms over his knees.

I notice the sweat over his lip and on his brow. He's wound tight, but he's holding back. As I look more closely, I can see all the signs.

The flush of his cheeks, the vein in his neck, the strain of his pants as he pulses within them. It's so hot. I'm doing this to him.

I tilt my chin up as that empowerment turns to emboldenment. I'm on a high as the air charges with the seduction this power owns. Ryan's eyes light up and he moves out of his chair lightning fast, places a hand in my hair and tips my head back as he takes my lips.

"There it is. That's what I want," he says against my lips. "You feel that? You see how much power you have over me?"

He doesn't allow me to answer as he kisses me hard once again. I can't help it. I cry out when he slides his fingers between my legs and pushes two inside me.

He chuckles and nips at my lip. "Shh, baby. I'm only getting started."

He isn't lying. I lose count of the orgasms he gives me as I kneel on the table before him. With every suck of my breasts, stroke of my clit, kiss of my lips, I pant with need and spiral into a world of awe.

Not once does Ryan touch himself or move to penetrate me. It's as I watch this that my love and respect for him go to a new level. This is for my pleasure.

He's ignoring his own need to bring me bliss. His face has turned red and his teeth are clenched. Even his chest looks flushed.

His body is coiled so tightly as he works me over. In this moment, I feel more powerful than I ever have. This man before me in all his glory is hanging on by a thread because of me, yet he's holding all that back because he wants me to be happy.

That's a heady mix that my mind trips over even as I watch the scene before me play out. This time when my orgasm hits me, I release a silent scream that carries with it all the feelings of helplessness. As one of the Mistresses said in a workshop, you will know when you find your place in this world.

The adrenaline and freedom will open the door you need, when you need it. The table is soaked beneath me. Ryan hisses loudly. He cups my face and kisses my lips.

"This is what I want for you."

He nuzzles my neck. Stepping aside and placing two fingers under my chin, he guides my head so I look into one of the mirrors.

"Carmen Nene Nash, that's what a woman with all the power looks like. I'm your slave and your master, as you are mine. Do you understand his restraint now?"

Yes, I do. I totally get it. I get this entire conference and everything I've learned. I think I'm ready. I can face my father. This is my life.

"Talk to me, baby," he says softly.

"Yes, I get it. More than you know."

CHAPTER TWENTY-EIGHT

Triple Play

Carmen

I was surprised when Ryan suggested we spend one of our last nights here in a nightclub. I almost begged off, but Roni talked me into going out. I'm glad I did. I've never been to a nightclub before.

There's so much to take in. Especially from the VIP booth we're in. Looking out at all the drunken bodies flailing against each other is quite amusing.

"You look like you're having fun," Ryan leans to whisper in my ear.

I turn to look at him. Something's not right with him. He's been in a mood since we arrived.

I'm not too sure what that's about. After all, this was his idea. He even provided the cute little black dress I'm wearing.

I was sure they were going to stop me and Roni and turn us away. Imagine my surprise when we skipped the line and walked right in. However, Ryan and John didn't seem surprised at all.

We were led right to our VIP table and a bottle of champagne sat waiting for us. I get the feeling the bottle wasn't the only thing waiting for us. The tension in Ryan and John leads me to think we're here for a reason.

"Yes, I am," I say with a smile. Reaching to cup his face, I tilt my head to the side. "But you don't look like you are."

He turns his face to kiss my palm. That smile I know him for spreads across his face. "I'm with you. I'm always having fun when you're near. I can't wait to have more fun later tonight." He wiggles his brows at me and leans in for a kiss.

He deepens the kiss, and I forget what I had planned to say. Ryan places his hand around my throat and gives a gentle squeeze, I almost come. All I feel is him and the thump of the music.

When he suddenly pulls away, I'm breathless and dazed. Wow. I still don't know what's wrong with him, but if it leads to passion like that.

I'm not too sure I want to fix it. He kisses my forehead before he turns his attention back out to the dance floor. I guess if he says he's fine, I should let it go.

"No Romeo No Juliet" by 50 Cent and Chris Brown blares through the speaker, hitting me in my chest. I cover my belly wondering if the baby can feel all the base surrounding me. A smile comes to my lips.

I go to say something witty to serve Ryan up some of his own sarcasm, but my words are cut short as my gaze lands on a sight I haven't seen the match of since watching the Blacks and their cousins all walk together at Toby's wedding. Now that was a sight.

However, these three who have grabbed my attention give off that dangerous vibe I get from Logan and Brooklyn. I don't know if it's the tats or their imposing height. Or it could be the way the crowd seems to part as they move through and the crazy swag they part the crowd with.

It's like the music has set the tempo of their moments. They all move in sync with each other. The two on the left and right look ahead toward the VIP area. However, the one in the middle has his head bent.

It's not until they get within a few feet of our table that he lifts his dark blond head. Those cold blue eyes beneath dark brows pin me and a chill runs through me. My hands itch to reach for my blades.

Only I don't have any on me. His lips turn up into a smile and I gasp. The gesture transforms his face and he's gorgeous.

Although, what blows me away is when I scan the faces of the other two. It takes a moment for me to realize I'm not going crazy, and I haven't been staring into the face of one person.

There are three of them identical and all with those breathtaking smiles and crazed looking eyes. The only difference is their hair and clothes. They all have neat quiffs like Ryan's usual hairstyle, but their shades of blond vary. From an ash blond to medium then dark. I get the feeling that only the one in the middle has his natural color.

It's crazy. All three lick their lips at the same time. It's hot and scary all at once. I don't realize I'm clenching the hem of my dress until Ryan speaks.

"Make me flatten this motherfucker. I'll put a bullet through all three of your heads at the same time," Ryan says without his usual taunting calm.

The three snort in unison and turn their mirth filled eyes on Ryan. "Ya do know we're distant cousins, mate?" the one on the right says with a faint version of the Australian-English accent I've heard since I've been here.

"We have no problem putting ya ass to sleep, ay," the one on the left says revealing the same accent, but I realize there's something else underneath.

"No problem at all," says the one in the middle with a sinister grin.

"And where exactly will I be?" John stands and says. He moves to the one in the middle and tugs him into a hug. They slap each other's backs good-naturedly. John turns to face us at the table. "Roni, Carmen, this is Alexander, the oldest of the triplets."

"G'day, love," Alexander aims at me and winks.

Ryan flies out of his seat so fast, I don't know it until he's standing behind Alexander with him in a headlock. "Keep playing with me, Lex," Ryan says before whispering something that brings a smile to Alexander's face.

Alexander shrugs Ryan off and fixes the collar of his white dress shirt that's rolled up to the elbows revealing two forearms full of tats. His black slacks and suspenders bring together his rough and sexy look. Funny, all three of them have on Converse. Even the one in the three-piece suit.

"I think ya've scared her," the one in the suit says as he pulls Ryan into a one-arm hug. He winks at Roni. "Good to see ya again, lovie. Ya look well."

"Good to see you without busted knuckles," Roni scoffs.

I turn to look at her. She doesn't seem half as concerned as I feel. Yeah, I get that Ryan and his brothers are all badass. However, this ... these three, they make me want to snatch Ryan and run.

"Yeah, that's always a plus. It's nice to meet ya, Carmen. I'm Maximilian, but everyone calls me Mil. Welcome to our playground."

"Thank you," I say as I find my voice.

"She talks," the last brother says with the slightest bit of amusement. He gives an exaggerated flourish of his hand. "Tobias."

"Nice to meet you, Tobias."

He nods. His personality seems as laid back as his black T-shirt and jeans. He moves to take a seat next to Roni and folds his arms over his broad chest. Maximilian takes a seat next to me.

I look to Ryan to make sure he's not going to flip out again, but he has his head bent with Alexander. The two look to be in a deep conversation. Alexander locks those cold blue eyes on me and finds me studying the two of them.

He tosses an arm around Ry and tugs him out of view. John reclaims his seat between me and Roni and takes a sip from his drink. When he turns those golden eyes on me, he gives me a broad smile and winks.

"Kind of hard to believe our entire family looks like supermodels." He chuckles.

Supermodel and unhinged, possible psychos. Something's different about these three. Wait, not only these three. I'll throw Logan and Cole in there too.

I'll admit. Sometimes my father can give off the same vibe. Honestly, in kindergarten when one of the little girls tried to cut my hair with scissors and pushed me off a swing because I told the teacher. I saw that dark look in my mother's eyes as she tried to beat the little girl's mother's behind. Something begins to nag at the back of my mind, but I lose the thought as Maximilian cuts into my musing.

"I can't believe my little cousin kept that smartass mouth closed long enough to snag a pretty girl like you," he says, smoothing out that accent.

"Did you not hear what I just said about our looks? No offense, Carmen, but you wouldn't have allowed him to get away with half the garbage that comes out of his mouth if he didn't look the way he does," John teases.

"Interesting, boss. Does that mean I allow you to get away with what you do because of your looks?" Roni chimes in.

"Out of respect, I'm not going to answer that," John says, putting his hands up in the air.

"Yeah, yeah. Your cock game is strong and you're kind of nice on the eyes. There I said it for you," she replies.

"Wow, ya weren't joking about her," Tobias says with his brows raised almost to his hairline.

Maximilian pulls a face. "Mate, that's mild."

"Yeah, that kind of is." I wince.

"We're not going to gang up on Roni," John warns and my heart swells. He says it with a smile, but I can hear the protectiveness and see it in his eyes.

"It was good to meet ya ladies. Since we're coming out of the shadows, I hope to see more of ya both," Tobias says and stands.

His words come off odd, but I don't have time to digest them. Alexander appears and the three walk off much the way they came. Ryan reclaims his seat, and something has definitely shifted with him. He's completely brooding at this point.

So much for a fun night out.

Ryan

I ended last night in a good mood. Too bad that didn't last into this morning. We leave in a few days, and I need to get things in order.

Carmen thinks we're returning home, but that's not happening, and I need to figure out how I'm going to get her to go along with a detour. On top of all of that, I needed to make this friendly visit to the three men I wanted to avoid. For a family that wanted to stay out of the Alliance, we Blacks just keep getting deeper into its bowels.

I don't know how we ever thought staying out of it was going to be possible. We're related to half the damn table. Our broken and large family tree has allowed for a lot of pieces to fall into place.

Logan is a genius. He connected all the dots for the ultimate takeover. I still will never know what triggered him and LaSalle to come up with all of this.

There's nothing I can do about it now. We're in this and we'll have to war through it with everyone else. Lex's words are still playing in my head.

"Listen, mate. Ya need to get out of the open. My boys had to break some necks right outside of Sydney.

"They weren't here as tourists. My girls on the inside of the Con say that some sod took special interest in one of the girls and took off a few days ago."

"Wait, one of the girls?"

"Ay ay. Ya know. I didn't think about it when the report came in. Now that ya bring it up, they weren't clear on which girl. Sorry about that, mate. A lot on my mind at the time. I didn't think about Roni."

"Thanks for getting in touch with me. We're not going to chance it either way. It's time to go," I reply.

"I figured you'd say that. My boys will see ya out tonight. We'll be in place at ya signal."

"Remember, she's not supposed to know about her father or what we're all involved in. Keep that slaughterhouse shit to a minimum."

Lex gives me that crazy grin, his eyes turning dark. "It's all we know, mate, but I'll tell my boys to reel it in." He cups the back of my neck and places his forehead to mine. "Good to see you, Ry. We won't be strangers much longer."

"We were never strangers. I'll see you back in the States."

We parted ways and he and his brothers left. I was in a shit mood for the rest of the night. I have too many questions.

Too many things out of my control. I might be the defiant child, but I don't like being defied. When things don't go my way, I feel like the world is out to defy me.

I can't afford that with my girl and my child's safety. Hell, my niece or nephew may be a target and that doesn't sit with me any better.

I sit on the foot of the bed stewing as Carmen uses the bathroom. I need to think fast. We have to go.

"What's going on?"

I look up to find Carmen standing in front of me. I didn't even hear her come out. She cups my face and searches my eyes.

I cringe inside at the lie I'm about to tell. "I left something at the beach house. Lex asked me for a favor, and I realized I left it behind."

"Is it important? Can we go back for it? You said the place belongs to your family, right? Would someone have been there already?"

Her genuine concern is like a punch to the gut. Placing my hands on her waist, I bury my face in her belly. These two are the reason I'm doing this, I remind myself.

Bile rises as the lie sits on my tongue. "I'm going to head back to see if it's there."

"I'll come with you. It's only one day. I don't think I'll miss anything. I have plenty for my story."

She falls right into my plan. I feel like I just used her love to manipulate her. I couldn't feel more like shit than I do in this moment.

"Yeah, sure." I stand and kiss her forehead. "I'm making some calls so we can head out. I'll be right back. Let me tell John we're heading out as well."

All lies, but I need a moment. Protecting Carmen is one thing. Lying to her is another.

It's time for some things to change. I'm not doing this shit anymore. I walk out of the room, ignoring her eyes on my back.

I pull my phone, but I don't call to make arrangements. I call the one person who has never told me a lie and who has instilled in me the morals that form me to my core.

"Hello, my babe," my mother answers.

"Hey, Mom," I reply. I realize the time in Cali and groan. "Did I wake you?"

"No, ye know I rise with the chickens." She sighs. "Talk to me. I can hear ye pain through the phone."

I rub a hand up and down my face. We don't usually drag Mom into our assignments. However, this one is personal.

I enter one of the empty conference rooms and start to pace. "Where do I start? The Alliance has cast the first stone, and the others are responding. Carmen's dad plays a huge role in all of this. She's not safe—"

"Ry," mom says softly. "I already know all of this."

I stop pacing and smile. Yeah, my mom is Cassy Black, and my father is Joe. I should have known better. My parents never reveal the depth of their relationship in public, but I think my mom has been counsel to my dad for years.

"It was my idea to take her away. That doesn't feel right anymore. I feel it. Things have changed and the game plan needs to as well."

"Ye have ye father's instincts. I believe ye, but what's truly the problem for ye. I can tell there's something else."

"She's lying to her dad, and her dad has me lying to her. I'm tired of it. It's making me sick to my stomach.

"I love her. She's pregnant with my kid. I can't have these lies between us. It's bullshit that her father has me in the middle of the lies he's feeding her," I say in frustration.

"Will the truth endanger her safety?"

"No. She's stronger than he gives her credit for. I think she'll handle the truth.

"It's not like it's going away. Like, what the fuck. He has a seat at the table. Did he really think he could hide this from her?"

"Aye, I think it's time I explain something ye will learn when ye have ye own wee loves. From the day that little one takes its first breathe, yer going to want to be everything to it. Ye will want to keep the world from harming that tiny being with everything ye are.

"Yer mistakes, yer dark moments, yer bad decisions will be amplified in yer head. And that's what will make ye wish ye never did those things and ye will be hell bent on yer little one never finding any of it out. It's yer way of protecting them. Do ye see what I'm saying?"

I take a deep breath as if inhaling her words. I get them. I understand what she's trying to say, but Kiyoshi made a choice. He knew that the Alliance would call to his door.

"I hear you."

"Do ye, love? She's his little girl. She sees her father as her world.

"I think ye figured that out by now. Yer father and Nash have been friends for a long time. Kiyoshi tried to leave the Matsumara world behind.

"After marrying Paloma, he counseled your father on leaving that world behind. It's how he gained his seat at the table. He couldn't leave the life, but he could make a difference.

"I think Nash has placed Carmen in one world and lives in the other. Sometimes we need a wee rude awakening to draw us into reality," she says with a bit of a hint in her voice.

"What do you mean?"

"If they don't want to tell each other the truth, maybe it's time we reveal the truth to them. My lads are not liars and ye shouldn't be forced to be one. Besides, I don't like this.

"Ye both should be home with family. That babe needs proper care and we're the safest place to be. No one touches me lads or me lasses. No one.

"Trust ye gut, Ry. Ye say the word and we'll come running."

I throw my head back and groan. Once I set this ball in motion, there's no turning back. Is this what I want?

Carmen is sure to hate me after I place her and her father in a room to allow him to see the truth. Didn't I just try to empower her? I feel like I'm about to ruin all of that.

"Like it or not, Ryan, they both need to know what the other's trying to hide. She loves ye. She'll forgive ye."

"That's a gamble I'm going to have to take. As selfish as it feels, I don't think I can keep this up. My gut is telling me this is the right thing to do."

"Our gut never steers us wrong. I'll tear the world down for ye, Ryan, I will. So do I call in the cavalry?"

"I'll take care of it. Thanks, mom. I love you."

"I love you too, my babe. I miss ye too."

I smile. "Yeah, I miss you all too. See you soon."

"See ye soon."

I hang up the phone with an actual plan in mind. Kiyoshi needs to know exactly what's on the line here. The heat has turned up and we need to mobilize.

"Hello, Dad," I say as my next call is answered. "I have a plan and I'll need your help."

CHAPTER TWENTY-NINE

Force of Hand

Kiyoshi

"There has to be another way to do this. I grow tired of this sit and wait, LaSalle. I agreed to this when I still had the drive for this type of thing. The years that have passed have changed the man I am," I say as I sit across from LaSalle Locatelli and Misha Krupin in the underground rooms of LaSalle's New York home.

His expression is tight. I know he has a lot on his plate with his wife's death and three small children to look after, but this visit is necessary. I need to know what we plan to do next.

It seems I am the first to be hit with assassination attempts on myself and my family. This cannot stand as it is. Changes will have to be made.

"You seem to be handling it all well," he says. "We're getting a little less resistance from the Yakuza after the message you sent with the Sato family."

"Da, this is what I think, no?" Misha adds.

I nod. "I have done what's necessary. I couldn't leave that situation unanswered."

LaSalle sits back in his seat and steeples his fingers together. His gray eyes are assessing as he thinks. I can't help but wonder where his other partner is. I came to see Logan, Misha, and LaSalle. However, Logan has not arrived.

"What do you want to do? It's a little late to pull out. That was what the meeting in Ireland was for." He tilts his head. "What do you think your options are?"

I look between the two men and their hard expressions. LaSalle once did not have this demeanor. At least not as a constant.

I can see things have changed for him. His eyes tell a story I know too well. I lean forward.

"I have all the options in the world," I say so we are clear this is a courtesy visit.

He mimics my gesture, sitting forward in his seat. "If you believe so but let me remind you of one thing. We chose each of you because we thought you had what it takes to see this through. Weak links will not be tolerated. You and I are similar men. We leave nothing to chance."

Ne sighs beside me. "May I speak?"

I look to my son and nod. LaSalle inclines his head as well. I think it's time my son step in.

In my old age, I have no patience for these young men who have never seen or done the things I have to survive this world. I'm old and set in my ways. I've had enough.

"It doesn't serve the Alliance if we begin to fight amongst ourselves," Ne says.

"This I agree with." LaSalle rubs his tired-looking eyes.

I look more closely and see a man who has a great weight on his shoulders. I remind myself of his challenges as he embarks on the great task of shifting the world of organized crime. It's a great thing LaSalle and Logan want to do.

It may look like we are all after power, but this is greater than power. This is an opportunity to restore some humanity.

"Da, I have not done this to fight amongst ranks," Misha mumbles.

"My father has not come to show disrespect or weaken the ranks. He's here to offer you a fresh option," my son continues.

"I'm listening," LaSalle replies.

"I will take his seat. All eyes will shift to me. I will be seen as the weak link and those who wish to challenge will feel more at ease to do so.

"We're forcing their hand in a way. My father will not actually be stepping away. He will operate more as my advisor.

"He will be our eyes and defense. You lose none of the resources or wisdom you chose him for."

Misha narrows his eyes. "This is an interesting card to play. You believe transition will not be questioned."

"We've thought of this. Yes, it's usual as my father is still breathing, but given the nature of what the Alliance is up against, it would make sense that I step in to take his seat. To everyone else Dad is old. No one thinks he's still getting his hands dirty," Ne replies.

"It's no different than what my father-in-law and Uncle have done." I turn to find Uri Donati has revealed himself from the shadows. I have known that he was there all along. "It's a bloody good idea if you ask me."

"Kiyoshi." LaSalle sighs. "You didn't have to come here for this. My uncles trust you and your judgment. You could have just told us this was what you wanted."

"Honor and respect bring me here."

Misha goes to speak, but the door bursts open and Logan storms into the room. He looks livid. I rest back in my chair and observe him. He looks around at the men in the room as rage fills his gaze.

"I told ya I was right. All this shit is enough," Logan grunts. "The late deliveries were one thing. I told ya I had a gut feeling they weren't a coincidence, but now two of my warehouses have been raided, the liquor license for the new pub has been blocked, and I'm being audited. Who the fuck do we pay to prevent this because they need to be fired and shot?"

I turn to LaSalle as he sits with an amused smile and raised brow. "I don't think you'll be shooting my brother or my sister-in-law. I'll have Bobby look into what's going on."

"It's obvious this has been done behind the scenes. Bobby keeps all our shit above board and has an eye on all legit actions. Give me a few hours to get this straight."

"Find out who initiated the raid and audit. I will find out whose payroll they're on and hush the problem," Uri says.

"So they're targeting our businesses as well," I murmur more to myself. "I am not the only target after all."

"Families for generals and finances of heads," Misha replies.

"Makes sense," Ne says. "So we agree. I will step in for my father?"

Logan takes a seat. "Hold on. What is this?"

"As we've told LaSalle and Misha. I'm the oldest member at the table. I agreed to this some years ago. I am no young man as the rest of you are. We have opportunity to take advantage of this."

"It will look like a weakness for me to step down while Ne takes my place and I advise him. More will become bold and we'll be done with this sooner."

"Aye, I will agree to this." Logan nods.

"It's settled," LaSalle says.

My phone rings, drawing my attention. When I see its Joe, I excuse myself. Thoughts of something happening to my daughter cause discomfort in my chest. None of this was meant to reach my wife and daughter, especially not my daughter.

I have regrets when it comes to Nene. I sometimes wonder if I've disillusioned myself by thinking I could create two worlds and keep Carmen from ever learning about the other.

Time and again I try to tell myself that I've done the right thing, but her lies about her schooling and the fact that she still hasn't told me about her boyfriend makes me question it all. I sacrificed respect for my secrets.

"Hello," I answer the call.

"I need you and Paloma on a plane with me and my wife ASAP," Joe says.

I knit my brows. Joe is one of my oldest friends. There are few men I give that title to. Though his request is odd, I will follow without question.

"I am in New York. I will return within the hour and can board the plane as my return flight lands. I will have Paloma meet me there," I reply.

"Cass and I will pick up Paloma. We will be waiting on the tarmac."

He ends the call and my curiosity has risen. I know this has something to do with my daughter. I don't have to ask.

"What have you done now, my spoiled one?"

LaSalle

"Speak your mind, my friend," Misha says as Kiyoshi and Nelson Nash leave.

I run a hand down my face. "This is what we wanted all along. The younger Nash. However, it's early in the game. Do you think he's ready? Does he have the ruthlessness of his father yet?"

"The apple doesn't fall for from the tree," Logan says, his accent thickening. I can tell he's still pissed about the play against his businesses. Sadly, this is only the beginning. "If he's not ready what's coming will make him ready. This road has scorched us all. It's our bones that will tell if we were made for this, not our flesh."

"I see him following in his father's footsteps." Misha shrugs.

"Your cousin still has his daughter with him?"

"Aye, Ry has been looking after her all right," Logan says with a grin.

"Not going to ask." I shake my head.

I have enough going on in my head. I need to get my house in order. Misha has been watching me and Monique's every move. Let's not even mention Monique. I run a hand through my hair.

"You know it's time," Uri says cutting into our chatter.

I work my jaw. "Yes, but not just yet. I will release you both soon enough. We don't want to play our cards too early. I get the feeling we haven't seen all the players raise their hands yet."

Kiyoshi is right in wanting to force our resisters out. I'm only making sure we have them all in view before we show our hand. Timing is everything. Every piece has to fit.

"If this is what you want," Uri replies. "We are ready when necessary."

CHAPTER THIRTY

Don't Know You

Carmen

I think the Universe hates me. As soon as we arrived in Barbados for the second time, I started to get sick nonstop. The little morning sickness from before we went to Australia was nothing.

For the last three, days I've been a mess. Ry has been worried about me becoming dehydrated and the fact that I haven't seen a doctor as of yet. I should have started my appointments around week twelve. I'm now moving through week fourteen or fifteen.

"Here, babe. Drink this," Ry says in my ear.

I groan and lift my head. I feel so weak. Reaching for the bottle of water, I bring it to my lips.

My tank top feels so tight. I start to tug at the front in annoyance. I want to go home.

I'm tired and this isn't as romantic as the last time we were here. Ryan can hardly touch me without me running to the bathroom. All my favorite foods have become my enemy.

"Thank you," I say softly after I down the bottle of water.

"You're welcome. Do you think I can carry you to the bed now?"

"I don't want to get in the bed again. Ugh, I'm so tired of being in bed. Can we sit in the living room for a bit? I want to be around people."

"Sure, I think they're watching a movie or something."

"I'll probably fall asleep."

"No different from John and Roni. I swear, we'll have to strain to hear the movie over their snores." He chuckles and lifts me into his arms.

The moment he has me held to his chest I feel safe and relaxed. My head stops throbbing and I feel like I might fall asleep on the way into the living room. Sure enough, we find John and Roni knocked out with the TV watching them.

John has his legs up as he lays with his head back over one armrest and Roni is lying the same way with her head on the other side of the couch.

I look out of the sliding doors and Torque is in the distance walking the beach. He does that a lot. I've become curious about him.

He seems to have a tortured soul at times. Others, you can't help but smile with him as he gives off a carefree vibe.

Ryan sits in an accent chair, pulling me down onto his lap with him. I snuggle in close and rest my face in his neck. I love that his cologne is subtle enough not to turn my stomach.

"This is perfect," I murmur before I drift off.

Ryan

She's sleeping so peacefully. I wish I could find some of that peace. Her father and mother will arrive with my parents anytime now.

I've second-guessed this plan so many times. However, when I last spoke to Kiyoshi I knew it was time. The old man sounded tired and frustrated.

Something I've never known him for. I know I give him shit, but I don't think it's right that Carmen hasn't at least told him she's dating.

Honestly, I think her father is hurt by that. He knows I care about her. I think he's been waiting to see if she will come clean at least about our relationship.

This is going to burn either way. There's a baby involved. John and Roni stir as the sound of tires crunching over gravel fills the air.

I stiffen and my body coils. I don't know if I should be ready for a fight. The two across from me wake and sit up, but Carmen is still fast asleep. I don't blame her. She's exhausted from retching all day and night.

"Showtime," Roni yawns out.

I heave a heavy breath, she's right, John walks to the back door as Torque signals that the cars are indeed our family. He's been on patrol out there.

Braxton's voice is the first I hear, causing me to groan. Why did I think my brothers were going to stay out of this? Turning my head, I find the entire Black clan filing into the house. Good thing this place is huge and we own the adjunct properties.

"Ry," Brax croons, coming to mess my hair and kiss my forehead.

I shrug him off as Carmen starts to stir a little. However, I freeze as Kiyoshi and his wife move farther into the room and take in me with their daughter in my lap. This is what I wanted.

I wanted Kiyoshi to come face to face with the truth. I guess what I wasn't expecting is the rage that I see in his face as he takes Carmen in. With her tank and shorts on, there's no mistaking her baby bump. I hadn't realized that I have my palm over it until her parents' gazes lock with it.

Her mother grins, but her father looks livid. His eyes are narrowed, steam seems to come from his ears and his head. Nelson moves into the house with that cute chick who's always with him and it's his reaction that seems to get the air flowing back through the room.

"Is she ... Ryan, is my sister pregnant?" Ne seethes.

"For what it's worth. She was pregnant before you asked me to watch over her," I reply.

"What?"

I close my eyes as Carmen's voice rings through the room. I know my girl. The amount of hurt and betrayal oozing from her confused voice slices through me.

She stiffens in my lap before she starts to slowly pull away from me. It's all happening so fast but in slow motion. I'm helpless to stop it. I open my eyes and the pain and confusion on Carmen's face speaks volumes.

This is about to be a total train wreck, but there will be no more lies.

Carmen

I'm still groggy from sleep, but I know two things. My parents and brother are here, and Ryan has been lying to me. What I'm confused about is why he would need to watch over me and what's my family doing here?

"You have been lying to me nonstop," my father bellows.

I'm stunned. While a stern man, my father has never raised his voice at me. I lift to my feet and wrap my middle protectively.

My mother takes off her sweater and takes a seat. She doesn't look surprised at all. Suddenly, I playback that day we worked out. I think she knew then.

"All of this, behind my back." My father waves his hands in the air at me. "School, travel, boyfriend.

"All of it lies. Lie after lie after lie. I waited for you to come clean, to stop treating me like I was born yesterday and here you are pregnant to top it all. I don't know you. Where is my daughter?"

"Kiyoshi," my mother says. "Come, sit."

My father turns to her with a sharp look. "You knew. Why didn't you tell me this?"

"Come, my husband. Sit next to me. You're going to give yourself a stroke."

"The women in my life are out to kill me. Why should I be concerned with anyone else? Grandfather, hm. She's twenty and makes me a grandfather without a husband."

My dad goes to sit next to my mother, opening his suit jacket and flipping it out at his sides before he sits. Mommy leans over and kisses his cheek before whispering something in his ear. He makes that sound in the back of his throat, but you can also see the slight change in his demeanor.

See, she has a way with him. It's like magic. I'm glad she's here because his words have sliced a hole through me. I can't even look at Ryan. I'm still confused.

"Daddy, I wanted to tell you. I planned to tell you. As soon as we returned home, I was going to tell you about the baby."

"We speak every other day. You had plenty of chances to tell me," he says bitterly.

My own anger rises. I'm a grown woman darn it. I'm tired of feeling like a child who needs my father's approval for everything. I won't live like this anymore.

"Listen, I messed up. I should have told you that while I did well in my Journalism classes and I actually liked them for the most part, I wanted to go into visual media. It may be against what you do at your company, but I like it.

"I was wrong for bringing Aunt Mariah into this as well. Yes, I should have told you that I have a boyfriend and I planned to spend the summer with him because we goofed up and I got pregnant, and we needed to get to know each other more. And I should have told you and mommy the moment I found out that I was pregnant.

"But I didn't. Ryan was able to tell his family right away and they accepted us. I didn't think I would have that. You've always made me feel like if I didn't do things a certain way, I would disappoint you.

"I've always felt like the black sheep of the family. Like I've never belonged. You take Ne to Japan all the time. I can't remember the last time I've gone there with my family. I'm always left behind." I huff and push a hand through my hair.

"So no, I didn't think I could tell you. It's been eating away at me that I couldn't pick up the phone and tell you I'm in love and having a baby. I'm happy and I don't think I'm going to finish school. At least not for journalism."

My stomach rolls. I barrel from the room to the nearest bathroom as fast as I can. Everyone moves out of the way.

I'm embarrassed and full of emotions I haven't yet been able to place. This is blowing up in my face and I still don't understand how. Did Aunt Mariah rat me out?

Why are the Blacks here with my family? What was Ry talking about? What the heck is really going on?

CHAPTER THIRTY-ONE

Honor

Ryan

Man, this is worse than I could have imagined. I go to follow after Carmen as she runs off for the bathroom. Kiyoshi stands to block the way.

"You will stay here."

I rock my jaw to hold back the words that are about to fly out of my mouth. I'm not in the mood. There's no telling what I'll say by the time I'm done.

"I will go," Paloma says and follows after Carmen.

"I'm going to take the girls next door and get them settled in," Felix says.

He and the ladies start to file out. My mother and father remain as do the rest of my brothers. Ne and the chick with him bend their heads together before she turns to follow after Felix and the others.

Kiyoshi takes his seat once again, but not without glaring at me. I cross my arms over my chest and glare back. Carmen's words are still slicing through me.

"Sit," Kiyoshi says sharply.

"Ry," my dad warns when I go to let him have it.

I blow out a breath and take my seat. Kiyoshi removes his suit jacket and starts to remove his shirt. I crack my knuckles. Bracing for a fight.

"If you want to get into a fight, we can, but I love your daughter so it's going to be a fight I'm willing to have over and over because I'm not going anywhere."

"Shut up!" he snaps. "You and Carmen think you know so much."

He tugs off his dress shirt and then the white tee beneath it, revealing a surprisingly well-toned and defined upper body for his age. However, that's not what grabs my attention. This man has more ink than I do.

On his torso, there's only a blank stripe down the center of his chest. There are dragons, flowers, Koi fish, even a Samurai on one side. The tats on his arms stop right at the wrists.

"I was a young boy when I lost my father. I was often picked on and teased after. One day I decided, no more.

"I wouldn't be made to feel any less than my empty belly and tattered clothes made me feel. I started to fight back. An acquaintance of my father's had been watching me.

"Genkei pulled me into his fold. Loyalty and honor became my life. My allegiance was to my *oyabun*.

"I cut myself off from everyone I knew to show my loyalty and respect to my new brothers. I didn't speak to my mother for years.

"Not until Genkei took her as his wife. That is a long story, but it caused me to become a different person, to question the choices I had made.

"Then Genkei was killed and I had to flee with my mother until I got her to safety. I was still a boy in the eyes of many. In

America is where my mother found true love and I find my truth.

"When I returned home alone, they were waiting for me to take Genkei's place. I did and I found out everything that had led me to my position.

"I had a score to settle, one that has bound me to this life until my revenge was complete, and well after. So when two babies came to me with this idea of an Alliance, I agreed," Kiyoshi says and stands.

He begins to remove his pants and I look to my dad and mom. They don't seem the least bit fazed. Stepping from his shoes, Kiyoshi drops his pants and turns in a full circle, revealing his back and legs covered in more tattoos. He has a geisha on his back and more of the dragon's body.

"This is a sign of respect and trust," Ne explains.

"Aye, it is," my father says with a nod.

"This is who I am. This is what I've kept from my daughter. The blood that drips from my hands and sword are things I never wanted her to know about.

"My mistake was thinking I could create two worlds without consequences or closing the door to the monsters who threaten the world I've created for my most precious treasures.

"This Alliance, it will do good things in our futures, but first it will reveal the things that go bump in the night. It will reveal us all as men. You want me to reveal who I am to my daughter.

"I want all of you." He looks around the room at my family. "To reveal to yourselves that you are as much a part of this as those of us at the table.

"I want you to reveal the young man you are meant to be. The young man I've watched since you were in diapers. The one who can be responsible and wise.

"My anger is not that my daughter is dating you, Ryan-san. It's that she kept it from me. Your father helped to save my life when I arrived in America.

"Any son of his is a son of mine. But what Carmen doesn't get to do is keep things from me that bring me joy and the humanity that I've so desperately clung to." He takes a pause as tears fill his eyes. I'm stunned. "Paloma brought me my first spark of joy. Then I had my children. My life was the reflection of hell before them.

"Not telling me about a film program that she's excelling in is a greater wound than those I've received in battle. Now, I am to be a grandfather, and it seems everyone has known except for me. The markings you see before you speak of pain, power, wealth, and strength.

"We do not show them to just anyone. You ... you Ryan are my family. It is why I've trusted you with my daughter's life.

"Your father says you have called me here." He gives a curt nod. "Thank you. Again, you show the man I know you will be."

"So he's off the hook. This is all on me?" Carmen gasps, making her return known. She turns her fiery gaze on me. "You were only watching over me for my father. For how long? Did any of this mean anything to you or was I a mistake? Oh my God, I feel so stupid."

"Baby, it's not what you think," I say.

"Save it. I know what those tattoos are. How could I be so blind? I spent years studying the Yakuza out of curiosity.

"I should have put two and two together. The way your men are. The trips to Japan without me. It's all clicking into place. Wow ... just freaking wow. You have a bodysuit."

"This is not something I wanted you to know. I ... I thought of what the Alliance could do to better your life. I never thought of how it would drag you into this life.

"No, wait. That's a lie. I didn't want to think about what it would mean. I wanted to believe I could protect you from all this forever."

"So those men in the parking garage, they were after me because of you?" Carmen says with so much hurt in her voice.

"Yes and no. This is so much bigger than me or you."

"I was pregnant then. Do you understand that I and your grandchildren were in danger because of what I didn't know?"

"You will lower your voice," Kiyoshi bites out. "You were never in any real danger. If Ryan failed to protect you, I knew your mother trained you well. You were walking out of there safely. Instinct would have kicked in."

"It did," I say. "She was amazing."

"Wait, you were there?"

"Yes, I took care of the other guy that was on his way after you."

She covers her belly with her hands. Her lips tremble. My heart breaks as I watch the hurt on her face.

"I was wrong for lying to you, Daddy. I am sorry for that, but you and Ryan have wronged me so much more deeply than that. While I was falling in love with him, I was only an assignment or charge or something. You've been lying to me all this time," she says.

I go to cross the room to her, and she takes a step back. "Carmen, please listen to me."

"No." She shakes her head. "I'll be going to stay with my mother and her family. Please stay away from me."

Carmen

I feel so hollow as I sit curled in a ball in the bed at my great-grandparent's house. My mother sits rubbing my hair as I try to stop crying. I'm so hurt and confused.

"You are mixing together two very different things, child," my mother says breaking into my thoughts. "Your father chose Ryan because of his love for you. Ryan agreed because he loves you. However, the boy didn't want to lie to you. He actually has locked horns with your father over the lies."

"Why didn't you tell me? You could've told me a long time ago. You were in on all the secrets."

"Girl, first, watch who you're talking to before I make you swallow your teeth." She kisses her teeth and rolls her eyes at me. "I agreed with your father. I didn't want you to be a part of that world either. Remember I told you about the day I met your father?"

"Yeah," I murmur.

"I left the restaurant with him, and we spent the day together. It was the best date I'd ever had, but that night was one of the worst nights of my life. Some men attacked me after he dropped me off."

Her eyes take on a distant look. I feel like I'm seeing my mother for the first time. She continues as if she's telling me the story as she relives that day.

"Lucky for me, your father doubled back in time to save me. He told me later that he returned because he regretted not kissing me goodnight." She smiles and gives a soft laugh, but it dies off and an almost haunted look takes over her face.

"To see your father in action. The man is deadly without apology. When he's Kiyoshi Matsumara, *oyabun,* he is a different man.

"I knew then that I was dealing with a dangerous man. He was tender with me long enough to get my tears to stop. After that, he demanded I pack a bag, and he had swords in my hands that very same night before he took me to his bed to claim me as his for the rest of my life."

"Ew, Mommy. Too much."

"Hush, I tell you this so that you know the true Kiyoshi. That night I watched your father tear in two. Kiyoshi Nash is the man who loves his wife and children and wants nothing but the best for them outside of the world he grew up in.

"Kiyoshi Matsumara is a man you never want to cross. He's ruthless, angry, and will destroy anyone who comes next to his family and thinks to harm them." She blows out a breath.

"Nene ... the man is right. You don't need any parts of that world, but you've gone and fallen in love with a part of it. The Blacks and their people ... they're as ruthless as your father.

"I don't know if we ever had a chance to keep you in the dark. You've been a magnet to it all since you were a baby."

"What? What do you mean?"

"You followed your uncle Kin around like a shadow whenever he came to America. Girl, anyone with half a brain would steer clear of that man. Not you.

"First time I ever saw him smile was when you placed your hand in his as he walked through the halls of the house."

I remember that. To me, Uncle Kin was always lonely. I needed to be his friend because no one else would be. I didn't see a dangerous man.

She continues, pulling me from my thoughts. "When men would come to the house to see your father, you would sneak to sit outside his office until I'd find you and drag you away. Never the businessmen who had no ties to his other life.

"No, you would go to the door when there were killers behind it. Then there were the swords. You took up Ne's wooden swords at the age of three.

"You're a better sword fighter than me or your father. You go to a place that looks so much like where your father goes. It's something in the eyes. You are his daughter."

She shrugs. I let her words sink in. It's a lot to absorb and I'm tired.

"You can't keep this baby away from its father," she says and lifts a brow.

"I don't know what I want to do about Ryan. I feel so betrayed. He hurt me."

"You're so hardheaded. He has done this because he was asked to. The boy loves you. Why make him suffer?"

I pout. I don't want to talk about this anymore. The same man I was falling in love with was lying to me. As he made me feel empowered to tell the truth, he also withheld the truth. That's where I have a problem forgiving him.

"I just need some time."

"You're going to do what you want to do. Just know it's going to come back to bite you. Eh."

CHAPTER THIRTY-TWO

Not That Man

Ryan

I'm not that dude. I'm not letting my girl and baby be away from me. Especially when their safety is in question.

We never went to visit her grandparents while here before because the area isn't as secure as I would like. I don't care if Kiyoshi and his whole fucking army are here.

Carmen and our baby belong with me. So I'm on my way to get my family. We'll just be mad together. It is what it is.

Paloma opens the door with a smile on her lips. "I knew it wouldn't be long before you appeared. You're just what my stubborn daughter needs," she says as she steps back and allows me to enter the house.

"How so?" I ask as I turn to face her once inside.

"Carmen will get in her own way because she's stubborn to a fault. She has her own rules in her head that make sense to her." She rolls her eyes and sucks her teeth. "She's also a people pleaser. In this case, I don't think she knows who to please. Which will keep that girl ignoring you for as long as you allow it."

She gives me a smile before she continues. "You're so much like her father in a lot of ways and she's exactly like the both of us. I too can hold onto something until its dead, man." She pats my cheek. "She's asleep in the back room on the left. I'll lock up once you leave."

With that, she turns to what looks to be the kitchen of the home. I start back for the room she pointed out. When I get to the door, Carmen is inside curled into a small ball on the bed with her arms locked around her center.

I lean on the doorjamb and take her in. She's in one of her deep sleeps. I'll have no problem picking her up and taking her back to the beach house. However, I want to look at her for a moment and absorb her.

There are certain things in life you can accept losing. For me, Carmen isn't one of them. We'll work through this.

Moving inside the room, I lift her from the bed and hold her to my chest. She stirs a little and snuggles into me, tossing an arm around my neck. Inhaling deeply in her sleep, she murmurs my name.

"Ryan." She sighs and settles.

See. We can work this out. I love her and I know she loves me.

Carmen

I wake and immediately know something is off. For one, the tanned arm across my middle doesn't belong to my mother. Second, the body heat and scent at my back are too familiar to be mistaken. Third, my mother wouldn't have morning wood stabbing me in my butt cheeks.

My eyes adjust and I look around my surroundings. I'm back at the beach house in the bedroom we shared. I go to toss his arm off me so I can get up and figure out why I'm back here.

"Don't move. I just started to fall asleep," he murmurs into the back of my neck, tightening his hold.

"Get off me. Why am I even here?"

"Because it's where you belong."

"No, I don't," I snap.

"Baby, I love you. Now, shut up and go back to sleep."

In a move so quick, his eyes open in surprise, I turn and flip him on his back to straddle him and wrap a hand around his throat. I glare down at him as my nostrils flare. With narrowed eyes, he glares back at me.

"Don't you ever tell me to shut up. I have feelings, Ry and you hurt them."

He begins to lift from the bed, ignoring the pressure I'm placing against his throat. He narrows those golden eyes back at me. Placing his hands on my butt, he comes nose to nose with me and squeezes.

"Hurting you was not my intention."

"Get your hands off me, Ryan," I say coldly.

"Is that really what you want. Your pulse is saying something else, but if it's what my baby wants ... you tell me."

"So you're suddenly ready to listen to what I want?" I snarl, in fact not wanting him to take his hands off me.

Truthfully, I want to bury my face in his neck and sob. My feelings were hurt by more than Ryan. My father said a few things that cut deeply.

Like, the fact that he doesn't know me. However, I'm not about to fall into Ry's arms so easily. He caused this.

"I always want to listen to your wants. The ones you say with your mouth and the ones that your body tells me," he says, dipping his head to capture my nipple.

"Ryan," I gasp-growl. "Stop it."

"I'm tired of being without you," he groans. "A day was too long."

I snort. "You were never with me."

He makes a disgusted sound in the back of his throat. "You don't even believe that BS. I can hear it in your voice."

He drags his hand up my back to cup my neck, with his other hand he reaches under my shirt and palms my breast. Before I can protest, he nips my lip and tugs. When he backs away, he has a grin on his lips.

"See, I love you. I'm willing to kiss you with that morning breath and all."

"Hrrr." I blow my breath in his face.

"Still not letting you go," he says and this time he takes my lips in a passionate kiss.

I try not to melt into him. I really do try, but my resolve is crushed when he flips me onto my back and pulls my legs around his waist. I whimper into his mouth and cling to his strong back.

He breaks the kiss and rubs his nose back and forth against mine. He stares into my eyes. "Talk to me. I'm listening."

"You should've talked to me. I would have told you that I planned to tell my dad," I murmur.

"Still wouldn't have forced the truth from him. You both needed to come clean. I hate lying, baby."

"I told you I don't have anything to hide. That's because I'm honest from go. You two put me in a fucked-up place."

"Lying to my girl. Hiding shit from the woman I love and compromising how I moved to keep her safe. I hated every minute of it.

"When I came to your apartment that first night, I was there to do a job, but I would have found out where you lived and popped up on your door regardless. We had agreed in Ireland I was taking you out for your birthday."

He cups my face and tips my head back, bringing his lips within a breath of mine. "I protect what's mine. You needed my protection.

"Falling in love with you was already in motion. The favor I did for your dad had nothing to do with us or my feelings for you, other than me taking advantage of spending more time with you."

"Ry," I whisper.

"Yeah, baby?"

"I'm overwhelmed. His words hurt and I don't know if I should trust you, but I want to."

He kisses my forehead. "You can trust me but first shut up until we get some toothpaste in that mouth."

I throat punch him, but with no real force behind it. He falls over to his side laughing with one hand over his throat and the other arm reaching to tug me into his side. I melt into his warmth.

"I'm going to warn you now. You keep putting your hands on me and my mother is going to kick your ass," he taunts.

"I'm sure she knows I could never do anything to hurt you. My love taps are just that. Nothing malicious behind them and not enough to make you flinch."

He chuckles. "Yeah, she knows and so do I." He kisses my forehead. "I'd never do anything to hurt you either, babe.

"I mean that. I didn't bring your dad here to hurt you. I did it because it was the right thing to do. You guys need to be honest with each other."

"Can I be honest with you?"

"Always."

"I don't like being away from you. I needed you and I couldn't run to you because you were a part of the pain."

"I'm so sorry." He sighs. "I'm twenty-four and I do asshole shit a lot, but I see us both growing.

"Stick with me. Grow with me and I promise we'll take the world by storm. You, me, and the kid. We're going to be fine."

"The kid," I say and giggle. "Maybe we should start thinking of names."

"Eric."

I burst into laughter. "I think you should be thinking more along the lines of Erica."

"Sean, Liam."

"Whatever," I mumble and go to move out of his arms.

"Where you going? You hate the names that much?"

I shake my head as I look down at him. "I have to go to the bathroom."

He gives me a smile and winks at me. "Brush them teeth while you're at it."

"Grr."

CHAPTER THIRTY-THREE

Not Funny

Carmen

Oh my God, I'm so hungry and we have so much to do today. First, we have to go to a doctor's appointment for the baby. Then we'll be heading out to Italy for an engagement party and wedding.

Italy was kind of a surprise and last minute for me. I'm a wreck because I needed to find something that would fit my six months—looking more like nine months belly. I think my butt is pregnant too.

I growl as my phone rings. I've been trying to make this pastrami and cheese sandwich for the last hour. Ryan went for a run, and I've been going in circles to get everything done.

I answer the phone and put it between my ear and my shoulder. "Hey, Mommy," I say into the device as I pull my sandwich from the oven.

It smells so good. I do a little dance as I slide it on a plate and sit it next to my juice on the countertop where I was sitting waiting. My mouth is watering as I look at it.

"Hey, Nene. What you up to? You get yourself packed?"

"Yes, I finally finished. It took getting Ryan out of the house. The man worries over everything.

"I couldn't lift a thing to get it done without him getting in the way or taking over. Men don't pack right." I frown as I think of the way Ryan had my suitcases looking.

My mother laughs at me. "Child, I could tell you some stories of when I was pregnant. Your father wouldn't let me out of his sight. Forget lifting a thing."

"I don't mind. Don't get me wrong, but I got twice as much in one bag. I don't know what he was doing when he packed it." I laugh.

I go to sit down and start on my sandwich, but my bladder tells me otherwise. I look at the sandwich longingly and mumble to myself. Reluctantly, I turn for the powder room. It's the closest and I'll be quick.

"What time is the appointment for the baby?" I grin to myself as her accent comes out on the word baby. It's more like a bae-bee in a singy kind of way. "Make sure to get the sonogram pictures for the album I'm making. I'm so excited. That baby will be here sooner than you know it."

"I can't wait. My feet have gone missing and my butt looks like a bus," I say as I try to tinkle quietly.

"You haven't seen nothing yet. You carry nicely though. You look beautiful."

I get all teary-eyed. I've been such a sucker these days. I'm ready to burst into tears at the drop of a hat.

"Thank you, Mommy. That means a lot today. I'm not feeling all that pretty. It took me forever to find a dress let alone two. I've been so frustrated."

She laughs on the other end. "Girl, you're gorgeous. I'm sure you're going to look stunning in whatever you found. Enjoy these days. When stained T-shirts and wild hair with lollipops hanging from it becomes your life, you'll be longing for today's troubles."

I flush and wash my hands as I finish up. My stomach growls. I look at the phone and see I need to hurry. Ryan should be back soon, and we'll need to head out as soon as he has a quick shower.

"Mommy, let me get off of here to eat before— No! That's not yours," I cry out as Ryan sits his sweaty butt at the counter eating my sandwich.

I burst into real tears. That was the last of the pastrami because his greedy-self devoured the pound and a half we just bought. I stomp my foot and ball my fists.

"I'll call you back, Mommy." I sob into the phone before I hang up.

Ryan looks at me with a mix of confusion and the look of a little boy caught with his hand in the cookie jar. I storm over and snatch the plate away. More tears fall as I look down at the demolished sandwich. There's nothing but a bite left. Barely that.

"Why? Do you know how hungry I am? What made you sit there and eat my sandwich?"

Ryan

Oh my God. I'm trying my damn best not to laugh. I feel so fucking bad, but she's crying and pouting and she looks so cute.

I'm going to make her another sandwich. I'll fix this, but she's so adorable as her nostrils flare at me. I get up and round the counter.

She gives me the evil eye as I get closer. Her lips are trembling as tears soak her cheeks.

"It was sitting there. I thought you were trying to feed me before we leave. I'm sorry," I say and reach out to tug her into me.

She knocks my hand away and stomps her foot. "This isn't funny, Ryan. I can see the laughter in your eyes. I was craving that sandwich all night and all day. I was finally going to get to eat it."

I reach to thumb at her tears. "I'll make you another one—"

"With what? Pastrami dust?" she snaps.

I snort out a laugh before I can hold it in. "What?"

"That was the last of the meat, you jerk. You can't make another one."

My heart actually sinks, and I feel like a big ass. "Aw, baby, I'm really sorry. I didn't know. I thought you left it for me."

"I'm not that good a girlfriend," she mumbles.

"Yes, you are. That's why I thought you made it for me. I'm so sorry. Come here," I coo.

"No. You stay away from me. I'm going to sit in the car. Take your shower and let's go."

"Babe—"

"No, Ryan. I wanted that sandwich. I knew I should've eaten it before I went to pee."

"You can have the last bite."

The glare she gives me causes me to take a step back. I place my hand on her belly and smile when the baby moves. I drop the hand away as Carmen narrows her eyes more.

"You don't get to smile at us. You just ate our baby's sandwich."

I wince. Damn. I feel really bad. She's totally pissed. That was a low blow. "I'll shower," I mumble and head for the bedroom.

Carmen

"What's going on? Where's Ryan?" My father jumps from his seat as I board his plane.

I refuse to fly with Ryan and his family to Italy. I'm still pissed about my sandwich. Not only did he eat it, but he burped the darn thing up all the way to the doctor's appointment, making me even more hungry.

I sat eating a bag of fruit that tasted like cardboard to my senses that were ready for my sandwich. That car ride seemed to take forever. I was ready to choke my sandwich back up out of him by the time we arrived. I could taste it in the air.

"I wanted to ride with you guys." I shrug.

"Right," my mother says as she gives me a knowing smile.

I called her and asked if I could fly with them. I need a break from my boyfriend before we get into a huge fight. My hormones are not making me a nice person and Ryan takes nothing serious.

"Hmm. I don't want to know," my father grumbles and takes his seat once again.

I take the seat next to my brother and he wraps an arm around me and tucks me into his side. Kissing the top of my head he holds me tight. There's nothing like having an older brother.

"I will get you that sandwich when we land. I know a place."

I turn my face up to look at him. He winks at me as he tries to suppress a laugh. I change my mind. I tug out of his hold and text Ryan right away.

Me: *You jerk. You told my brother.*

Ryan: *I'm trying here, babe.*

Me: *You should've tried not to eat my sandwich, doofus.*

Ryan: *Hahahaha. I'm sorry. Stop being mad at me. I love you.*

I don't reply. I don't want to stop being mad. I want my sandwich.

CHAPTER THIRTY-FOUR

Fix This

Ryan

"You all right?" Felix says in my ear. "Nick and Sephora are here and you're not over there busting his chops."

I snort and nod my reply. I can't take my eyes off the woman in the bronze-colored dress who's turning me on. Her skin is glowing, and her legs are revealed, looking longer and sexier than ever.

Just look at her. She's lighting up the room. At six months there's no mistaking it, she's swollen with my child growing inside her.

It looks so hot on her. My cock stirs beneath my kilt. It's been two days too long since he's gotten some attention.

I'm not interested in servicing my own piece. That's for Carmen and Carmen alone. However, I know I'm not suffering alone. The lust filled looks she gives me say it all. No matter how hard she tries to hide them.

She's been dodging me since she ditched me to fly with her parents. I'm still pissed she gave me the slip while I was taking a shit. That sandwich has been the bane of my existence since I ate it.

My mother laughed her ass off on the plane ride here after I told her why Carmen wasn't with me. Twelve hours of my mother ribbing me and my brothers joining in on the laughter. My father's face turned so red as he tried not to laugh, he looked like a tomato.

For once I wasn't the one with all the jokes. I'll give it to her, my mother had some good ones. Yes, I did learn a valuable lesson. You do not eat a pregnant woman's food.

Carmen has refused to be in the same room with me without her parents or brother around. She's even slept at a separate estate for two nights. If I wasn't needed by Toby and this Alliance shit, I would have put a stop to this two nights ago. Carmen's smart. She figured that out fast and used it.

I didn't think she would carry this out this long. I was sure at the doctor's visit she would have cooled off. Especially once the baby came up on the ultrasound. I was so sure she was going to give in.

"Would you like to know the sex of the baby?" the doctor had asked.

My eyes were glued to the screen in awe. Our little creation was on there, sucking their thumb. It couldn't have been more real for me than in that moment.

I turned my gaze to Carmen to see her reply. Her eyes softened as she looked from the screen to me. I bit my lip as I shook my head no.

I wanted it to be surprised. There's the bet we made, but I wasn't ready to settle it. I think she read my mind.

Her lips turned up into a soft smile. It was the first smile she gave me since I had left the house for my run that morning.

"No," Carmen answered the doctor.

I reached for her hand to squeeze it and just like that, the shutters came down. It was as if we hadn't had that small moment. She's as fucking stubborn as her father.

I, for one, am over it. I thought the sandwich was for me. It was just sitting there.

How was I supposed to know she was in the bathroom? Was I wrong for laughing? Yeah, but I'm me. I'm a dick. That shit was funny.

I most likely wouldn't have laughed had I realized I had eaten all the cold cuts the night before. I woke up starving in the middle of the night. Honestly, I had my own craving.

However, I think this is way worse than how mad she was about me having her dad come to the Barbados beach house. I admit I sort of screwed that up. I could have handled it a little more smoothly.

Hey, shit happens. If everyone around me weren't playing a game of Pinocchio, I wouldn't have had to play my hand. Yet, that blew over a lot faster than this.

All over a sandwich.

Watching her greet LaSalle and Tasha across the room with her family doesn't even make sense in my head. She belongs standing with me and my family. She's a Black and so is our baby.

She would be my wife already if it were up to me. The world should know she belongs to me.

"You two still haven't fixed that shit?" Wyatt says in my ear.

I roll my eyes. He knows we haven't. Carmen would have been on the plane with us if we had or at least at the Château we've been staying at.

She would also be over here in my arms. I turn to lock gazes with my brother. He has the perfect little family.

Nora and Evan keep a smile on his face. Nellie is always right beside him. There isn't a thing more he could ask for.

I haven't seen him happier. That's what I want for me and Carmen. I've gotten used to her living with me.

I love waking to her smile. I turn to look back at her. She doesn't look happy at all. That fake smile isn't fooling anyone.

"No, but I'm done waiting her out," I reply.

"I'm surprised it took you this long. You two look like two sad puppies," he says, a hint of a smile in his voice.

I turn to look at Wyatt again and find Noah and Braxton with their eyes on me as if they're in agreement. I love my brothers, but I'm glad they haven't stuck their noses into this. That would only make it worse.

I think she's still pissed because I told her brother. The asshole was only supposed to get her a sandwich, not snitch me out. While she's been steering clear of me, I have texted Carmen every day and I call to leave messages every night since we've been apart.

She gives one word responses unless I ask about the baby. I'm not going to lie. I miss her. I miss the fuck out of her.

"It's time ye go get me daughter-in-law. Go be a Black. You'll have her in your arms in no time," my mother says as she cranes her neck to look up at me.

I smile, wrapping an arm around her shoulders and give her a hug. "You know I love you, right? Even though you were relentless on the plane."

She turns and kisses my cheek as she chuckles. "Aye, it was fun though. Always good when you're on the other end of the jokes. That smart mouth gets ye in trouble all the time. How's a taste of ye own water?"

I plant a sloppy wet kiss on her cheek.

"Ach, gross. Ye little fucker."

I burst out laughing as I give her a little squeeze. She reaches to mush my face away as I laugh. Mom is strong as heck.

"Go get yer lass before I hurt ye. Carmen has baby brain. I would stay mad at ye father for the dumbest crap for weeks. I see the way she looks at ye, the lass is ready to give in."

I release my mother and turn toward Carmen again. I catch her looking at me for the hundredth time. She's been sneaking peeks since we arrived.

My lips turn up. Yeah, it's time. I'm not returning to the Château without her in my arms. Next time I step into my bedroom, it's going to be with my girl in my arms.

"Sucks to be you," Brax taunts behind me.

I shrug. "You worry about your own house."

"Nothing to worry about in my house," he scoffs.

"Oh yeah? I hope your kid looks like its mother. You're the only one of us who came out ugly."

"You wish. Suck my ba—"

"Braxton, ye better not say it," my mother chides, bringing a wider grin to my lips.

I toss up my middle finger and saunter after Carmen who has slipped out of one of the side doors. This is one of the safest places she could be, but I'm leaving nothing to chance. Besides, it's time we talk.

I've had enough.

Carmen

Inhaling deeply, I fill my lungs with the fresh night air. Something about the grounds here reminds me of the ones in Ireland. I haven't put my finger on it yet.

I look around trying to get it to click for me as I work to clear my head. I turn to look over at the gardens and think about walking into them. Now that's something that wasn't on the property in Ireland.

I wonder what they look like during the day? We'll be here for a few days. I'm sure to find out as we come back here for the other festivities.

So much has changed as I take a look around our world. Things I didn't notice before stand out as clear as day. Like my mother's companions.

I hadn't noticed how watchful they are. Now I see that they're like two secret service women. They move when she moves.

There's so much I've observed, but what sticks out most tonight is that I'm in love with Ryan Black and that kilt and tuxedo jacket are going to be the end of me. How does he make a kilt look so sexy? It isn't the first time I've seen him in one, but it's twice as sexy tonight for some reason.

I'm blaming my stupid hormones. I pout and blow out a breath. I should probably head back.

However, I realize my mistake when he covers my belly with his strong hands and buries his face in my neck. I know it's Ryan because I know his cologne and the feel of his arms around me. I chide my body for melting into him so easily.

The baby moves as if knowing its father is near. Ryan's lips turn up against my skin. He gives a small chuckle.

"At least one of you misses me."

"The baby is a traitor."

I swear. Since the first time Ryan felt this kid move the baby moves for him when he's near. I've woken to him talking to my belly. It's only been like a week since he's felt it, but it's been the same.

Ryan gives a full belly laugh and tugs me closer to his front. His warmth cradles me, and I can't deny it. The baby isn't helping. I feel guilty as if the two have missed each other.

"I missed you," Ryan says in my ear before nipping it.

He turns me in his embrace. I keep my eyes on his chest, closing them when he kisses my forehead. I shouldn't crave his touch.

I want to stay in my feelings. It's like I can't resist him for long. He pecks the side of my lips.

"Ryan," I warn.

"Carmen," he mocks my voice. "I miss you, baby. I know you miss me too."

He glides his hands down my back and I shiver. I'm annoyed with myself. It's becoming harder to ignore him.

He starts to sway me from side to side. I'm tired. I'm tired of fighting him. I'm tired because this baby is taking everything from me.

Plain tired. In this moment, I can't even remember why I'm so darn mad at him. Before I can protest, he crushes his lips to mine.

I resist for all of two seconds. I moan into his mouth and lock my fingers into his hair. He deepens the kiss, taking my breath away.

Wow, two days *has* been too long. I need to remember not to get so mad for so long. It's only torture for myself.

"This dress looks so good on you," he says against my lips. "Your legs are sexy as fuck. I can't wait to wrap them around my neck."

He squeezes my butt in his big hands. I can't help but wonder how long we have to stay here. His length is pressed into me as if his mind is in the same place.

"How long is the party going to be?"

"Doesn't matter. We're about to miss at least an hour."

"What?"

He takes my hand and places it under his kilt. My mouth pops open as my hand meets bare skin. I wrap my hand around him and smile.

"You're not wearing any underwear?"

"Surprise," he says wiggling his brows. "Now come on. I have something I want to show you."

I laugh but follow him as he tugs me along. I don't know where we're going, but it feels right to be at his side. The most complete I've felt in days.

CHAPTER THIRTY-FIVE

Pushing Too Far

Johnathan

Walking out onto the second-floor balcony, I inhale and blow out a long breath. I scan the vast grounds and shake my head as I see my brother and his girl below, disappearing into the gardens. His kilt and Carmen's bronze dress are my first clue that it's the two of them.

The next is the fact that Ryan is towering over her. At six seven, my little brother is probably the tallest guy here. Carmen is half his size.

I'm glad they're working things out. The kid truly cares about her. Usually, Ry could give a shit about anything.

I have my own shit I need to smooth out. Enough is enough and there are times when I'm pushed too far. This is one of those times.

"You going to tell me what's going on with you?" I direct at the person I've been looking for.

"Nothing," she says in that detached way of hers.

I place my arms on either side her of her, caging her in as I grasp the railing. The fruity smell of her perfume is intoxicating. This dress that's encasing her curves and full pregnant belly is one of my favorites I've seen on her.

It's simple, yet the black fabric accentuates all the right features. Her hips, legs, ass, and breasts. All the curves I've come to know so well.

I press closer, allowing my heat to engulf her. The move draws a shiver from her. Looking down at the side of her face, I study her.

She can hide from everyone else, but not me. That's not going to work. I place my chin on top of her head, bringing one hand to her belly.

I often wonder how we got here. This wasn't at all how we started. However, I saw it coming a mile away.

"I'm not having that. Talk to me."

She sighs and shifts her weight in my hold. I wrap my other arm around her, trapping her to my body. I latch my lips onto her neck, dragging a moan from her lips.

"John," she whimpers.

"Tell me what's wrong."

"Unless that's an order, no," she replies.

I think for a second. I'm tempted to give the command, but I don't. I turn her to face me instead. Her dark eyes lock with mine and I search them for answers.

I purse my lips. "You're pregnant. There's nothing we can do about it right now."

"I'm going to do this, John."

"Not while you're pregnant and having complications, to begin with. Let it go."

"Let it go," she seethes. "Do I have to remind you what was done to us?"

"No," I say tightly. "You don't have to remind me of—"

I cutoff and claim my temper. Last thing I want is to start a heated argument with her. She shouldn't be stressed. I run a hand through my hair and close my eyes.

"You don't have to worry. I'm not going to disappear. Not today, but I have a lead. I want to look into it before it's too late," she says, causing me to pop my eyes open and glare at her.

"What is it? I'll handle it."

"No," she says firmly.

"It's that or nothing. You decide."

She works her jaw with her stubborn ass. God, this woman means the world to me, but she drives me up a freaking wall. I cup her face in my hands and lean in until we're breath to breath.

"Your choice. You can't have your cake and eat it too."

"What if I hadn't made it out of that warehouse? What if that Russian guy hadn't helped me escape death? What then?"

"Are you asking yourself those questions?" I say against her lips.

"Maybe."

I lick her plump lips. "We'll never know because you were meant to survive. You need to stop beating yourself up because you did. I promised you we'd settle the score. You know I've been trying to find her. I've been digging, baby. For two years I've been looking everywhere I can."

"It's been three since I last saw her. What if she met with the fate I escaped? Here I am in this fancy dress and shoes, at this fancy party and she could be dead or worse, living through hell."

"You have to stop blaming yourself. Where is this coming from? You've been fine for months now."

"You think I was fine. It's what I want you to believe."

"Bullshit. You're racking up punishments, baby. I've counted two lies so far. Keep playing with me."

Lust fills her eyes. I would kiss her, but that would be what she wants. I won't allow the distraction.

"I should've kept pushing you away," she whispers. "I don't deserve you."

"Lie number three. We'll have to wait until we return home for what I have planned for you." I circle her lips with my nose. "I can't wait until we can return to full play. I think you forgot a few things in the last few months."

"The only thing I've forgotten is what my mission was. I never should have gotten sidetrack—"

I cut her off with my lips. We've been here before. Not recently, but when she first realized she was pregnant.

I'm not sorry that it happened. Roni has been on a death mission from day one. The revenge she seeks is likely to get her killed. Nate never should have allowed her to start training.

He saw his error too late. When I stepped in to do damage control, we all knew it was too late. She trusts no one and has scars so deep I don't know if I'll ever reach them to heal what's been done. No matter how much I wish I could.

She moans into my mouth and melts into me. The demanding kiss is just the thing I need to get her to relax and let go of her thoughts for now. I deepen it and relish in the feel of her warm body against me.

We're different. We show our emotions differently. I understand what she needs and because of that, I'm one of the few who has completely earned the ounce of trust she's willing to give. Or so I hope.

You never know when she'll turn the tables on you. I've come to expect that and accept it. When Roni needs me to prove myself, I always do.

"John." She breaks the kiss and places her head to mine. "What if this all falls apart? What if our baby—"

"Shh." I kiss her forehead. "Our baby will be fine. You're thinking too much. Seven months. You've made it this far, we'll have our baby and everything else you'll leave to me."

She nods and purses her lips as tears build. It takes a lot for Roni to cry. I think the pregnancy has gotten to her.

"Hey, I'm here. I'm always here. You're not alone."

She nods her head again.

Roni

I nod my head because I can't tell him how scared I am. Have I gotten a lead? Yeah, but that's not why I've been distant with John.

So we can add a fourth lie to my punishment. If I weren't ready to lose my mind, I'd be more excited for him to make good on that promise. However, I'm having sharp pains.

They're not that often, but it happened this morning and not too long ago while we were greeting the guests of honor.

I'm trying my best not to freak out. This pregnancy has not been easy. I don't even want to think of why because the rage will fill me up and consume me again.

"Baby, are you sure you're all right?"

"Yes, a little hungry. But fine."

He narrows his eyes on me. I can't let him see too much. If I do, he'll read all the way through me.

It's one of the things that draws me to him. He sees me. John has seen me from the first day we crossed each other's paths.

He opens his mouth to say something but changes his mind and kisses my forehead. I'm grateful. I don't want to ruin this trip for everyone. I'm already the odd one out.

Well, I like spending time with Carmen. The others don't give me shit, but they've had their clique before I came around. I tend to feel out of place with them, I know it's not them, they try. I'm the one who's closed off.

"Come," he says in that deep voice, and I shiver. "Let's get you something to eat."

I start to walk off the balcony quickly. So quickly, I run into someone as I move through the doors. I look up into those blue eyes and I know it's him.

I never thought I'd see him again. He narrows his eyes at me and removes the phone from his ear. The way his gaze sharpens on me makes me feel like he's peeling my skin back.

"Hey, Misha. Sorry about that," John says as I stand speechless.

"I know you, da? From where?"

I don't answer. I fight against the memories as they try to push themselves forward. I lick my dry lips and stand straighter. I'm not that same girl.

"No, I don't think you do," I reply with more confidence than I had seconds ago.

He narrows those icy blue eyes farther. "Da. I do. Your face. I remember your face."

His brows furrow. He's working overtime to place me. He may have saved my life, but I still don't know what he was doing there that night.

I won't risk being dragged back into that hell by telling him the truth. John moves behind and wraps his arms around me. His warmth and strength are just what I need at the moment.

Pain starts to trickle across my back, increasing by the second. I bite the inside of my cheek. The pain passes as fast as it comes. I think about telling John, but I remember we're here on business and pleasure. He's needed here.

"I don't think you've officially met," John says to this Misha guy. "This is Roni."

"Roni, this is Misha Krupin."

Misha reaches for my hand and brings the back to his lips. "It is pleasure to meet you. I will figure out where I know you from. It will come to me."

With that, he turns and leaves. I tilt my head back and look at John. He shrugs.

"That's Misha for you. Do you know him?"

I shiver. The answer is yes, but again I'm going to add a lie to the list. I turn my attention to my purse as if I'm looking for something.

"No, I don't."

John tugs my body close and leans into my ear. "You have told me at least six lies this evening. We will talk about them all. Every single one as I make you come so much you beg me to stop, or should I hold them from you? Hm. We will see, won't we."

CHAPTER THIRTY-SIX

Triggers

Carmen

I jump for the third time as a random sound outside triggers me. It's been this way since Italy. I never thought I'd attend a wedding that was shot up.

That's stuff I've seen in movies. A world I'm so far removed from. I think I now understand why my father wanted to keep me in the dark.

"Hey," Ryan says into my ear and wraps his arms around me. "You're safe. I'll never let anything happen to you."

I nod my head slowly and reach for the cup I dropped into the sink before the loud sound. My hands are shaking. It's been almost a month and I'm still jumpy and nervous.

All I can remember is Ryan shielding me with his body. At one point, someone gave him a gun, and he stood ready to return fire. I think my brain shut down after that.

It was such a gorgeous wedding. Days of food and celebrating. I would love a weeklong wedding like Tasha's.

We were having so much fun as the reception started to wind down. And then the first shot rang out. I still feel for Tasha's sister.

She lost someone. At least from what I gather, it was someone important to her. Me and the other ladies were pretty much rushed into cars that sped off to get us to the château.

Once there, we all packed our things to leave. I was a nervous wreck until Ryan and his brothers came storming in the doors with their dad. It wasn't long before we were on a plane returning to the States.

Ryan covers my shaking hand. "Hey, are you listening to me? I'll always be here to protect you."

"You can't promise that," I choke out.

"Yes, I can. I don't like lying, remember? I'll always do whatever's in my power to live up to that promise."

He shuts off the sink and turns me to face him. I look into his eyes and see the sincerity of his words. When he cups my face, I nuzzle into his hand.

"What if you're not around?"

"Babe, I've developed a sixth sense when it comes to you. If I'm not there, know that I'm on my way and I'm going to get there right on time."

I wrap my arms around his waist and hold on tight. As tight as I can with my bump in the way. If I hadn't seen the sonogram myself, I'd swear we're having twins.

"Everything has been so scary. The wedding, Roni going into labor early. I feel like we haven't had time to breathe. Something is always coming at us," I murmur as I press my cheek to his chest.

"It comes with the life. Quiet always makes me ... I don't know. It's like I'm more watchful when it's quiet.

"The silent moments are when the plotting is going on. I never trust silence."

"Oh God. So you're fine with all this chaos," I groan.

He reaches to pinch my chin and lifts it. "You have the safest seat in the house. The chaos has to go through me to get to you."

I want to believe him. In this moment, I latch onto his words like a safety blanket. It's the comfort I need.

Everything has changed. I haven't been to my parents' house since we returned. Oddly enough, they haven't pressed for me to come by either.

Which speaks volumes. This is all so much bigger than I comprehend and for once, I'm not itching to know the story.

"Ry?"

"Yeah."

"I want her to learn to fight and stuff. Like my parents taught me. Maybe you can teach us to shoot too."

He snorts. "Yeah, I'll teach you to shoot. That's not a problem and when *he's* old enough to start *his* uncle Noah will be ready."

"Noah is good with the kids. So *she'll* be in good hands." I laugh.

He gives me a little squeeze. "It's good to hear that laugh. I'll be happy either way.

"Boy or girl. Although, I don't think God would do that to me. Do you have any idea how crazy I'd be about my little girl? Like she'll have trackers in her sneakers and shit."

I bury my face in his chest to stifle my laughter. I've seen how protective all the guys are. They hover around Lulu and Nora to make sure they're safe.

It's kind of comical and I don't think they notice that they're doing it. I can only imagine Ryan with his own daughter. I look up at him and place my chin to his chest.

"I think you're going to make an amazing father."

"What about husband?"

My lips part. I blink at him as if my brain has taken an exit and left me to fend for myself. I don't know what to say to that.

I mean, it's not the first time he's said it, but things are so much more serious between us now. We're having a baby together. I've all but moved out of my apartment to start living with him.

Have I thought about marriage? Yeah, once or twice at the wedding in Italy, but I never let myself get carried away. After all, he hasn't mentioned it since we returned home from the Barbados.

Ryan laughs. "What happened? Cat got your tongue."

"I ... I don't know what to say. I ... well, I hope you will. To whoever you marry."

He frowns at me. Cupping the side of my face and brushing his thumb over my cheek. His gaze is so penetrating, I feel like I'm frozen in place.

"You still haven't figured out who you are to me?" he asks almost as if he's having the realization for himself.

"Ry, some days I still wonder why you're with me. I still think you're way out of my league," I say and bite my lip.

It's the truth. I sometimes wonder if he's still with me because of the baby. Ryan is so much more experienced than I am.

He's four years older and his life is in order. Like, he loves his job, and he has this forever home that he'll raise a family in.

I've never once been arrogant to think that will be with me and the baby. I don't want to just be his baby mother, but I'm well aware that it could come to that. We've truly only been together for barely seven months, if that long.

He nods. "Okay." He gives another nod. "All right."

"What?" I ask in confusion.

"Nothing," he says and kisses my forehead. "I'm going for my run. I'll see you when I get back."

I'm left looking after him as he walks out of the kitchen and heads out of the house. I'm not sure what just happened, but I get the feeling that a whole lot has changed in that one conversation. I'm not sure if that's a good or a bad thing either.

Ryan

"What's up?" Brax asks as he jogs beside me. "You've been in your head since we met up."

I needed someone to talk to after my conversation with Carmen this morning. I called Brax and we met up between our houses. I was grateful that I could find the perfect house close to all my family. I live within blocks of Brax and less than a three mile radius away from everyone else.

"I think it's time I go shopping for a ring," I blurt out.

Brax slows to a stop. I stop and turn to look at him. He has a crooked grin on his face as he places his hands on his hips.

"Thanks," he says.

My brows pinch. "For what?"

"You just won me a stack from each of our loving brothers." He smiles like an idiot.

Figures. I'm not surprised at all. It's something I absolutely would have initiated.

"You all bet a grand that I'd propose?" I scoff. "Who doubted that shit?"

"Nah, wasn't about if, it was when. Wyatt and Noah didn't think it would click until after the baby."

I run a hand through my hair and laugh. "I can't be mad. I've lost money on both of them."

"All jokes aside," Brax says more seriously. He folds his arms over his chest. "Why not? I mean, you guys live together already. The baby will be here in a few months. You're crazy about her, kid. We all see it. Heck, she's crazy about you for some reason I don't understand."

"Fuck you. You do know Heather is just as crazy as your ass. It's the only reason you two are married."

He shrugs. "What's your point? Besides, I heard all about Carmen. Bro, if you're not careful she might kick your ass."

I lift a brow. "This is true. She flipped me and choked me one night, I swear I was about to nut."

"Oh come on, I don't want to hear that shit. And I thought John was bad." He shakes his head.

I wave him off. "We're getting away from the point. I need to get a ring and I have to figure out when and how to propose."

"You know you're asking the wrong brother, right? I didn't do any of that shit."

I groan. He's right, but he was my go-to. I totally should have called Felix or Noah.

Fuck.

I draw a hand down my face. I'm sweating and not from the run. Knowing how Carmen feels I don't want to mess this up. I need to show her once and for all that I'm not out of her league. She's everything I've ever wanted before I knew what I wanted.

"What's this about?"

I look my brother in the eyes and debate on whether or not to reveal this. It's not like my family hasn't known that I've been after Carmen and that she was set on avoiding me in the beginning.

"She still thinks I'm out of her league. It's bullshit. That girl is amazing and I'm lucky I found her. I need her to see I'm in this. I love the fuck out of her. She's perfect."

Carmen can be shy, nerdy, fierce, and she's so damn smart. Not just book smart. I've dated girls who don't have half the common sense that Carmen has.

She's been on top of so much with the baby. Our house is baby proofed. She's been looking into daycares and a pediatrician. All shit I haven't thought once about, and I know these aren't things her mother has told her to do because I've heard them on the phone when her mother has brought these things up after the fact.

Twenty and she blows my mind with her thoughtfulness and her attention to shit. She's more my equal than she will ever know. Which pisses me off even more that I didn't notice that she's still not totally secure in our relationship.

I have to fix that. It will be my job from today forward. She will forever know that I'm in love with her for life.

"So you want to propose so she doesn't leave your ass?"

"You know what … never mind. Forget I mentioned it," I grumble.

"Relax," Brax says as he laughs. I glare at him. "I'm busting your balls. I'll help. I didn't do the big proposal, but we both know I nailed it with the wedding."

I roll my eyes. "Dork. Do you have any idea how stressed I am?"

"Yeah, I do. That's another reason I know you're crazy about her. Come on. We can brainstorm while we finish this run. I'll call the jeweler that set Heather's ring. We'll have you straight in no time."

Brax pulls me into a hug and pats my back. I'm so glad I can count on my brothers when I need them. I seriously don't know what I would do without them.

I want to do this one right and for all my smarts, I know when it comes to Carmen I can goof shit up. My direct approach can use a little finesse this time. I plan to be her husband, not some dude she sleeps with who got her pregnant.

Operation Mrs. Carmen Black has been in session. Now it's time I close the deal.

CHAPTER THIRTY-SEVEN

See Me Clearly

Carmen

"Carmen, get that ass naked and in my bed," Ryan calls through the house.

I nearly spit my juice across the living room. He has returned from his run with a box in his arms. I look at him curiously.

He has a sexy smile on his sweaty face. His hair is wet and plastered to his forehead. He's sexy even fully dressed.

His white hoodie with the red embroidery fits his sculpted body with love. Those sweatpants should be outlawed. I frown.

It never occurred to me before that he goes out with that print showing. Has he lost his mind? Now I know why the neighbor always smiles when she sees him.

"Have you tried compression shorts or something under your sweats?" I don't realize how hard I'm frowning until he starts to roar with laughter. I force myself to focus. "What's in the box?"

"Some goodies I ordered before we left Australia. I'm going to shower. You get that ass in bed. Daddy's going to give you some special attention."

I burst into laughter. "Did you bump your head on that run? Daddy?" I give him a pointed look.

"I'm someone's daddy, woman. Stop with all the mouth. I'm horny just thinking about all the shit in this box.

"Don't you dare take those glasses off. Let's go," he says and starts for the bedroom as if I'm supposed to follow without question.

I shake my head. He's crazy. However, I'm curious as to what's in the box. I didn't know he made an order before we left. We had to leave so abruptly.

It dawns on me now that we didn't have to leave because he left something behind. Which takes my thoughts back to the nightclub and his cousins. I've wondered how they fit into all of this.

I could spend hours falling down that rabbit hole, but instead, after a few minutes, I scoot off the couch and follow after Ry. Or should I say, I wobble after him as best I can. I wobble a lot these days.

When I enter the room, the big box is on the dresser and the shower is running. I tip the opened box over and peek in. Oils, lotions, ropes and a few other things are piled high. I grin and shake my head.

However, I do begin to strip from my dress. Who am I to deny the pleasure I know Ry is about to bring? Once I'm down to nothing but my birthday suit, I climb onto the bed to wait.

All thoughts of positioning myself in some sexy pose go out the window when I topple over onto my side. I can't help but laugh at myself. I start to snort and all, causing myself to laugh more. I'm so busy laughing, I don't notice the shower cut off.

The room fills with music. I laugh to the point of tears when Jodeci's "Freek'n You" starts to play. I turn over to find Ryan in nothing but a towel around his waist.

He licks his lips as he looks over my body. I don't know how he still gets turned on by all this. I wiggle my toes that I can't see and shyly wrap my arms around my belly.

He moves to the bed, dropping his towel on the way over. He's so hung it's ridiculous. Irrational jealousy feels me, and I vow to burn *all* his sweatpants.

The thought is quickly forgotten as he captures my lips in a passionate, toe-curling kiss. I cling to his wet hair as he steals my breath away. I gasp when he moves to kiss my neck.

"Ryan," I whimper.

"I love you so much, Carmen." He moves to plant a kiss on my belly before licking it from the bottom to the top. "All of you."

I may not be able to see my vagina, but I know it's wetter than a waterfall. He reaches for the nightstand and that's when I see he placed a few bottles from the box there. Biting the plastic from around the cap, he tears into a bottle of oil.

Unscrewing the cap and replacing it once the safeguard is removed, he hovers on his knees and pours some of the oil on my belly. With one hand, he rubs the oil in. The scent of apples reaches me, bringing a smile to my face as I look him in the eyes. There's so much heat there. Promise of so much to come.

We have a wordless exchange that causes me to squirm. The baby pushes back at Ry's hand, making me laugh. Ry gives me a brilliant smile.

"Come on, little guy. You're going to mind your little business in there. Don't be trying to cock block."

"Ryan," I chide. "You can't say stuff like that to the baby."

He gives me a look. "Seriously, babe. Have you not been around my family? This kid is going to hear a lot worse."

I cover my face and groan. Ryan's potty mouth will corrupt this poor baby before it gets here. I can only imagine after it arrives. Shoot, I have found myself cursing way more since we've been together.

More oil hits my skin. I peek out through my fingers. Ryan has poured it between my breasts. He puts the bottle back on the nightstand and massages and kneads my mounds. I forget what we were just talking about.

Moans float from my lips as I arch up off the bed. My skin is slick enough that he's able to spread the oil over my arms and then down my legs. My senses are on overload by the time he decides to give me a reprieve from this torture.

"Oh, yes," I cry out when he lowers between my thighs and sucks my lower lips into his mouth.

"Mmm, that's my girl. You taste so good." He parts my folds with his fingers. "Let me hear it."

I rock my hips against his face as I continue to cry out. I claw at the sheets and bite my lip. Ryan grasps a tight hold of my thighs and pushes his face in deeper.

I close my eyes tight and beg for mercy in my head because I know to say it out loud is useless. I shudder as he brings me to my first climax.

When I open my eyes it's like snowflakes are falling in my vision and I swear my glasses are fogging up. My heart pounds so hard, I tighten my grip on the sheets.

"Ryan, please. Not again," I plead.

He chuckles. "Find your center, baby. I'm just getting started."

Oh God. Help me now.

Ryan

When I arrived and found that box on the front porch, I couldn't wait to get into the house. After spending time with Braxton and shoring up my plans, I was stoked. I'm going to propose. I hope to have a ring picked within the week.

"One more, babe," I croon as I finger her sopping wet pussy.

I've been keeping them coming. The sheets are drenched and so is my face. I lick around my mouth as I watch her come apart once more. Damn, I love this pussy. I'm so hard, I can't wait a second more to have her.

Lifting to my knees, I know exactly how I want her. Placing a hand on her belly, I gently roll her onto her side and then to her knees. Her juicy ass bounces as I put her in position. My cock starts to leak.

"Damn," I groan to myself.

Reaching for the oil again, I can't take my eyes off her fat dripping cunt. I finger the dripping juices and bring the delicious essence to my lips. I groan around my digit as the taste of my girl and the oil mix.

I'm reckless with the liquid as I pour it on her back and ass. I want to watch her ass glisten as I move in and out of her. It's all I've been able to think about.

She lowers her torso to the bed and tucks in, lifting her globes higher as if in offering to me. Yeah, my baby knows her man. I give her cheek a slap and watch it vibrate.

"Fuck this."

I grab my cock and glide right into her. Her tight heat sucks me right in and my eyes roll in my head. If my girl weren't already a perfect ten her pussy would make up for everything else. I lie to you not.

This shit has the power to shut my brain down. I groan and grunt as I move in and out of her slowly. When I look down at our connection, I have to bite my lips to keep from coming.

Each time my pelvis bumps up against her cheeks, it ripples. Her thick ass is so sexy around my pale rod. Damn, I love fucking her and watching her pussy swallow my dick.

Carmen gasps, and I freeze. "Are you all right?"

"Please, don't stop. So good, baby. Please," she says as she turns to look over her shoulders.

I nearly bust out laughing while gritting my teeth as I see I've knocked her glasses askew on her face. They're crooked and barely holding on.

Sexy.

I grasp her tits and pull her oily back to my chest. Sitting back on my heels I start to drop her up and down on my shaft as I thrust up. I look down at her in awe.

"You belong to me. This dick belongs to you," I say huskily in her ear. "That's it. Gush all over me. Mark me as yours. I'm going to coat them walls with all this cream."

She sucks that full bottom lip into her mouth. I groan and dip my head to nip the top one before moving to stare down at her again. Although her glasses are tossed across her face, when she looks up at me with a world of trust in her eyes, something inside me catches.

I realize that her trust is what I want most. I want to look in her eyes and see that she knows I'm here for her. I'm the one who will do anything for her. There isn't a man on this earth who will love her the way I do. It's not possible because I love this woman more than life itself.

As our eyes connect, I tell her all of that without speaking a word. I don't have to. She gets me. When she cups my face, I see the same look in her gaze.

"I love you too," she says softly, confirming what I already know.

I fix her glasses with my teeth before placing my forehead to hers. I ease us into making love. Her body moves against mine easily.

I palm her stomach and breathe her in. For once, I think we're both seeing things clearly. I've opened my heart to her, and I have no plans of ever closing it.

"I love you more than you could ever know. Today, tomorrow, and forever, I'm yours."

CHAPTER THIRTY-EIGHT

We're Here

Carmen

"I've been wanting to ask you guys about something," I say quickly, like tearing the band-aid off.

"What's up?" Roni says as she breastfeeds the baby.

I pause for a moment as I watch her and her little one. Those cute little fat cheeks. You would never know Roni was nearly two months early.

I lift my gaze to Roni. She's different. At times she's still distant, but she's happy. True happiness lives in her eyes. It's not something that was there before.

I shake those thoughts off before I chicken out. Chewing on my lip, I try to decide how to say this. It's been gnawing at me for weeks.

"Well, it seems like I'm the only one who was freaked out by the shooting," I say and pause looking around at everyone.

Nellie pushes her glasses up her nose as she holds Evan against her shoulder burping him. Heather sits back looking as if she's ready to pop. She's due any day now.

Bean looks exhausted as she holds her newborn son in her arms. She even nods a bit before catching herself. I purse my lips not to laugh.

That will be me in two more months. I'm not going to make fun of anyone. I continue as my thoughts come together.

"You guys handled the situation like it was just another day at the office."

Roni shrugs. "It was."

"Yeah, we've been through worse," Nellie says.

Kamara comes from the kitchen with a tray of pastries and fruits. My stomach growls on queue. Leaning in, I snatch a tart before the tray hits the table.

"I think we have all become desensitized. You know. We've been kidnapped and attacked before. Now the instinct is to protect ourselves and our children," Kamara says.

I scrunch my face up as I think on that. I guess that's sort of how I felt the day I was attacked. I went into survival mode.

"I guess I can understand that."

"Listen, Carmen, a lot has changed and will continue to change," Roni says. "We'll be ready for whatever. There are a lot of us having babies or who just had babies, but the ladies in New York are waiting on us to start training like they have. If we're going to be a part of this, we're going to be ready."

"Oh man, why do I feel like y'all are about to get me in trouble with Wyatt?" Nellie groans.

"Trust me. He'll get over it. If what I know is coming, is coming, you're going to want to hear Val out. We all have a role to play and I, for one, would rather be ready when the time comes."

"I don't know," Kamara says, wringing her hands. "Toby is already going to be angry when he finds out what I've been up to."

"So what's a little more trouble. Besides, I'll take the rap for whatever. I can handle John," Roni says.

"What's the deal with you two?" Heather blurts out as she locks her gaze on Roni.

"We are what we are," she replies. "He gets me, and I understand him."

"Ah," Heather says, not sounding too convinced.

"Anyway, if you're not comfortable, Carmen, it will come. You sort of grow into it. I know a lot of us have been around the Blacks for forever, so we're used to it, but I think you'll be fine," Bean says.

"Yeah," Kamara says. "Once you decide you want to be a part of this family everything else grows on you."

"Like she has a choice." Bean giggles. "Ryan has it bad. I think he's fallen the hardest of all the brothers. The guys have been up to something, and I think it has something to do with you."

"Hush," Roni hisses at her.

I narrow my eyes. Ryan has been acting a little strange the last few days. At first, I thought it had something to do with work. However, this morning when he practically rushed me to get dressed to come hang out with the girls, I got a little suspicious.

I don't normally go out much. I've taken a break from NY/LA Connection. I'll decide if I want to go back after the baby.

"Ugh, does this little girl know that she can't stay in my ribs like this," Heather groans.

"I so don't miss that," Nellie laughs. "Wyatt mentioned another baby this morning and I swear I almost threw a butter knife at him."

"Toby has been hinting, but I am not listening." Kamara chuckles.

"I'm surprised you guys haven't had another baby. I thought for sure you two would have had more by now," Bean says tiredly.

"I think we have had enough on our plates. Things are only beginning to settle in my home. We have time."

"Are you guys thinking of moving there?" I ask.

"I don't know. We've talked about it."

"I'll be sad if you guys go," Nellie says.

"Nothing has been decided. We don't have to rush to leave for now. We will see what happens," Kamara says.

I look around at all these women I've come to call friends. Their friendship feels different from what I had with Courtney. I don't have to question this group. They are all down to earth and will stick up for each other.

I commented on one of Courtney's pics on social media and her mean girlfriends made a few snide comments. Once Courtney said nothing, I realized that she never would. To stay with the in-crowd, she will always be silent and go along with whatever their silly behavior is.

I'm fine with that. We're adults and I have adult things going on in my life. These women understand that and have welcomed me into their friendship.

"Are you okay?" Nellie asks as she comes to sit closer.

When I look up from my thoughts, I see that Kamara has taken the baby. I turn to Nellie. Am I okay?

"Yeah, I think I am. I think I've found what I've been missing. I wasn't looking before, but I found it somehow."

Ryan. He brought a whole new world with him. A world I was already connected to without knowing. Funny. It feels right.

Nellie places a hand on my knee. "We're here if you need us. We're family. We're always here," she says the words to me, but I catch that something passes between her and Roni.

"Thanks," I murmur as a chill runs through me.

It's eerie. I can't place it, but I get the feeling those words will ring true one day. I shake the feeling off, I'm being silly.

Ryan

"Is that the one?" Dad asks as he pats me on the shoulder.

I look at the ring in my hands. It's one in what seems like a million sitting in the black velour cases in front of me, but I think it's *the* one. It's no small rock.

Carmen deserves the best and I'm going all out. However, my baby isn't flashy, which makes this ring perfect for her. It's simple, yet stunning.

The blush-colored diamond in the center says it all as smaller white diamonds form elegant leaf like designs on either side of the band.

"This is one of my favorites," Tanya, Braxon's jeweler says.

"So, kid?" Noah says.

The room is filled with anticipation. I asked my parents and brothers to be here with me when I picked the ring. I look to my mother and hold my breath as we lock gazes. For me, this is the one, but if she says it's wrong, I'll pick something else.

"Ye be a nasty little fucker," she says with a smile on her lips. "I know why ye picked the blush diamond. Aye, it's a grand ring, but yer as filthy as they come."

Dad snorts. "I don't want to know. And I wouldn't be so sure about that, lass. They're all nasty. The things I spare you."

I can't help smiling back at my mother. She's right, I did pick this one for a reason. Most likely for the same reason she's thinking.

Carmen giving me her virginity was a big deal to me. I will cherish that for the rest of my life. Whenever I look at this ring, I'm going to think of that.

"This is the one," I say.

Everyone cheers and Brax pops a bottle of champagne. Now all I have to do is finish working on my plans for the proposal. I look at my dad and groan.

I have one more thing to do before I propose, talk to my future father-in-law. If that stubborn ass comes up with a reason why I can't marry his daughter, we're going to have a problem.

I sometimes regret pissing him off so much in the past. He's hell bent on fucking with me now.

"I'll talk to him," I say to my father.

He pats my back. "Aye, I know you will. You're a good kid, Ryan. He's been waiting for you to come to him the right way."

"Yeah, yeah, I know."

"We're here if you need us," he says. Then he turns to us all. "I'm proud of my boys. You all have become fine lads."

"Aye, ye all make me proud," Mom adds.

CHAPTER THIRTY-NINE

Time for Us

Carmen

"It feels like forever since we've had time alone." I sigh as Ryan rubs my feet.

A lazy day on the couch. It's all a girl could ask for. A moment to be still.

"Yeah, I know. I'm waiting for your mom or mine to jump out and start barking orders. I had planned to paint the nursery."

I start to laugh. "Right, but you were taking too long. I can't believe your mom. She's the best. I love the color and the furniture. It's perfect."

He lifts my foot to his lips to kiss. "You're happy. That's all that matters."

"Yeah, I am happy."

"Good. What should we do today? Quick before one of our phones rings."

"Ugh, as long as I don't have to move off this couch, I don't care," I groan.

He chuckles and moves on to massage my other foot. This is paradise. I could stay like this forever.

"Hey, I almost forgot to ask. Did you get things cleared up with finishing your degree online?"

"To my father's great pleasure, yes. I can complete both degrees online. I've gotten through most of the film courses that aren't available online, which means at some point I will have to attend one or two brick and mortar courses, but there's no rush for that.

"Honestly, I can finish both programs faster this way. I was already moving at an accelerated pace. I'll start classes next week and should be able to graduate around the same time," I say and shrug.

"You sure this is what *you* want?"

"Yeah, after thinking about it. I at least want to finish what I started. I think that will bother me more than anything.

"I'll think about what's next after. Daddy and I still haven't had the time to sit and talk about what my place will be within Nash Media."

"Cool, whatever makes you happy."

"You know something. I've wondered if I was confused and undecided about everything because of the baby." I laugh.

"Oh, shit. I didn't think of that. You were totally sold on your career path in Ireland." Ryan snorts. "My little monster has caused a whole lot of trouble."

"Our baby is not a monster." I nudge his thigh with the foot he's not working on.

"It's a Black. Trust, that little child is a monster."

My lips turn up. It's the first time he hasn't called the baby a he. I think it's starting to sink in that we're in fact having a girl. I know we are.

"So you're finally seeing that we're having a baby girl, are you?"

His eyes widen and he looks at me in mock shock. "Those words have never left my mouth. Nor will they ever. We're having a healthy baby and I'm winning the bet."

I laugh and toss my head back against the arm of the couch. This feels so right. I push down the nagging feelings I've been having the last few weeks.

I don't know what it is. It's like something big is coming. I haven't been able to explain it or put my finger on it, but it's been gnawing my nerves something awful.

"I think everything will settle into place like it should. You don't have to rush things with school. If it's what you want, I'm here to support you.

"I'll help with the baby when you need to study. I've been talking to Dad about how I can fit into the team again once things die down—"

"Wait, about that. Like, you still work for my dad?"

I bite my lip. I've been wanting to ask this question for a while. I still don't know how I feel about it.

"Technically, I've never worked for your father. It was a favor. I still work cases for Black and Lock, but I've been doing a lot remotely since you've been living with me. Felix is a beast with drones. I've done a ton of surveillance right from this couch. I still clock billable hours."

"I haven't been on a bounty, and we haven't been called in for any of the heavy stuff we specialize in. So Dad hasn't needed me there," he explains.

"But you could be called away?"

I don't know why that thought makes me so nervous. The thought of not having him around puts knots in my belly. I search his face for the answer as I hold my breath.

"Yeah, but it would have to be for something big, and you would be protected. I'll never leave you unprotected."

I fall into silence as I think this over. I don't know if I've gotten used to the reality of my life yet. I'm trying, but at times I feel so disconnected from what I know and what's real.

Ryan's stomach growls, drawing me from my thoughts. I look at him incredulously. He lifts his shoulder. I can't help but laugh.

"Dude, we just ate."

"I'm a big guy. I need my nourishment."

"But you had the equivalent to two stacks of pancakes and like a pack of bacon to yourself. Where does it go?"

"First, it was that turkey bacon shit you eat. I farted that out two minutes after eating it. Second, I burned the pancakes off as you were riding my cock not too long ago."

"Once I flipped your ass over to put you to sleep, I used up all that fuel. You're forgetting that you just woke up from a nap. It's been a minute since we ate," he says with a cocky smile.

I palm my forehead. "Why? Why do I get myself into these conversations?"

"I'll order some Chinese. You want to watch *Goonies*?"

"How is that your favorite movie?" I say through my laughter.

"I was annoying as fuck when I was little. I got on everyone's nerves, and they'd come up with shit to get me back. Noah and John thought locking me in the room in the dark to watch it would scare me."

"I freaking loved that movie. *Chewy*." He mocks the movie, causing me to laugh more. He starts to laugh with me as he continues the story. "They got in so much trouble. Mom was the one to find me locked in the dark."

"Oh my God. That's so bad. I know she kicked their butts."

"You have no idea, but I wasn't done with them. I pissed in Noah's bed a few days later. When Mom went to put away his laundry while we were at school, she smelled it."

He falls onto me as he laughs, cupping my belly. He looks up at me with tears of laughter in his eyes. I'm trying my best to hold my own laughter in.

"When we got home, she lost it on him. '*How ole are ye? Ye pissed the bed and didn't have enough sense to pull off the sheets to put in the wash?*'"

"'Why are ye pissing the bed? Someone fucking with ye at school? Do I need to come up there? Ye need to see a therapist?"

"We all had our ears pressed to his bedroom door to listen as she reamed him out. I swear, he sounded so confused. He had no idea what she was talking about, which only pissed her off more. She thought he was lying to her." He gasps with laughter.

"That was mean and nasty," I say as my laughter gets the best of me.

"You have seven boys, you will learn that we do some of the nastiest shit ever. Especially to each other. I could tell you some stuff that would totally gross you out."

"Please don't."

He kisses my stomach. "I know that I mentioned it before, but I hope you're up for more than one. I know you want a career and have dreams, but I'm willing to do whatever we need for you to have support. I'll be a stay-at-home dad if I have to. These last few months have shown that it's an option," he says with a plea in his eyes.

His golden puppy eyes nearly have me promising him as many babies as he wants. However, I stop myself before I can make that promise. The truth of the matter is, I'm scared out of my mind as it is.

"I've yet to figure out how to be a mom. I might suck at it," I murmur.

He moves up my body to my lips. Placing a gentle kiss against my mouth, he says, "I think you're going to be an amazing mother. I put my life on that. Think about it. We can visit this discussion again after we're married."

With that, he gets up from the couch and leaves me stunned. I look after him as he saunters away as if he said nothing at all.

Married? He's serious about that, isn't he? It's not the first time he's mentioned it.

Hello, Carmen. Ryan Black is in love with you, and he wants to get married. Time to let that sink in.

CHAPTER FORTY

Inevitable Paths

Carmen

"I hope she made some curry goat and rice and peas," I say as I rub my belly. We pull up to my parents' house and my stomach agrees with me. "Oh God, if Daddy made Miso soup or Yakitori I'm bringing the entire pots home. You have my back, right?"

Ryan laughs and shakes his head. My parents invited us over for dinner. I'm excited and so ready for time with my family and some good food.

"I'm sure your mother went all out. As much food as she brings to the house, I can only imagine what she'll do from her own kitchen," he says and leans to kiss my cheek before he gets out of the car.

I dig in my bag for my phone. Heather had promised she'd text us all a few pictures of the baby. She and Braxton are going out tonight and she dressed their little doll up and couldn't stop gushing about it.

She's such a cute little girl. I poke my lips out when I don't find any pics. I was hoping they'd come in before I get distracted with my family.

I'll have to check again after dinner. Ryan helps me out of the car and we head into the house hand in hand. I lean into his side. He squeezes my hand and kisses the top of my head.

I look up and smile, those golden eyes beam back at me. Placing a hand on my belly, reality hits me. I'm walking into my parents' house with my family.

He kisses my nose. "What?"

"Nothing." I shake my head as we cross the threshold.

I stop in my tracks as we round the corner into my parents' living room. There's a house full of people looking at us. Pink and blue balloons are everywhere.

Ryan moves behind me and wraps his arms around my waist, palming my belly. "Surprise," he says in my ear.

"Surprise," everyone else cheers.

"He didn't want us to scare you." Braxton laughs. "He was afraid we were going to stress you and the baby."

"Do you ever shut up?" Ry snaps back at him.

I turn my head up to look at Ryan. He looks down at me and smiles. I guess now I know why he was acting all nervous today. I thought it was about having dinner with my mom and dad.

"You did all of this?"

"Ha. Hell no. My mom and yours did. My job was to get you here."

"You tell a lie," my mother says. "He has been in on everything we've done. He picked the cake and made the guestlist."

"Aye, he did his fair share to make sure it was perfect for ye, lass," Cass says.

"Thank you," I say to Ryan, lifting on my toes to kiss his cheek, he bends for me to reach, but turns his face after my lips brush his skin to peck my lips.

"You're welcome."

"Hey, we didn't come here for that," Roni says.

The crowd laughs, causing me to look around at all the smiling faces. So many people. I can't believe how many people are here.

Faces from the wedding in Italy, even Gigi is here. I'm overwhelmed with a sense of family and friends. This is beyond what I expected for my baby shower.

Ryan

The smile on Carmen's face is worth dealing with my mother and hers. They were going to drive me crazy with this shower. I've been distracted from planning our engagement as I've helped them out with the little details, they asked me to see to, but that smile is worth everything.

"Does this mean you'll stop harassing my wife?"

I turn to look at Nick and give him a cocky grin. "What? And leave you to raise my kids. I think not," I taunt.

"You know, one of these days I'm going to forget who you are and kick the ever loving s—"

"Nick," Sephora says in warning as she walks up.

She places her hand on Nick's chest and the man melts under her touch. I smile as I watch the gesture. I don't blame Nick for his possessive ways at all.

"I get it now. I know exactly how you feel," I think out loud.

"I can see it in your eyes," Sophie says. "She's good for you. I like her."

I turn to look across the room where Carmen is talking with Val and Tasha. I narrow my eyes and tighten my fists. Not the most innocent women in the room.

LaSalle can fool himself if he thinks his wife, isn't a killer. I smell that shit on her. It's only a matter of time before that side comes out around here.

It's been two months since Italy and Carmen has finally stopped jumping out of her skin at the smallest sound. I'm not so sure I want her getting too close to danger. Don't get me wrong, I like Val.

I'm still getting to know Tasha, but she seems cool if you look past what lies beneath the surface. Nick places a hand on my shoulder.

"It's nothing we can avoid. We've brought them into our world, now we teach them to survive within it."

"For the record, she was in it before me. Even if it was without her knowledge. And I never asked to bring her into this world."

He snorts, causing me to turn and look at him. "You think this is a choice. We were all destined to be right here. She's Kevin Briggs's niece.

"That links her to Nate. Nate's wife is good friends with Uri Donati, which links her to Val." He nods to the women across the room. "They were going to cross paths. This, my friend, was inevitable."

I look around the room. There's a good portion of the Alliance here. Nick's words couldn't be truer. We're all connected in some way. Six degrees of separation.

This has been in motion since way before Toby requested his seat. As I told Carmen before, I hate the silence and it's been too silent concerning this Alliance. I'm not naïve enough to believe that it's all been squashed so easily.

"We're not here for any of that today. Can we not talk about anything other than babies and happy things?" Sephora says.

"You are right," Nick says as he smiles at her.

"Come, I want to play the next game, and I need a partner."

I watch them as they go before turning to look across the room again. The group of three has grown. My mom and Carmen's have joined the group along with a few other women.

"What's with the look?" Wyatt asks as he walks over and hands me a bottle of water.

I notice the label on the bottle and smile. *Baby Black*. It has one of the sonogram pictures I provided my mother with on it as well.

I nod toward LaSalle, Uri, and the group they're standing in. "You ever think Toby getting involved was a bad idea?"

"We were never going to avoid getting sucked in. I've come to grips with that. All we can do now is protect our own.

"It's been quiet, but we're still watching and waiting." He bumps me with his shoulder. "Forget all that shit. This is your baby shower. You have a beautiful girl and a baby on the way. You'll pop the question soon and we'll be having another wedding."

"I can't believe the baby will be here in a month. I don't know if I should get excited or puke."

"A little of both," he says and smiles. "It's the best feeling in the world. I can't explain it. It's like watching the perfect sunrise, catching the perfect wave, and falling in love all rolled into one."

"They're everything to me. Carmen, the baby. I knew she was going to be a part of my life from the first time she fell into my arms, but this has become surreal.

"I'm going to be a father. Fuck. Who let that happen?"

"Bro, I've been asking the same thing," he teases.

He tugs me into a head-lock and kisses the top of my head. "You're going to make an awesome father," he says in my ear. "If you fuck this up, the six of us will be here to kick your ass until you get it right."

I shove him off, but I'm smiling as I do. "Five hundred says my kids are the least screwed up when they grow up."

He barks out a laugh. "You're so on. Hey, Noah, John," he bellows across the room. "Get over here. You're going to want in on this one."

I shake my head as all my brothers, not just John and Noah head in our direction. If this is what my future looks like, I'm fine with that. I can handle whatever comes to my door.

CHAPTER FORTY-ONE

Private Calls

Ryan

"We had so much fun," Tasha says at LaSalle's side. "I'm so glad we were able to make the trip."

"Thank you for coming. It was so nice getting to know you more," Carmen says with a huge smile on her lips.

"Likewise, I'm happy to gain another little sister."

"Be lucky you live in California," LaSalle says as he looks down at his wife lovingly. He places a hand on her belly and leans to kiss her lips. "We have a hard time finding our wives in New York. Maybe this baby will slow this one down."

Carmen gasps. "You're pregnant?"

"Yes, and I thought we agreed to wait to announce it," she says as she glares at LaSalle with no real heat at all.

These two make a perfect couple. That hidden look I see in Tasha's eyes; I also see in LaSalle's. There are people who are dangerous, but not smart when it comes to the execution of their transgressions.

Then there are those that will wait you out, plot their move, and have all the pieces move toward their desired outcome without anyone being the wiser. The King and Queen on the Chessboard. If I had to pick who to watch in this group, these two would be the ones.

"I'm a proud papa. I wasn't going to hold it in much longer." LaSalle gives her a smile and all the little frustration she may have had seems to melt right away.

"Well, since the cat is out of the bag. I'm exhausted. We're going to be going soon."

"Come, we want to take a picture with all the girls," Tasha says, grabbing ahold of Carmen's hand and calling for the others to join them.

LaSalle moves in closer, catching my gaze. "You are one of the youngest who have fallen under my covering, but you're bright. Kiyoshi sees this too. He talks about you as much as Ne."

I turn to look at my soon-to-be-father-in-law. Well, that's still a conversation I need to have. He sees us and lifts a glass in our direction. I nod before turning back to LaSalle.

"I've gotten to where I am because of my brothers. My brothers have watched my back for as long as I can remember. Toby is lucky to have you.

"When he becomes distracted, you will see for him. You're the observer. I'm trusting that.

"The Alliance won't work because of its leadership, it will work because of its foundation. That foundation is all the men around each member at the table. You need anything, you come to me. Never hesitate to ask."

"Can I ask why I'm getting this offer?"

"My son has mentioned you by name. You and your family. It's the first time he's been so specific about details so far in the future.

"A member of your little family is important to him." He smirks at my confusion. "I'll explain one day. We'll talk more soon. Congratulations. For now, *addio*."

I'm left totally confused as I look after him. I'll be asking more questions soon. I rub at my chest as it grows tight. I've heard about Ellen and her gift.

Is he telling me his kid has the same gift?

Man, I don't know how I feel about that or if I want to know what that kid has seen about me and my family. I look toward Carmen. That happy smile is still there.

I can't see my life without her. Whatever that kid has seen has to be some good shit because I'd lose my mind if anything happened to her or our baby. I shake the eerie thoughts off as Roni catches my eye.

She nods at Val a second before she starts up the stairs behind the group picture taking. No one has had access to the second level. Everything has been down here.

Paloma has set up a nursery here for the baby. I've been here a few times to help set it up. She revealed it to Carmen earlier tonight while everyone was distracted with food and drinks.

It's possible that Roni could be headed up to take a peek, but I doubt that. Something else is up. I can feel it.

I'm too nosey to let this go. I take out my phone as if I'm focused on it and ease my way around the room. I'm almost to the steps at the back of the house through the kitchen, when Paloma appears.

She beams from ear to ear. I curse in my head, knowing I'm not going to get upstairs in time to find out what Roni's up to.

"Ryan," she says, tugging me in with a smile. "My daughter found a man as pretty as she. Come, let me fatten you up."

My greedy stomach wins out over my curiosity. I follow her right over to the food. What can I say? This woman cooked so much good food, I'm not passing up thirds.

Roni

It's been two months since I've had the baby and for a while, I thought I'd give this all up. That is until tonight. When Val gave me this phone and told me to answer the text, I have to admit I was curious.

Val has been one of the few in New York who I've allowed to get close to me. It's something in her eyes that made me trust her. I was relieved when she started training for the Briggs.

There was always something different about her. However, I did question who the phone was from. Her answer pulled me in, like a hand grasping my neck and demanding I follow.

"A friend from Russia." Her words sent a chill down my spine.

When the text came to answer in five, I looked over to Val and she nodded her head. Anticipation coiled in my belly as I turned and crept up the stairs to find privacy. I figured I'd go to the nursery Carmen has gushed about in case someone finds me up here and questions me.

My palms are sweaty as the FaceTime call comes through. The room is dimly lit by a cute little lamp that casts stars and hearts on the ceiling. I look around as if someone's watching me before I answer the call.

"I was right. I know you. Took moment to figure out, but I remember," he says before I can state a greeting. "We go back to beginning, Da."

I look into his cold blue eyes, and I'm still surprised that this is the man who saved me. I've looked into the eyes of men who are monsters, men who are dangerous. His are no different from theirs. Yet, he's the reason I made it to be rescued with the others.

"I don't know when the beginning was for you, but that wasn't it for me."

"Da, but we have history." He sits forward in his chair with his words. "Your enemies are my enemies."

"Is that so? What do you want?"

"Direct. This is good. I have something you need to do for me."

"Why would I do anything for you?"

"Call it a favor for your life," he says with a vacant tone.

"Will that make us even?"

He remains silent for a moment. Pulling a complicit face, he nods. "Da, you owe me nothing, but this favor I ask is not for me. It's for everyone."

"What?"

A smile comes to his lips. "You are not as safe as you think. Too many questions, you and your friend expose us all to people you should want to hide from."

"And?" I lift a brow. "Do I look scared? I'll be ready."

"You can't be ready for something you don't know."

"Will you stop talking in circles?" I snarl. "What do you want?"

He laughs but cuts off abruptly. "Make young boy stop. He doesn't know who he's pissing off. Your little friend has made waves."

"What?"

"Don't play fool with me. John is friend, but I give you courtesy of call. I am not ready to play hand. He stops or I stop him."

"What makes you think I have any control over him?"

He cuts a hand across his neck as his face grows angry. "Don't lose respect I have for you. I will not play this game. You want little friend you search for, you stop boy. Now."

I gasp. "What little friend?"

"Girl you risked your life for. I can help you find her. Torque, that's boy's name, da? He makes too many mistakes. Call him off. I will make sure you get revenge you seek, but not at cost of everyone."

I can't breathe. If he can find Natasha, I can go for her. I can save her. I hold back the tears.

"How do I know you're telling me the truth. I need proof she's alive."

He shrugs. "She lives for now. Smart girl. She survives off brain, not body. I will make my business to help her once you handle other friend. Be quick before he tips everything."

I clench my teeth. He's given me nothing to go on, but my gut tells me to trust him. Especially if Torque has gotten himself on the radar of men like him.

He gives me an evil grin. "You think too much. It's simple."

"Stop boy, help girl, keep shit from our door. You are smart too. Too smart not to make right choice. You are tangled in a mess greater than you and friends."

"Fine." I nod. I furrow my brows. I don't know if he has the power to answer my next request, but I try. "But I need one more thing. I want to know the truth. How did I get there?"

He sits back and steeples his long fingers in front of his lips. This guy would be a gorgeous man if he weren't an asshole. I can't stop gritting my teeth as I wait for his answer.

"Da. This I will do. I will give you answers when you solve problem."

With that, he hangs up the phone. I'm going to kick Torque's ass if John doesn't find out and do it first. I swear, that kid drives me nuts.

"There's always something." I blow out a breath.

I pause and a shiver takes over me. Who is Misha Krupin? How the hell did he know to call me and not John about Torque? I look down at the phone.

Val.

She knows all her soldiers. I should have known.

CHAPTER FORTY-TWO

Restless

Carmen

"Hey, Ry?" I call out as I come from the bedroom, headed for the kitchen.

I can't sleep. I've been so tired the last few days, but sleep has alluded me. I want to close my eyes and fall asleep so bad.

"Ryan?"

I smile when I find him on the couch with the remote control to the videogame console in his hand and his headset on. However, he's fast asleep. He's been trying to stay up with me to keep me company as I live through this misery.

Not wanting to wake him, I turn for the kitchen and get a glass of water. I nearly spit it out when Ryan starts to snore like a buzz saw. He's super loud.

I feel so bad. He has to be exhausted. He never snores like this.

I finish my water, then waddle over to turn the game off and toss a throw over Ry. I bend a little to reach the console and that's when it happens. My eyes grow wide and my lips part in a gasp.

The floor beneath my feet is soaked instantly. "Holy shit," I cry out as a sharp pain shoots across my back.

Ryan jumps up from the couch with a gun in his hand. I have no idea where he pulls it from, but the moment he sees me hunched over holding my belly, he tucks it away and leaps over the coffee table to reach me. I look up at him with tears in my eyes.

"I'm not ready," I whisper through the pain.

"Yeah, well, you better get ready. This baby is coming. Come on. I'll get you dressed and call your doctor."

I nod my head as the pain subsides a bit. He takes me by the arm and leads me toward the bedroom. I guess I'm moving too slow for him because he lifts me into his arms and carries me.

Placing me on my feet in the bedroom, he peels my wet panties down and goes to get me a fresh pair. I take off his shirt I wore to lie down in. Once he gets me into my panties, he rushes to the closet for something for me to wear.

I go to tell him to grab a dress, but my words are snatched by searing pain. Oh my God, why didn't anyone tell me there would be this much pain? This is insane.

My eyes cross and I double over, reaching for something to lean on. Somehow, I find the bedpost and wrap an arm around it. I clench my teeth and fight through.

"Breathe, baby. You've got this," Ry says in my ear.

I look at him and glare. "Got what? You feel this? You know this pain? What I got?"

Ryan's eyes widen in surprise. Yeah, I might sound like my mother, but this pain is no joke. He can't tell me what I've got. My back is trying to split open with his child.

I close my eyes and try to breathe. Ryan doesn't say another word. Once I can stand again, I straighten and hold my hand out for the dress he's holding.

He shakes his head and starts to dress me. If I wasn't so tired, I might fight him on this. Instead, I allow him to place the dress on and then my shoes.

Ryan gets my baby bag and rushes me to the car as fast as my legs will take me. As soon as I'm inside the pain hits again. I brace myself against the dashboard and growl through the pain. Ryan jumps in and starts out of the driveway.

"Holy shit. Motherfucker," I yell.

Ryan lets a laugh slip, and I turn to glare at him. "That's the most you've cursed in the same hour since I've met you," he says, with a sheepish look on his face.

I don't have it in me to fuss at him. I close my eyes and try to filter out some of the pain. It does little to help.

"This can't be normal. Is this normal? Call Dr. Omid. I want Dr. Omid."

"Babe, I already called Dr. Malcolm. He's on his way."

"I said call Dr. Omid. Your big head baby is trying to rip its way out of me. This. Shit. Ain't. Normal. Call Dr. Omid!"

"Calling Dr. Omid," he mutters.

When Wyatt's voice comes through the phone, I glare at Ryan. He holds his hand up at me. I hold back the string of curses ready to fly from my mouth.

"Bro, I need a favor," Ryan says.

"We're already on our way to the hospital. Mom called."

"No, Carmen doesn't feel right. She thinks we need to call in Omid."

"On it. Hold on, I'll call him now." There's a pause as he places us on hold. "Ry, I have Omid on the line."

"Dr. Omid. Something's not right. I can feel it," I say before Ryan can speak up. "Please. Can you help me?"

"Carmen, I need you to relax. I'm already here at the hospital. I'll be waiting for you when you arrive. Ryan, how far out are you?"

"Ten minutes, but I'll be there in five."

"Drive safely. I'll be here."

"Carmen," Nellie's voice comes through the speaker.

"Yes," I pant.

My face is covered in sweat and tears. Ryan reaches over and rubs my back with one hand. It doesn't ease the pain, but it makes me feel a little better. We stop at a light and he leans to kiss my head.

"I love you," he whispers in my ear.

Nellie's soothing voice helps me to keep from freaking out as she starts to coach me through. I'm so grateful to her in this moment. I know this is my first baby, but I'm not sure it should feel like this.

I rock in my seat as I continue to cry. I sob so much this baby could be baptized in my tears. I try to wipe my face, but it's useless. Sweat and tears cling to my cheeks and run down my chin.

"Ryan," I whisper.

"Yeah, baby."

For weeks I've been having this feeling like something bad is coming. It's been nagging me hard in the last few days. I clench the dress around my belly.

"I'm scared."

Ryan

I've never felt more helpless in my life. Yeah, I was there for John and Roni when their baby came early. We all were, and we stood by to support them any way we could.

John wasted no time calling Omid when they first found out Roni was pregnant and that may have been what saved the baby's life. Dr. Omid would have been my first choice had Carmen not had her own doctor already.

However, hearing my girl ask for Dr. Omid now, after she has trusted her own doctor all this time has me damn near shitting in my pants. I reach for her hand and lace my fingers with hers.

"I'm here. I made you a promise remember. Nothing is going to happen to you or our baby."

"You don't—"

"Carmen," I say in warning. "Nothing is going to happen to you guys. We're having a baby. We're finally going to find out what we're having."

"We never picked a name," she sobs.

"Okay, that's fine. We'll pick one when we know what she looks like," I say and turn to peek at her.

She turns to me with furrowed brows. I wink before turning back to the road. I sort of gave up on thinking it's a boy.

Mom told me straight out I could forget it. She hasn't missed once. John had a girl just like she said he would so I guess I'm having one too.

I've come to accept it. She'll be spoiled as fuck, but who cares.

"You think we're having a girl? Ryan Black, did you have the doctor tell you without me? I swear—"

"Babe, relax. I don't know for sure. It's a feeling. We'll have a boy next time."

She kisses her teeth long and hard. "Next time. I'm not doing this again."

I pull up to the hospital and lean to kiss her lips. "Let's not rush things. You said you weren't going to be mine before and look at us now. You're about to have my baby and you love me."

She frowns at me and pushes me away when I try to kiss her again. "I should have listened to my first mind. Look at what you've gotten me into. Trouble, I knew you were troub—Oh God, get me inside, please."

I jump from the car to find Dr. Omid with a nurse and a wheelchair waiting for Carmen. I freeze for a second as it sinks in. We're here to have a baby.

The little person I've been talking to in her womb will be in my arms soon. I'm someone's father.

Ah shit. Who let this happen?

CHAPTER FORTY-THREE

It's A Girl

Ryan

"It's a girl," I croon as I rush out into the waiting room. "8 pounds and twenty-two inches long. My baby girl is gorgeous."

I wipe at my face, trying to hide my tears. She's so fucking beautiful. She also scared the shit out of us all.

Carmen was right in asking for Dr. Omid. The cord had wrapped around the baby's neck. That man is gifted.

He was able to get her out without a C-section. Our next pregnancy we're going to him from go.

My brothers surround me and draw me into a hug. I break down. The weight of the last eight hours setting in.

"I thought I was going to lose them both," I sob.

"You did good. You were strong for them both and they're healthy," Wyatt says.

I still don't know where I pulled the strength from. I wanted to freak out right along with Carmen, but I held it together until my girls were both safe. Hearing her little cry helped ease the tightness in my chest.

I swear, I couldn't breathe until I heard her take her first breaths. Holding my little girl for the first time was amazing. She was so tiny in my arms.

She's not even an hour old, but I can see her mother and me in her face. She's going to be gorgeous when she grows up. I wish I could keep her small and in my arms forever, but I'm excited to watch her grow and become amazing at the same time.

In this moment, I feel like the baby. Like the little brother who would come to them when I needed them to have my back. I absorb their strength as my fear and exhaustion hits hard.

"Let me in, let me in," my mother says.

I chuckle and wipe at my face as John and Noah step back. My mother looks up at me with pride shining in her eyes. I bend down to wrap her in my arms.

"I'm so proud of ye," she says, her voice filled with emotion. "Yer going to make such a good father."

I get choked up all over again. I turn toward my dad as he pats me on my back. This is what I want for my little girl.

If she ever needs anything I want to support her like this and if I can't be there, I want her family to be there.

"I don't know about you guys, but I need to talk to my swimmers. What's with all the girls?" Brax says and groans.

Everyone laughs and the tension leaves the room. Ne and Kiyoshi are the next to pull me into a hug. I'm surprised by the long embrace from Kiyoshi.

It reminds me that I have one more step before the proposal I now have to move back a week or two. I've been putting this off long enough. I turn to look toward the room where Carmen and our little girl are.

Her mother is there with her. They'll be fine for now.

"Can we go for a walk?" I say to Kiyoshi.

"Yes." He nods his head.

Dad pats my back again as I start off with Kiyoshi. I don't know why the heck I'm so nervous. I guess it's because this is the only thing keeping me from proposing.

It will all be a reality once I get his blessing and I'll be making the next biggest step of my life. I think of my little girl's face. I know I'm ready.

"What have you named my granddaughter? A strong name will build strong character," Kiyoshi says as I gather my thoughts.

"We haven't settled on a name yet. I like Cassidy after my mother or Carrie. Carmen's isn't sold on either."

"Cassidy is nice, but that's some tough shoes to fill. Did your father ever tell you about the time we got drunk and had a bar fight? I was more afraid of your mother when we returned with busted knuckles and cuts she had to stitch up." He chuckles.

"Nah, never heard about that. I think my little girl can hold her own with the name, but she probably should have her own identity."

"Yes, this is true. What would you like to talk to me about, young Ryan?"

I stop and turn to face him. "I'm going to propose to Carmen. I have the ring, and I was planning to do it this week, but since the baby is a week early, I'm going to push it back a bit. I wanted you to know."

He laughs at me. Looks in my face and laughs at me. I ball my fists at my sides in frustration.

"You still come to tell me what you will do. Never once have you asked? You two are same coin different sides."

I sigh. He's right. He has a point. I rub the back of my neck.

"Your daughter means the world to me. I love her with everything I am. When I thought I was about to lose her earlier, all I could think about is that I didn't make her my wife. I didn't show her how much she means to me.

"So I'm sorry. I've approached this wrong. I would like to marry your daughter with your blessing. May I have your blessing?"

"You know, in the Yakuza when we feel we've been dishonored we cut off your fingers. I may let you marry her if you part with a pinky."

I search his face to see if he's serious. He gives nothing away. His face is straight as fuck.

I shrug my shoulders. "If that's what it takes. Your blessing is important to her. I know she won't marry me without it."

He laughs again and pats my cheek. "You, my son, will make a great husband. Keep your fingers. Babies have a lot of snot. You will need them to clean it up."

I chuckle and tug him into a hug. "I've always liked you."

"Yes, and I you, Ryan. Now, let's go see my granddaughter. She needs a name."

Carmen

Oh my God. She has a set of lungs on her. This latching business isn't as easy as I thought it would be and she's hungry.

"Be patient, Nene. She's learning just like you. She's just as frustrated as you are," my mother coaches.

I take a breath and nod. I want to burst into tears, but I hold them back and try again. I yelp in triumph when she latches on this time, only to clamp my mouth shut when I startle her.

"It's okay. She's got it," my mother coos and strokes the baby's cheek.

"Ruby, do you like Ruby?"

"Child, don't do that to the girl. No."

"Ugh, I don't know. Why is it so hard to name her?"

"Probably because you're trying to do it without me."

I look up to see Ryan standing at the foot of the bed with his hands in his pockets. He looks tired, but like a tired supermodel. I don't even want to look in a mirror. I can only imagine what I look like.

"I was thinking that's all. Ruby isn't so bad." Ryan gives me a pointed look. "Okay, okay."

"You know that joke about how you never know a baby named Keisha. Ruby is the same thing. I don't think I know any babies named Ruby." I release a small laugh as I look down at my daughter sucking emphatically on my breast. "She's tearing that tit up."

"Ryan." I look up at my mother and groan. She laughs and shakes her head.

"He's right. She must be very hungry."

Ryan moves closer to kiss the top of my head, then the baby's. "How are you feeling?"

"I don't know. It doesn't feel real yet."

"I'll leave you two to have some alone time. Everyone else will want to visit soon. They already have a text loop going with pictures of her from the nursery," my mother says.

"Oh, I want to see those. Send them to my phone."

"I will," she says and kisses my cheek. "I'm so proud of you. She's gorgeous."

"Thank you."

I smile as I watch her leave. When she's gone, I look at Ryan who has taken a seat on the bed. He's staring at our little girl with a smile on his face.

"What now?"

He lifts his golden eyes to me. Bouncing his gaze across my face, he lifts a hand to cup my cheek. My heart is pounding and I don't know why.

"Now, I finish what I started," he says and kisses my lips.

He then leans into my ear and whispers a name. My heart swells. It's perfect. I love it.

"Yes, yes. That's perfect. Hey, cutie. Your name is—"

"Ryan," John calls as he rushes into the room. "We need to talk."

"Now?"

"Right now."

CHAPTER FORTY-FOUR

Called Away

Ryan

"Babe, stop crying. Your mom and dad are going to take you to the hospital. I'll meet you guys there," I say into the phone.

"I'm sorry. I'm such an emotional mess. She's coming home. This is the first time I haven't been there first thing," she sniffles.

We had a five-man recovery assignment come in from the government. One of those tricky assignments that they call us in for specifically. It needed to be quick and have no ties back to the government.

We were in and out. Once back to our secure location, I jumped in the car with Wyatt and Felix to head straight to the hospital. I had planned to bum a ride in the helicopter with Roni and John, but they're still working shit out from the bomb that landed in John's lap.

I'm not in the mood to be in the middle of that. I'm exhausted, but I'm not even changing out of my gear before heading to my girls. I'll be there soon. However, Carmen is upset because her breasts hurt, and she knows the baby is hungry.

"It's okay. I understand and I want to cry a little with you." I get a laugh out of her, and it brings a smile to my face. "Baby, let your parents take you to the hospital. You're already at their place. I'm en route, I'll get there around the same time. See you as soon as I get there."

Carmen pumped for the nurses at the hospital to feed the baby when we're not there, but I understand. She wants to be with our little girl and make sure she's eating and okay. It was hard for us to leave the hospital without her in the first place.

Complications from the cord and some other things Dr. Omid wanted to keep an eye on caused the baby to have to stay for another two and a half weeks. We'll be bringing her home today.

"Okay, love you."

A smile spreads across my face. "I love you more, babe. Kiss our girl for me. Tell her Daddy's coming," I say before ending the call.

I place my head back against the headrest in the backseat and close my eyes. The last thing I wanted was to take off on an assignment, but I was the only one able to complete the team in time.

Noah, Brax, and Toby were all coming back in from assignments, but wouldn't arrive in time. Dad is out of town and Rob hurt his back. Don't ask.

These old dudes are as bad as the rest of us. I'll never tell what I saw my mother and father doing once. Shit scarred me for life.

If I have one secret from my brothers, there it is. The one time being the nosey one got me burned. Never went to find out what those weird sounds in the house were after that.

"We'll be there soon. Man, I remember how hard it was for me to leave Nellie and Nora the first time. I swear, I sat in the nursery smelling Nora's neck until the very last minute. I wanted to commit the scent to memory," Wyatt says.

"This shit is killing me. Her tears, knowing that she can feel the baby but she's not with her. I feel like they both need me and I'm failing already."

"You're not failing, dude. Ease up on yourself. Besides, I told you we would've made this work without you."

"It wasn't safe. You needed a full team and I'm glad I followed my gut. John almost walked right into a bullet," I mutter.

My brother was distracted. It's not like him. Roni has been on missions with us before, she's highly trained.

So I know her presence wasn't the reason for it. However, I'm pretty sure I know what it is that has him distracted.

Those two are complicated and I still don't get them. They have this connection that you can feel pulsing between them, but if you don't know any better you would think they're not a couple. I don't know how to explain it.

It's like they guard their relationship from the world. No one gets a view of their intimate moments. I thought that would change once Roni got pregnant, but it hasn't. I gave up trying to figure them out.

"Yeah, I'll talk to him later," Wyatt mumbles as if he's in thought. "Did you see what actually happened?"

"No, I reacted before it could happen."

"You did good. I'm thinking it's time we start doing team drills again. We're slacking and I don't like it. We should be more focused than ever."

"I can set up some training times in the schedules. Dad asked me to design a safe room at the office that could double as a nursey. I have the logistics down, I just need to check with my architect to make sure it can be done the way we need," Felix says.

"Smart. I like that idea," Wyatt replies. "Nellie has had to work from home a few times that we've needed her in the office.

Back in the day that wasn't a big deal. We've grown as a team, but our needs are all changing."

"We sound like old men," I groan.

"We sound responsible."

"Exactly, I rolled over for sex this morning and remembered she couldn't. I wanted to talk her into it anyway, I was so damn horny, but responsible me cuddled instead."

Both of my brothers burst into laughter. Fine, they can laugh. That was a test of my will this morning.

It took everything I had not to seduce her. Especially knowing the bleeding has stopped.

"TMI," Felix says.

"Not going to lie, I've been there." Wyatt chuckles.

I shift in my seat as I start to become uneasy. My stomach turns and I feel like I want to throw up. Something's not right.

"Yo, how much longer until we get to the hospital?"

"Fifteen minutes," Wyatt replies.

"Can you cut that in half? Something's not right."

CHAPTER FORTY-FIVE

Awakened Beast

Noah

I step out of my Hummer and all I can think about is kissing my son and fucking my wife. She needs to spend some time on the throne today. I'm horny and missing her warm pussy something fierce.

I grab my cock and squeeze as I walk to the front door. I don't care what's going on, Brodie is going down for a nap. I walk into the house and groan.

My son is screaming his head off. There goes my plans. I drop my bag and toss my keys in the bowl.

My stomach starts to growl as the smell of bacon and eggs float through the house. I find Rebecca and Brodie in the kitchen. She's bouncing our son while piling food on a plate. When she looks up, she has a big smile on her face as if our kid isn't screaming in her ear.

"I knew you were on your way, so I made you breakfast. Eat and take a shower. I'm going to change him and get him down for a nap," she says happily.

Yeah, marriage looks real good on Bean. I love this woman more and more each day. Before she can hurry off, I pluck our son from her arms and wrap her in my embrace.

Brodie quiets down as soon as I have him. I love this kid too. He's the reason I want another one.

I capture Rebecca's lips and devour her with all the hunger that's been building inside over the last two days I've been away. Reaching to squeeze her ass, I bring her closer into my body. Brodie starts to whimper a little, which is the only reason I let her go.

"You go take a shower and breathe for a bit. You've been here with him on your own for two days. I can wait," I say against her lips.

Her face lights up. "A shower," she says with excitement in her voice. "Do you want me to change him first?"

"No, I got it. Take your time."

"God, I love you so much right now. Don't worry about me, I already ate. All of that's for you."

I kiss her forehead. "Thank you. I love you too."

The smile she gives me tugs at my heart. I don't know how to not love her. She's everything to me and more. That smile completes my day. No wonder I've been in a shitty mood for the last few days.

She kisses the baby's cheek and takes off like she has fire on her heels. I pull out my phone and order two-dozen roses because she deserves them. Once that's done, I snatch a few pieces of bacon before getting to work on Brodie's diaper.

I probably shouldn't have eaten first. I nearly gag as I open his diaper, and his little creamy covered ass comes into view. "Damn, what are we feeding you?"

I work quickly to change him and dispose of the bomb he left. My nostrils are on fire. Shaking my head, I scoop up the kid and head to the powder room to wash my hands.

"If this is what your mom has been dealing with, I need to do more than order flowers." He looks up at me like, *Daddy, who the fuck cares, get over it.*

I chuckle and kiss his cheek. I sit killing a plate of eggs as I hold my son when my wife returns and wraps her arms around me. Those soft breasts press to my back and I get hard instantly.

"Want me to put him down for a nap?"

"What are you really offering?"

She laughs in my ear and nuzzles my neck. "I was hoping you'd be offering me something," she replies and reaches to squeeze my grown cock.

I push my plate away. "Let's go, you get him down for a nap and I'll get in the shower. Teamwork, baby."

She laughs and takes the baby. I get ready to follow her, but my phone buzzes in my pocket. I take it out and see it's the house's security system. Pulling up the cameras, I see guys dressed in all black surrounding my home.

"Baby, get down and get the baby to safety. Don't come out until I tell you to. You got me."

Fear fills her eyes for all of a second. She nods and takes off with our son. I knew shit was too damn quiet.

I roll my shoulders and pull the two pistols in the hustlers at my back. With what has become a sixth sense to me, I aim and fire. All hell breaks loose as the others start to fire back.

I return fire, taking down a few more of their guys. I growl as I'm grazed in the side. This is not what I wanted to be doing with my day.

And they brought this shit to my door. Yeah, this isn't going to end well for them. I fire at the shadow that runs across the side of the house right outside the kitchen. I drop him, but more fire is returned.

I drop to the ground and roll, landing on the balls of my feet behind the kitchen island. I'm sure by now my house alarm has notified my brothers, but I don't have time to wait for them.

The sound of something sliding across the floor causes me to jerk around and aim. When I see the semi-auto stop in front of me, I groan. My wife ... why did I think she was going to listen?

I hustler my two pistols and pick up the weapon she's offered. "Bean, get your ass to our son," I snap.

"As soon as we take out the trash, babe. Back up isn't coming. Everyone's hands are tied. Let's get this shit done, so I can stop our son from crying."

"Bean," I warn.

"Noah, focus. Do you hear that?" She whispers for around the counter. "You have to be kidding me. These fuckers again."

The amount of rage that fills me can't be measured, but I don't have time to register or suppress it. Bean starts to fire, causing me to roll my eyes. She would have one of the big boys. This place is going to be a fucking mess.

CHAPTER FORTY-SIX

Roaring Blackout

Braxton

I feel like I haven't slept in days, but I need to get these reports in and get this footage loaded up for Felix. I'm so glad I wasn't in town for that government job. My head and body aren't in for any of that shit.

I need food, ass, and some sleep. Doesn't have to be in that order, but it needs to happen soon. I drag my tired body into the office, but as soon as I see my wife at the front desk, I beam from ear to ear.

I've missed her and our little girl. Heather gets up from her seat as I round the desk and drop my bag. My arms are around her before I can think twice.

God, I love this girl. I devour her sexy mouth and groan. The way she sucks on my tongue has me hard as a rock. I squeeze her plump ass and back her into the desk.

"Who's here?" I breathe against her lips.

"Nellie is in the back. Other than that, just me."

"Get her to cover the desk. I want to take you downstairs for a minute."

She gives me a mischievous smile. "We'll have to be quick. My mom needs me to pick up the baby early today."

I lick my lips and look down at her breasts. "Yeah, I can make that happen. Or you can call Kaye. See if she'll pick the baby up for us. I'll babysit for her whenever she wants in return."

Heather reaches for my swollen cock. "You need me that bad?"

"I've been gone for a week and a half, what do you think?"

"I'll make that call. You talk to Nellie," she says.

I release her and start for the back. "I'm on it."

I find Nellie in one of the back conference rooms talking to herself as she looks at a computer screen. I lean in the doorjamb and watch her. She's truly a genius with these computers.

I would love to see her, Felix, Wyatt, and Sephora go at it in some type of challenge. They all are freakishly talented when it comes to electronics. She turns to me and smiles, pushing her glasses up her nose.

"Welcome back. What's up? You need something processed from your case?"

"Not at the moment. Was wondering if you could do me and Heather—"

My words are cut off as the lights go out. The backup generator kicks in after a few seconds. I look at Nellie and she has the same look as I do. She taps at a few keys on her laptop.

I know shit is about to get real as she pulls a Glock from one of the hustlers we strap under the table. We keep them for times like this when the girls are working alone. They can always place a piece where they sit for safety.

"We have company she says. Get Heather."

She doesn't have to tell me twice, I was already out the door when I took a look at her screen. Guess I'm not getting that food or that pussy anytime soon. Great.

I get to the weapons room and find my wife right where I knew I would. She tosses me my bag I dropped by her desk. "Thought you might need that," she says.

"Thanks. You two stay back here."

"You smoking?" Heather says and rolls her eyes.

If this situation weren't so serious, I'd laugh. There are times when her time in New York slips through and it's amusing. Not today.

"Heather—"

"We don't have time for this. Let's get it done, B."

I grit my teeth but nod. We don't have time. I unzip my bag and suit up.

Nellie appears and gets into a vest. My brother will kill me if something happens to her. I'm so frustrated, but I need to focus.

Noise comes from the front of the office. It's showtime. I signal for the girls to spread out.

They nod and I head to the front. I roar as I see the first red dot appear next to Heather's desk where she was sitting not too long ago.

Nah, this shit ain't happening. Not on my watch. I don't see anything after that.

Toby

"Yes," Kamara cries out.

I groan as I find my release. Man, if this is what happens after a few days away from home, I'm taking on more away assignments. My wife attacked me as soon as I walked into the door.

I lie on my back dripping in sweat. Kamara has been working out, but that still doesn't explain the new acrobats she's been pulling off in bed. I can barely catch my breath.

"Babe, I think you're trying to kill me," I pant.

She laughs and sits up. Her dark skin is glistening with sweat, making me hard again. Damn my wife is sexy. I cup her breasts and knead them.

She turns toward the bedroom door. "Why must they play with the TV so loud? I should go make them turn it down."

"They're fine. We used to play with the TV that loud too. Come on, one more," I groan as I lift and bury my face in her neck.

She giggles and gasps as I suck on her salty, sweet, wet skin. I grasp her waist as she starts to rock her hips into me. Her thick thighs are pressed against mine and feel like silk brushing against me.

"Yeah," the twins cheer from the living room.

We both freeze. We know our kids. Something about that cheer is off. I groan as I release Kamara.

"I'll check on them," I mumble.

Something crashes and we both kick it into gear. I toss on my shorts and grab my Glock to place it in the back of my shorts just in case. The feeling in my stomach tells me not to leave the room without it.

"Stay here," I say to my wife.

I rush from the room as my twins come running to me with wide eyes. "Bad guys. We got two but one broke through the window."

"What?"

Kamara comes running from the room with a gun in her hands. A gun that she's actually holding with the look of experience. She gestures with it for the twins to go inside our bedroom.

"Go, hide," she says in a rush. The twins hurry into our bedroom. "Let's go. The camera shows six more. We can handle this. Everyone's under attack. We need to get to your mother."

"What the fuck—"

I don't get to finish. With the look of training that has my brother written all over it, my queen runs forward with her gun lifted and lays down two bodies like it's child's play. I'm in total shock.

"Toby, snap out of it. Your mother. We have to get to your mother."

Her words snap me into action. I pull my gun and move to shield my wife with my body. I notice two things at once. One, the guys are arguing amongst themselves. Two, they're not doing it in the same language. They don't understand each other.

Two are shouting in a Spanish dialect and one other is shouting back in Russian. It seems whoever was interpreting for them has gone down.

I turn and fire. The fourth one I was listening for tries to sneak us. Wrong move.

I turn back for the others and signal for Kamara to follow my lead. She nods and we move for the front of the house. I take in the remote controls to the cars that Felix gave the twins. Noah has been playing with them and those cars a lot when he's here.

"Those assholes," I mutter to myself.

"Those assholes are protecting our family," Kamara snaps.

"Later," I hiss and point to my right for her to take down that guy while I get the other two. "Now."

We both fire at the same time. I move outside to make sure the coast is clear. I find the remote control cars along with the bodies my entire family has just accumulated.

I don't have time to be pissed. I turn to Kamara as she runs out of the house with the kids heading for the car. She tosses me a T-shirt and shoes. She has my workbag with more ammo and guns on her shoulder.

"Let's go," she calls as she gets the kids in the car.

"What's going on with Mom?" I ask as I get into the car.

"She's not answering the phone. Faith and Jennifer aren't answering either. Everyone has been hit and your Dad's not here. We need to get there and make sure they're all right."
"Fuck," I bellow. "You and the kids stay in the car when we get there. I'll park somewhere safe."

CHAPTER FORTY-SEVEN

Mama Bears

Wyatt

I've finally pulled up to the hospital. The anxiety coming off Ryan is palpable. I hope this is some new father shit and not what I think.

I know that uneasy feeling. In fact, my stomach is in knots. I guess I'm feeling my brother's pain. I got us here in less than ten minutes after he asked. He goes to step out of the car as all our phones start to go off.

"What the hell is going on?" I bark at Felix as our phones go crazy.

"I have no fucking idea. That's the office and … holy shit. We're being hit from every side."

"What—"

"Hey," Ryan bellows as two things happen at once. Glass explodes at the front of the hospital and shots ring out. Ryan takes off running.

I don't think twice. I release my seatbelt to get out of the car and place my earpiece back in my ear. "Felix, get us all live. I need to know what's going on."

"On it."

Cass

"Ye picked the wrong door to come knocking," I snarl as I pump my shotgun and fire.

"Cass, you're hit," Jennifer calls.

"Ha! Took me first bullet in junior high. I'm fine. It's these fuckers on my doorstep about to die, dead ye be ye hear."

I fire again. I'm so mad I could spit. My shoulder burns, but I'm not ready to die today. If my name be Cassy Black I got this shit. I didn't raise seven boys to be men just to die now.

"Get down," Faith calls. "I got this."

"I got you covered," Jennifer says.

I go to reply, but someone grabs me by my injured shoulder and squeezes. "Motherfucker," I cry out.

Now, I'm a wee lass and many underestimate that. I was picked on in school until I let everyone know I followed behind me brothers from the time I could walk. I was one of the boys.

Like this melter with his hand on me, they learned the hard way. I flip the shotgun in my right hand and catch it. Turning quickly, I ram it into this wanker's nuts. My left shoulder burns, but I can still use me arm. I take the shotgun in my left and put it in his belly.

"Tell the devil Cass says hi." I pull the trigger.

Feeling someone at my back I turn and aim. I sag in relief when I lock eyes with my son. He fires a few shots before rushing to me. I grab the back of Toby's T-shirt as he wraps me in his embrace.

"I'm here, Mom. It's okay. I'm here. It's over."

I shake my head. "No, no, this is the beginning. This is what's been coming. Call me boys. Check in with yer brothers."

When he stiffens, I look up at him. His eyes are hard and haunted. Fire only a mother in rage could know fills me.

"What?"

"Nothing, let me get you to a medic."

"What, Toby? I have a bullet left. Ye'll be getting stitched up with me."

He blows out a breath. "You weren't the only one targeted."

Tears fill my eyes. "Christ. What aren't you telling me?"

"Ry needs us."

CHAPTER FORTY-EIGHT

Team Matsumara

Kiyoshi

"Hmm."

"That's the third time you've made that sound. What is it?" My wife asks as we walk into the hospital with our daughter to pick up our granddaughter.

I roll my shoulders and place a protective hand on her back. I smile as I feel the scabbard there. My little warrior is always prepared.

"Something is off here. We've been coming here for more than two weeks. I've learned the staff by face. This is not the staff we know," I whisper to my wife.

"Is everything okay?" Carmen asks.

I move to kiss my daughter's forehead. "Everything is fine. Go get your little one. She misses you. Bekia, Calu you go with her, we'll be right behind you."

Carmen smiles and nods. My wife's companions also nod at their instructions and follow my daughter into the elevator. I've trusted them with my wife's life, I know they'll take care of my daughter.

"You are right. Something is amiss. It's too still in here," Paloma says at my side.

"Yes, this is what I've noticed," I say to her in Japanese.

I narrow my gaze and look around. I pull my phone out to mobilize my men around the hospital. As I send the text, I see the security guard who's approaching me from the corner of my eye.

I lift my head as he stops before me and Paloma. "I'm going to have to ask you to put that away. No cell phones are allowed inside the hospital."

I clench my jaw as I note the others who are on their devices. That's not the only thing I take notice of. While I note this guard's heavy Latin accent, I also take in his tattoos that stick out of the collar of his shirt and cover his knuckles.

To my right, there are two other guards hovering who I've never seen before. The one with the ash blond hair catches my attention. He keeps looking between the exit and the elevators my daughter just went to.

"Sure, that is not a problem," I say with a smile as I place my focus back on the guard in front of me.

He looks to my wife and narrows his eyes. Meanwhile, one of the other two starts for the elevators after the doors close behind Carmen and the others. My cheek twitches.

I unbutton my suit jacket and nod to my wife. She tosses her duster and moves to stand back-to-back with me. At once the room reveals itself as others who were sitting as if innocent visitors, stand to their feet. I shrug from my jacket and wrap the sleeves around my fists.

"I warn you now this isn't wise," I say in a claim that is completely deceptive.

"We'll see," the guard says before lunging at me.

I sidestep him and wrap my jacket around his neck. My wife pulls her Kodachi blades and runs for the guard by the elevator as he tries to step in a car. I snap the neck and dispose of the guard in my hold as one of the false visitors attacks me.

Whipping the jacket at his face, I spin into him and thrust a hand into his throat. Two others charge me, and I take them down just as quickly. Paloma is handling her own as well.

She fights her way back to me and we work together on those who have surrounded us. My men have arrived to do their part.

"Block the elevators," Paloma commands. They move into action at her word.

My wife and I don't slow. We stand back-to-back like warriors in sync, breathing one breath. I duck and she flips over my back to slice at the guy wielding a machete.

When I stand to my full height, I wrap an arm around my wife's waist, and she flips in my embrace while spinning her blades.

When she lands back on her feet right side up, we switch positions, and I thrust my palms into the chest of one of the men still standing after her attack. He falls to the ground as a big guy appears. He's wide and tall. A brute of a man.

He claps his hands together and rolls his big shoulders back. I grunt and snort. Then I groan as I hear my wife's battle cry. I brace myself, knowing what's coming. She runs up my back to propel herself in the air and comes down on him with her blades aimed at her target.

His focus is on my wife, giving me the opportunity to take him by surprise. I spin around him and thrust my palms into his back in a one, two combination. He stumbles right into Paloma's attack.

However, when she draws back, he's still standing. He stumbles a little as a growl comes from him. I go to kick his mid-section, but he blocks the blow.

Paloma lands a kick to his stomach and I spin in the other direction, landing a kick to his other side. He stumbles to the left and we both attack relentlessly. I throw an uppercut and he flies back through the glass front doors.

I see the man with the gun seconds before I toss my body over my wife. Pain sears my side, but I grit my teeth against it. More gunfire rings out, but it doesn't register as being aimed toward us.

"Kiy, are you all right?" Paloma says beneath me.

"Yes, I'm fine."

"Where's Carmen?" I lift my head and find Ryan over us with a gun in one hand and the other outstretched to help me up. I roll from over my wife and watch as Ryan's eyes narrow. "Shit, you're hit."

"Flesh wound. Get to Carmen and the baby. We will finish this."

"I'll go up with him," my wife says.

I nod. "Yes. Hurry."

Carmen

I chew on my lip as we step off the elevator. Something wasn't right in the lobby. I could tell by the look in my father's eyes.

I'm anxious to get to my baby and make sure she's okay. However, as we step off the elevator something's off. There are more guards on the floor than usual. Calu and Bekia both stiffen at my sides.

I see Dr. Omid as he walks briskly in our direction. He grabs my elbow and covers me with his body before anyone else sees us. He shoves me into a nearby room which turns out to be a closet.

My eyes widen when the terrified nurse holding a baby in her arms comes into view. When I realize the baby in her shaky hold is mine, my knees nearly give. I look up at Dr. Omid.

"When I stopped by for rounds, I knew something was off right away," he whispers. "Nurse Beckett here heard one of the guards asking for baby Black several times. She grabbed her and hid before contacting me."

The shivering nurse starts to cry. "She's been so good. I was so scared she'd start crying and they'd find us."

I lick my dry lips and nod as I start to make a plan in my head. "We need to distract them and get them away from the baby. Calu, you're going to stay with nurse Beckett and the baby. Bekia, you come with me."

"What can I do?" Dr. Omid asks.

"When the coast is clear get my baby to safety."

He nods. "I can do that. I'll get her away from here."

"Okay, everyone. Bekia, let's go."

I step out of the closet and look around. There's even more activity than earlier. Everyone seems to be moving in confusion.

I step away from the closet my daughter is in as if nothing is wrong. Moving toward the nurse's station, I paste a smile on my face. I'm halfway there when one of the guards turns in my direction.

He freezes and narrows his eyes on me. When he starts toward me, I see the malicious look in his eyes. I start to back away and Bekia pulls her swords.

"Run," I call out.

She hesitates for a moment but turns with me to lead the guard and the others around the nurse's station away. I head for the staircase. We can run down to the main floor where my parents are.

As we run my phone starts to ring. I wrestle it from my pocket not pausing for a single step. Hope fills me when I see Ryan's number.

"Ry, we need you," I puff into the phone as I keep running.

"Where are you?"

"We're being chased on the sixth floor. I'm heading for the stairs with Bekia."

Once in the staircase, I start down, but commotion below causes me to look down. There are men running up the stairs. "Shit, go, go, go. We have to go up," I say to Bekia.

We turn and the guards from the nurse's station are filing into the stairwell. Bekia takes a stance to guard me. It looks like we gave my daughter a path to safety all right.

"I have this. You head up," Bekia says. "Get to safety."

"I can help," I say.

"No, this is my job. Run."

I hesitate. "Carmen," Ryan calls into the phone. "Listen to her. I'm coming. Run."

I don't want to leave her, but I nod and take off. I go up a few floors and peek my head out to see if the coast is clear. It's not. A dark-haired guy locks his eyes on me and starts to run toward me.

"Crap. Ryan," I huff out. "I'm headed for the roof. I'm being chased."

"I'm … baby." My phone starts to break up as I run farther up the stairs.

My lungs burn as I push forward. When I get to the top, I push through the door and stumble out. I look around for someplace to hide, but there's nowhere to go.

The door behind me bursts open and the tall dark-haired guy comes through. I back up looking for a weapon. There's nothing I can grab. I'm going to have to fight him hand-to-hand.

He laughs as he moves forward, and I back up. Fear starts to rise, Ryan better hurry up. I don't know how long I'll be able to fight this guy off.

He swings at me, but I duck out of the way and kick at his leg. Surprise is clear on his face as he stumbles. I gain a little confidence and bounce on my feet.

Mom has always drilled into me that I'm to fight to the death, even if my blades are lost. I dig deep ready to fight back as I realize that I wasn't trained for sport but to protect my life. I move forward swinging, taking advantage of the element of surprise.

I land two more blows before he blocks the third and punches me in my chest. The wind is knocked out of me. I take a few steps back as tears well in my eyes.

"You make lucky hits, little girl. It won't happen again," he growls with a Russian accent.

He charges me. I block his hits, but I'm unable to counterattack as he tries to overpower me. I'm forced back toward the edge of the roof with each blow. In my head, I plan to use that to my advantage.

He rushes me and I make my move. I duck and flip him over me. However, the momentum takes me over the edge with him.

In a swift move, I hook my arm over the edge and catch myself before I drop off to the ground below. My skin burns and my muscles scream in protest.

"Oh God," I cry out as my grasp slips.

I'm not going to be able to hold on. This hold is awkward at best, and I don't have the strength to pull myself back up. My heart sinks.

I'll never get to see my little girl grow up. I'll never get to see where my love for Ryan will take us. My aching breasts are a reminder that I'm leaving my baby behind.

Tears run down my face as I fight to hold on, too scared to move an inch to try to pull myself up. How did I get here?

CHAPTER FORTY-NINE

Don't Let Go

Ryan

Paloma and I charge off the elevator and rush straight toward the staircase where all the commotion is coming from. As we approach, Bekia comes into view fighting in the tight space.

She kicks a guy in the chest and he comes flying out of the stairwell. There are more of them rushing to attack. Paloma pulls her swords out and looks me in the eyes.

"Go, find my daughter."

I nod and move forward shoving a guy out of my way and down the stairs before I leap over a body that's already still on the ground. I take the stairs two at a time, headed for the roof. Noise below has me looking over the rail, but the space is too tight to shoot down to help.

However, Paloma and Bekia seem to be handling their own. I grind my teeth and start back up the stairs. Carmen needs me. I can feel it.

I have to get to her like I promised I always would. I push my long legs harder than I've ever pushed them before. When I clear the exit to the roof, I look around and see nothing.

"Carmen," I bellow as my heart races.

"Ry," she whimpers.

I feel like I'm going to be sick. I rush in the direction of her voice and her arm comes into view. She's slipping as I dive for the edge.

I grab her arm in a tight hold right as she loses her grip. Her scream rings out as I lock my fingers around her forearm. I've never hung onto anything so tight in my life.

Our eyes lock and she looks at me with a mixture of relief and fear. "Hold on for me, baby," I say as I try to pull her up. "Fuck."

"Ryan, please," she cries as she clasps my forearm.

"I've got you. Don't let go." I remember the earpiece I never took out from our mission. "I need some help up here. Carmen's hanging off the side of the building and I'm holding on for dear life. Wyatt, can you get here, bro?"

"My hands are a bit full down here. I'm trying."

"Fuck," I bellow again.

"Ry, this is John. Roni and I are in the bird. We're headed your way. You hold on. We're coming."

"Shit, if you can speed the fuck up that would be great."

"We're coming."

I angle my body and steady myself to throw my other arm over and grasp her with both hands. It's not the best grip, but I've got her and I'm not letting go. My nostrils flare as I try to lift her toward me, but that causes me to start to slip. Carmen starts to freak out and kick her feet.

"Baby, relax. Be still for me."

"Ryan, I don't want to die," she sobs.

"Who's dying? How many times do I have to tell you I've got you?"

"Ry—"

"Nah, baby. I've got you. Don't you let go. We're getting married and we're raising our little girl together. Don't you fucking let go," I demand.

She sniffles and nods. I see when she gets ready to look down. That's a bad idea.

"Hey, look at me." She snaps her head up. "That's my girl. You keep those pretty eyes on me."

"Ry, I'm scared."

"I'm not letting you go. Do you know how much I love you?"

She slips a little more in my hold. "Ryan."

"Sh, baby, I've got you. If you would have let me suck some of that tittie milk out this morning you would be lighter."

"Seriously," she chokes out, her eyes widening.

"I'm just saying."

"This is not the time for that."

"I totally agree," John says in my ear.

"We've broken through," Felix says next. "Wyatt and I are on our way."

I grind my teeth and try to tighten my hold. John's ass better get here fast. My body is clenched so tight my muscles are twitching.

"John?"

"Almost there."

I look out and the chopper comes into view. We're not in the clear yet, but I have a little hope. I look back into Carmen's eyes and I can see the panic.

"Come on, baby. Stay with me. I've got you."

"I'm trying."

"Try harder. Don't you fuck this up. I have a big ass rock waiting for you. I'm going to marry your ass as soon as we find someone to do it."

She gives a short laugh. "Only you can make jokes at a time like this."

"Who's joking? We're getting married, baby. If we have to fly to Vegas tonight. I'm marrying your ass once I get you on solid ground."

"I don't want my baby to grow up without me."

"Don't do that shit, Carmen. I swear, baby—"

She slips a little more and screams. I'm starting to sweat and my hands have become slippery. We both fall silent as we look into each other's eyes.

I silently tell her I love her and how much I need her. I'm not losing her like this. I can't.

The sound of the helicopter gets closer. It's like my heart beats to the sound of the propellers. Everything slows down. I'm aware of every muscle in my body. Carmen's hold on me starts to slip as the force of the wind from the chopper makes my hold unsteady as well.

The bird gets closer, and I can't hear my own breathing over the sound. I look Carmen in her fear-filled eyes. "Don't. Let. Go."

Blue Collection Character Tree

Legally Bound 1
Bobby Mairettie and Paige Kemble-Mairettie *father and mother of:*
    *Peyton and James Mairettie (*twin boys*)
    *Sydney Mairettie and Maria Lynn Mairettie (*twin girls*)

Legally Bound 2
Marcus Mairettie and Rita Briggs-Mairettie *father and mother of:*
    *Daniel Mairettie
    *Hannah Mairettie

Legally Bound 3
Nathaniel (Nate) Briggs and Pamela (Pam) Kemble-Briggs *father and mother of:*
    *Tiffany and Tracey Briggs (*twin girls*)
    *Nathaniel Briggs Jr.

Legally Bound 4
Jasper Briggs and Marie Mairettie-Briggs *father and mother of:*
    *Clay Briggs

The Mairettie Family
Grandpa Marcello Mairettie and Grandma Marie Ann *father and mother of:*
    *Marcello Mairettie Jr.
    *Andrew Mairettie
    *James Mairettie
    *Jessie Mairettie
    *Lynn Mairettie

*Gianna Mairettie
*James Mairettie and Minnie Mairettie *father and mother of:*
    *Bobby Mairettie
    *Sam Mairettie – (Ellen Kensington-Mairettie, *wife*)
    *Marcus Mairettie
    *Marie Mairettie

The Briggs Family
Thomas Briggs and Raquel Marinos-Briggs (**Deceased**) *father and mother of:*
    *Nathaniel Briggs
    *Rita Briggs

Earl Briggs (Thomas' younger brother) and Caitronia Marinos-Briggs (twin sister of Raquel) *father and mother of:*
    *Kelly Briggs-Fecteau (Alexie Fecteau, *husband*)
    *Jasper Briggs

The Kemble Family
Peyton Kemble and Davina Kemble *father and mother of:*
    *Pamela Kemble
    *Paige Kemble

Other Important *Legally Bound* **Characters**
Camille (Cam) Mc Wien-Carter (Seth Carter, *soon-to-be ex-husband*) *father and mother of:*
    *Seth Carter Jr.
    *Eddie Carter
    *Aiden Carter

Austin Mc Wien (*Camille's father*)

Baroness Olivia Kontos (Baron Kontos' widow; Jasper's ex-lover; Thomas Briggs' new love interest)

Vanessa (Julissa) Smith-Mims (Patrick Mims, *husband, Deceased*)

Hush 1
Uri Donati and Valentina Caprisi-Donati *father and mother of:*
  *Vita Khayla Donati
  *Nori Donati
  *Inzo Donati
  *Eva Donati

Hush 2
Luca Donati and Shannon Caprisi-Donati *father and mother of:*
  *Carlo Donati (Introduced in **Ballers 2**)

The Donati Family
Angelo Uri Donati (***Deceased***) and Donatella Manzo-Donati-~~Zuko~~ *father and mother of:*
  *Uri Donati
  *Nico Donati ~~Zuko~~
  *Annabella Donati ~~Zuko~~ (*Nico's twin sister*)
  *Michael Donati – ~~Zuko~~

Nicholas Donati (Angelo Donati's brother) and

Ava Donati *father and mother of:*

  *Luca Donati

The Caprisi Family
Vincent Caprisi and Khayla Grant-Caprisi (***Deceased***) *father and mother of:*
  *Valentina Caprisi
  *Lissette Caprisi (***Deceased***)
  **Shannon Caprisi (*Vincent's daughter*)

Other Important *Hush* Characters
Uncle Valentine Caprisi (*Vincent's brother; head hitter*)

Iman Grant (*Khayla's sister;* ***Shannon's mother;* **Deceased**)

Roberto Donati-Zuko (*Donatella's husband;* **Deceased**)
***Posed as Dale the accountant from Legally Bound 3*

Cole 'Brooklyn' O'Brien

DJ

Ballers 1
Bradley Monroe and Tamara Hathaway-Monroe *father and mother of:*
    *Brielle Monroe
    *Ashley Monroe and Ashton Monroe (*twins*)
    *Corey Monroe (*Baby Tam is pregnant with at end of **Ballers 1**)

The Monroe Family
Vernon Monroe and Gloria Monroe *father and mother of:*
    *Trevor Monroe (Donna, *soon to be ex-wife*)
    *Bradley Monroe
    *Ann Monroe (*Bradley's twin sister; Tom, husband*)

Trevor Monroe and Donna Monroe *father and mother of:*
    *Jessica Monroe
    *Toby Monroe and Paige Monroe (*twins*)
    *Jonathan Monroe
Tom Rivers and Ann Monroe-Rivers *father and mother of:*
    *George Rivers and Melissa Rivers (*twins*)

*Amy Rivers

The Hathaway Family
Byron Hathaway and Fiona Hathaway *father and mother of:*
  *Ellerie Hathaway
  *Tamara Hathaway

Other Important *Ballers* **Characters**
Stacey (Tam's best friend)

Reese (Tam's best friend; Nico's girlfriend in *Ballers 1*)

Alee (Tam's best friend)

Cyrus Pierson (Tam's boss) *father of:*
  *Tommy Pierson
  *Carey Pierson
  *Stephanie Pierson

Ballers 2
Nico Donati and Reese Bridges-Donati *father and mother of:*
  *Nico Donati Jr.
  *Lanya Donati
  *Orso Donati
  *Santo Donati
  *Stefano Donati

Other Important *Ballers 2* **Characters**
Tiberius Roman (Reese's ex-husband)

Symphony (Michael's right-hand)

Brothers Black 1

Wyatt Black and Lanelle (Nellie) Bryant-Black *father and mother of:*
   *Nora Black
   *Evan Black

The Black Family
Joseph Black and Cassidy Black *father and mother of:*
   *Wyatt Black
   *Noah Black
   *Johnathan Black
   *Felix Black
   *Toby Black
   *Braxton Black
   *Ryan Black

The Lockhart Family
Rob Lockhart and Faith Lockhart *father and step-mother of:*
   *Heather Lockhart

Steve Lockhart and Nora Bryant-Lockhart (***Deceased***) *step-father and mother of:*
   *Lanelle (Nellie) Bryant-Black

Chase Lockhart and Jennifer Lockhart *father and mother of:*
   *Rebecca (Bean) Lockhart (Noah's best friend and love interest)

Other Important *Brothers Black 1* **Characters**
Missy (Johnathan's ex-girlfriend, ***Deceased***)

Lucy (*Heather's girlfriend*)

Barry Coleman (***Deceased***)

Brothers Black 2
Noah Black and Rebecca (Bean) Lockhart-Black *father and mother of:*
  *Brodie Black
  *Connor Black
  *Baby on the way

Other Important *Brothers Black 2* Characters
Joshua (*Deceased*)

Carmen (Nene) Nash (*reporter; niece of Mariah Briggs from Yours Series; Ryan's new crush*)

Logan O'Brien

Brothers Black 3
King Toby Black and Queen Ogeima Feechi (Kamara) Abioye-Black *father and mother of:*
  *Lulu Black
  *TJ Black
  *Baby on the way

Other Important *Brothers Black 3* **Characters**
Missy (Johnathan's ex-girlfriend, *Deceased*)

Lucy (*Heather's girlfriend*)

Barry Coleman (*Deceased*)

King Elijah Abioye aka Mr. Naidoo

Queen Ada Catherine Naidoo-Abioye

King Kwäzē Naidoo-Abioye

Celeste (Kwäzë's ex-girlfriend)

King Afafa (*Deceased*)

Missy (Johnathan's ex-girlfriend, *Deceased*)

Lucy (*Heather's girlfriend*)

Barry Coleman (*Deceased*)

Joshua (*Deceased*)

Carmen Nash aka Nene (*Reporter, Mariah Briggs, from Yours Series, Niece, Ryan's new crush*)
Logan O'Brien

Dylan O'Brien

Jamie O'Brien

Cole 'Brooklyn' O'Brien

Uncle Jonah McGowan

Uncle Jack McGowan

Uncle Raymond McGowan

Uncle Ronan McGowan

Carrick McGowan

Malcolm McGowan

Graham McGowan

Jeremiah McGowan

Reilly McGowan

Brothers Black 4
Braxton Black and Heather Lockhart-Black *father and mother of:*
   *Riley Black
   *Rowen Black

Other Important *Brothers Black 4* **Characters**
   Debbie ~~Lockhart~~-Kline (Rob's ex-wife, Heather's Mother)

   Lucy (*Heather's pretend girlfriend*)

   Amanda Kline (Heather's half-sister)

   Ernest Kline (Heather's Stepfather, *Deceased*)

   Eugene aka Crooked Nose

   Logan O'Brien

   Dylan O'Brien

   Jamie O'Brien

   Cole 'Brooklyn' O'Brien

   Uncle Jonah McGowan

   Uncle Jack McGowan

   Uncle Raymond McGowan

Uncle Ronan McGowan

Carrick McGowan

Malcolm McGowan

Graham McGowan

Jeremiah McGowan

Reilly McGowan

Nicholas Lincoln

Sephora Lincoln

Thomas Briggs

Brothers Black 5
Felix Black and Kaye Porter-Black aka Kaye Blaze *father and mother of:*
    *Dashawn Black
    *Second child unannounced

Other Important *Brothers Black 5* **Characters**
    Lakia Redding (*Kaye's writer friend*)

    Dean (*Kaye's writer friend*)

    Hayidah (*Doll for Club Desire*)

    Pastor Wayne Porter (*Kaye's father*)

    Danesha Porter (*Kaye's mother*)

Danny Porter (**Deceased** *Kaye's brother and Felix's best friend*)

Grandma Reid (*Kaye's grandmother*)

Grandpa Reid (*Kaye's grandfather*)

Alberto Perez (*Felix's best friend*)

Jacob McTavish (*Lead actor in Kaye's movie*)

Mona Richards (**Deceased**, *a fan)*

Logan O'Brien

Dylan O'Brien

Jamie O'Brien

Cole 'Brooklyn' O'Brien

Connie O'Brien

Kate O'Brien

Uncle Ronan McGowan

Carrick McGowan

Brothers Black 6
Ryan Black and Carmen Nash

Other Important *Brothers Black 6* **Characters**
Kiyoshi Matsumara-Nash (*Carmen's father*)

Paloma Matsumara-Nash (*Carmen's mother*)

Nelson "Ne" Matsumara-Nash (*Carmen's Brother*)

Yui (*Nelson assistant*)

Bekia

Calu

Mariah Briggs (*Carmen's Aunt*)

Gigi (*Carmen's roommate*)

Torque

Alexander (*Oldest Triplet*)

Maximilian aka Mil (*Middle Triplet*)

Tobias (*Youngest Triplet*)

Austin Mc Wien (***Now Deceased***)

Logan O'Brien

Misha Krupin

Dr. Omid V-Shah

Connie O'Brien

Kate O'Brien

Don LaSalle Locatelli

Tasha Locatelli

Valentine Donati

Uri Donati

Yours Series
Nicholas Lincoln and Sephora (Sophi/Soph/Lilla du) Emilsson
father and mother of:
    *Nicole Lincoln
    *Nadia Lincoln
    *Nicholas Lincoln Jr.

The Lincoln Family

Dean Lincoln and Shelly Lincoln (***Both Deceased***) *father and mother of:*
    *Nicholas Lincoln
    *Rick ~~Carbon~~ Lincoln
    *Gavin ~~Carbon~~ Lincoln

The Emilsson Family
Liam Emilsson (thought to be deceased) and Faraz Emilsson father and mother of:
    *Lucian Emilsson
    *Ettie Emilsson
    *Sephora Emilsson

Lucian Emilsson and Kimberly Ann Clove *father and mother of:*
    *Lilla Emilsson

Other Important *Yours* Characters
Mark Fienberg (Sephora's best friend)

Ivana Graves (Nick's ex-girlfriend; ***Deceased***)

Bianca (Liam's mistress; ***Missing***)

Winton (Nick's driver and security)

Jillian Carver (Nick's ex-temporary PA; *Deceased*)

Harvey Carver (Jillian's father; Nick's family friend; *Deceased*)

Bailey Wilder (waitress; Mark's girlfriend)

Dylan O'Brien

Nick's Crew
Wyatt Black
Kevin Briggs (Mariah Briggs' husband; Nick's PA)
Craig Hilton
George Ligal
Lucian Emilsson
Andrew Connor (Ettie's husband)

Be Yours Series
Prince Omid Arman Vahid (Dr. O.V-Shah) and Divine Favors
father and mother of:
   *Prince Firuz Arman Vahid
   *Princess Fairuza Araz Vahid

The Vahid Family

Javed Vahid and Hana Vahid (**third wife**) *father and mother of:*
   *Prince Omid Arman Vahid
   *Prince Bazar Vahid
      Padma Vahid *first wife and mother of:*
         *Prince Paiman Vahid
         *Princess Yasmin Vahid

Other Important *Be Yours* **Characters**

Prince Jahan Vahid

Prince Remi Vahid

Prince Ramses Vahid

Sassa Vahid (*First wife of Javed Vahid*)

Marica Thompson (Divine's cousin)

Dr. Nobi

Gretta (Medical Assistant)

Navid (Omid's advisor)

Dada (Divine's best friend)

ACKNOWLEDGMENTS

Oh Lord almighty, you gave me strength! This book was out to challenge me from go. So many moving pieces that will culminate in book 7 and flow into other series on top of Ryan's personality. Anyone that knows me knows I hate every book while writing it and I won't put it out until I love it. I love this book. It was fun capturing a younger couple coming into their own.

I'm so happy about the end of this series. Don't be mad at me for the cliffhanger. I'm already working on book 7. Which I'm sort of sad about. I love this family and this is the last brother. Although, not the last you will see of them.

Thank you so much to all the readers that have been willing to take this journey with me. Thank you for your patience and support as well as your kind words, emails, posts, comments, and shares. You make this thing I do bring a smile to my face on days when it's not so easy.

Shout out to my team. My husband has been waiting on this one for a while. Thanks to my authors that sprint with me and work as hard as I do.

Now hold on. Let me stop and stand to give God these praise. I already see what God is up to in this year and I'm here for it, Lord. I thank you. For every lesson, every blessing and every opportunity to show Your Glory and live in Your Grace. Thank you.

Next! We're here all year. LOL.

ABOUT THE AUTHOR

Blue Saffire, award-winning, bestselling author of over thirty contemporary romance novels and novellas, writes with the intention to touch the heart and the mind. Blue hooks, weaves, and loops multiple series, keeping you engaged in her worlds. Blue is a hybrid author, writing for Sourcebooks and for her own publishing company Perceptive Illusions as Blue Saffire as well as Royal Blue.

Blue and her husband live in a house filled with laughter and creativity, in Long Island, NY. Both working hard to build the Blue brand and cultivate their love for the artists. Creative is their family affair.

Blue holds an MBA in Marketing and Project Management, as well as a MED in Instructional Technology and Curriculum Design. She is also an NLP Master Practitioner.

Wait, there is more to come! You can stay updated with my latest releases, learn more about me, the author, and be a part of contests by subscribing to my newsletter at www.BlueSaffire.com
If you enjoyed *Brothers Black 6: Ryan the Joker*, I'd love to hear your thoughts and please feel free to leave a review. And when you do, please let me know by emailing me TheBlueSaffire@gmail.com or leave a comment on Facebook https://www.facebook.com/BlueSaffireDiaries or Twitter @TheBlueSaffire

Other books by Blue Saffire
Placed in Best Reading Order
Also available …

Yours 3: Life Mastered

Ballers 2: His Final Play

Legally Bound 5.1: Tasha Illegal Dealings

Brothers Black 2: Noah

Legally Bound 5.2: Camille

Legally Bound 5.3 & 5.4 Special Edition

Where the Pieces Fall

Legally Bound 5.5: Legally Unbound

Brothers Black 4: Braxton the Charmer

Broken Soldier

Brothers Black 5: Felix the Watcher

A Home for Christmas

Doctor Feel Good

Brothers Black 6: Ryan the Joker

Brothers Black 7: Johnathan the Fixer

Wild Hearts

Pieces of Trevor's Heart

Ballers 3: His Team

Ronan Book 1: Kings of New York

Coming Soon …
King of Gods Book 4: Immortal Iron Brothers Series
King of Past Book 5: Immortal Iron Brothers Series
Dylan Book 2: Kings of New York Series

Other Blue Saffire Series

Hold On To Me Series
My Funny Valentine
Be My Valentine

Hitter Squad Series
Remember Me

Work Husband Series
Unexpected Lovers
My Best Friend's Wish
The Ones Left Behind
The Last Ones Standing

The Lost Souls MC Series
Forever
Never
Always

The Moran Brothers Series
Love Notes
Stay With Me

The A**hole Club Series
Pit Book 1: The A**hole Club
Ox Book 5: The A**hole Club
Kelex Book 6: The A**hole Club

Immortal Iron Brothers Series
King of Knights Book 1
King of Inferno Book 2
King of Tides Book 3

Check out Blue Saffire exclusives on the
BlueSaffire.com website
The Fixer
His Miracle Baby
Razor
Dane
Trip
Professor Jones
Room 112

Other books from Evei Lattimore Collection Books by Blue Saffire
Black Bella 1

Destiny 1: Life Decisions
Destiny 2: Decisions of the Next Generation
Destiny 3 coming soon ...

Star

Other books from Royal Blue Gay Romance Collection written by
Blue Saffire
Kyle's Reveal
Beau's Redemption

www.ingramcontent.com/pod-product-compliance
Lightning Source LLC
Chambersburg PA
CBHW071246250626
47163CB00002B/356